She hadn't recognized that it was a setup, and now her friends were in danger...

Two cars pulled in while she munched on the first of two candy bars—she couldn't make up her mind so she bought both. A van pulled in. The driver got out and talked to the driver of one of the other cars. All the passengers in the two cars and four more men from the van got out. She couldn't see what the men at the rear of the van were doing, but the men in the cars had the trunks open and they were gearing up. Strapping handguns to their thighs. Putting something over their heads. She had seen that before. Even in the dark, she recognized body armor. One of the men turned and *US Marshall* reflected in the pale light. *Someone's getting arrested tonight.*

She took a casual bite of her candy bar. It felt weird to be this close to men who would arrest her in an instant if they knew who she was. It was exhilarating and heart-stopping at the same time. There but for the grace of—

The men got into the van and took off in the direction of the dirt drive toward the safe house. *Oh, shit. They're going to get Durham Security.*

Joan pulled out a burner phone she had taken out of the cache, dialed Kearney's number, and started jogging toward Darren's car. "Pick up, pick up, pick up," she begged out loud, hoping he would answer a call from a number he didn't recognize.

She nearly choked on a small chunk of candy bar when she heard him answer.

"Yeah."

She dropped the remainder of the candy bar. "Feds are heading toward the house. Get out. Go out the back. They're—"

"Whoa. Slow down. What's this again?"

"You have no time. *No* time." She picked up her pace, and her words breathed out between her panting. "I'll get Darren's car. Go out the back. Go now."

Yelled warnings, scuffling, a door slammed, then the phone went dead. Joan broke into a run. Darren's car came into sight. She slowed for a quick scan. The feds had over-looked putting a guard on the car.

But the doors were locked. *Shit, shit, shit.*

Six months ago, Joan Bowman's fiancé, Duncan Archer, was shot during an ATF sting operation in Arizona. He'd left a message with a friend that, if anything happened to him, she was to call a certain phone number. That led her to Yonkers, New York, and Duncan's longtime friend, Jeb Durham, who has control over Duncan's estate. Their understanding was that, if Joan called, something had happened to Duncan, and she was to inherit the money.

Duncan's plan was for Joan to use the money so she could buy a new identity and disappear. However, Jeb has other plans. He can't accept the fact that his friend is dead and believes Joan had something to do it. He gives the money to her in advances only large enough to live on. If he keeps her close, he can play her, befriend her, and get her to open up to him and confess her part in Duncan's demise. But Jeb has yet to learn what Duncan knew well: never play a player…

KUDOS for *The Only Sin*

In *The Only Sin* by Janet McClintock, Joan Bowman is on the run from the law. With her lover Duncan killed in Phoenix, Joan has gone to New York to find his friend Jeb, who tells her that she is to inherit Duncan's estate. But Jeb is suspicious and only gives her a monthly allowance until he can be sure that she is not the one responsible for Duncan's death. But Jeb's plan backfires when Joan goes to work for his security company and he finds out that deceiving Joan is a very bad idea. Like the other two books in McClintock's Iron angel series, this one is filled with wonderful characters, fast-paced action, and more than a few surprises. ~ *Taylor Jones, The Review Team of Taylor Jones & Regan Murphy*

The Only Sin by Janet McClintock is the third book in this talented author's Iron Angel series. Joan Bowman, on the run from the law after a sting in Arizona, has fled to New York to a friend of Joan's lover Duncan's, who was killed in the Arizona sting. Jeb, Duncan's friend, gives her money from Duncan's estate to get set up in New York, but not enough to disappear and start a new life with a new identity. Jeb convinces Joan to go to work for him in his security business in an effort to discover her role in Duncan's death. He doesn't want to release all Duncan's money to Joan until he is sure that she was not responsible for his death. But Joan doesn't trust him. She knows he is up to something, and she has no intention of getting stung by someone else's agenda. *The Only Sin* has some big shoes to fill, following the first two books in the series, but McClintock doesn't disappoint, delivering another page turner that will keep you on the edge of your seat. ~ *Regan Murphy, The Review Team of Taylor Jones & Regan Murphy*

THE ONLY
SIN

Book 3 of the Iron Angel Series

JANET MCCLINTOCK

A Black Opal Books Publication

GENRE: THRILLER/SUSPENSE

THE ONLY SIN
Copyright © 2017 by Janet McClintock
Cover Design by Jackson Cover Designs
All cover art copyright © 2017
All Rights Reserved
Print ISBN: 978-1-626947-59-7

First Publication: OCTOBER 2017

Published by Black Opal Books **http://www.blackopalbooks.com**

"In self-defense and the defense of others,
cowardice is the only sin."
From *The Darkest Night* by Dean R. Koontz

CHAPTER 1

Joan scurried across the street, mixing her footprints with those already in the light snow that had fallen during the night. She quickly covered the half block to the subway entrance and ducked down the stairs. With each step, the cold city streets disappeared above her and relief filtered through her body.

The station platform was a hodge-podge of light and dark. Several lights were out, which created shadows between areas of bile-colored light, as if they were human fly strips. She pulled up her scarf, checked for surveillance cameras, found a dark area near the tracks, and slipped into the gloom.

A half-turn one way, and then the other way revealed a deserted platform except for a man sleeping on a bench. If law enforcement found her and confronted her in this murky tomb, she would have nowhere to go. She looked down the tracks into the darkness.

Where was a train? The station serviced both uptown and downtown trains. She would hop on the first train that came along to put much-needed distance between herself and the federal agents who were probably blood-hounding through her apartment at that very moment.

She pulled out her phone—one bar. She frowned and returned it to the front pocket of her black, leather jacket. It would be dangerous to call anyone until she determined how the feds had located her.

She thought about the cryptic phone call that had sent her scrambling to pack her few possessions. A man's voice had said she'd been made. She had five minutes to get out of her apartment. It didn't take five minutes to pack the few things she owned. Fugitives traveled light.

Loneliness ached in every joint of her body. If Duncan were alive, he would have known what to do. But he was dead, killed by federal agents in another city during a sting operation. Her shoulders slumped. Life sucked for the last man standing.

Her once-sharp instincts were muted by grief, making sorting out who she could trust tricky at best. It had been foolhardy to come to the New York Tri-State area where she had a connection—maybe that was how she had been located. That mistake could not be undone but, heartache or not, she needed to get her head above the quicksand before the law sucked her down.

How in God's name did the feds find her in New York City? Only three people knew where she lived. Three people out of a country of over three hundred million. How hard could it be to find three people she could trust?

She peered into the darkness. *Come on, train. Where are you?*

She leaned a shoulder against the cold, iron support beam. Only two people knew her number, and neither of them gave her the warm-and-fuzzies. They both had been Duncan's friends, which didn't necessarily make them hers. Kearney had been a brutal enemy for a couple years, leaving her with physical and mental scars. Then, out of a misplaced sense of duty, she saved his life, and now he spent every waking hour trying to make up for the gruesome things he had done to her.

The jury was out on Jeb. Duncan had left his sizeable estate in Jeb's hands on a handshake—some kind of spec ops honor thing—with instructions to give it to her if something happened to him. Jeb had handled her inheritance with integrity. Yet, something about him did not foster reliability.

He controlled her inheritance, so she had to stay close to him.

She looked down the track again. How fucked up could one life get?

She wiped the nervous sweat off her forehead with the back of her hand. Her hat. In the rush to get out of the apartment, she had forgotten the ball cap she always wore. That bill would come in handy to block her face from surveillance cameras. She couldn't do anything about it now. She set down the duffel, slid off the backpack, and did shoulder circles to loosen them up. No rumble came from the tunnel, but footsteps scraped down the stairs. Joan glanced over her shoulder to get a glimpse of a man's legs descending to the platform. The pant legs had a stripe down the side, like those on a uniform. *Don't act nervous.* She turned to stand with her back to the beam, pulled up her collar, and looked down at her bags. *No one knows you're here. You're waiting for a train like anyone else.*

Should she have stayed up above ground? The city streets were not alien to her, but she felt alienated by them since she had returned. Staten Island and Manhattan had been her playgrounds. Saturdays of museum trips with her mom dotted her memory of pre-teen years. Later, she went to Manhattan by herself and spent many hours in the great libraries surrounded by books where she soaked up the quiet and safety. She loved books, but to a fugitive they were anchors.

A wry smile started at one corner of her mouth as she thought about the time she had obtained a false ID. She had partied with the best of them—until her dad found out and grounded her. She had screamed at him that he had ruined her life. As it turned out, her dad had not ruined her life. She quite efficiently made waste of it all on her own. Sure, she could have said "no" at any time. She even did once, but she could never say "no" to Duncan. And now he was dead and she might as well be.

She pulled out her phone and popped it out of its holder.

A business card fell out and fluttered to the ground. She squatted to pick it up, but a man beat her to it. She looked up into the eyes of a Port Authority Police Officer.

Her mouth went dry, and for an interminable two seconds they looked into each other's eyes.

Joan broke the trance by smiling at the officer and thanking him for picking up the card for her. She stuffed it into the front pocket of her leather jacket.

"Is everything okay?" the police officer asked.

Joan beamed her sweetest smile. "Oh…yeah. My boyfriend kicked me out." She shrugged. "His loss."

The officer gave her the once over then turned and walked away. Joan closed her eyes and released a giant, silent exhale. Out of all the stations he could be on duty, why the one closest to her apartment? The self-help book she was reading at the moment, *Getting Past Your Past: Take Control of Your Life* by Michael A. Singer, suggested quieting the mind's narration of the outside world and experiencing the world. She closed her eyes. This storm passed, and she had one more hour of freedom, maybe even a day— or two if she was lucky.

The faint rumble of an approaching train picked up her heart beat. A downtown train came to a stop in front of her. She jockeyed her bags through the door and took a seat with her back to the platform and the police officer. Out of the corner of her eye, she watched him roust the sleeping man. He had fallen asleep on a bench under an advertisement for No-Doze. Joan half-smiled. You couldn't make this stuff up. She pulled up her collar and tucked her chin into the olive green scarf. The train pulled out of the station and her thoughts returned to her predicament.

Everything had happened too fast for her to think about what the feds were doing in her apartment. She mentally scanned her apartment for anything she may have left behind. A potentially damaging note. A forgotten weapon. Secreted cash. Her damn hat. Her body reacted first with shaking that rippled through her body. She rubbed her face with her hands and tried to think of her next step. What would Duncan have told her to do? Get on the next train—check, did that—and call him. But she couldn't call him. Because of her shortcomings, he was dead.

She tried to ignore the card in her pocket, but it beckoned her, as if it were vibrating. She pulled it out and thumbed the raised name and numbers. Jeb Durham had written his private number on the back and given it to her in case she ever needed his help with anything. "No matter how large or small," he had told her.

Giving her the card turned out to be prophetic or a coincidence, but she did not believe in either. She thought about it while she flicked it with her thumbnail. Jeb had given her the card. He knew her phone number. He topped the short list.

She put the card back in her pocket.

Time to make a plan.

CHAPTER 2

Jeb leaned on the window sill to the side of his desk. He winced. Two decades ago, while a mercenary in Sierra Leone, he had taken a bullet to the hip. It had ended his soldiering career but set him on the path that brought him to this imminent junction with Joan Bowman. He looked at his recon specialist. "So I take it you don't approve of what I'm doing."

Colavito leaned back in his chair and straightened his legs. "I don't understand what you're doing, so I can't approve or disapprove" At five-foot-ten, he stood four inches shorter than Jeb. Half Italian, half something else, his skin was lighter than olive, but darker than most. "You don't trust Joan, but you want her to work for you. That doesn't make any kinda sense to me. Why don't you just give her the money that was left to her and cut her loose?"

"If I control her money, I control her."

Colavito raised his brows and tucked his chin.

"It prevents her from disappearing until I'm satisfied that what she and Kearny told me is the truth." Jeb ran his hand over his gray-flecked, brown hair and watched a garbage truck back into the dumpster in the alley below. He turned back to his recon specialist. "C'mon, 'Vito, you don't think there's something odd with their story about what happened in Phoenix?"

"It was a sting. Shit happens."

"All these years, all the crap Archer'd been through, do you think he'd fall for a sting? Then get himself killed?" Jeb slurped his coffee. "And she was supposedly engaged to him, but she doesn't wear a ring, and doesn't call him by his real name. She calls him Duncan? What's that all about?"

"If you ask me, you're scraping the bottom of the peanut butter jar. You're gonna wind up with fingers smeared with foul smelling shit. Let. Her. Go." Colavito emphasized each of the last three words.

"I can't. If I don't make sure she's four-square, I feel like I'm doing Archer a disservice."

Colavito shook his head and walked across the thick carpet to get himself another cup of coffee.

"And she's friends with Kearney," Jeb said. "Either there's something going on between those two—" When Colavito turned, coffee pot in hand, and opened his mouth to disagree, Jeb hurried on, "not anything romantic, a partnership, affiliation, or whatever it is. Either that or Archer lied when he told us what Kearney did to her."

"Why would he lie about that?"

"My point exactly," Jeb said. "Archer wouldn't lie about that, which casts a bad light on the connection between those two."

"You think their story is a cover?"

"I'm sure of it."

"A cover for what?"

Jeb pressed his lips together. "That's what I'm going to find out."

"You think she had something to do with Archer's death?"

"I don't know. I just can't shake this suspicion that…" He shook his head to clear it. "Maybe it's nothing. All I know is I have to be sure before I hand over all his money."

Colavito crossed his arms and watched his boss walk stiffly to his chair. "Okay, let's say I agree with you that something is going on. How are you going to pull the truth out of her? Because we both know you won't get anything out of Kearney."

"Kearney's a former interrogator. He'll see me coming a mile away." Jeb folded his well-built frame into his soft-leather desk chair. "But Joan, she's a different story. I can work her." He made the motion of hooking a fish and mimed reeling in a catch.

"What are you going to use?" Colavito smirked. "Your rugged good looks and your irresistible charm with women?"

"I thought about it."

"I was joking."

"I'm not."

"Well, George Clooney extraordinaire," Colavito said. "How are you going to charm her into your confidence? Unless you want to be left unconscious on the side of the road like the last guy who tried to make her do something she didn't want to do, you're gonna have to get her to come to you."

A phone rang in the reception area. Jeb looked up in anticipation. The secretary's soft voice filtered through the closed door. The soft clicks of the keyboard started again.

"Joan is going through a rough time," Jeb said. "Losing her fiancé, living on the run, law enforcement after her. I'm going to be there for her."

"You can't make a pass at her," Colavito said. "It's too soon. I haven't seen any signs of her moving on."

"I'll put a wedge between her and Kearney. She'll need someone to talk to. I'll be a man friend. Women like that, right?" Jeb leaned his elbows on his desk. "I'll get her to relax around me and open up. When she's ready to talk, I'll be right there." He smiled. "Her best bud."

Colavito returned to the chair in front of the desk. "In answer to your question a few minutes ago, I don't like what you're doing. Leading her on that you're her friend is just plain wrong. That said, it still leaves the problem of getting her to come to you."

Jeb put his chin in his clasped hands.

"You've done something."

Jeb frowned and nodded.

Colavito gestured for Jeb to explain.

"I had someone warn her that federal agents were on their way to her apartment."

"Were they?"

"How the hell would I know?"

"Why would you put her through that anxiety? She's a grieving woman—Archer's widow."

"They never got married. She's not—"

Colavito stood, stopping Jeb in midsentence. "The long-time woman of any other operator—married or not—would be considered a widow and reap the benefits of that status."

Jeb rubbed his jaw. "You're right."

"And you're screwing around with *Archer's* widow." Colavito walked to the window. "You better hope he doesn't find a way to reach out from the grave."

"I just wanted to see who she'd call. I wanted her to come to me."

"Did she call you?" Colavito asked over his shoulder, still looking out the window at the snow that had turned to slush in the warming morning air.

When Jeb did not answer, Colavito twisted at the waist to look over his shoulder. Jeb sat rubbing his index finger across his upper lip, staring at a point midway across his desk.

"Jeb, did she call you?"

"She may have called Kearney."

"You're playing with fire. You know that, right?" Colavito shook his head. "When did you call her?"

Worry etched furrows across Jeb's forehead. "About five."

"That was over five hours ago. That's a long time to not hear from somebody in trouble."

Jeb's desk phone let out three electronic chirps, indicating he had an in-house call.

He picked up the handset. "Yeah, Claudia…" His brow smoothed and he looked at Colavito. "Joan Bowman is in the outer office? Is that right?"

છ્ગ્છ્ગ

Claudia looked up at Joan. "He'll be just a few minutes."

"Thank you." Joan flopped onto the chair closest to where she had set down her bags. She watched Claudia working at her desk. She could be anybody's grandmother. *I'll bet she's seen and heard a lot. Probably tougher than she looks, too.*

"There's coffee in the corner. Help yourself."

The coffee sounded like pure bliss after five hours in the cold streets, but Joan didn't get up to get any. It seemed like too much work. The adrenaline had worn off, leaving her wrung out. Her morning had been spent riding the subways and walking the streets, watching for a tail and staying invisible in a city peppered with surveillance cameras—lugging those bags the whole time. The thought had crossed her mind to ditch the bags, but they were all that remained of her life. Her whole life in two bags. Only five months ago she wouldn't have believed she would sink so low. No, scratch that, she hadn't sunk to any depths. The person she had been back then continued to exist. Her horizons had simply shrunk.

The warmth in the building, welcome at first, now made Joan too hot. She took off her jacket. Claudia cast a long look then went back to her work. Joan looked down. Dammit. She had fled her apartment without putting on a bra. Fatigue and the sense of safety in Jeb's building made the situation funny, and Joan chuckled out loud. She shook her head. What a messed up day this was turning into.

"You have time to go the ladies room, if you'd like," Claudia said without looking up.

The thought of picking up the duffel bag and trudging

down the hall to the ladies' room sounded like too much work. It would be easier to put on her jacket.

Before she could convince herself to make the effort, a phone buzzed on Claudia's desk.

"You can go in now," she said. "You can leave your bags there. No one will bother them."

"I'd rather keep them with me," Joan replied. "Never get separated from your gear—you know how it is."

The old army adage had served Joan well, except for the one time she hadn't stuck by it.

That had been another messed up day on foreign soil a long time ago. A time when she would have been considered a normal person, living a normal life, or as close to normal as army life could ever be.

Hoping her plan would do its job, Joan maneuvered her bags through the door into Jeb's office.

He pushed on his desk to stand up. "Joan, come on in. I didn't expect to see you today."

She placed her bags to the side of the door and turned to greet him. "It was a spur of the—" She stopped mid-sentence. Jeb didn't act like he noticed her lack of a bra, but she knew that he did. *Damn men and their peripheral vision.* "—moment thing."

Jeb offered Joan some coffee. "It's better than Claudia's. Hers is like cat piss."

"I heard that," Claudia said, reaching for the door to close it. She looked at Joan. "I use his coffee as nail polish remover."

A tired smile wrestled its way onto Joan's face at the banter of people who got along.

Jeb extended an arm toward a man pouring a cup of coffee. "This is Colavito, my recon specialist. 'Vito, this is—"

"Angel," Joan interjected. "I'm going by Angel now."

Jeb rubbed his upper lip with his finger. "Since when?"

"Since this morning. A lot has happened." Her eyes traveled the room and settled on the chairs facing the desk. She chose the one on the left, which she considered "her chair," because she always sat in it when she came in to see Jeb for the monthly allotment of her inheritance.

Jeb came from behind his desk with a slight limp. He turned the other chair so that when he sat in it, he faced her. "You look tired."

"I don't sleep well."

Colavito handed Joan a cup of coffee and gave Jeb a quick look. He didn't directly look at her chest, but she felt it. She swallowed her self-consciousness. The morning had been devastating. And tiring. The look could have meant anything.

She should have put her jacket on when she had the chance.

She sipped the coffee and her eyes flashed up to Colavito's. He had made it perfectly: milk with one sugar and one packet of sugar substitute. "How did you—" The smile on his face stopped her. She looked at Jeb, then back to Colavito.

"Let's just say my specialty is noticing details," Colavito said.

"But how would you—" She scowled at Jeb. "Has he been following me?"

"I just wanted to be sure you didn't live a risky lifestyle that would jeopardize my company."

"I never said I'd work for you." Every time she had come in for her monthly allotment, he had asked her to work for him in the covert division of Durham Security. Working with a vigilante organization was not a quiet life living under the radar.

Jeb talked over his shoulder to Colavito. "Why don't you go get us some breakfast?"

"What do you want?"

"Surprise us."

Joan's gaze tracked Colavito across the room. "You should know what I like for breakfast."

He turned and flashed a smile, winked, then left the office.

"I can use someone with your skills. Martial arts, firearms, great instincts. And some jobs require a woman's touch." Jeb leaned his forearms on his thighs, closing the gap between Joan and him. "You're the kind of person who has to be busy. Working for me would be good for you. Is that why you're here, to accept my offer?"

Joan eyed his clasped hands just inches from her knees. He had never sat on the same side of the desk with her before. He knew something was up. She silently scolded herself for being overly sensitive. Jeb was being friendly. He couldn't know she was in trouble. But then, when you walked into someone's office like a hermit crab, carrying the totality of your wretched life on your back, it howled trouble.

"Joan? Is everything okay?" he asked.

She had taken too long to answer. She bit down on her emotions and said, "Can we talk about that later? I'm in a jam."

"Fair enough." He tapped her knee with his fingertip. "Tell me why you're here."

That small gesture made her cringe inwardly. Jeb had always been aloof and professional, which made the nature of that gesture all the more disconcerting. She pulled her gaze from his finger to his eyes. "I got a phone call this morning warning me that federal agents were coming for me. I packed as quickly as I could and got out of there."

"Did you recognize the voice?"

"No. But only you and Kearney know my number."

"Where's your phone now?" he asked.

"I removed the SIM card and destroyed it. Then I tossed it into the nearest trash can and the phone in another."

Jeb pushed himself out of the chair and walked around his desk. He pulled a cheap cell phone out of the bottom drawer. "This is a burner. I'm the only one who knows the number." He motioned for her to take it.

"Thanks." She slid the phone into her jacket pocket. "Any ideas about how the feds found me?" Her eyes followed him hitch around his desk and sit on the edge.

His foot brushed hers when he extended his legs. "Someone may have recognized you. This damn 'see something, say something' campaign catches people like us in the nets along with the terrorists."

Joan fought the reflex to pull away from the touch. He seemed to be playing a game. A year ago, when she was at her lowest point, Kearney had encouraged her to "play the game," and she had proven herself to be a solid player.

Okay, Jeb, let's see what you got. "I know coming here could be dangerous for you and your business," she said. "If you want me to leave—"

"Don't even talk like that." He sat in the other chair to be eye-to-eye with her again. "You did the right thing by coming here."

Joan sipped her coffee and contemplated his face more than she had over the past five months. His eyes radiated the hardness of a man who had seen combat. Duncan's eyes had shown it, too. She wondered if her eyes gave away the horrors she had been through.

"Do you know where you're going to stay?" he asked.

"I thought I'd hole up in one of those cheap, cash-only hotels for a few days."

"I have a two-bedroom townhouse in Staten Island. The guest room is begging to be used. It's not much, but you're welcome to stay there until you get your feet under you."

"Let me think about it." Living in Jeb's house would give her a better chance to find out what made him tick. But Staten Island was still part of the city, and that would do nothing to lower her anxiety level.

A commotion erupted in the outer office. Claudia's raised voice came through the closed door telling someone to stop.

The door opened. Kearney strode across the room. "Are you okay?"

"I'm sorry, Jeb, he walked right past me," Claudia said.

"It's okay, Claudia. I'll take care of it." Jeb frowned at Kearney. "Come on in."

Kearney ignored Jeb's sarcasm and knelt next to Joan's chair. "Do you know how they found you?"

"We were just discussing that," Joan said with a glance toward Jeb. "We thought maybe someone recognized me."

"Or maybe through her phone," Jeb added. "I gave her a burner, just to be sure."

"You can't be too careful." Kearney spotted Joan's coffee cup. "Any more coffee?"

Jeb pointed behind Kearney. "Help yourself."

While Kearney poured his coffee, Joan said, "Jeb offered to let me stay with him in Staten Island for a while."

Kearney hesitated then finished pouring the coffee. He returned to Joan's side before saying anything. "You can stay with me. I have an extra bedroom."

"Staten Island is populated enough that she won't be noticed," Jeb said.

Joan sipped her coffee and watched the two men.

"The city is going to be hot for you for a while," Kearney said.

"It's on the other side of the river. Far enough away to not raise any flags."

"It's still the city," Kearney said to Joan without looking at Jeb.

Interesting. Since Kearney had entered the room, Jeb talked to him about her, but Kearney talked to her. His conversation leaned more toward securing her future freedom. Jeb seemed more interested in what he wanted. This plan to get both men in the same room seemed to be working.

Jeb's offer to move into his house offered an opportunity to learn more about him and his motivations. The memory of Duncan's strong embrace made her sit back in her chair. She wasn't ready for this, but a gentle refusal might get Jeb to reveal something she could use.

"Thanks, Jeb," Joan said. "I appreciate your help, but I think I'll take Kearney up on his offer."

Jeb pinned Kearney with his gaze, stood, and walked around his desk, closing the blinds on his way past the window. "Are you sure that's what you want?"

"Walking around the city this morning made me realize it makes me uptight. A stint in the suburbs might do me some good."

"You ready?" Kearney said, heading toward Joan's bags.

"I...uh, Colavito..." Joan looked at Jeb, not sure what to do. "Colavito went for breakfast. Maybe we should wait for him to come back."

"Don't worry about it," Jeb said. "Go ahead and get settled in."

Joan stood.

"Wait." Jeb slid open a door on the credenza behind his desk. After spinning the dial on a safe, he pulled out a couple bundles of cash. "Here take this. You're going to need a car if you live upstate."

Joan thought of the wad of cash in her backpack. And the three fake ID's.

"Take this." Jeb raised the cash a few inches, a gesture to accept it. "Let me feel like I've done something to help you."

When Joan reached for the cash, she took the chance of turning it into an intimate handshake by putting her other hand on his. "Thanks, Jeb. I'll pay you back."

A dimple appeared next to his soft smile. "I'm counting on it."

Joan smiled back. Jeb had yet to learn what Duncan had known: *Never play a player*.

CHAPTER 3

Jeb struggled to get his six-foot-two frame out of the driver's seat and cursed his hip. He ran his hand over his hair and examined the 1940s bungalow where Joan and Kearney lived. It had the appearance of an afterthought, plunked down on the side of the hill. The land sloped away from the foundation to the gravel drive that served as a driveway for this house and the identical one farther down the lane. The land continued sloping forty yards downward to Route 32.

He massaged the back of his neck before reaching across the front seat and pulling out a bag of bagels and a cardboard tray with four cups of coffee tucked into the wells. He set the bag in the center of the tray, closed the door, and limped toward the back of his SUV to meet up with Colavito, walking up the gravel drive toward him.

"Is my car okay here?" Jeb asked.

Colavito took the tray from Jeb and nodded his chin toward the next bungalow. "The neighbors are rowdy twenty-something guys. They came in at about four-thirty. They won't be moving for several hours."

Jeb studied the house and the surrounding area. "What's the back like?"

"The same. Steep slope. Lots of underbrush. There's a pull-off where they park their vehicles. Want to move your car back there?"

Jeb eyed steep wooden stairs to the front door of the

bungalow. He adjusted his stance to ease the pain and briefly considered the idea. Deciding against babying his hip by
moving his car to the rear of the house, he said, "This is
good."

Colavito headed toward the bungalow, but Jeb stopped
him. "Did you learn anything about their plans?"

"Plans?" Colavito rubbed his brow. "No plans. They
seem to argue a lot, but my parabolic receiver only picks up
so much. Most of the reception is muffled."

"You didn't get any transmitters on the windows or inside?"

"These two are too savvy for that," Colavito said. "I had
to use Twentieth Century technology."

"Did you get a chance to check around inside?"

"The close call with the feds must have spooked Joan.
She stays inside ninety-nine percent of the time. She only
leaves the house to go for a run, I can never be sure how
long I'd have. I don't want to get caught nosing around."

"Well, while we're in there, do the best you can to check
things out."

Colavito headed up the stairs verbally noting the peeling
paint, a couple of weak steps, and the weeds growing out of
the gutters. "I don't like any of this," he said, looking back
at Jeb. "It's poorly maintained, probably with plywood
walls. The thick undergrowth surrounding it would make it
difficult to defend, if it ever came to that."

Colavito shook his head and opened a shabby screen
door with squeaky hinges. The top half of the front door
consisted of nine glass panes divided by rotting wood. He
rapped his knuckles against one of the panes. It rattled under his touch. "We have to get her out of here."

"That's my plan." Jeb nodded and frowned at the ripped
screens and uninhabited wasp nest in the far corner. "I'll
make some calls. If we separate them, I can cozy up to
Joan, and maybe we can turn one against the other to find
out what really happened in Phoenix."

"You still think their story is a cover?"

Jeb pressed his lips together and took another look around. "Why would she have chosen to live here rather than in my house?"

Colavito shrugged. "She knows Kearney better?"

"Yeah," Jeb snorted. "I'll bet that's it." He shook his head. Archer had survived many deployments as a mercenary, even the last one in El Salvador when his whole team perished. He was a survivor. Then he met Joan. Then he wound up dead. Colavito could have been right when he said that shit happens. But what if it turned out to be something else?

Their monthly allotments from Archer's estate were certainly enough for better accommodations. Using this for a temporary residence until they made their escape could explain their choice. It affirmed his decision to retain control of Archer's estate to force Joan and Kearney to stick around.

Jeb knocked against the wooden bottom half of the door and cupped his hands to see inside. "Are you sure she's home?"

"Been home all night."

He saw movement. "Here she comes."

Joan shuffled across the living room and closed a door on the left, just inside the front door.

He raised his voice to be heard through the door. "Good morning, Iron Angel." When the door opened a crack, he smiled, hoping to get a smile on the sleepy face in front of him. "Didn't you get my text?"

She yawned and glanced at the cheap, plastic clock on the wall above the television. "Yeah, I got it," She said with a raspy, sleep-filled voice. "Keep your voices down. Kearney's still sleeping."

"We brought bagels and coffee," Jeb said without lowering his voice.

"Come in. Next time use the back door," she grumbled, opening the door wider so the two men could enter the rundown living room of the rented bungalow. She looked up at

Colavito and said, "So you've decided to come in rather than sit in the woods and watch us."

His face froze. "You knew I was watching you? I set up way across the…how long have you known?"

"Archer said you're good," Jeb said to Joan.

"Is there anything he didn't tell you?"

"You'd be surprised how much he told us about you."

She changed the subject. "I was tempted to invite you in during that freak ice storm a couple nights ago, but hell, who am I to interfere with someone doing his job?"

"You coulda brought me some hot coffee," Colavito said. "We could have huddled together to keep each other warm. And—"

Jeb shot a warning glance at Colavito. "Ditch it, 'Vito. She's a widow for Chrissake."

A boyish grin flashed on Colavito's face. He held up the cardboard tray. "Where do you want this?"

Joan ruffled her short hair and padded across the room. "Bring your stuff over here. There's a table and chairs."

On the way across the small, sparse room Jeb said, "Don't mind Colavito. Flirting is the only way he knows how to talk to a woman."

Joan snatched up the newspaper Kearney had left on the chipped Formica table and cleared a stack of self-help books from one of the chairs. After a brief search, she dropped them on a table at the end of a beat up, second hand couch. She brushed an orange and white striped cat off the table, but it quickly enthroned itself on the back of the sofa.

"What's the cat's name?" Colavito asked, rubbing its head and chin.

"I have no clue. I never saw it before." She remained standing, looking wary of the purpose of this meeting.

Jeb raised his eyebrows. "You're pretty casual about a cat you've never seen before."

"It's just a cat. I'm sure the mystery will unravel itself in time. If there was a man standing in the corner with a three-foot sword, I'd be concerned about that." She put her hands on her hips. "What do you want?"

Jeb limped to the nearest chair and slumped into it. Slouching eased the dull ache. He had a prescription for the pain, but preferred to stay alert during the day. He cleared his throat. Joan's unexpected grouchiness made him unsure where to start.

"Archer wasn't much for pleasantries either," Colavito said to no one in particular. He wandered around the room, checking the windows, peaking into the tiny kitchen, listening to the light snoring coming from Kearney's room. He scanned the line of the ceiling, the slanted wood floor, the stained plaid couch. Something in Joan's bedroom caught his eye.

Colavito rubbed his stubble. "Interesting."

"What's interesting?" she asked.

"Your room. It's bright and clean. The bed is neatly made. Doesn't match the rest of the house."

"The bedroom is important to me. It's the first thing I see in the morning and the last thing at night."

Colavito nodded. Years of surveillance carved deep creases into the skin at the corners of his brown eyes. He moved toward the chair opposite Jeb, with the efficient, wary movement of a wolf.

Joan picked at the cracked vinyl on the back of the chair in front of her. "Spending the money Duncan left me feels like giving parts of him away," she explained. "Kearney bought just the bare essentials until I find a job and can—"

"Colavito isn't judging you," Jeb assured her. "Recon is what he does. It's so entrenched, he couldn't stop if he wanted to." He hesitated. "Like you."

She lifted her chin. "I quit that life."

He caught the tell, the almost imperceptible tightening at the outer corner of her eyes that told him she wasn't being entirely honest. "Is that right?" He pulled a cup of coffee out of the cardboard carrier. "Sorry about the surveillance, but I had to be sure you and Kearney didn't live in a way that could jeopardize Durham Security."

"This constant surveillance has to stop, Jeb. Don't you have other projects or jobs or whatever you call them? My life is boring." She turned toward Colavito. "Isn't it?"

Instead of answering her question, Colavito blew on his coffee.

She glared at Jeb. "And I haven't said I'd work for you."

Jeb lifted the lid off the paper cup and blew on the black, steamy liquid. He glanced up at her without lifting his head. "You haven't said 'no.'" He continued blowing on his coffee.

"Maybe I should have. Maybe I thought you'd take the hint."

"Maybe you need help saying 'yes,'" Colavito said in a low tone, as if talking to himself.

Joan squinted at him, but he was struggling with the tab on a creamer. When Jeb started speaking she turned her attention back to him—eyes first, then a slight turn of her head.

"Iron Angel, you are going to work for Durham Security." Jeb took a slurping sip of hot coffee. "I know it. You know it. Let's skip the bullshit and get down to business."

"I won't do it unless you hire Kearney, too," Joan said. Kearney had been turned down by Jeb many times. If she hooked herself to Kearney, possibly Jeb would stop hounding her.

"Durham Security has a great reputation of clean, surgical ops. He doesn't fit the business model."

"When he gets involved in an op, it gets messy," Colavito added.

Jeb rubbed his upper lip. "But I might be able to find something for him to do."

So much for calling off the relentless job offers. The possibility remained that if she said "yes," no job would materialize for her to do.

"Do I smell coffee?"

Their heads turned toward the sound of Kearney's voice.

A bare-chested Kearney walked toward them, tightening the drawstring of his sweatpants. He wasn't in particularly good physical condition—a small roll of flab ringed the elastic waistband. His specialty, enhanced interrogation, required intricate skill not physical prowess.

He said quick hellos on the way to the table. Grabbing one of the cups, he pawed through the bag of bagels like a hungry boar. "What's up?"

She decided against answering him, and instead addressed Jeb. "You should know, up front, that I have Iron Angel Bad Karma—things always go to shit around me."

"Is that right? Well, you should know—up front—that I don't believe in that crap."

"You will," Kearney said, picking up a plastic knife and preparing to cut a bagel.

Jeb's mouth formed a mocking, flat smile. "Is that right?

"I've sworn off killing. I won't kill anybody." She looked down at her hands. "I want to get that out. Just so you understand."

"Agreed."

"And I don't want any leadership responsibilities." She made a horizontal slicing motion with her hand to emphasize her point. "None."

"Got it."

Kearney stopped slicing his bagel. "What's going on here?"

She turned her head to take in her meager surroundings. She could use some earned income. Jeb had been right, that day in his office, having nothing to do made her feel useless, and it made her treadmill lifestyle—training, eating, sleeping, and training some more—borderline masochistic. She studied the faces of each of the men. The quiet ticks of the plastic clock broke through the thick silence, marking the seconds marching into the past.

She exhaled heavily, locked eyes with Jeb, and answered Kearney. "I got you a job at Durham Security."

A broad smile crimped a dimple to the left of Jeb's

mouth. He pushed out the chair in front of her with his foot. "Take a seat, we have important ground to cover."

She sat down and grabbed a cup of coffee. Kearney settled on the arm of the couch behind her, petting the cat that rubbed up against him and purred.

Colavito slid his chair back from the table. "Well, boss, if you don't need me, I'm going to go home and get some sleep."

"You earned it. I'll touch base in a couple days."

After quick good-byes, Colavito disappeared into the kitchen to leave by way of the backdoor as Joan had suggested when they arrived.

Jeb waited until Joan finished preparing her coffee before beginning. "Okay. You two will be part of the covert division of Durham Security. You'll always enter via the back entrance, through our private club, Notches. And then go directly to the second floor via the back staircase."

Joan sipped her coffee and picked at a bagel. "What's wrong with going in the front?"

"It's my regular part of the security business: loss prevention, armed security guards, bodyguards. I don't mix the two. They aren't allowed in Notches unless they're invited by me for a specific event."

"Why not?"

"My operatives work hard, play hard, and drink hard. They need a safe haven to unwind and talk freely about problems without fear of revealing what they do for a living. Their preferred liquor is always kept in stock at no charge. It's a perk of employment." He smiled, scooped a few crumbs off the table into his other hand, and put them in the empty cup tray. "I've already told the bartender to order a case of Patron."

A hint of a smile on Joan's face caught his eye. "What's so funny?

"You were so sure I was coming on board you already ordered a case of Patron?"

"Absolutely. Is that a problem?"

Joan relaxed back into the chair. "I like confidence. It's the sharpest tool in anyone's arsenal. I'm not as confident as I used to be, but I'm working on it."

"That's not what I saw in the office a couple weeks ago. You were a woman who had just gotten chased out of her home with nowhere to go, yet you didn't skulk into my office begging for help."

"She's getting better every day," Kearney said, leaning forward and squeezing her shoulder.

Joan turned her head slightly, but not enough to see his face. Jeb watched the interaction between these two adversaries who had become allies. It looked like compliments from Kearney were rare, and she didn't know how to respond to them. Or Kearney's friendly touch was something Jeb was not supposed to see.

"Good," Jeb said to keep the conversation moving. "Because I have a job for you right away. It's a simple bodyguard position a couple nights a week—nothing too demanding. I want you to get your feet wet, feel your way around, see how we do things."

"So I'd go through the front office then?"

"No. You're an operative. You always use the back, always report directly to me." He leaned forward, resting his forearms on his thighs. "Now let's talk money."

❦❦❦

After Jeb left, Joan tidied up. While putting the empty coffee cups and used napkins in the trash can she asked over her shoulder, "What's with the cat?"

Kearney flashed his big toothy grin. "I'm watching it for my girlfriend while she's on vacation."

"What's her name?"

"Elaine."

"And she's your girlfriend?

"Evidently."

"What does that mean?"

He licked the cream cheese that oozed from between two bagel halves. "Who knew that one movie date, plus two dinner dates, plus a night of sex equals a relationship?"

"You're kidding me, right?" She stopped wiping her hands. "Wait…you got a woman into bed?"

"Contrary to your personal opinion, I am not repulsive. You know the difference between a good interrogator and a great one?"

She shook her head.

"A great one is able to get into someone's head. Once inside their head, you can manipulate them." He leaned against the refrigerator and crossed his arms. "Me? I'm a great one."

"So you got her into bed under false pretenses."

"I prefer to think of it as mindful seduction." He raised his eyebrows. "However, the pretenses after I got her there weren't false."

Joan turned to put the leftover creamers in the refrigerator. "I don't even want to know what that means. Do you know anything about her?"

"Well, she says she married young. She dedicated her life to her husband and two children—"

Joan squinted her eyes. "Where's the husband now?" A scorned husband in a love triangle could be dangerous—not just for Kearney, but for both of them.

"That's the sad part of her story. The day they dropped off their youngest kid at college, Hubby Dearest told her he was divorcing her. At first, she was broken up about it, but now she's resolved to live her life to the fullest."

"So what I'm hearing is she wants a bad boy." *She had to start with the worst man on the planet? Good luck, honey.*

He chuckled softly. "Yup. That's me."

Smug bastard. "You're going to straighten out this relationship thing, right?"

He took a bite from a garlic and sea salt bagel and

munched on it while he thought about it. "I like her. Maybe I'll play this out and see where it goes."

"Well, be careful. The wrong word in the wrong ear can bring us down." Joan rubbed her eyes. It had been her deposition as a state's witness that took down the Constitution Defense Legion, but Kearney seem oblivious to the implication of her words.

He took a big bite, and with a mouthful of bagel said, "It can work."

"Suddenly I'm not worried. You're a pig. When she realizes that, she'll be gone." Joan walked past him. "I'm going for a run to clear my head."

She went into her bedroom to change. Should she tell Jeb about Kearney's girlfriend? How did he survive on the run for so long when he could be so irresponsible? After she got him the job he wanted at Durham Security, he seemed hell bent on blowing it over a woman.

On the way past her bedroom door, he raised his voice to be heard through it. "Maybe she likes men who are pigs. And you hang out with me."

She yanked the laces on her left sneaker so hard they broke.

CHAPTER 4

A week to the day later, Joan eyed the monster of a man standing at her kitchen door, blocking the late morning light. If Jeb hadn't called to tell her he sent Carmine to help her move, she would have grabbed a knife. But even a knife would be little use against a man his size.

He wasn't looking through the window in the door. Instead, he stood with his back toward her, checking the surroundings.

He turned when she opened the door and said, "You must be Carmine."

"You must be Angel." No smile. His upper eyelids were at half-mast shading dark brown eyes, giving them a dreamy appearance. He stood at least six-foot-four. A round belly peeked out between the lapels of his sport court. But he wasn't out of shape. The loose-fitting jacket didn't hide his broad shoulders, massive chest, and pumped up arms.

"I'm already packed."

"You haven't seen the place yet, and you're ready to move?" He dipped his head to avoid messing up his black, wavy hair when he walked through the door and then tugged on his lapels to straighten his jacket. Before he closed them, she saw the holstered semi-automatic on his hip. He noticed her staring at his hip. "What? Did you think Jeb sent me to strong-arm ya?"

"It crossed my mind."

"If Jeb was gonna strong-arm you, he'd send multiple

operatives, and he'd surprise you. Trust Jeb. Once you're on the team, he's there for you."

"I want to trust him, but I don't think he trusts me."

"What makes ya say that?"

Joan shrugged. "I don't know. Just a gut feeling."

"He had me find this nice place for you to live. I'd say that says something about him and what he thinks of you." Carmine looked around the small, dingy kitchen. "I'll bet you're anxious to get away from Kearney, after what he did to you. I never understood that about Archer—if Kearney had done to my girlfriend what he did to you, he'd be taking a long swim at the bottom of the East River. You know what I'm talkin' about?"

"You know what Kearney did?" Was there anything Duncan didn't tell these people? And as for how Duncan tolerated Kearney, he owed the bastard his life. Kearney had saved Duncan's life twice—once literally and once by getting Duncan off the streets to get treatment for his PTSD.

"Well, not exactly," Carmine said, showing no signs of discomfort. "But I heard stories of Kearney's gruesome handiwork."

"Well, forget about it. I have."

Carmine scrutinized her face. "No. You never forget stuff like that. How do you live in the same house with the guy?"

"It's called forgiveness."

"How can you—"

"It's not easy." She rubbed her thighs over the worst scars. "You are right, though—I can't forget what he did to me, but the forgiveness allows me to move on."

Forgiveness. Moving on…Something more than grief tormented her. More than missing Duncan's presence and touch. More than the aching hollowness in her life. If it were simply grief she could handle it, but something more haunted her.

"Where's your stuff?"

Her thought process interrupted, she'd think this through

later. "I'll get it." She returned with faded army duffel bag, a backpack, and a gym bag.

"This it?" He took the bags and smiled. "Ya'd think you were a fugitive or somethin'." When he smiled, his taciturn expression disappeared and his olive skin visibly brightened. His eyelids drooped a little more giving the impression of sharing a private joke.

She relaxed. The giant Italian seemed affable and maybe even safe. "I thought we'd make a second trip for my weight set and motorcycle."

"No need for a weight set. There's an exercise room. Wait'll you see this place."

After loading her bags in the spacious trunk of Carmine's big, black Cadillac, she settled against the luxurious passenger seat.

As she reached for the seatbelt, she asked, "What model is this?"

He turned the ignition key. "A '68 Eldorado." The engine rumbled to life, sending vibrations through the floorboards. "If you like this car, wait till you see Claude's car—a sweet '39 Mercury."

"Who's Claude?"

"My teammate." Carmine hooked his seatbelt. "Know anything about cars?"

"Not really, but I recognize a souped-up engine when I hear one."

He snorted, shifted the car in reverse, put his arm on the back of her seat, and looked over his shoulder. The transmission whined when he sped down the narrow drive. "Souped-up. I haven't heard that expression for a while." The bumps and ruts of the drive turned into a gentle rocking motion by the Caddy's suspension. When he pulled out onto Route 32, he floored it. The powerful engine responded and the speedometer needle arced to eighty-five miles per hour, pinning Joan to the soft leather seat that wrapped around her.

"Whaddya think?"

"Off the ledge," she said in a breathy voice, as if making slow, sensual love.

He chuckled. "I like you, Angel. No fear. Pure appreciation of power and speed. You should see your face." He slowed when they approached a vehicle driving the speed limit. "And Jeb says he found a nice place for you to live and you pack up your shit and go. No questions. I like that. I bet you don't even know where you're going."

They rode in silence for several minutes. Joan saw things on the landscape she hadn't previously noticed. They passed a housing project under construction on land that had been farm land not so long ago. A ramshackle barn with no visible means for keeping it erect stood as a lone sentinel to the past. Driving a motorcycle took too much concentration and alertness to notice the signs of progress around her. The smooth ride and the relaxation of not having to drive lulled Joan into a dreamlike state.

"You know, Archer really loved you," Carmine said out of the blue. "I mean: Really. Loved. You."

"What makes you say that?"

"A couple-three years ago he said he had met a mouthy woman who—"

"Mouthy? He actually used that word?"

"I think he said, 'cocksure,' but don't quote me on that." He glanced at her before returning his attention to the road. "From that moment on you were all he talked about. We know everything there is to know about you."

So much for a private relationship. If he was here, I'd strangle him. "Oh, yeah? What color underwear am I wearing?"

Carmine shifted in his seat, shook his head and said, "Cocksure," under his breath. After a long side-wise look he said, "Bikini. Black. No lace." He palmed the steering wheel to send the Caddy up the entrance ramp to Route 17, heading toward Goshen.

She turned her head away and fought a smile, wondering what word Duncan would have used to describe Carmine.

She watched the backyards of houses and small businesses pass by. The buildings were built before the four-lane lured the traffic from the original two-lane road. Their front yards opened onto the local road—a road with sharp curves and uneven surfaces, known only by locals.

"This is our exit, 128. There might be a better way, but I'm showing you the way I go. This is Craigsville Road." He checked both ways for traffic and made a left at the end of the ramp.

"It looks almost rural."

"Jeb didn't tell you anything about the place?"

"He just said I'd be housesitting in return for free rent and utilities."

A mile later, he turned left. "This is Greycourt. We'll be making a right turn onto private land in a couple seconds."

He turned onto a short access road with an abandoned, cinderblock gatehouse on the right hand side just far enough in that a truck could pull in and not block Greycourt Road. Beyond the gatehouse a road curved away from them in both directions. A chain link fence extended around the land on the opposite side of the road.

Carmine edged the Caddy left onto the curved road. The fencing circled the property on her right. Weeds bordered two rusting steel Quonset huts. A small, neglected vineyard languished on the west side of the buildings. When the car slowed, she looked past Carmine to pastures surrounded by gleaming, white, board fencing.

"This isn't one of those awful dude ranches where they ride horses to death, is it?" She didn't know much about horses, but those places that rented horses by the hour seemed cruel to such beautiful animals.

"No. These are Standardbreds—bred for racing—pacers and trotters."

"Like with the sulkies behind them?"

He glanced at her and smiled. "You're brighter than you look."

"Yeah," she said sardonically. "So bright I'm a fugitive from justice."

"You're a fugitive, not an inmate," Carmine said. "I call that some pretty smart thinkin'." He eased the car onto a driveway flanked on both sides by the white fences. "Do you play the horses?"

"No. I don't gamble."

"Oh, you're a gambler, all right—just not with money. I'd bet my life on it. Maybe I'll take you to Monticello sometime and show you how to read The Sheet that gamblers use to choose their bets."

You're a gambler all right—what could she say to that? For a fugitive, every day was one big gamble with no happy ending. Failure to use a turn signal could initiate a traffic stop, and she'd spend the rest of her life in jail. A life sentence for a moving violation. She shook her head. No wonder she couldn't sleep.

After a quarter mile, the fencing opened up to reveal a typical farm house. White. Wraparound porch with requisite swing. To the left of the house a broad, dirt parking area abutted a stable and behind it sat a horse transport the size of a bus. Beyond that a pasture extended to the far tree line. No rusting machinery. No piles of junk. The patches of grass around the house and along the stable were green, lush and recently mowed. Impressive for an absent owner.

Carmine rolled up to the left of the house and parked.

He started talking while he got out of the car. "There's a guy who maintains the property, but he's only here two days a week. And there's a guy who takes care of the horses. He's here twice a day, but doesn't pay attention to anything but the animals. The doc wanted someone here every day to keep an eye on the house. He's put a lot of money in it...well, you'll see."

He walked up to a mullioned door on the side of the house. "This is the entrance you'll use."

The door opened into a fifteen-by-fifteen foot living room with a breakfast bar on one side. A refurbished galley kitchen could be seen under overhead cabinets. A hallway extended past the kitchen and past a small bathroom—also refurbished. And beyond that, the hall ended at a bedroom the same size as the living room.

"This addition was added for a housekeeper's quarters." Carmine opened a door. "It even has a...whatcha-call-it?... walk-in closet."

Joan eyed the ornate, antique brass bed. "This is beautiful." She fingered the rosettes and filigree surrounding them. "Does it take a lot to keep it shiny like this?"

"I think I remember Doc sayin' his wife had it cleaned and sealed. So all you have to do is bring in your belongings and you are open for business." He cleared his throat. "I didn't mean anything by that. I hope you didn't take offense."

She patted him on his rock-hard upper arm. "It takes a lot to offend me."

"Let me show you the rest o' the place." He talked over his shoulder while leading the way to the main house. "You have free rein. You can use the media room and the exercise room that I told ya about. I don't know if you cook..." He turned to see her admiring the roomy, renovated kitchen with commercial grade appliances. "...but you can use the kitchen—unless the owner is here, which he never is. When's your first job for Jeb?"

"Tonight."

"Too bad. I woulda cooked you a great Italian dinner and we coulda watched a movie together later."

She craned her neck to see farther in the house. "Let's take a look at that workout room." While she followed him through the house, she silently chastised herself for being too casual and familiar with a man she didn't know that well. She hoped his intentions were friendly. Anything more than that would make working with him uncomfortable. She rubbed her eyes—the last man she got too close to got killed.

Later at Notches, she would get a better feel for this man's intentions and do some damage control, if necessary.

❧❧

Joan's few clothes looked lonely in the large closet, but at least her folded clothes held their own in the hand-carved chest of drawers. The apartment wasn't home yet, but it wouldn't be long before this new place offered her the comfort and familiarity of home. She searched for a hiding place for her genuine identification, the two remaining false ones, and the cash. Before she could look, someone knocked at the door. She stuffed the documents into the duffel bag and toed it under the bed.

Carmine must have forgotten something. Two hours ago, he had dropped her off at Kearney's bungalow to pick up her motorcycle. She had driven her bike back to the farm, blessing the salesman every minute for insisting on keeping the fairing and windshield on the front of the bike—it had protected her hands and legs from the icy blast when she drove at highway speed.

She hung back at the sight of a man standing at the door. The man cupped his eyes to see in the door. Jeb. The man all but lived at Durham Security. What was he doing here?

She opened the door without a greeting.

"Hi," he said, looking past her into the room. "I just thought I'd check out Carmine's choice for you."

She stepped back to let him in.

He took in the bare walls and beige, once-overstuffed couch. "It's not very big, but it's nicer than the bungalow, right?"

"It's nice." She studied him. "Thanks for your help getting this place." Jeb had left his business in the middle of the day and traveled at least an hour to check out her new apartment. An unusual act for him.

"Oh, yeah," he said, as if finally remembering he had a

box under his arm. "I bought a coffee pot for you for a house warming present. And there's some sugar substitute you like in this bag. I put some of my favorite coffee in there, too."

Joan thanked him and he followed her to the kitchen. He muscled open the stapled flaps and worked the coffee maker and packing material out of the box.

"I was hoping I could talk you into making me a cup of coffee and showing me around your new digs."

"Digs? What are you—stuck in the Sixties?"

He bumped her shoulder with his. "You know what I meant."

"I didn't think you were that old." Teasing Jeb came easy. He had always been all business, professional in his dealings with her. Now he was acting buddy-buddy, ever since that phone call that blew her out of her comfort zone and into his office.

"Here," he said, handing her the glass pot. "Rinse this out. Let's get this baby fired up."

While he scooped the coffee into the filter, he chatted about why he preferred drip coffee. He pushed the button and they waited in silence for the gurgle that meant coffee was only minutes away.

Joan kept her eyes on him.

"What are you looking at?" he asked.

She smiled to cover getting caught in the act of studying him. "Nothing."

A slow smile tugged at his mouth. "Okay. Show me around."

"There really isn't much to see. This is the kitchen."

"Is that right?" he said, looking around in feigned wonderment.

Joan slapped his arm and squeezed past him to the hallway and pointed. "Living room, with basic furnishings: couch, two chairs, and coffee table. No lamps—overhead light only, with fan."

Jeb stood, rubbing his upper lip. "Is that right? No TV either."

"Yeah, I'll pick one up this week some time."

"I gotta see that: a flat screen strapped to your back as you bike down the highway."

"It's amazing what you can transport on a bike with a little ingenuity."

Jeb snorted. "I have an extra one. I'll bring it up for you to use."

"You don't have to do that."

"Chalk it up to concerns for road safety. I don't want to lose my newest operative."

She pointed out the bathroom, but when she reached the bedroom door an uneasiness settled across her shoulders. A bedroom. A man other than Duncan.

Jeb must have felt her discomfort because he said, "I guess that is the bedroom." He turned and walked to the kitchen where he turned to face her. "Nice...digs." He flashed his dimple at her and winked. "Let's check on that coffee."

Her uneasiness drained away and she joined him in the kitchen. Too much time on the run could be fueling her skepticism of Jeb's intentions. Her positions in the resistance group and the militia required sharp insight for things that could go wrong or actions that didn't fit the situation. Jeb had been right a week ago when he said she couldn't change if she wanted to.

"Mmmm," she said, inhaling deeply. The aroma of coffee made her new apartment feel like home.

"You're easily pleased." Jeb filled two mugs.

Joan reached for a packet of sugar substitute. "There were times when coffee was my only friend."

He bumped her shoulder again. "Now you have a new one." He headed to the living room, mug in hand.

Joan poured milk into her coffee and thought how different he acted when he wasn't being her boss. Without the weight of his responsibilities, his conversation became light-hearted. Almost playful. More seemed to be going on with him than appeared on the surface. He could swing from harsh to kind to intense to friendly. She still didn't like him, but if he wanted to be her friend, she sure could use one.

Jeb flopped into one of the chairs. "Tell me something about yourself, Joan."

ᘓᘓᘓ

Special Agent Woyzeck flew into New York City from Pittsburgh that morning, shaved with an electric shaver over a sink in the men's room on Concourse A, hailed a cab, and went to the Federal Building without checking into a hotel. If the task force didn't take on his case, he'd check into that hotel anyway. He wasn't leaving New York without Joan Bowman.

He passed out photos to the federal agents seated at the conference table. "This is Joan Bowman, a fugitive I've been chasing for two-plus years. She cooperated at one time, and was instrumental in bringing down the Constitution Defense Legion."

The Senior Supervisory Agent Danielson fingered through the photos. "I heard of that. She never made it to prison."

"Yes, sir. That's right. She was abducted out of my car by masked men with assault rifles."

"What happened to her? Do you know?"

"She joined up with another group in Arizona…with the guy in the photos."

Danielson leaned back in his chair. "I'm assuming you're here because you believe she's in the New York area."

"Yes, sir. She thinks her fiancé is dead, she's on the run, alone. In desperate times, people go home." He looked at Danielson with a confident smile. "She grew up in New Jersey."

"What's the story with the guy?"

"That's Dennis Maurice Archer. We arrested him in Phoenix for running a paramilitary group called the Counter-Insurgency Army. He escaped from the hospital where he was recovering from gunshot wounds. We don't know where he is, but if Bowman is here, and he's alive, this is where he'll be, too."

"What kind of charges are we looking at?" Danielson asked.

"Terrorism, sedition, murder, illegal arms dealing, to name a few."

"I'll hook you up with our contacts in New Jersey." The Senior Agent nodded toward the female agent across the table from Agent Woyzeck. "Agent Merrill will work with you. Give her everything you have. If they're here, we'll find 'em." He stood to indicate the meeting was over. "These are dangerous people. Let's get them off the streets."

CHAPTER 5

Later that day, sitting in a café in Yonkers, Joan looked past her reflection in the tinted window. Twilight filled the avenue, lengthening shadows that swallowed the office building across the street. That building was the address Jeb gave her for her first job for him. Its windows, now bright in the ending day, showcased the people inside like G-rated peep shows. She watched it while she waited for her coffee to cool. Her mind wandered to the apartment Carmine showed her that afternoon. Jeb had made a wonderful gesture to make her feel at home. It was the best welcome she had received in a long time, although his intentions had not yet come into focus. If he was offering friendship, she'd take him up on that, because living alone was a relatively new concept. If Jeb's intentions were something more intimate, that would have to be considered with deep thought.

She missed Duncan. Dating him had been straightforward. He liked her. He said so. They became a couple. No room for misinterpretations. Easy. She picked up her phone to ask Kearney his opinion, but decided against it. Instead, her eyes wandered to the last of the commuters lingering at a bus stop in front of the café. Some of them puffed on their cigarettes, getting in the last drags before the next bus arrived.

The conversation with Jeb, telling him she swore off killing, popped into her head…

I am not a killer.

Special Agent Woyzeck would disagree, as would seven-teen dead men. And then there are the six women who died, not at my hands, but because of me. The one man I should have killed died at my feet from bullets fired from someone else's gun. But I'm not all bad. I saved Kearney, and now he feels obligated to save me, but he's just being a pain in the ass.

Khalil Gibran got it right: "Out of suffering the strong-est souls emerge; the most massive of which are seared with scars." Seared with scars. I don't know how strong I am, but I sure got the scars part right. As bad as the scars are on my body the worst ones are on my heart. I managed to save Mr. Pain In the Ass, but I couldn't save the life of the man I love. If only I had been stronger or faster or a better leader...

She leaned against the back of her stool in the rundown café. She bent her knee and braced her shin against the counter. The café manager walked up and wiped the already clean counter a few feet away—his way of telling her to sit up. She nodded at him, put her leg down, and leaned her elbows on the edge of the counter.

People who know me back down from me, or don't face off with me in the first place. But Duncan, he stood between me and myself...my worst self. He never backed down—the only person brave enough to stand up to me. But he's gone. Because of my shortcomings...

Joan closed her eyes and imagined his strong arms around her. Their strength were her strength, their warmth her warmth—or had been. She groaned inwardly and took a sip of her Americano. And winced. *Still too hot to drink.* She leaned back and studied her reflection in the glass that separated the café from the deepening dusk...

People who've done the things I've done say they don't recognize themselves when they look in a mirror. I have no misgivings about who I am. I am not a naïve, run-of-the-mill productive member of society. And I no longer envy them while they go about their lives blissfully unaware of me and people like me. Looking back, at some point I made the fateful step over a line...no, through a gate that swings one way—from average worker to specialized operative...

Joan pulled off the top of her cup and blew on the liquid fire inside....

*Am I an operative? Well, I don't flip burgers...*She glanced over her shoulder...*or serve coffee for a living, that's for sure.*

I am who I am, and I'm comfortable with that.

I have to be.

But Kahlil Gibran was talking about souls. Well, my soul is scarred, too. At night, when all I want to do is let go of my empty world, ghosts of my victims remind me of the things I've done. I'm never fast enough or smart enough to silence them. Their taunts force me to do things I can't stop myself from doing, force me to be someone I am not.

I am not a killer—not anymore...

She dispassionately studied the other side of the street and spied a froth of curly, brownish-copper hair. She sat upright. *Duncan.* Her heart drummed against the inside of her chest. She grabbed her backpack and ran out of the café. A bus pulled up to the curb with the breathy squeal of air brakes. Taking quick side steps, she darted around the back of the bus and crossed the street, dodging the front end of a sedan that skidded to a halt.

There. To the left, bobbing away from her. A flash of copper. She pushed her way through the crowded sidewalk. The copper curls disappeared in the middle of the next block. She wanted to scream at the people to get out of her way. She jostled and shouldered her way through the crowd. Duncan would not get away this time.

She stopped at the spot where she had lost sight of him and looked up the street. She twisted to check out the opposite side of the street. Nothing.

She entered the alley and crept along the brick wall on her right. She glanced over her shoulder, took a few more steps, and stopped. Only normal city sounds filled the air. She darted across the alley to a green dumpster. Her fingers swept the rust-roughened metal while she slipped along its length to the far corner.

She took the last step around the corner. "Duncan." His name slid between her lips—breathy, certain.

There was no one there. She looked around. The alley dead-ended at an eight-foot chain link fence. Only a tangle of weeds and scattered pieces of broken brick were on the other side. Other than the dumpster there was nothing else large enough to conceal a full-grown man.

Her scalp prickled. She backed up a few steps. *You aren't fast enough.* She ignored the thought. This was no time to acknowledge her haunting memories. She ran her hand over her hair until her palm pressed against the skin at the base of her ear, at the edge of her jaw. She turned to leave. A man blocked her exit.

"Duncan."

It wasn't Duncan—too flabby. Too much of a pain in the ass.

"Shit, Kearney, you scared the living daylights out of me." She checked the alley again. "Why the hell are you here, sneaking up on me?"

"I saw you take off out of the café, like someone's life was in danger. I followed you in case you needed backup." His eyes checked the area behind her before narrowing and settling on hers. "What's going on?"

"I saw Duncan."

Kearney exhaled loudly and shook his head. "No. You didn't." He reached out to rub her arms.

She batted his arms away. "I know what I saw."

"Everyone grieves differently," he said. "But constantly watching for him is not good. Moving on won't diminish your love for him."

"I saw him."

"Sometimes I think I see him, too."

"You do?"

He put his hands on her shoulders. "It's a trick our brains play on us when we miss someone. We want to see him, so we do—in a crowd, in a reflection."

"I don't need any of your mind-shrinking mumbo-jumbo."

He put an arm around her shoulder to guide her toward the street. "He's alive in our hearts, right?"

She nodded. *Yeah, he's alive in my scarred, beat up heart.*

"Let's go to Notches. You look like you could use a drink."

"I'll meet you there later," she said with one last look over her shoulder. "There's something else I have to do first."

They stopped where the alley met the sidewalk. "Did Jeb give you an assignment already? I told him to go easy with you for a while."

She shoved him. "Who are you to tell anybody what I should or shouldn't be doing? Don't talk to Jeb on my behalf. I'm not a...project." She pushed through the crowd. He was coddling her because she fought phantoms, or saw a...dead man. She didn't need protection—not his, anyway.

She'd be late, if she didn't hurry.

Kearney rushed up to walk beside her. "You saved my life. I feel obligated...I have the skills to help you. I'd never forgive myself if I didn't."

"Go away."

"Duncan would want me to help you," Kearney said, moving to block her path.

She pushed past him. "That's getting old. It doesn't work on me anymore."

He caught up to her. "Why else do you think he gave me the contact information for Jeb? Why didn't he give it to you?"

"That doesn't work anymore, either." She stopped to check the number on the building on her left. "Stop the bullshit, K. Go away. I have work to do."

Kearney put up his hands in mock resignation. "Okay. But I'm here for you if you ever want to talk about it." He backed up a few steps. "And don't forget. Notches later. Jeb says everyone has to be there."

She crossed her arms. "Got it."

After he disappeared around the corner at the end of the block, she opened the door to the building and quietly climbed the staircase to the room number on the piece of paper in her pocket. On the landing outside Room 3A, she almost collided with a woman built like a dancer. Joan moved to the side and watched the petite woman glide down the stairs, a giant gym bag slung over her shoulder.

Joan listened for any unusual noises. Two wannabe gangsta teens lumbered down from the fourth floor. On their way past her, they made sexist remarks followed by kissing sounds. It was typical New York nonsense. She shook her head and went into Room 3A.

"Hello," a dark-skinned Indian woman said, greeting her. "I am Nirmala. Are you here for the meditation class?" The woman's voice was smooth, exuding peace and an inner calm.

Joan scanned the room. "I'm Angel from Durham Security."

"Oh, yes—"

A man walked in carrying a foam pad. He smiled. "Hi, I'm new." A boyish smile lit up his face. "I'm Rob." He pushed up the wire-rimmed glasses that had slipped from the bridge of his nose.

"Two new students in one night. How wonderful," Nirmala said in her soft, mildly-accented voice.

The man looked at Joan. "You're new, too?"

"I—" Joan looked to Nirmala, not sure of the cover story she wanted to use.

"Yes, this is Angel. She will be joining us for a few classes."

When he moved away to set down his foam pad, she said to Nirmala, "Can we talk a minute?"

They walked through the doorway, into the privacy of the hall. Joan was only five-foot-five, but she towered over the kind-faced woman. She leaned in to talk to Nirmala in a lowered voice. "If I'm lying on the floor with my eyes closed, I can't protect you."

"Have you ever meditated?"

"I don't see—" Joan studied two students who had just arrived.

Nirmala greeted them. She motioned for Joan to move farther along the corridor. "When you meditate your senses are heightened even though you are relaxed and in an altered state of consciousness."

"I'd feel better standing and alert with my eyes open."

"Why don't you try it? Besides nothing has ever happened in the classroom. It's always on the way to the car that…well, things get scary."

"Can I be sitting, at least?"

"Whatever is comfortable for you. Meditation is a personal activity."

"I'll sit on the floor with my back to a wall for support."

Nirmala smiled, patted Joan's arm and returned to the classroom. "That can work, if it makes you more comfortable." She entered the classroom and greeted each student by name.

Joan unzipped her backpack and pulled out the rolled up, thick blanket. She laid it down next to the wall right inside the door.

Nirmala lowered the lights and turned on a CD player. Calming sounds of nature filled the space.

Fifty minutes passed in a snap. Joan had participated in the prompts for relaxation, breath control, and mind emptying. Her thoughts had wandered to past mistakes and her shortcomings, but she pushed them away each time. She stood up and stretched, exulting in feeling more relaxed than she had in ages. She would look for a book on meditation tomorrow.

She accompanied Nirmala to her car. Out of the safety of

the building, Nirmala showed signs of nervousness, jumping at every sound. Joan didn't see anything out of the ordinary, but she understood other people's fears. The glow and roar of fire filled her thoughts. She shook her head to chase away the memory of the fire that had trapped her in a bar in Phoenix. She asked questions about meditation in an attempt to distract Nirmala and get her mind to release its grip on fear. The questions distracted Joan's mind as well, and her own memory faded. Once someone was scared by something, everything became a boogeyman. If she could impress upon Nirmala it was all in her head, she could wrap up this job for Jeb.

When Nirmala was safely in her Subaru and had pulled into the nighttime traffic, Joan's job was done for the day. Nirmala's stalker had never bothered her once she left for home. Joan wondered if the threat was real or a waste of time. She corrected herself—overcoming the bumps in the night was never a waste of time—real or otherwise. She'd have to find a way to convince Nirmala there was nothing to fear, but allaying fear of a non-existent threat was proving a negative. It'd be less problematic if there was a concrete fear that called for action.

Something clattered behind her. The sound, though not loud, stood out in the quiet of the night.

She spun around to face the rear of the small parking lot. She pulled a knife out of the sheath in her boot and moved to the safety of a Ford pickup on her right. She knelt down and peered across the undercarriage of the truck to the cars beyond. No feet, but that didn't mean no one was there. As she crept from vehicle to vehicle, the cool spring air sent a shiver across the base of her neck. The sound of her breathing filled her ears. Using the breath control techniques Nirmala had taught in the class, she focused on the car in the far corner of the lot. She moved in a crouch across the front of a car grill and peeked around the fender. The area was empty—except for a stray dog scavenging for food.

The dog retreated to the far corner and made a movement to go under the car, thought better of it, circled, and then settled on warily watching Joan. It was ready to scurry under the car to safety, if necessary. Talking in soothing tones, Joan slowly shrugged off her backpack and reached into one of the pockets for a partially-eaten muffin. She pulled it out and tossed it half the distance to the dog.

She left the hungry dog to its dinner, shouldered her backpack, and walked toward the street. A shadow moved on the other side of the parking lot. Her mind told her it was Duncan's silhouette, but Kearney's words earlier in the evening squelched the thought. Damn him—he was right. She had to stop seeing her own boogeyman everywhere she looked. She rolled her shoulders to relax and headed toward Notches.

A deep melancholy wrapped around her, hunching her shoulders. Her pace slowed. Duncan would never again fight his way through an unruly mob to get to her. Or hunt for her until he found her stuck in the desert, out of gas, guarding an unconscious Kearney. No one else understood that even a strong woman had her weak moments and need-ed to be strengthened by strong arms and encouraging words. She had led a normal life at one time. Held a secre-tarial job. Owned a home. Worked out in a gym. It had been solitary, but never lonely. But having had strong man in her life, it made her feel all the more alone now.

A police car slowed next to her. Her heart froze in her chest and she spun around to look for a place to hide. She faced a shop window and watched the cruiser pass by in the reflection. It turned the corner and sped down the side street she had just crossed. Speaking of a normal life: Welcome to your new normal. You are where you are because of choic-es you made. Duncan is gone because of choices he made. Accept it. Embrace it one last time. File it in a locked com-partment in the far corner of your mind. Move on.

It sounded easy enough, but easy didn't have a place in her life.

After walking a few blocks, she turned down an alley

and stopped midway. In front of her was a godforsaken, easily overlooked door in the dark, litter-strewn alley. Behind her a full, secluded parking lot sat in shadows. The gray steel door had peel-and-stick lettering that spelled out "Private Club" and below that: "NOTCHES" or more specifically, 'NO CHES'. The empty space between the "O" and the "C" was the same shade as the rest of the door—the "T" had disappeared a long time ago without leaving a trace. Joan hesitated, hand on the weathered brass door handle, fixated on the blank space. A part of her wanted to be that blank space. Gone and forgotten. But there'd always be someone looking for her.

She opened the door.

CHAPTER 6

Led Zeppelin rock music thrummed through the din of lively conversations at Notches, but Joan's blues clung to her like the odor of wet clothes. The spirited bells and dings of the pinball machine did nothing to draw her in. She felt like an outsider.

She hesitated to walk into the room. Notches was usually a sleepy little bar, but tonight it was more crowded than usual. Most of the tables between the booths and the bar were occupied by men in all shapes and ages who gestured broadly. One of them yelled a good-humored insult at the dart players. The other guy feigned throwing a dart at him. Both groups laughed and returned to their conversations. Kearney had his back to her, playing an antiquated pinball machine while a tall blonde woman looked on.

Joan steeled herself and zig-zagged through the tables toward the far end of the bar where a man called Champ sat. She had seen him before, sitting on the same stool. Those times, she had tried to talk to him, but someone always blocked or distracted her. He always looked so sad. If they shared their sadness it might lessen their heavy loads—birds of a feather, and all that. Their eyes met and hope curled through her body.

Colavito, who had been talking at one of the tables, stood up in front of her. "Jeb's been looking for you."

She sidestepped. "Okay. In a minute."

"It's not a good idea to make the boss wait," he said, stepping to block her.

Blocked again.

Jeb appeared behind Colavito. "Why don't you come over and tell me about Nirmala and her problem."

Joan looked past Colavito at Jeb. "Sure. Give me a sec."

"It's going to be a long night." He flexed his fingers in a gesture that indicated for her to come toward him. He guided her toward his stool at the opposite end of the bar from Champ. "Let's get business out of the way first. Then you can enjoy the rest of the evening."

Joan placed her order with Tony, the bartender, and turned when loud laughter erupted from the rear of the room. The darts players were joking with each other—something about their game. Kearney gave her a chin nod before turning his attention to the blonde working the flippers and racking up points.

Tony free-poured a generous double shot of tequila and placed a frosty mug of ice water next to the glass. She thanked him. He nodded and walked a discreet distance away.

"How did it go tonight?" Jeb asked.

"It went okay. I didn't see anything, but something has scared the piss out of Nirmala." She sipped the silver Patron. While it burned a track down her throat, she turned around and leaned both elbows on the bar, opening up to the buoyant atmosphere, hoping it would lift her mood.

"If there's anything going on, I know you'll take care of it." He reached for his glass. "Like you did in Phoenix."

"Take care of it?" she asked, echoing his words. "Does that mean put an end to it? If there is anything, that is."

Jeb rubbed his finger on his upper lip and remained silent.

"How far do I go?" Her role had been described as a bodyguard. Bodyguards didn't usually neutralize a threat. They protected the client. She understood vigilantism, and this sounded a lot like it. Her role and its expectations needed to be defined. This level of confidence and responsibility so early was unexpected. Operating in a militia was a team effort. Being the Operations Chief for the Legion had been a self-starter position, but her actions still had to be part of a group effort. Acting as a lone wolf was new territory and outside her comfort zone.

"Do whatever you would have done in Arizona," Jeb said, watching her facial expressions closely. "Just keep me in the loop."

Joan nodded, made a mental note to nail down the parameters of this job. "One more question."

"What's that?"

"Do you still have someone tailing me?"

Jeb rubbed his upper lip with his index finger. "No. Why? Do you think you're being followed?"

"I get that goosey feeling, but I don't see anyone. Maybe I've been on the run too long."

"Do me a favor? Keep your eyes open. Let me know if you see someone. I'll put a guy on it."

"Thanks." She looked around the room. "Did I miss something? This looks like a celebration."

"Claude is getting released from jail," Jeb said. "He took one for the team. Never gave up any information on Durham Security."

"I can relate."

He rubbed his index finger over his upper lip. "Yeah, I heard."

Of course. Joan snorted, never taking her eyes off the room crowded with boisterous, self-assured men—and a couple women. She hadn't given it much thought before tonight, but she hadn't expected there to be other women operatives.

"Who are the women?"

"The blonde playing pinball enlisted in the marines. She leaves for basic training in a couple weeks. I'll miss her. She's a great operative. But she'll return to us combat-ready. That brunette is the wife of one of the operatives.

She worked for me until she got pregnant with their first child."

A numbness, deeper than any tequila could deliver, immobilized her. This was a complete world with families and camaraderie. Why hadn't Duncan shared this world with her? She had trusted him unquestioningly. Had she been wrong? Joan pinched the bridge of her nose to stem the stinging.

"Archer didn't tell you about us in order to protect you," Jeb said, as if reading her mind. "He wanted to insulate you from any fallout caused by the jobs he did for me—if it ever came to that."

Yet he sent me here. She gave Jeb a weak smile and downed the remaining tequila. He had handled Duncan's estate impeccably. Duncan had entrusted everything to Jeb on a handshake—a special ops code of conduct. To raise questions would dishonor Duncan and, even in death, she wanted to believe in him. Her faltering trust in him knifed her aching heart.

Kearney joined them and distracted her from her self-castigation. He talked hogwash about the CIA, El Salvador, and an exotic *señorita* he met there. She hadn't known that he was a Master Diver until he described the Great Barrier Reef in exquisite detail. Tales of surfing the Pipeline in Oahu created a vision of a younger, long-haired Kearney wearing flowery board shorts, rushing into the surf with a surfboard under one arm. The absurd image of him as a dashing, American James Bond ladies' man made her smile, finally crushing her melancholy. The music worked its way into her tapping feet.

Several large pizzas showed up, borne by a cocky, foulmouthed operative she hadn't previously met. He handed the pizza box to Jeb and joined some friends at a table before introductions could be made. After three hours of pizza and tequila, the long day hit her. She was ready to go to her new home and climb into bed. "I'll meet Claude another day. I'm gonna jump."

"It won't be long now," Jeb said. "They're released one minute after midnight. It would be rude to not be here."

His comment stung. Jeb didn't mean it that way, but he pointed out something she was ashamed she had forgotten—it would be rude for a member of the team to be absent at the return of a loyal colleague. She pasted a smile on her face and listened intently to more of Kearney's escapades.

A half hour later, the door opened and Carmine entered the bar followed by a man who was two inches taller, had a shaved head and thick, hard muscles—the result of many hours in the jail's weight room.

The room erupted in cheers and clapping.

Claude and Carmine walked toward Jeb shoulder to shoulder, moving in unison, like defensive linemen. A football coach had once explained to her that defensive linemen depended on knowing each other well to be successful players. The smallest movement of one prompted a reflexive response in the other. To reach this point, they spent a lot of time together on and off the field. They could often be seen walking together, side-by-side, in sync, just like Carmine and Claude were doing now.

Over the short distance to the bar, several men stood and clapped Claude on the back and either gave him a quick embrace or shoulder bump. They exchanged words only they could hear. When he stopped, Carmine stopped, too. When he moved on, Carmine was right beside him. The sight of this tight-knit two-man team flipped a switch in Joan. She felt pulled into the fold of the Durham Security family, like they were now doing with Claude. By the time the prodigal operative received a warm, sincere greeting from Jeb, she felt connected to the group, which included Claude whose gray eyes had just settled on her.

He offered his hand. "You must be Angel."

She fought the urge to step back. In Phoenix, an outlaw biker friend had been the size of Claude. She had withstood a harsher gaze from Duncan. Yet, something caused her stomach to clench.

As her hand disappeared in his, she was not surprised he would know who she was. She was family. "Yes. It must feel great to be free again."

He reached past her to get a bottle of beer from Tony. "Indescribable," he said over the din that had resumed. He raised the green bottle to eye level. "I've waited a year for this."

Jeb stood to get the attention of the rowdy group. The room fell silent in waves. One or two people yelled for the oblivious talkers to shut up. "Everyone grab a drink."

Joan panicked because she had finished her drinks, but Tony had placed a fresh shot of Patron next to her refilled mug. She smiled her gratitude at him. His face remained neutral.

Jeb raised his glass. "Tonight we welcome the return of one of our own. To Claude!"

"To Claude!" everyone replied in unison. Whistles and hoots erupted.

"I have a toast," Claude said. He raised his glass and hesitated for effect. "To time off for good behavior."

The room burst into applause with catcalls alluding to past questionable conduct and misdeeds.

"Let's go sit in the booth," Carmine said.

Claude nodded at him and asked Joan, "You coming?"

Joan sent a look to Jeb to ask if they were done with business. He nodded a gesture to go ahead and join Carmine and Claude.

"Sure. I'd like that."

Carmine pointed her toward the large corner booth by the dart board and pinball machine. Claude got held up greeting everyone between the bar and the booth. When he finally sat opposite her, Carmine appeared with a handful of shot glasses filled with an amber liquid.

Carmine slid into the booth beside her. "No sissy tequila tonight, lovely lady. It's Jack Daniels all around."

"You're crowding me. Can't you sit next to Claude?" she teased before taking a sip.

"No sipping, lovely lady." He downed a shot. "Sure, I could sit next to him, but we're so big our thighs would touch, and he'd get all hot and bothered. I'd spend the rest of the night fighting off his advances."

"In your dreams," Claude responded. "When was the last time you had a woman make advances at you, eh?"

"I get more than my share, eh," he answered emphasizing the last word. At Joan's puzzled expression, Carmine explained, "He's our token Canadian."

When Claude got up to get a round of drinks, she noticed a narrow waist. She bet he had six-pack abs under his fitted polo shirt—no pasta belly like Carmine's paunch. When he returned he held six shot glasses in large hands. A pinky ring that would have slipped off her thumb flashed in the light. He sat down and studied Joan with eyes surrounded by a hardness she had seen on the faces of others who had spent time behind bars. His scrutiny was long and penetrating. His intensity unsettled her.

"So you are the famous Iron Angel," he said through the burn of the JD he had just chugged.

"I don't know how famous I am."

"Archer worried over your body count. How high was it?"

Her eyes flashed up to his. "I didn't keep track. What kind of a question is that?"

He chuckled. "Everyone keeps track. How many?"

This was not a conversation she had expected or wanted to have. She studied him. He had to be joking, so she gave him chin nod and a half smile. "Are you wearing a wire?"

He lifted his shirt, exposing rock hard abs. "No wire. I'm just trying to get to know you."

She sipped the Jack Daniels while she took stock of the situation. No one talked about people they killed. If this was some kind of jailhouse conversation, she didn't like it.

"He's feeling you out in case we ever have to work together," Carmine said, giving Claude a hard look. "Aren't you?"

Claude tossed back a shot. "Yeah, that's it. Don't get your panties in a twist, eh."

She downed a shot and looked at the empty shot glass. A dangerous cocktail of discomfort and anger bubbled inside her. If she hadn't been pinned in, she would have gotten up and left. Who were these guys to belittle her? After a long inhale and a longer exhale she said, "I never sought out trouble. I committed the cardinal sin in self-defense—I let the other guys make the first move." She looked up at Claude. "They weren't as good at fighting as they thought they were."

"And you think you are?"

"I know I am."

Claude raised his glass in salute before chugging its contents. "I bet you are."

"So what do you guys do for Jeb? Or am I not supposed to ask?"

Carmine straightened in his seat and checked behind him, as if their jobs were a secret. "We're what ya'd call a roving overwatch. When you guys go in and do the detail shit, we hover around the periphery to make sure no one crashes your party, if you know what I mean."

"Do you even know the meaning of periphery?" Claude asked Carmine.

Joan relaxed. The bantering lightened the conversation that had started out too serious for comfort.

"Yeah, we're like satellites."

"If the mission goes to hell, we come in and get you out," Claude added. "You always hope we don't have to do anything, eh?"

An upbeat song came over the loudspeakers. Carmine grabbed her wrist. "Let's dance."

She shook her head. "There's no dance floor."

He dragged her to an open area near the front of the room. Evidently, titans didn't take no for an answer. When the song was over, Claude brought a shot glass to the dance floor. After she downed it, she danced with him. Then Carmine did the same thing—another shot another dance. Between dances, she'd try to break away to talk to Champ, but some guy named Patch, Colavito, or other men, whose names she couldn't remember, would show up with a shot. And so went the evening until three in the morning. The crowd had thinned to a handful of hardcore partiers. The honoree had disappeared earlier in the evening. Colavito sat at one of the booths in a deep conversation with the blonde. Carmine had excused himself to go to the bathroom, and hadn't returned. Kearney had left without saying good-bye.

She rebuffed the foul-mouthed operative and found herself standing next to Champ.

"Looks like you're having fun tonight." he said.

She leaned into the bar, misjudged the distance and fell against it. She nodded. "Yes. I had fun for the first time since…you know."

Champ motioned for Tony to bring a mug of ice water. "Feels good, doesn't it?"

"Yeah." She hiccupped. "Yeah, it feels good."

"Someday you'll have to tell me what happened in Phoenix."

"Why is everybody so interested in what happened in Phoenix?"

"Everybody loved Archer. They just want to know."

"Well, I don't like to talk about it."

"Why?"

Joan tried to focus. He could not have just asked her why she did not want to talk about the end of Duncan's life and the life they had had together. "Kearney likes to talk about it. Ask him."

"Talking about it will lessen the pain," Champ said, taking the mug of water from Tony. He swiveled on the barstool and handed it to her. "Drink this…all of it, or you'll be in a world of hurt when you wake up."

"Damn. I had so much to drink I think my tonsils are pickled." She took a long pull.

Champ chuckled. "You got Jacked."

She raised her brows in question, but kept drinking the refreshing water.

"Claude and Carmine do it to every newbie. They feed them shots of Jack Daniels until they're shitfaced. It means you are officially accepted onto the team."

The icy water cleared her head, but not enough. "How am I going to get home? I drove my bike down here." She held up the mug to get Tony's attention.

"I live up your way. I could give you a ride."

"I think I'll take you up on that. Can I ask you something?"

"Anything."

"Why haven't we had a chance to talk before this? It was like all evening was designed to keep me far away from you."

"Just being protective, I guess."

"Protective?" She hiccupped again. "Of who?" She picked up the mug of fresh ice water and took a long drink. "You look like you can take care of yourself."

"Did you ever think it might be to protect you from me?" He glanced past her then leaned in conspiratorially. "They must have realized we're talking." When he leaned back there were mischievous creases at the outer corners of his eyes. His smile was sweet and coy like...no, she wasn't going there.

He looked past her. "Why don't you ask Colavito yourself?"

Colavito put an arm around her shoulders. He swayed and leaned on her. "What are you two talking about?"

She twisted out of his arm and poked a finger into his chest. "How come you guys didn't let me talk to Champ?"

"Well, I'll tell you one thing. You are not driving upstate. You are drunker than I am. And I'm wasted." He twisted around to get Tony's attention. "Give me a key to a room." He turned back to her. "We have rooms on the third floor for members who've had too much to drink. We don't want anybody getting stopped by the cops for DUI."

Colavito took the key Tony offered. It had an old-fashioned oval fob with a number on it. "Let me take you up there."

"Oh, no. I'm not going anywhere with you. Champ offered to give me a ride home."

"I'll take her up," Jeb said from behind Colavito. Without hesitation, Colavito dropped the key into Jeb's hand, gave him a sloppy salute, and left through a doorway at the rear of the bar.

Jeb put a hand on Champ's shoulder. "We'll talk in a couple days. Drive safe."

"Good night, boss," Champ said, standing up. He winked at Joan. "We'll talk again, lovely lady."

What? Are these guys miked? Carmine called her lovely lady once, and everyone else seemed to pick up on it. A dozen ways to kill Carmine sloshed around her head while watching Champ walk away. His gait was smooth, cat-like. She rubbed her eyes to clear her mind of Duncan's agility and smooth gait.

Jeb's loud voice brought her out of her thoughts. "Finish up your drinks, folks. Pick up a key if you need one. Bring your mug upstairs with you if you want," he said, guiding her toward the door through which Colavito had disappeared. "Let's get you settled in."

They walked through an unused kitchen lit only by the emergency light over a door at the far end of the room. She ran her fingers along a stainless steel work station to prevent staggering and focused on the emergency light, using it to guide her along a straight path.

The door beneath the light opened into the familiar stairwell she used to get to Jeb's office on the second floor. They struggled up the first flight in silence. Joan tried to act more sober than she was. Jeb moved clumsily because of his stiff hip, and drinking all night did not make it easier for either of them. At the first landing, she stopped to study the next flight of stairs and wobbled backward. "I had fun tonight," she said before pushing her weight forward and starting the climb.

"It was the first time I saw you smile—really smile," Jeb said. "You always look so sad."

"I am sad. He was right about moving on, though. It doesn't lessen my love for Duncan."

"Is that what you and Champ were talking about?"

"No. That's what Kearney tells me." A loud hiccup echoed in the stairwell. She stifled the boozy giggles that rippled through her body.

They reached the top of the stairs and started down the hallway. Jeb grabbed her elbow to stop her in front of a door with a metal 'Five' on it. He stepped in closer to her. "What were you and Champ talking about?"

"Nothing in particular. Just chit chat."

"Just chit chat?" Jeb echoed. "Are you sure?"

"Why don't you guys want me talking to him?"

"We don't…what do you mean?"

"Whenever I headed down to his end of the bar, someone always blocked my path."

"It's just your imagination." His breath brushed her cheek when he spoke the last two words because he staggered and fell toward her. He caught himself and braced his forearm on the wall above her head.

"He thought you might be protecting me from him. Why would he say that?" There was no logical reason why they would have to protect her from Champ. She didn't know him, and it seemed no one wanted her to get to know him. And what the hell was Jeb doing, hovering over her?

Jeb leaned in closer. "He can be a dangerous man."

"That's what everyone said about Duncan, but…well, he was different with me." She pressed her fingertips against Jeb's chest and stole a glance at the door. "Do you have the key?"

He straightened. "Sorry. You're probably tired. Moving into a new place, working your first job, then getting Jacked by Carmine and Claude. You've had a busy day." He unlocked the door and pushed it in. He lifted one of her hands and placed the key in it. "Lock up. These are good guys, but they've had a lot to drink tonight. They may get lost going to and from the bathroom. I'll be in Room Eight if you need me for anything." He turned to go to his room.

"Hey, Jeb. Where's the bathroom?"

He pointed down the hall. "Last door on the right. It's co-ed. And no showers. This isn't a hotel."

"Got it. Good night."

"Good night."

She shut the door and checked out the room. Two single beds framed a window with a small night table under it. There was a forlorn, white sink on the right wall with a couple folded towels on one corner. To the left was a bare rectangular table that might have held a TV at one time. She pulled aside the curtain and looked down at a quiet alley.

Was Jeb about to make a move on her? She dropped the curtain. Nah. He was drunk and not thinking clearly—being a man, doing what men do. While she sipped her water she promised herself no more alpha males. *They're always too centered on other things: the group, the surroundings, possible threats, new conquests.*

After finishing the water in her mug, she set it on the night table. She toed off her boots and fell onto the bed fully clothed. Tears burned her eyes.

"Dennis Maurice Archer, come back to me." He was an alpha male, but it was safe to want him. He wouldn't be coming into her life. Tears rolled down her cheek onto the pillow. "Life's so empty without you."

For a change, her nightly phantoms kept their distance and respected her grief.

ოჲო

Her phone vibrated on the night table. She eyed a full mug of water next to it, trying to remember when she put either one there. She picked up the phone and swiped the message icon.

Kearney: *Where are you? You okay?*

Joan: *I stayed in a room above Notches. I feel great, in view of how much I drank.*

Kearney: *I'm here, too. Want to meet for breakfast?*

Joan: *Okay. The CCD in ten.*

Kearney: *CCD?*

Joan: *Cate's Corner Diner?*

She rubbed her sour stomach and shuffled to the sink to splash some water on her face. Kearney was grieving, too. Maybe she should try to connect with him. He certainly was trying to make up for their bad history. Her phone beeped indicating she had a message.

Kearney: *Oh. K.*

෫ઝ෫ఐ

Kearney was already seated at a booth when Joan arrived at the diner. She saw the double take before he watched her walk the length of the aisle between the stools at the counter and the booths along the outside wall. Her movement was confident, graceful, leonine. He wiped his face to hide a smile.

Joan slid into the booth across from him. "What are you smiling about?"

"You look chipper today."

"Yeah, I'm all bright tailed and bushy-eyed," she replied with a hint of a grin. "I got Jacked last night. I'm surprised at how good I feel this morning." She motioned to a wait-ress.

"Give it a couple hours. You haven't sobered up yet."

"You're so full of shit." She smiled up at the waitress when she arrived with a white mug in one hand and a pot of coffee in the other. Joan ordered a toasted bagel. It would be better not to overtax her stomach. "I hope you're paying. I forgot to go to the ATM yesterday."

Kearney chuckled and shook his head. "You're like a helpless lamb."

"Duncan called me that once, except he had said, 'a helpless lamb with a killer instinct.'" She shook her head to clear it. "So what did you think of Claude?" she asked, plucking a packet of sugar and a packet of Equal from the ceramic holder.

"His intensity pegs the meter. Why?"

"That's what I thought, too. I wanted to be sure it wasn't just me." The falling granules from both packets were fascinating to her tired eyes. She reached for the creamer. "Jeb said he didn't give up any information on Durham Security when he was inside."

"That's what I heard." Kearney hesitated before continuing. "That makes him a stand up guy."

She sensed a reservation in Kearney's estimation of Claude. "But?"

"You think something's up with him?"

"He's intimidating as hell," she said. "Is that his normal nature or is it a ploy to cover up something?"

Kearney shrugged it off. "Time will tell."

It seemed to be enough of an answer, and a comfortable silence fell between them. They drank their coffee and watched the people rush past the window on their way to their final workday of the week. It had been years since Joan had experienced a work week. How did they do it? But then, how many of them could live her lifestyle? The waitress broke into Joan's thoughts when she brought their breakfasts and topped off their coffees.

After a couple bites of the bagel, Joan put her elbows on the table and gripped the mug with both hands. She opened her mouth to say something, thought better of it, and took sip instead. Finally, she said, "Is the offer to help me still open?"

"With what?" Kearney asked without looking up from loading a fork with scrambled eggs. When she didn't answer, he looked up and stopped with the fork halfway to his mouth. He studied her face, looked into her eyes for an extra beat, then shoveled the eggs into his mouth.

She sat without moving while he chewed his food.

He swallowed and wiped his mouth before answering. "Why now? What changed?"

"I—" She cleared her throat. "I feel like I'm being followed." She put her mug down and looked out the window. "I know what you're going to say. Jeb had Colavito tailing me—us—but Jeb said he pulled him off. "

Kearney placed his fork on his plate and leaned against the back of the booth. "Have you seen anyone? You spotted Colavito that last time."

Joan shook her head.

Kearney noisily cleaned his teeth with his tongue and watched Joan trace the rim of her mug. When he was ready to speak, he leaned forward on his elbows. "Does this have anything to do with your Duncan sighting last night?"

He didn't gesture air quotes around the words "Duncan sighting," but Joan heard them and felt their impact. "Fucking psychiatrist," she muttered before nibbling on her bagel.

"Psychologist. What were you thinking right before you thought you saw him?"

"Okay, Mr. Psychologist." She smirked and locked eyes with him. "I was thinking how much I missed him and how good he had been for me—how safe he made me feel."

Kearney didn't say anything while the silence increased the impact of her words. His eyes didn't leave hers.

"I know what you're going to say," she said. "I was thinking about how much I wanted him back in my life, so my mind produced an image. Blah, blah, blah."

"What do you say?"

"I say I saw him." Joan slumped back in the booth. The reality of Duncan's presence faded under Kearney's scrutiny. She swallowed hard. Damn Kearney. She knew this would happen, but she had brought up the subject anyway. When would she ever learn?

"I can help you, but you have to want the help," he said.

The waitress placed the check next to Kearney and asked if their breakfasts were okay. He looked up at her, checked her nametag and winked. "Perfect, Lisa. Thank you." He watched her while she topped off their coffee mugs and removed the dishes.

He turned his attention back to Joan, but she had closed down mentally. He glanced over his shoulder in the direction of the waitress then back to Joan.

He narrowed his eyes. "That Lisa Brown thing still bothering you?"

"No," Joan said a little too quickly.

"I want to help you, Joan. But you have to want the help, and part of that is being honest with me and, more importantly, with yourself."

She pressed her lips together while she sorted through her feelings. She had already asked him for help. She could back out, but backing away from difficulty wasn't her style. His help could put to rest her guilt about Duncan's death. After a slow wag of her head she looked into his eyes. "Yes, it bothers me. It should bother you, too."

"I gotta hear this. Why?"

"You were the one who gave me the fake ID with that name."

Kearney leaned forward so his head was halfway across the table. "Listen to me, Joan Bowman," he whispered. He tapped his finger on the table for emphasis. "You are not responsible for their deaths. I am not responsible for their deaths. The men who hunted them down and killed them are responsible."

"But I gave the deputy that name—"

"And he released that information to the wrong people. If anyone is complicit in their deaths, it's him. Not you." He waited to let his words sink in. "And as far as I know, you didn't kill anyone who was not threatening you or someone else. Am I right?"

She wondered why she had asked him for help. "Will you help me, K? I can't work through this by myself."

"I've wanted to help you for a long time. It's the one thing I can do to make up for—"

Joan waved him off and slid out of the booth.

Kearney grabbed the check, left a substantial tip, and paid the bill. He walked Joan to her bike, listening to her scratch the surface of her feelings. She watched his eyes, and he seemed genuinely interested in what she had to say.

She straddled her bike while it warmed up, and brushed non-existent dust off the tank. "Thank you for not judging me."

"I've never been judgmental."

She gave him a You Have Got To Be Kidding Me look before pulling on the helmet.

He leaned on the handlebar and smiled. "Well, maybe in the beginning, before I saw how you handled what I did to you. But not lately...not for quite a while. And especially after how you handled yourself at the end in Arizona." He tapped her arm with his index finger. "Your street name is Iron Angel for a reason. Remember that."

"Then you don't think I'm crazy?"

He flashed his white, toothy grin. "I didn't say that."

She grinned. "We have to be crazy to do what we do, right?" It felt good to smile. Maybe relying on Kearney was going to be all right. There was hope for starting over, making a new life, maybe even planning a future. "But just one question: when is my life going to get back to normal?"

"You've already started down that path."

She raised her eyebrows. "I have? When?"

"You got yourself a new job. You've moved out on your own. Ain't no stoppin' you now. You're on the move. Aow!" Kearney spun in a circle and put one hand on his hip the other straight up in the air like something out of "*Saturday Night Fever.*"

She laughed at his off-key singing of the Luther Vandross song and his silly John Travolta move. She righted the bike and heeled up the kickstand. "And I was worried that I was the one who went into the weeds."

He stepped back. "I'll text you later. Get some rest. Hey—" He pulled a wad of cash from his pocket and peeled off two twenties. "Here. I don't like the idea of you going all the way upstate without any money in your pocket."

"Thanks, but I'll stop at an ATM on the way."

"You're tired. And you're going to sober up about the time you jump onto Route 6. Take these. You can pay me back later."

She stuffed the twenties into a front pocket of her leather jacket. After a quick chin nod, she zipped away down the alley.

CHAPTER 7

On the ride to Yonkers for Nirmala's Monday night class, Joan settled back in the driver's seat of Kearney's freshly-detailed Wrangler and thought about her relaxing weekend getting her new apartment in order. Rob's face popped into her head. She had Googled bookstores and by pure chance had picked the store in Beacon where Rob worked. He had helped her pick out a couple books on meditation then asked her to a poetry reading. Two lines of poetry written by her mother, and suppressed twenty-five years ago, had burst into her head: *I saw a flashing light of darkness, as hands, unloving, grabbed and stole me…*

Words that reminded her of her mother's death. Words that prompted a harsh turndown of Rob's invitation—even now she gripped the steering wheel tighter. After Rob's awkward, hesitant invitation, the harshness crushed him, and it showed on his face and the slump of his shoulders.

What kind of a person had she turned into? Thoughtlessly, and even more tactlessly, shutting down a man's simple invitation. It was time to put past losses into perspective and move forward. She accepted his invitation—it was just a poetry reading, not a date, and she had two weeks to bail on him if she changed her mind—then returned home to read her new books and practice meditating.

Traffic was heavier than usual and she arrived at the class right after Nirmala turned on the CD of relaxing music. Joan placed her new foam pad where she had sat before, and was surprised at how quickly her breathing came under control. Keeping thoughts from entering her consciousness was still difficult, but sweeping them away seemed easier. Evidently, her phantoms were no match for a quiet mind. Who knew? She relaxed and absorbed the normal sounds of the city and the quiet breathing of the people in the room.

Footsteps on the stairs brought her out of her meditative state—Nirmala had been right about heightened awareness. They weren't the normal sound or cadence of steps. They were quiet and stealthy.

She tensed, opened her eyes, got to her feet, and stood just inside the doorway. She motioned for Nirmala to move into the corner out of sight of the door. Joan's heart raced. She quieted it by inhaling slowly through her nose then exhaling through her mouth.

The footsteps crossed the landing on the third floor. Rob's head appeared in the doorway. Joan exhaled loudly and motioned to Nirmala that everything was okay.

"What are you, the hall monitor?" Rob whispered.

"Why were you sneaking up the stairs?"

"I wasn't sneaking. I was being quiet so I didn't disrupt the class." He slipped past her a little too close for her comfort. He smiled at her. "But so much for that."

Joan ran her hands over her short hair. "Yeah, well…" Yeah, well, what? Was she too edgy? No. Nirmala's situation had worsened and she couldn't let down her guard for a second.

Rob picked a spot next to Joan and smiled. "I'll be noisier next time, if that will make you feel better."

She glared at him and mouthed the words, "I'm sorry," to the other students before closing her eyes to sink back into the cool serenity of quieted thoughts.

When the class ended, Joan rolled up her mat and approached Nirmala to talk about how the rest of the evening would pan out. Because she hadn't talked to Nirmala before class began, she didn't know how much Nirmala knew about the Jeb's suggestions or his new strategy in handling her stalker.

Joan stuffed her mat into her backpack and waited until the chatty students finished talking to Nirmala. When the room was empty she said, "Jeb called and said things have escalated."

"Yes," Nirmala said. "After the last class, I was followed to my house."

"How do you know that?"

"He brazenly parked right in front of my house and watched me close the garage door."

"Was there any other contact? Door knob rattling, phone call, anything like that?'

"No nothing. Just watching."

"And he never did this before?"

"No. Never. I always felt safe at my home."

They headed toward the door. Joan said, "You said he watched you walk inside. Did you get a good look at him?"

"It was dark. The nearest streetlamp was out."

"How long was the light—"

Rob waited in the hallway. How much had he heard? Nirmala looked up at the sudden end to Joan's sentence. She saw Rob, looked at Joan, then busied herself with locking the door to the studio.

"I just wanted to walk you ladies to your cars." He looked from one to the other, evidently feeling their tension. "There've been some purse snatchings in the area."

Nirmala forced a smile. "Well, thank you, Rob. That is quite nice of you." She headed for the stairs.

Joan fell in beside her. Rob walked down the stairs behind them.

Joan prickled at the idea of Rob behind her. Trouble always came from behind, out of sight, undetected. She smiled over her shoulder a couple times to check on him, but he stayed a couple stairs back, not crowding the two women.

When they reached the street and headed for Nirmala's car, Rob hitched up next to Joan. "So what do you do when you aren't taking meditation classes?"

"I clean offices." She didn't like where this was headed, and said the first thing that popped into her head. Personal questions were never a good sign, at least not for a fugitive. Agreeing to go to the poetry reading with him didn't give him a free pass into her life.

"Why do you come all the way to Yonkers to take meditation classes?" he asked. "There must be others in Orange or Rockland Counties."

Joan's blood turned cold, but she kept her voice casual. "How do you know I don't live in Yonkers? Or somewhere else in Westchester County?"

"Here's my car," Nirmala said. "So you will follow me to my house so I can give you that book I told you about?" She must have picked up on Joan's apprehension about Rob, and thought of the ruse to cover Joan following her home. She was impressed with Nirmala's ingenuity.

Joan stepped between Rob and the car while Nirmala slipped into the driver's seat. "I'll be right behind you," she said to Nirmala over her shoulder. She turned her attention to Rob. "We'll be okay now."

"Okay," Rob said in resignation. "I'll just make sure you get into your car safely."

Joan knitted her brow. His response wasn't what she expected. He looked disappointed. She'd have to have Colavito check him out. If there was anything she needed to know about Rob, it was important to have it.

"That's really not necessary," she said, brushing past him and heading toward the Wrangler. In that quick pass she had checked for weapons. Nothing in his waistband, but that didn't mean he wasn't armed.

"I take Tae Kwon Do classes," he said coming up beside her. "I can protect you. Prevent someone from grabbing your backpack."

Tae Kwon Do? Really? Better let him be the man. "Oh,

in that case, I drove that Wrangler over there." Joan pointed across the small parking lot.

"Is this your boyfriend's car?" Rob asked.

He was fishing for information. Could he be more obvious? "Uh…no. I don't have a boyfriend. My fiancé died a few months ago."

"Oh, I'm sorry." He shoved his hands in his pockets. "I can't imagine what you're going through."

Joan unlocked the car a slid behind the wheel. "See you at Thursday's class?"

"Yeah, I'll see you then."

Joan started the engine and backed out immediately, forcing Rob to step back to avoid getting run over. When she shifted into Drive she saw him give a small wave. She pulled forward and flashed her lights for Nirmala to pull out of the parking lot.

In her rearview mirror, Joan saw Rob climb into a white Hyundai SUV. When the women turned right out of the parking lot, Rob turned right, too.

Joan's heart rate picked up. Who was this Rob guy? She analyzed what she did know. He worked in a book store and, with his shock of curly, dark blond hair and wire-rimmed glasses, he looked the part. He asked too many personal questions. He was too nice. Too perfect.

At the next intersection, she glanced in her rearview mirror. Rob flashed his headlights a couple times and turned left. Did he flash good-bye? Who does that? Nice people, or people pretending to be nice. A sweeping check of the traffic behind her didn't send any red flags. They weren't being followed, but then the stalker knew where Nirmala lived. He could already be there—or on his way there.

During the drive to Nirmala's home in Scarsdale, Joan mused about Rob. He had the nice guy act down. Hands in his pockets. He offered a sincere "I'm sorry" when she told him that her fiancé had died. He was kind of cute and was about Duncan's height, five-eleven, but skinny compared to Duncan's boxer physique. He was boyish with a hint of a dimple when he smiled—it could charm a less cynical woman. It was a grin really, an impish grin. He could genuinely be a nice guy. She didn't have a lot of experience with nice guys, and maybe she wouldn't recognize one if he plopped into her life. She was used to hard-hitting, gun-toting men. How does a woman act around an average guy? Joan smiled. The poetry reading in ten days would be an excellent time to find out.

The smile flattened. He knew she lived upstate. Why couldn't anything be easy? Her headlights swept a wide arc when she turned into Nirmala's driveway. She would get Rob's full name from Nirmala and ask Colavito to check him out and find out more about him than he would want anyone to know. It was a perk of working for an established organization. Joan turned off the engine and got out of her car.

Nirmala's garage door went up revealing a neat, well-lit area in one half of the two-car garage. Nirmala pulled in, got out of her car, and stood in the light.

Joan headed for the garage, turning and taking a few steps backward to survey the neighbors' yards. "Where was the stalker the last time he was here?"

"He was parked directly across the street." Nirmala opened the rear door of her sedan and started to remove her CD player and mat. "Maybe he took tonight off."

"Yeah, or maybe he changed his MO." With one last turn to check the street, Joan walked into the garage. "Do you mind if I check your house? Make sure he didn't get inside."

"I don't think it's necessary, but if it will make you feel better."

"It will make me feel better."

How would that look if she watched Nirmala walk into her house alone to find the stalker in her living room? Jeb would want to know how his client had been harassed, beaten, kidnapped, raped...or worse. Nirmala's safety was on the line, along with Joan's future with Durham Security.

The last thing I need is another ghost in my head.

Nirmala led Joan through a mud room and laundry area that rivaled Joan's living room in size. They stepped into a beautifully renovated kitchen with cherry cabinets that reflected dim light tucked under the upper cabinets. Joan wanted to soak up the beauty of Nirmala's house, but she had to ensure her client's safety.

"Check all the windows and close the curtains," Joan said. "I'll go ahead and check the rooms and closets."

Joan checked the hall coat closet beneath stairs that went to the second floor. The living room was quiet and undisturbed. She wove her way through the downstairs checking behind furniture and in closets. She headed upstairs and checked the upstairs bedrooms and bathrooms. All was in order. She relaxed and headed for the top of the stairs to return to the first floor. Nirmala called her name.

Joan's heart rate kicked up and she bolted down the stairs. "What is it?"

Nirmala stood in the shadowy vestibule at the bottom of the stairs squinting through the beveled glass in the right sidelight. "He is there. Across the street."

"Let me see." Nirmala stepped aside and Joan took her place. She moved her head to find the piece of glass that would allow her to see across the street the best. "That's him in the SUV?"

"I don't know if it is the same guy, but it is the same car."

Joan looked around for a safe place for Nirmala. Every room had floor to ceiling windows that, in a safer time, would be beautiful. Tonight, they were a defense nightmare. She chose the family room off the kitchen. The family room curtains were drawn and the kitchen windows were small. The hearth at the far end of the room caught her eye. The fieldstones surrounding the fireplace, combined with the distance from the rest of the house, provided the best protection.

"He has never come in the house before." Nirmala spoke

confidently, but Joan knew she was struggling to believe her own words and stay calm.

"A few days ago, he had never come to your house." Joan put her hands on Nirmala's shoulders. "Stay here so I won't be distracted by wondering about your safety."

Nirmala nodded.

"Where does this back door go?"

"To a small yard and a tall privacy fence."

"Your neighbors over there," Joan pointed to their left, "do they have a dog?"

"No. Just a couple kids."

"Everything's going to be okay, Nirmala."

"Should I call the police?"

"Not yet. Wait by the fireplace. If I'm not back or don't call in five minutes, you can call the police then, okay?" Joan walked over to the back door and unlocked it. "Lock this door after me and don't let anyone in, no matter what, unless it's me or the police. If you have to call the police, take your cell phone and go directly to a bathroom upstairs, and lock that door. Okay?"

Nirmala nodded. "But what are you going to do?"

Joan looked into Nirmala's nervous eyes. "I'm going to rock his world."

CHAPTER 8

The next afternoon, Joan paced in the reception area outside Jeb's office. Claudia shot fitful glances at her. *You'd think she'd be used to high-strung operatives.* Joan kicked at a bump in a rug to flatten it. *I feel like I've been called to the principal's office.*

The first time she had been there was a several weeks after Duncan's death. She and Kearney, wound tight from a constant state of vigilance, had just arrived in Yonkers after taking a circuitous route from Phoenix to throw off their pursuers. Jeb had taken a framed photograph off the wall and handed it to her. She smiled at the thought of the picture of Duncan as a young mercenary. It was now on her bedside table with a votive in front of it, a bottle of Jack Daniels behind it, and flanked by two shot glasses—one for Duncan that was never empty and one for her that she filled and emptied every night.

The smile faded from her face when she thought about the previous night. The stalker had been unaware of her approach. The dumbass—it had not been Rob—didn't lock his doors or wear a seat belt, and she easily opened the driver's door and pulled him out of the car. The look on his face had been one of surprise which turned to fear when he realized she wasn't the police, but something else. Something worse than being dragged downtown and booked.

She slumped into a chair and pulled out her phone. She texted an insult to Kearney. It was a new way to relieve tension and while away dead time. If anyone read their texts they'd think they were about to kill each other. She smiled inwardly, stood, crossed the room, and leaned on the reception counter. If she wanted to kill Kearney, he'd be dead. If he wanted her dead, he would have done it in that motel room when he had the chance. *We've buried the hatchet, but I can't forget where it is*. She rubbed her brow and thumbed her phone.

An older man came in, breathing heavy from the exertion of walking up the flight of stairs. *What the heck could he be guarding?*

Claudia looked up and smiled at him. "How's your wife doing?" She handed him a thick envelope.

"Much better. Thank you for asking." He smiled at Joan. "Spring's coming."

"Not a moment too soon," she replied before looking down to get Kearney's return text.

"I don't think I've seen you around before. I'm Edgar. Are you applying for job here?"

"Just starting.

"Do you know where you'll be working?"

"Personal Security." Edgar was on the second floor, but he didn't look like an operator. Being here didn't mean he knew about the covert division of Durham Security.

He nodded. "Ah, I should have recognized it."

"What's that?"

"Your no-nonsense toughness. If I was a bad guy, I'd think twice about attacking anyone you were guarding."

She smiled at him and shook her head. "If only it was that easy."

Jeb's office door opened, and she stuffed the phone into the pocket of her cargo pants. Colavito walked out of the office with a serious expression. He saw her and hesitated. A quick smile appeared then dropped off his face. "I'd love to stop and talk, but I gotta run." He breezed out of the reception area.

Joan stood, mouth open, waiting for his usual arm

around the shoulder accompanied by the inevitable romantic suggestion. Her standard response would have been a dig about his manhood or intelligence, but the words died in her mouth. His flirtations were merely a form a communication with no serious intent to follow up on them. It had become a game between them, but not today. Today he left a cool eddy of air swirling around her.

She shut her mouth and turned to ask Jeb what was up with Colavito, but he was talking to Edgar.

"I'm glad to hear your wife is home from the hospital," Jeb was saying.

"I want to thank you for that time off with pay." Edgar gave the envelope a short wave before putting it into his pocket. "And that extra financial support keeps us in our house. It means a lot to her...and me."

Jeb put a hand on Edgar's shoulder. "It's the least I can do." He guided the man toward the door. "When do you think you'll be returning to work?"

"Maybe not for another week or two, if that's okay with you."

"Take as much time as you need. And if there's anything else I can do, anything at all, just let me know. Okay?"

"You've already done more than any other employer would have. You've been good to us. Thanks again."

Jeb watched him leave. After he closed the door, he turned to Joan. "Go ahead into my office. I'll be in after I get my messages."

Joan shivered inwardly from Colavito's iciness and headed into the office. The thick carpeting made her feel like the floor was fluid. The office's woodsy aroma reminded her of patchouli—spicy and irritating. With a glance at the empty space on the wall where the framed photo of Duncan had been, she slid into her brown leather chair on the left. It was the chair she sat in when she was told about Duncan's estate. She sat in the same chair every time she was there. She thought of it as her chair.

She looked over her shoulder and an uneasiness coiled

through her. Jeb was taking a long time in the outer office. She shook off the nervousness and settled back in the chair to wait.

"Angel," Jeb said, walking across his office. "Want some coffee or water?"

Joan shook her head. He used her street name instead of her given name. That meant this was business.

"Some Scotch?"

"No, thank you." She watched him walk around the end of his desk. Offering scotch in the afternoon should have been accompanied by his grin and dimple, but he was serious. Did she go too far with the stalker? Not far enough?

He sat down with a grimace.

"Hip bothering you today?" she asked.

He shrugged. "Not more than usual." His gaze was intent, unwavering. "How are you doing?"

She sat up straight at his piercing scrutiny. Fun time was over. "I'm okay." Her answer rang flat and…careful. She resisted squirming. He had said she could handle the situation anyway she saw fit. The words had been loose, but the message had been clear. Had she misunderstood?

Musical notes emanated from Joan's cargo pocket. She ignored it.

"You want to get that?"

"No. It's Kearney being a pain in the ass. We were trading—"

"I think you should get it." Jeb watched her intently.

"Nah, it's just…" The heat of Jeb's gaze kindled a spark of caution. She pulled the phone from her pocket, saw it was from Kearney, and turned it off without checking the text.

"It might be important."

Joan locked eyes with Jeb. "We were trading insults while I was waiting in the outer office. When I don't respond, he'll know I'm in conference with you."

The seconds ticked by.

"Is there anything you want to tell me?" Jeb asked.

"I confronted the stalker last night." Something had changed Jeb from the friendly guy to this intent, tense man. She couldn't think of anything that she would have said or done to make such a drastic change in him. It had to have something to do with the case she was working. She inwardly kicked herself for not clarifying Jeb's instructions for handling the Nirmala case.

"We'll talk about that later." Jeb tapped a pen against the desk. "Is there anything else going on that I need to know about?"

Joan narrowed her eyes in thought. *If it's not the case it might have something to do with Kearney.* Kearney would not have told Jeb about her hallucination—would he? Damn him. Psychologists were supposed to be able to keep confidences, especially one who was a fugitive and a spook. But her gut told her to let Jeb reveal his information rather than spit out something he didn't already know.

"If there is something going on, now is the time to speak up," Jeb said.

"I don't know what you mean."

"I have zero tolerance for bullshit from my operatives. Even less for secrets."

"Secrets? I don't have any secrets. Tell me what the hell you're talking about."

Over the past few weeks, Jeb had hinted that she should distance herself from Kearney, but he was the only person left alive who knew what she had been through over the past couple years. Jeb was controlling with his business, but there had been no hint that he would try to control her personal life, telling her with whom she could and could not be friends.

His gaze didn't falter.

Joan willed herself to sit still and wait for Jeb to open up and tell her what was going on. The one to speak first usually speaks from the weaker position.

"At one time or another," Jeb said, "we've all questioned a plan or even our actions. Questions are good. They keep us honest." He paused before continuing. "Sometimes we find ourselves in situations that seemed okay at first, but then we have second thoughts. If you find yourself in that kind of position, you know you can talk to me, right?"

"I'm not having second thoughts about working for you." She had no idea what made him think she did not like her job at Durham Security. She leaned back in her chair and draped her arms on the armrests.

"That's nice to know, but that's not what I was referring to, and I think you know that."

Joan didn't reply. This was a fishing expedition pure and simple—a new side of Jeb. He had made it a point to be friendly. They had several conversations where they shared things about each other. She had become relaxed around him, and looked forward to their conversations—until now. Fishing was a study in patience, and she had nowhere to be.

He looked at the empty spot on the wall where the photo of a younger Duncan had hung before he gave it to Joan. "I wanted to trust you." He must have reconsidered his words because he looked at her and added, "I can trust you to tell me anything, even if it's hard to talk about?"

Kearney and his loose lips are dead. "Sure. But I'm okay. Really."

"If you think I might get upset, you can always talk to Colavito. Sometimes he's easier to talk to than me."

What the hell? "Okay. I'll keep that in mind." She had no idea what subject could be easier to talk about with Colavito. If she kept calm and let Jeb talk, maybe he'd slip or open up, and the pieces of this puzzle would fall into place.

After a full minute of scrutiny, Jeb said, "Tell me about last night."

"Okay, but before I do let me say I have no idea what you're driving at. If it's important to our business relationship, speak up now, or I'll consider it unimportant and move on."

"Is that right?" he said, rubbing his upper lip with his index finger. He sat up in his chair and switched direction. "Nirmala called me this morning. You want to tell me what happened?"

"Did I do something wrong?" At Jeb's impassive expression, she continued, "Everyone is so serious. First Colavito, now you."

Jeb looked at his desktop and rubbed his forehead. "Something's come to my attention. It's a shifting landscape, and we've been caught off guard."

"Does it have to do with me?"

Jeb's eyes flashed up to hers and hardened into a stare. "Do you have something to feel guilty about?"

Joan wanted to say something, but couldn't formulate a cogent thought before Jeb spoke again.

"Internalizing will sap your strength."

"Good advice. I think I'll take it."

Jeb nodded and offered no more information. His eyes bored into her.

"About Nirmala," Joan said, doing her own switchback. "I've given her some pointers on staying safe when one of us isn't with her. And like I said, I met her stalker."

"She told me. She said you wouldn't tell her anything that happened when you went out to confront him. Want to share the details with me?"

"I simply explained why stalking Nirmala was not a good idea, and not particularly good for his health or longevity."

Jeb's jaw tightened. "How did you explain it to him?"

"Well, actually, my knife did most of the talking."

"You didn't—"

"Kill him? No. Like I told you when you hired me, I swore off killing." The words were casual, but her nervousness deepened.

Colavito's awkward detachment put her on edge. Jeb's ill-temper set her nerves on fire. *Relax. He said it has nothing to do with me.* Joan knitted her brow. Was that what he said?

She pulled on the cuffs of her leather jacket and shifted in her seat.

"After what could only be described as a killing spree in Arizona, why swear off killing now? What happened to make you change direction so fervently?"

"I can't—" Joan shook her head to clear it of the vision of blood spatter and the raw meat smell. "Enough is enough, that's all."

"Whatever you did, you can tell me." He rubbed his hand over his jawline, as if rethinking his words. His features softened and his voice took on a pleading tone. "Talk to me.

"Don't say that." Joan gripped the arms of the chair. "That's how Duncan always answered the phone."

Jeb put his hands up. "Whoa. Calm down. We're all…" His voice trailed off and his gaze shifted again to the empty space on the wall.

She followed his gaze. *We're all what? Friends? On the same team? Yeah? Well, why can't you say it?* She looked sideways at Jeb. His shoulders looked stiff. His whole demeanor screamed that he was wound tighter than a bear trap. This would be a good time to stay calm. No sense getting everybody riled up because they both were off their strides today. She took a deep cleansing breath.

Jeb's eyes softened. "Tell me what's going on with you." He took a deep breath before continuing. "You seem…stressed."

"I'm okay." She wasn't okay, or anything close to it— Colavito's fake smile, Jeb's odd behavior—as her anxiety level increased, so did her struggle to stay on an even keel. She straightened the collar of her jacket.

He rubbed his finger on his upper lip for a couple seconds before continuing. "Back to the stalker. How exactly did you explain to the stalker that it wasn't beneficial for him to continue to stalk Nirmala?"

"I put a knife to his throat."

"Did you cut him?"

"It's hard to put steel to flesh and not draw blood."

Jeb frowned. "I don't like your flippant attitude."

Holy shit. That was out of character. "Yes, sir." Joan answered the question again. "I cut him a little. Just enough so he'd feel the blood trickle down his neck."

"How did he take that?"

"Not so well. He tried to hit me, so I put him down."

"Put him down?"

"You know. A blow to the carotid. Puts their lights out every time."

"You didn't slash his throat."

"What if I did?" Joan winced at her sharp words, but Jeb didn't snap at her this time. "Nirmala is such a sweet lady. She doesn't deserve that petty, annoying, rat-shit gnat buzzing around her."

Jeb's face flushed from a fast influx of blood. "Did you slash his throat?"

"No."

"Why not? I bet you wanted to."

Joan met his eyes. "If I wanted to slash his throat, I—"

"Why not?" His voice was hard, demanding.

Because I can't stand the smell or feel of blood. Because slashing a throat means lots of it. In spurts. Her respiration rate increased. *And it would kill him.* She tightened her jaw. "Because I didn't."

"Come on, Angel. We all know it would have been so easy…especially for you. Nothing is too low for you."

"Especially for me? Nothing is too low—what the hell does that mean?"

"I think you know what I'm talking about," Jeb said.

"No. Tell me." Joan moved forward in the chair and leaned on the desk. "If you have something to say, say it."

"I should say the same thing to you."

"What?" He was baiting her to spill information. If she knew what he wanted to know, she'd tell him so they both could relax. This conversation sounded eerily similar to a method of interrogation where it circled back to some vague point over and over again, but from a different direction each time.

After a long, hard stare, Jeb stood and leaned with both hands on the desk. "Did you want to kill him?"

She stood and mirrored his stance. "I turned over a new leaf, Jeb. No more killing."

His eyes tracked down her face, from her brows, to her eyes, to her mouth. "Trust me, Iron Angel. We have to trust each other. That's how this business works."

"I trust you." Or did, until this conversation. But he stopped trusting her. It was time to find out what had changed. "Is this about how I'm handling Nirmala's stalker?"

His glare cut through her. "I think you know it isn't."

He's not sure… a shifting landscape. "Is this about my physical or mental fitness for this job?"

"Are you mentally and physically up for this job?"

"Yes." She surprised herself by how quickly she answered. A refreshing wave of confidence radiated through her body and her mind welcomed it. Her shoulders levelled and her lungs filled with air.

"Then I think so, too," he said. The sharp edge to Jeb's voice was gone, as if this interaction had been what he wanted all along. A glimmer of anticipation lit his eyes.

The subtle change in Jeb's mood encouraged her to continue. She was hesitant to ask the next question, and she formed the words slowly. "Does this have anything to do with Kearney?"

The door opened and a man who could have appeared on the cover of GQ magazine strode into the office without shutting the door behind him. His stride indicated a self-assured operative comfortable in his abilities. Confident no one could stop him from doing anything.

Jeb frowned at the interruption. He shook hands with the man and after a brief, friendly interaction, he nodded toward Joan. "Darren, this is Iron Angel—Archer's widow."

Darren offered his hand. "I'm sorry for your loss. I never

had the honor of working with Archer, but I heard a lot of good things about him."

"Thank you."

"Darren is from the Chicago group," Jeb said.

"Chicago group?" she asked.

"Durham Security is part of a national network of security firms under an umbrella organization called Stillwater," Jeb said.

"As in still water runs deep?" Joan mused aloud.

Darren's face lit up. "Most people don't get it right away. You are one sharp lady."

"So I've been told." She looked back at him unamused. If he hadn't interrupted the exchange with Jeb, she would have figured out what was on his mind.

"I hear you now work for Durham Security. So what will you be doing?" Darren licked his upper lip and smirked. "Mall security?"

She smiled. "Fuck off."

He let out one, loud laugh. "You're going to fit in around here." He turned to Jeb, all business. "I was supposed to meet up with Colavito, but I missed him."

"He's heading back to his place. Call him on his cell." Jeb rattled off a phone number.

Darren repeated the number and left after quick good-byes. He closed the door after himself this time, and the office fell into a brief where-were-we silence. Joan settled back into her chair, frustrated at the disruption to the delicate rhythm into which she had led Jeb.

"Jeb, I want things to be right between us again."

"Me, too." Jeb sat down and leaned back. "We'll let time do its thing. When Colavito and Darren get back, we'll bring this up again."

Joan's lips tightened. Her instincts came to life. Jeb would not accuse her outright, which suggested he was unsure of his position. Colavito's mission had something to do with her. His specialty was surveillance. Darren was an out of town asset.

The pieces didn't fit together, but they were related. She was sure of it.

A cloud must have moved from in front of the afternoon sun because the room brightened, and the sunlight eased the heavy silence between Jeb and Joan. Muffled office noises filtered through the door. A siren wailed somewhere outside the window.

Jeb must have sensed the same change in the room's atmosphere. His tone was soft when he spoke. "Do you have anything else for me?"

"We should talk about the next step in Nirmala's protection." Joan's voice sounded harsh in the deadened room.

"You think the stalker will come back after your conversation with him?" The lack of hesitation or inflection when calling Joan's knife-to-throat encounter "a conversation" spoke volumes.

She pressed her lips together and nodded. "Unfortunately, yes. Stalkers think differently from normal men. He won't scare that easy. He might skip a couple nights to lick his wounds and make his plans, but he'll be back." Discussing work relaxed her, and she slipped into a new conversational rhythm.

They brainstormed possible scenarios. The stalker could become more covert. Or he could amp up his actions or recruit someone else to watch Nirmala while he remained in the shadows. Each situation required a different response. They had to be ready for anything.

Joan liked their plans and wanted to spend more time fine tuning them, but Jeb's direct gaze troubled her. He got lost in thought for a second or two, then honed in on her like a laser beam.

Joan's gut tightened.

"You're good? Sleeping well?"

"I'm on the tracks. Why?"

"I have a bodyguard job. A family. There's a young girl, and the male bodyguards make her nervous. I told the client I would have a female bodyguard available soon."

"What will it entail?" A minute ago she was knee deep in shit, but he just offered her another job. The flip-flop led her to believe she wasn't the only one in the room with a lot of questions.

"You will be part of the mobile team," Jeb said.

"Mobil team, what does that mean?"

"There's a team that protects the family when they are home. I have to keep a team there twenty-four-seven. When a member, or members, of the family travels outside their property, I have another team on call that covers that. That's the team I think will work for you."

"So who is this family, and why do they need protection?"

"The mother is a well-known television personality who tackles controversial topics on her show. There have been death threats."

"Any idea who made the threats?"

"No one is sure, but it would be wise to expect a well-trained opposing force."

"Like radical Muslims?"

Jeb rubbed his upper lip and watched her facial expressions. "I'll hook you up with the owner of the bodyguard school I use. He'll get you up to speed."

"You're going to put the safety of this family in the hands of a rookie?"

"You won't be on your own. This is a team situation. And I know you won't panic or run if shots are fired."

"Shots? I don't have a permit to carry a piece in New York City."

"I'm working on getting you a carry permit, but it will take time. But for this case, I don't want you to have a gun. They scare the little girl. You'll be in charge of keeping the family calm if a situation arises. Get them to safety—that kind of thing." He fingered through the papers on his desk and looked anxious to get back to work. "Anything else?"

She would have left at that time, but there was one more thing.

"I have something for Colavito, but it should probably go through you first."

"Probably. What is it?"

"There's this guy, Rob. His full name is Robison J. Reddington and he's a student in Nirmala's class. He's acting hinky. I thought Colavito should do a background check. You know what I mean?"

"Colavito is busy." Jeb moved his mouse, clicked it a couple times, then typed a few words. "That's R-o-b-i-s-o-n?"

"Yes."

"And Reddington is spelled like it sounds?"

"Yes." Joan spelled out Reddington anyway.

"I wonder what the 'J' stands for," Jeb mused.

"Jerk-wad."

Jeb glanced up at her, fighting a smile. "I think the word is 'dickwad.'"

"Not in Jerk-wad's case."

"You have a way with words."

Joan smiled. "It's part of my charm."

He raised his eyebrows, shook his head, and exhaled loudly. "Yes, it is."

Jeb's mood seemed to be lightening. The grilling, demanding part of this conversation could have been simply a test to be sure she was ready for this other job. That offer spoke of confidence in her abilities, but she couldn't shake the feeling that something happened to cause him to lose his trust in other areas.

There was something he wanted to know from her, but was not willing to come right out and ask. He was a confident man, but his actions spoke of a man who was being safe.

She racked her brain trying to find something that would have changed his opinion of her. She wanted to believe Kearney would not have revealed what she told him in confidence. If it wasn't that, she had nothing.

He typed some more on his computer with a final tap. "I

sent an email to Champ. He'll check this guy out, see what comes up."

"He can do that?"

"Anything anybody can do, Champ can do it better, faster, and more thoroughly."

"Why didn't you just text him?"

Jeb rubbed his upper lip with his forefinger and stared at his laptop, as if trying to make a decision. He finally looked up at her. "You're telling me how to do my business?"

Another evasion. Still water may run deep, but a turbulent river has undercurrents.

☙☙☙

Agent Liz Merrill and Special Agent Andrew Woyzeck stopped work long enough to grab a late lunch at the Irish pub around the corner from the federal building—he was buying to celebrate the information he just discovered.

The pub was dark with well-placed lighting. The hanging lamps over the bar produced pools of light, creating small, cozy areas. Agent Woyzeck chose a wooden table between the bar and the booths around the perimeter. Agent Merrill joined him.

He was anxious to follow up on the lead he had discovered buried deep in the file the US Marshalls had on members of the Constitution Defense Legion. He could barely contain his enthusiasm while he studied the menu. He had worked tirelessly for the last four days. The Fugitive Apprehension Task Force had given him access to databases and Liz had helped in areas where he was not granted access—four days spent searching and coming up with nothing. Then today after one last look through the file, he had found it. Joan Bowman's connection to the Tri-state area. There was still no connection for Dennis Archer, and the man who went by Kearney had no connection to New York City or any of the surrounding area. Zero. And the mystery of his true identity was even more enigmatic. He had to be a product of black ops or some uber-secret agency.

But Woyzeck had a lead on Joan. If she was here, he'd bet his Steeler season tickets Archer was here.

The waitress appeared. He ordered a salad with grilled chicken. Liz's order went on forever, or at least it seemed that way. He wondered how she maintained her weight, but his thoughts circled back to Joan Bowman and his dilemma in locating her. Four days with no leads. If nothing had surfaced, he would have been on the first flight back to Pittsburgh on Saturday morning. Just the hint of a connection between his fugitives and the New York tri-stare area set his hunt into high gear.

Movement at the door caught his eye. Two employees from the federal building came in and, after searching the faces in the pub, joined some co-workers in one of the booths.

"Your lead isn't going to pop out of existence in the next few minutes, Andrew," Liz said, taking a sip of her soda—the real stuff, not calorie free. "Try to relax."

Woyzeck took a long pull from his glass of water. "I can't believe we missed the connection."

"That's why they call us investigators. We don't stop investigating."

Special Agent Woyzeck mumbled an affirmation, and the conversation changed to the weather, and turned into a friendly debate about who would have a better season, the Mets or the Pirates.

Their meals arrived. Tiny Liz Merrill had ordered a hamburger deluxe with an extra side of greasy onion rings. Bulky Andrew Woyzeck looked down at the salad with grilled chicken in front of him. Diets sucked. Summer was only a few months away, and if he didn't shrink his paunch, it would feel even worse than it did now. Diets not only sucked, but they were an evil form of torture for the hard-working. He poured raspberry vinaigrette over the three kinds of lettuce.

The next time Woyzeck looked up, Agent Merrill's boss, Special Supervisory Agent Danielson, was heading toward them. He pulled out a chair and sat down.

"You took time out for lunch?" Agent Merrill asked her boss. "I feel special."

"Well, I have good news and bad news for you, Woyzeck." Danielson looked over his shoulder at the waitress. "I'll have what he's having."

Well, at least I'm not suffering alone, Woyzeck thought.

"But add a side of fries," Danielson said.

What's the bad news? I'm the only person in Manhattan on a diet?

"So...the good news is we have eyes on your girl."

"You do? Where? When can we pick her up?"

"Not so fast, Steelers fan," Danielson said. "I said there was bad news."

Agent Woyzeck's mind raced. If they knew where she was but there was bad news, she could be dead. That would be terrible—all this time spent tracking her down. Or she's in jail. Too bad he didn't put her there himself. Or—

"We've been told to back off the investigation."

And then there's that—a power move by a ranking agency. It wouldn't be the first time this had happened to Agent Woyzeck, but it would be the last. Retirement loomed in the not so distant future.

"I'm sorry," Danielson continued. "But we've been shown the exit ramp."

"Who told us to back down?" Agent Merrill asked before chomping a big bite from her hamburger.

"I can't tell you that."

"Do you know why?" Agent Woyzeck asked, his mouth watering at the sight of Liz's juicy burger.

"Yes, but I can't tell you that either.

"What can you tell me?"

"Agent Woyzeck, go home. Go back to Pittsburgh and work your other cases. Kiss your wife. Hug you dog if you have one, but there's nothing else for you to do here."

Agent Merrill wiped her mouth with a napkin and swallowed her food. "Come on, boss. Can't you tell us something?" She gestured with her eyes toward Woyzeck as if to say, "Throw him a bone."

Danielson's coffee came and he took several sips. He placed the cup in the saucer and repositioned it in the indentation in the center while he thought about his answer. "I'm not supposed to tell you this, so I didn't tell you—if anyone asks. During an undercover investigation by another federal agency—and no, I won't tell you which one—Bowman popped up. Her identity has been confirmed. That's all I can tell you."

"How did they know to look for her?"

"They got wind of our manhunt and, as a favor to me, they asked their undercover to make the ID."

"So she's still here, and she's not the subject of their investigation…" His voice trailed off, thinking of the possibilities. This could be good news. He could check around on the sly. See what he could shake out of the tree.

"When this group goes down, they'll get her, if she's still around."

"Then we should nab her while we can."

Danielson pierced Woyzeck with a hard stare. "Did we fully cooperate with you?"

Woyzeck didn't answer.

"We assigned an agent to assist you in your investigation. Gave you space to work. Accompanied you to check out possible locations. Did we do everything to help you in your investigation?"

"Yes, sir. You did."

"Go home, Special Agent Woyzeck. Don't do anything that'll make me look bad." Danielson leaned toward Woyzeck. "Don't screw around with this case. Do we understand each other?"

CHAPTER 9

An unexpected knock raised Joan's heart rate. Since the early morning warning to abandon of her Manhattan apartment, a knock at the door changed from the joy of a friendly visit to the gut-clenching threat of an arrest warrant.

With knife in hand, she looked out each window before approaching the door. Standing to the side, she nudged the edge of the curtain with the tip of the blade. Her shoulders slumped and her head dropped to her chest.

Jeb had called that afternoon to invite himself over to her place. She had politely declined. The harsh words and innuendos in his office the day before still echoed in her head. She did not need Round Two. She had begged off saying she felt a cold coming on, which she immediately regretted because he wanted to rush over with some chicken soup. In time, he gave up, and she had enjoyed a rare afternoon relaxing on her comfortable bed, alternately napping and reading.

She opened the door just wide enough to look out. "I thought we agreed you were *not* coming over."

He held up a bottle of red wine. "I want to make up for the way I talked to you in the office yesterday. I was having a bad day, and I took it out on you. Let me make up for it."

"No need. You have a lot of responsibilities and we all have bad days."

He leaned on the doorjamb, so that his face was just

inches from hers. "C'mon, Joan. Just a couple glasses of wine then I'll go."

"You were not invited."

"I know, but I'm here now. And did I tell you I have a bottle of wine?" He held it up and swung it from his fingertips.

Joan frowned at him.

"I know you want me to come in."

"Is that right?" she asked with a hint of mockery.

"If you didn't, you would have already shut the door in my face."

"I can't do that."

A slow smile pushed up one corner of his mouth. "Why not?"

"Because you're my boss."

"But I'm not here as your boss. I'm here as your friend."

"In that case…" Joan shut the door and leaned against it. The shock on Jeb's face before she closed the door on him made her smile. She glanced over her shoulder at the door. This could be a good time to find out what he was up to. She opened the door. He had started to walk away, so she quickly said, "You give up awfully easy."

He turned and smiled at her. "Damn, you are a hard woman."

Melancholy smothered her playfulness. "Duncan told me I had gotten hard."

"Hey," Jeb said putting a hand on her shoulder and bending his knees to be eye-to-eye with her. "I was just kidding. I didn't mean to dredge up bad memories."

"None of my memories of Duncan are bad, except…" She brushed his hand off her shoulder and headed to the kitchen.

He followed her. "Except for what?"

"I don't want to talk about it." Joan shook her head and grabbed two water glasses out of the cabinet. "I hope these are okay." Her breath caught in her throat when she turned toward Jeb. The intensity from the day before had returned to his eyes. She cringed inwardly and vowed one drink and she would show him the door.

She reined in her emotions. "I don't have any wine glasses."

"They'll do the job." In the few breaths it took to say those words, the intensity disappeared and Jeb's demeanor softened. "I have something else for you. Mind opening the wine while I get it?"

By the time Joan had opened the wine, Jeb had brought in a large, narrow cardboard box that looked suspiciously like a *new* flat screen TV. Before she could turn down the gift, he disappeared saying something about another box. She strode out of the kitchen to put a stop to his unwanted generosity. She met him at the door.

"What good is a TV without a DVD player?" he asked, slipping past her.

"Take this stuff back out to your car." She put her fists on her hips. "Jeb, I can't accept these gifts. I have plenty of my own money to buy what I need."

"I know. But I was harsh with you the other day. Let me make it up to you." He slid his hand along her neck and rested it on her shoulder before turning to open the box holding the television.

Joan stepped backward and put her hand where Jeb had caressed her neck. The way-too-intimate gesture required her to say something. "Jeb, we have to talk."

"Sure. Let's get this set up first." He pulled the Styrofoam spacer out of the box. "Where's the wine?"

"Now. We have to talk now."

He wrinkled his brow at her. "Talk about what."

"This." Joan gestured toward the boxes, then pointed a finger back and forth between them. "What is going on here?"

"I'm being a friend." He walked toward her.

She took a step back.

"I just wanted to make it up to you. I was out of line."

"Friends don't buy expensive gifts for each other. That's

what a…" If another word for it existed, she couldn't think of it at that moment. "A boyfriend does. And I'm not ready—"

"That wasn't my intent."

Joan narrowed her eyes. "Really?"

"No. I just wanted to make things right between us again."

"What would you have done with your male friends?"

Jeb slid his hand over his slicked back hair and looked around at the boxes. "I went too far, didn't I?"

"The wine would have been sufficient."

"Point taken. What do I do with all this shit?"

"Well," Joan said. "It's here. Might as well set it up."

Jeb smiled at her.

"But I'll pay you for it."

"Okay. You're the boss," Jeb said and started pulling out components and setting up the TV and DVD player.

❧❧❧

If Joan had helped him set up the television and DVD player, he would have finished earlier. He looked over his shoulder in time to see her pouring a second glass of wine. The bending and reaching made his hip throb, and he plopped into the chair to survey his handiwork. Without cable hook-up or a movie to play, it sat like a glaring monument to his error in judgment. He propped his feet on the coffee table. "So what do you want to talk about?"

"You're the one who came here saying you wanted to make amends. Maybe you have something to say."

"Fair enough." He raised his glass for a toast. "Here's to better inter-personal, social skills."

She raised her glass. "To thinking before throwing yourself into a pile of shit." She clinked his glass and took a sip. "This is good."

"It's from Colavito's stash at Notches."

"Damn, Jeb, you didn't buy the make-up wine?"

"Since the company buys all the liquor at Notches—" he swirled the wine in the glass. "In a roundabout way I did buy it."

Joan snorted. "You'll spend the time and money to get a television and DVD player, but won't spring for a bottle of wine? I hope you don't run your business the same way."

"Can we agree to stop beating a dead horse? I give up. I made a mistake."

The corners of Joan's mouth twitched under wine-induced, rosy cheeks. She took a sip. Her smiling eyes above the rim of her glass remained on him, softening his perception of her. If she were anyone else, he would have been charmed. He reminded himself to stick to the plan. Having fun at his expense meant he was on the right path.

Joan tucked her legs up beside her on the couch. The frowns disappeared, replaced by smiles. She seemed to laugh more easily.

He imagined traversing a minefield when talking to her. He hoped wine was her kryptonite.

When she laughed at his jokes and talked about bikes and guns, he could see why Archer had fallen for her. She was genuine and straightforward. He had suggested they play cards to while away the evening, but she said she didn't play cards, or any games—cards or otherwise. Good. If she was not a player, it would make his job of getting to the truth much easier.

Interacting with Joan was tricky and tantalizing at the same time. He found himself thinking more than once that if he could get her to cry, he could put his arm around her to console her. Feel her in his arms. In the protective circle of his embrace.

Making a widow cry. What kind of man makes a woman cry just to get his arm around her? If thoughts alone could send a man to hell, he was on the express elevator to the depths of depravity.

Her words faded while he studied her facial expressions,

looking for the tell, the minute movements of her eyes or mouth that indicated deception.

She brought up The Constitution Defense Legion and he guided her into talking about Archer. Her smile turned soft and coy when she talked about how they met. Her love for him radiated from her watery eyes and in the softened tone of her voice. No deception there.

She spoke highly of Kearney, but a dichotomy of revulsion and neediness emerged in her minute facial expressions. Kearney did not control her. And he did not intimidate her. Reading her face became more difficult when she tried to explain why Kearney had to be in her life, and that gave him a lot of information to work with. It was a weakness ripe for exploitation. She went on to say she had forgiven Kearney for all he had done to her.

His suspicions softened. He saw the woman that his friend had fallen in love with so deeply that he left two-thirds of his seven-figure estate to her. She never questioned getting a monthly advance on the estate. Jeb silently reproached himself for not handling the estate as Archer had requested. He had failed his friend, and he had failed his friend's widow. She had called him reprehensible. He deserved worse than that. He lacked any salient worth. No more than fly spit on a pig's ass.

He missed the connection, but while he had been lost in thought, Joan had started talking about her undercover work for the Legion. His ears perked up. She could live a lie—maybe even a lie about Archer's death. He struggled with his rising anger. Anger at himself for being beguiled by her. Anger at her for what she may have done to Archer. Anger at the untimely loss of his longtime friend.

Archer had said no one could bluff better than Joan. Was she deceiving him about forgiving Kearney for torturing her. Or loving a man so completely that every memory of him is good. Or being straight forward and sincere.

"Jeb? Are you okay?" Joan asked.

He wrestled with his anger and loosened his clenched

jaw muscles. His friendly face appeared. "I'm fine. I was just thinking about what those federal agents did. Shot in the back, did you say?"

"I didn't say." She bit her lip. "But, yes, he was shot from behind."

"Tell me how it happened."

"I don't talk about what happened. To anybody. Not now. Maybe not ever." She slipped her feet off the couch and put them on the floor. "Maybe it's time for you to leave."

"No." The truth was so near it prickled his skin. If he backed off now, he may never know. "I want to know what happened."

After Joan rubbed her face as if in thought, she stood and stared pointedly at his legs. He did not move them, blocking her path. She would not get out of telling him what happened.

She stepped one leg over his.

Before she could lift the second leg over, he grabbed her wrist and looked up into her eyes. "He was my friend. I deserve to know."

She yanked her wrist from his grasp. When she shifted her weight to lift her leg across Jeb's, she lost her balance. After a couple steps and a wobble, she regained it, turned, and headed down the hallway toward the bedroom.

"I'll be right back," she said over her shoulder.

Jeb pushed himself out of the chair and followed her. She would not walk away from this confrontation. To hell with the plan. He would get answers before he left.

He stopped just inside the bedroom. "What's that?"

Joan looked genuinely embarrassed when she gestured toward the makeshift altar. "For months, wherever I lived, this has been on my bedside table." She picked up the frame and looked at the photo under the glass. "This photograph of Duncan has been propped up by a bottle of Jack Daniels. These two shot glasses in front of the photo...one is his, and is always full. And the other I fill and—" Her voice shivered with emotion. "I toast to his memory every night." Her chin quivered when she picked up the bottle and gently laid the photo on the table. She touched the glass over Duncan's face.

"I—" She swallowed hard. "Let's go in the living room and drink to Duncan."

Jeb stepped aside with his arms crossed, glaring at her. She slipped past him and led the way to the living room. She had pulled him in before. Tears and fake emotion would not draw him in again. He wanted the truth, and he would get it.

Joan splashed a shot of whiskey into each water glass. She raised her glass. "To Duncan."

"May he rest in peace."

They clinked glasses and Joan began her version of what happened in Phoenix.

"It was supposed to be an arms deal. We needed weapons and ammo bad. Duncan had this policy of using weapons once then getting rid of them to hinder ballistics evidence. That emptied our arsenal like an airplane toilet." She poured another glass for each of them. "Anyway, I warned him not to go through with it—"

"Why? What was wrong?"

Joan waved her hand as if to bat away the details. "Our regular sources dried up or weren't dealing with us. Then this new supplier came along with everything we needed. It stunk, and I told Duncan that. He overruled me, and there we were."

"Where?" Jeb sat up and leaned forward, eyes pinned on Joan.

"This half-deserted industrial park. Me and Duncan and our small team were supposed to extract Kearney if things went bad." She took a sip. "And things went to shit right away. With all our planning with teams and communication and…we even had a drone. With all that, we were deep in the weeds—too many party crashers."

"Party crashers?"

"It was an ATF sting, but *Le Espada* got wind of it and they showed up. And, as if that wasn't enough, the Demon Brotherhood Motorcycle Club decided to take that time to get their pound of flesh."

"Bikers? What was their problem?"

"I left their president unconscious in the middle of an Arizona highway, then stole his bike to get to Duncan." Joan hiccupped and held up a finger to make a point. "If it makes any difference, Duncan had been injured and that bastard was taking me out to the desert to," she curled her fingers in air quotes, "talk to me."

"So that's the guy you left unconscious in the middle of the road. The president of an outlaw motorcycle club?"

"That's the guy."

"You have balls. I gotta hand you that."

"Yeah, well anyway, we were in one building and Kearney was in the other. We had to get to him to get him out of there, but we had to cross a big open space. We sent a couple guys to create a diversion on the other side of the building we were in, but it didn't work. The agent on top of our building stood his post and fired, hitting Duncan and this girl, Dee Dee, a member of our team."

Jeb's muscles tensed. "That's how he got shot in the back."

Joan pressed her lips together and nodded.

"You didn't shoot back and maybe a stray bullet—""

"No. I didn't fire my weapon until later when I crossed paths with the members of *La Espada*." Joan stared at the Jack Daniels bottle. "I—" She licked her lips and when she looked at Jeb her eyes were glassy. She swallowed the rest of the whiskey and fingered the empty glass. "I know you shouldn't stop in the thick of a firefight to pack wounds, but I couldn't just leave him there. I dressed his wounds as fast as I could. He was barely alive when I left him." She looked over at Jeb. "I had to leave him. He was too heavy to carry. I had to get to Kearney to get his help."

Jeb studied her. From her emotion, it was obvious she

loved Duncan, even if everything else she told him was a lie. He had to stay aloof. If he got caught up in her emotions, it would wash him away, and the moment for the truth would be gone. And in its place would be a lack of resolve to stay away from Joan. She had an irresistible quality—caring, friendly, but ready to gear up and watch a man's back in an instant.

She had no need for make-up or fancy clothes. And she kept her body in perfect physical condition. For the right man, she would be a handful, but worth every minute. Jeb rubbed his eyes with his thumb and index finger.

"It sounds like you did everything right," he said, hoping a hint of support would help her continue with her story. Between the liquor and the emotion, the confession would come. "You can't blame yourself."

"But I can." Joan pulled her feet up to the edge of the couch and hugged her legs. She rested her chin on her knees. "I told him I would come back for him." Her face collapsed into grief. "I couldn't get back to him." Her shoulders shook in silent sobs.

Jeb hesitated, unsure of what to do. If he moved to sit next to her on the couch, she might push him away and the delicate connection he had so deftly woven would be broken. If he stayed where he was, there would be no connection. He might never learn if what she said was the truth. He reached over and squeezed her arm.

She shook her head and said between sobs from behind her knees, "Dee Dee was there—Kearney killed—there were gunshots."

Jeb knitted his brow. He had drunk some wine, but not enough to garble Joan's story. "Who shot Archer?" he asked again, to see if Joan's emotions would cause a crack in her story. He did not believe a federal agent would shoot someone in the back. If he got her to continue her story, the truth just might emerge.

The door swung open and Kearney strode into the room. "What the hell?" He walked around the coffee table and sat on the couch next to Joan. He looked at Jeb. "What did you say to her?"

"What are you doing here?" Jeb asked. Kearney's arrival gave Jeb the perfect opportunity to enact part two of his plan: put a wedge between Joan and Kearney. It could not have happened better if he had planned it.

"Every Wednesday we get together to talk." Kearny put his arm around Joan's shoulders. "What happened?"

"I was telling Jeb what happened in Phoenix." Her muffled voice was thick with emotion.

"I was bringing her along slowly." Kearney glared at Jeb. "When did you get a psychology degree?"

"She told me you killed Archer," Jeb said.

"I don't believe it," Kearney said.

Joan raised her head and wiped her eyes. "I didn't say that." She glared at Jeb. Her voice lowered into a growl. "I told you the ATF agent killed Duncan."

"You said Kearney did it."

"Why would you say that?" Kearney jumped to his feet. "After all I've done to help you…I can't believe this. You want to talk to Jeb? Have at it."

Joan stood to face Kearney. The rapid rise, coupled with the wine and whiskey, affected her equilibrium. She teetered, regained her balance, but by that time Kearney had made his way to the middle of the floor.

Jeb pushed himself out of the chair and faced off with Kearney. "You better leave before I do something I'll regret."

She turned on Jeb. "You put one hand on Kearney and it'll be the last move you make."

"What?" Jeb pointed at Kearney. "If you want to be mad at anybody, he's the one you should take it out on."

"Fuck you, Jeb." She turned to Kearney. "Don't go. You know I would never—"

Kearney slammed the door on his way out.

Joan started after Kearney.

Jeb grabbed her arm. "Let him go. Hanging out with him is dangerous."

She used Jeb's grip for balance, pivoted, and kneed him in the hip. He doubled over and groaned. She wrenched her arm free and ran after Kearney.

Jeb held his hip and balanced on his good leg, cursing under his breath. He looked up when Joan walked in and slammed the door behind her. Although she had had a lot to drink, her eyes were now focused. When he took a step and winced not even a flicker of compassion crossed her face.

"This is your one chance to tell me what just happened," she said.

"Kearney ran like a little girl when faced with the truth."

Jeb took a hesitant, flinching step toward her. He stood helplessly while her eyes filled with tears.

This would be the time to talk her down and comfort her, but the pain in his hip prevented him from doing that. In the presence of her flaming anger, the logic of his plan melted before his eyes. She had become heartless, or if she still had a heart, it had turned to ice. He stood face to face with the danger he had feared existed behind her kind, playful demeanor.

"You need a man around who will speak the truth and stand by it," he said.

"I can't believe you just said that. You know I didn't say Kearney killed Duncan. Why would you say that?"

"You inferred that was the truth."

"I did not. You wouldn't know the truth if it had yellow eyes glowing out of the darkness."

He put his hand out to her. "Joan." He hopped once on his good leg and winced.

She crossed her arms. Her facial features changed from anger to something more unnerving, a neutral, flat, expressionless face. She was closing down, and he got stranded on the outside.

"Don't let him put a wedge between us." He took one agonizing step. "Joan, help me to the chair."

"I told you what happened in Phoenix." She opened the door. "Now get out."

CHAPTER 10

The next night, Joan continued her job guarding Nirmala. Joan had texted Jeb earlier in the day to tell him she would finish the job for Nirmala, but when it was completed, she could no longer work for Durham Security. A strong connection had developed between her and Nirmala, and she wanted to see this job through. She didn't think of Nirmala as the client, but rather as a mentor and friend. Besides, Joan wasn't a quitter—well, she would quit Durham Security, but she would stick with Nirmala to the end.

She was in the car ahead. Joan checked the traffic behind her, banished any thoughts of Jeb from her mind, and instead thought about Rob. The background check had come back clear, indicating he might be what he appeared to be— a kind, book-selling Boy Scout. A Boy Scout, she reminded herself, who had checked into where she lived.

He had caught her off guard when he asked her to the poetry reading, and she said agreed to go with him to spare his feelings. Poetry. What kind of guy would ask her out for poetry? And when had being friendly become suspicious? Maybe she had been part of seedy, underground subcultures so long she didn't believe in the existence of a courteous, sociable man.

And how should she act on this…date? *It's not a date. It's just an afternoon of poetry. And I'm not acting girlie for anyone.* She would be pleasant, only laugh at his jokes if they were funny, drink her coffee, and use the time to do an offhanded, subtle exploration. If he was hiding anything, she would find out. And even if she didn't uncover any evidence, she would get a sense if something was not quite right. Today was Thursday, which gave her until Sunday to devise a plan. Her confidence in herself and her instincts had returned. If he had an angle, she would ferret it out.

She glanced in her rearview mirror and frowned. The stalker was in the SUV behind her. She knew it was the same vehicle because the headlights were the new blue tinge style—rare enough to know it was the same car. She had hoped for a longer reprieve, but they were on his clock. And it had become clear over the years that nothing was ever easy.

She speed-dialed Nirmala. "Hey, Nirmala, I don't want you to get upset, but our friend is behind me." She had been right when she told Jeb that the guy would not give up easily.

"Oh, no. I thought he gave up."

"I had hoped so, but these guys aren't like regular guys." Joan checked her rearview mirror. "I want you to stay calm. When you get to your house, drive directly into your garage and put the garage door down immediately."

"What about you?"

"Don't worry about me. I'm prepared."

"What do you think he is going to do?"

"I don't know, but he'll have to get through me to get to you, okay? When you get in your garage I want you to stay in your car."

"Why? I'm not safe in my house?"

"Until I check it out, let's assume it isn't safe. Stay in your car and keep the doors locked."

"Okay, if you say so."

"And call my cell if anything at all happens. Whatever I'm doing, I will stop and get to you."

"But how will you get into the garage?"

"Open the garage door if anyone threatens you."

"Oh, yes. I'm so nervous, I didn't think of that."

The garage door was going up before Nirmala pulled into her driveway. Joan looked to the left and checked out the garage as she drove past. It looked clear. When she reached the end of the block, she watched the garage door descend—and the stalker park across the street. It was a bold move that hinted of a plan.

She turned right and pulled past shrubbery so the stalker couldn't see her vehicle. "Stay in your car, Nirmala."

"Yes. I will."

Joan eased out of the car and stood with the door open for added protection. She scanned the area around her several times looking for some minor detail change—a deepened shadow, a moved branch, an outline that wasn't there on a previous pass—it would stand out like bolded print on a typewritten page. Satisfied, she closed the car door until there was a soft click, and pulled her knife from the sheath in her boot.

After one last look around, she crouched and slipped between the shrubs on the corner lot. She held knife in a reverse grip so the blade would be hidden behind her arm until she wanted to brandish it. The element of surprise was a powerful attention grabber, almost equal to the feel of cool steel against the skin.

Her heart beat sped up. She wiped her palms on her pant legs. If they were sweaty, the grip on her knife wouldn't be secure. The adrenaline seemed to sharpen her vision, and she kept her eyes on the surrounding shrubs with quick glances at the interior of the SUV parked directly across the street from Nirmala's driveway. The dark form in the driver's seat looked like the same guy.

Joan stopped at the edge of the trees. The stalker was being obvious. It was a trap. But if she stayed alert, she could foil his plans. His actions up to this point showed a lack of honed techniques, and she could only hope he hadn't sought the help of someone who had more experience. If he had done that—

She inhaled deeply and blew her breath out between her lips.

She hugged the shadows and approached the SUV from the rear. When she passed the rear fender, the driver opened the door. The door shut behind him, she grabbed his collar, pushed him backward, and swept his feet out from under him with her foot. She dropped to one knee, adding to the momentum. The back of his head to hit the ground with a loud crack.

"What is it going to take to convince you to stop stalking Nirmala?"

The man moaned and looked at Joan with unfocused eyes. He tried to roll away from her. She kneeled on his arm. He winced and moaned louder.

She shook him and said through clenched teeth. "You will stop stalking Nirmala."

The man's words were articulated moans. "I don't know what you're talking about. I was just checking the map on the navigation app on—"

"Shut up." Joan pressed the knife against his throat. "We both know what you're doing. This isn't a—" She felt something cold and hard, like a gun barrel, at the back of her head.

"Stand up slowly," the newcomer said. "Slow. No funny stuff."

Funny stuff? Joan stood gradually and faced the armed accomplice. *I still have the knife in my hand. Is this guy for real?* The stalker scuffled to his feet behind her.

"Drop the knife," the gunman said.

Joan bent slowly and flicked her wrist so the knife skittered under the car, out of the reach of the stalker. The gunman wasn't any more skilled than the stalker. He stood within arm's reach of a person who was obviously highly trained, which was an indication of stupidity or false confidence. Behind her, the stalker laughed a derisive chuckle. It was premature and an outward sign of inexperience.

Joan smiled inwardly. "What now?" she asked.

"Turn—"

Joan grabbed the barrel of the gun and twisted. His trigger finger snapped. She hit him behind the ear with the butt of the revolver. He fell stiff and inanimate like a tree— holding his broken finger.

She spun around, grabbed the stalker, and pressed the barrel of the gun against the soft spot under his chin. "Laugh again, you no-good piece of shit."

Surprise, shock, fear all made their way across the stalker's face. He stood frozen in place. Beads of sweat appeared on his forehead. Something warm spread across Joan's thigh that was pressed against his groin.

She fought the revulsion of the man's piss on her leg. "Laugh. Come on. You're a big, brave guy stalking a small, sweet lady." She pressed the barrel harder against him. "Laugh. No? How about a giggle?"

He shook his head in short jerks. Fear squeezed a tear from the corner of his eye. Sweat dripped down the side of his face. His mouth opened and his lips moved, trying to form words, but nothing came out.

"Give me something. Give me a reason to pull this trigger."

"I'll stop." His voice was a whisper.

"What did you say? I couldn't hear you."

He cleared his throat. "I'll stop. I won't stalk her anymore."

The sound of an approaching car pumped up Joan's adrenaline. "Listen, asshole." Her voice came out in a growl that surprised her and, by the look on the stalker's face, it surprised him, too. "This is all I know how to do without hurting you."

His eyes moved to look at his moaning, barely conscious friend, who had gotten to his feet only to lose his balance, slam into the rear fender, and fall against the tire.

"Look at me." She jerked the front of the stalker's shirt and pressed against him harder. "Pay attention. If I see you again, things aren't going to turn out very well for you and any friends you want to take to the grave with you. Catch my drift?"

He nodded.

She shoved him toward the door of his car. "Get out of here."

"What about him?" he asked looking at his friend.

"We'll see that he gets home.

The stalker swallowed hard. "We?"

Claude got out of the sedan that had parked behind the stalker's SUV. He bent over the moaning man.

The stalker's eyes widened at the big man. He yanked open the door and all but jumped into the driver's seat. He fumbled with the ignition key.

Joan rapped on the window with the barrel of the revolver and made a circular motion with it to tell him to roll down the window. He rolled it down two inches.

"Go straight home. Your friend is going to need you when we're done with him."

"But—" He licked his lips. "But he was just helping out. He never stalked Nirmala."

Joan smiled a half-smile. "That's why he's the one who'll pay the price. If we make you pay, you may not learn the lesson. You might fall back into old habits later on, we won't know how many accomplices you'll have. If we make your friend pay, and you fall back into old habits, we're assured no one will step up to help you again."

"Don't do anything to him. Let me take him with me."

"You really are new at this. The person with the gun calls the shots—no pun intended." Joan stepped back and pointed the gun at him. "Now would be a good time to leave."

The SUV sped off.

Claude had the moaning man's wrists zip-tied behind him. He held him on his wobbly legs, supporting him with an arm linked through one of the man's arms. "I'll take it from here."

Joan opened the cylinder and let the rounds fall into her

palm. She gave the gun to Claude and dropped the rounds
into the pocket of his windbreaker. He shoved the man toward his car and roughly pushed him inside, zip-tied his
ankles, and slammed the door.

Joan picked up her knife. "I'll just check on Nirmala,
then call Champ so he's ready to clean up anything we
touched."

"Don't worry about Nirmala." Claude leaned back
against the driver's door. "Carmine is getting her settled
in."

Joan looked down at the wetness on the front of her
thigh and shook her head.

Claude followed her gaze. "Are you gonna be okay?"

"That rat bastard pissed on me." She looked up at the
sound of Nirmala's front door opening. Her jaw dropped at
the sight of Carmine with a Ziploc baggie of baked goods.

Joan put her hands on her hips and watched him walk
down the front walk. "I never got any cookies."

"I must look hungry." Carmine held out the baggie.
"Want one?"

She shook her head and headed into the shadows. When
the darkness melted around her, the adrenaline began to
drain from her system, and her hands started shaking. It
spread to her arms. Rubbery legs carried her through the
shrubs toward her car. She looked back to see Claude gesture for Carmine to get in the sedan.

Before pulling out, Joan grabbed her cell phone and dialed Champ's number. She would get back to the locker
room before the guys finished doing whatever they had
planned for the accomplice. This would be an excellent opportunity to talk to him one-on-one, without interruption
from the others.

෴

A half hour later, Joan walked into the briefing room and

stopped short. Jeb sat at the long, wooden table, arms crossed, legs comfortably relaxed. Sirens and other city sounds filtered through the dark windows behind him. The yellow light from above gave him an unspoiled appearance of tranquility in the midst of chaos.

He nodded his head toward a door to his left. "There are fresh clothes on the bench." He pushed a folded plastic bag across the table toward her. "Put your clothes in this bag and leave it in the room."

Joan laid her knife on the table. It had traces of the stalker's blood on it, and it would have to be thoroughly cleaned.

"Put it back in your boot."

She watched him out of the corner of his eye while resheathing the knife. "But—"

"No 'buts. If there was DNA on the knife, it's in the sheath. Champ will have to open it up."

"Where's Champ?"

"Get changed. Then we'll talk."

"I'm not sure we have much to say to each other. Like I said in my text this morning, I'll finish up this thing with Nirmala, but I don't think I can continue to work for you after that."

"We have to talk about what happened last night."

"No we don't."

"Get changed and hear me out."

She picked up the bag. "You're the boss." She walked through the door into a room that had been turned into a locker room.

Beat up, second hand lockers lined the walls on either side of the door. Some had locks. The doors hung open on others. The far wall held hooks to hang clothes. Lengthwise down the center of the room wooden benches had been placed end to end with an opening in the center. At the far end were three piles of clothing. Joan grabbed the pile of women's clothing.

She toed-off her boots and put them into the bag. The weighty silence was unnerving. She raised her voice to be heard through the wall. "Socks and underwear—do I keep them or put them in the bag?"

"In this case, you can keep them on."

She undressed, stuffed the clothes in the bag, and pulled on sweat pants. She pulled a faded NYU sweatshirt over her head she said, "So Jeb, what are Carmine and Claude going to do to that guy?"

"What guy?"

She pulled the drawstrings of the bag shut. "The stalker's friend. They hogtied him and threw him in the back seat of a car."

Jeb chuckled lightly before answering. "They're up to their old tricks."

She checked for any forgotten items and headed out of the locker room. "What tricks are those?"

"They'll just—" He lowered his voice when she appeared in the doorway. "—scare the shit out of him and send him on his way."

"Like, how?"

Claude and Carmine strode into the room laughing about some inside joke. They stopped in the mid-laugh and looked from Joan to Jeb. Their wide-eyed, slack-jaw expressions indicated they had heard what happened at Joan's apartment the night before.

Jeb gave them a chin nod. "Iron Angel wants to know what you did to that guy."

Carmine came to life first and reached out to rub Joan's head. "Don't you worry your crazy little head about it."

She ducked away from him, batting his hand away. "I'm just asking."

"We just scared him a little," Claude said.

"Like, how?"

"If you had to guess, what do you think?"

"I really don't know. I don't know how to scare someone without hurting them."

Carmine snorted. "Yeah right. From what I heard, you did pretty good scarin' that stalker without shooting him.

I'll bet he was pissin' his pants when he took off out of there."

"He pissed himself before—"

"I don't even know why we were there, eh," Claude said. "You took care of those two guys like they were little old ladies." Claude looked at Carmine. "We coulda been at Notches getting drunk." He licked his lips. "Speaking of which," he pushed Carmine toward the locker room, "I hear a bottle of Jack Daniels calling my name. Let's get changed, eh."

The two Titans disappeared into the locker room, and the room seemed to double in size after their departure.

The curved neck of a cane hung on the edge of the table. Joan's throat tightened. She leaned on the table and hunched into the chair across from Jeb. "Jeb, I am sorry about your hip. I didn't mean to injure you. I was so—"

"I deserved what I got." He leaned forward. "I was out of line."

"I—" Joan glanced at the door to the locker room. Sounds of clanging metal doors punctuated Claude and Carmine's continued banter and put-downs.

"I don't see how I can stay at Durham Security."

"I don't want you to leave," Jeb said. "I have a body-guard job you'll be perfect for."

"I don't think it's a good idea."

"Look, I know I'm not the easiest person to work for." He spread his hands on the table and studied them. "And maybe I pushed too hard to be your friend. It's just that you looked so sad and lonely and I wanted to cheer up the wom-an who was the best thing to ever happen to my best friend."

That kind of cheering up I can do without. But Joan's heart leapt against the walls of her chest at Jeb's words that she was the best thing that ever happened to Duncan. But it recoiled at the memory of Jeb's mean and harsh words— and his lie to Kearney. If she wanted to find out what was going on in his mind, what motivated him to reach out in friendship one day, and what motivated a smack down the next day, she had to accept his apology and keep up the mask of friendship. The key would be to stay distant and objective. And vigilant.

Claude looked around the corner from the locker room. "It's awful quiet out there. Everything good?" He looked from Jeb to Joan then stepped into the room. He had changed his pants, but was shirtless, revealing a muscular chest with several nasty-looking scars. Carmine stood a few steps behind Claude to see what was going on.

Jeb leaned forward on his elbows, hands clasped at his chin. He kept his eyes on Joan and said, "Good as gold."

Carmine pointed the finger of shame from Joan to Jeb and back to Joan. "You two play nice." He pushed Claude's shoulder. "Let's pack up our shit and get down to Notches."

The deep murmur of men's voices floated from the locker room.

Joan eyed the opening to the other room. "I'm not the easiest person to work with either."

"Really? I hadn't noticed." One corner of Jeb's mouth curled up.

"Smart ass." She smiled and looked at his cane. "I'll take your crutch. Then what will you do?"

Jeb exhaled a quick breath through his lips and shook his head. He looked serious, but his eyes gave him away. "And you would, too."

Joan leaned back and crossed her arms. "Try me."

"Seriously, though, let me make it up to you."

The mood lightened. Joan softened. "Oh, shit. What gifts am I going to have to pay you for this time?"

"No presents. I *am* trainable, you know."

"If you acted right in the first place, you wouldn't have to keep apologizing."

Carmine and Claude lumbered into the room, preventing a Jeb from making a comment.

"Just leave our clothes in there?" Carmine asked.

"Yeah," Jeb said. "Champ will get it later."

"See you at Notches?" Claude asked looking from Jeb to Joan.

"You bet," Jeb said.

"Nah," Joan said. "I have to get home and get some sleep. Jeb has another job for me."

Claude pushed Carmine out of the room.

"Sure you won't stop in for one?" Jeb asked when they were alone.

"There is something you can do for me, that is, if you want to make up for what you did last night."

"Anything."

"You have to set the story straight with Kearney. He won't answer any of my texts."

"Tell me something first. Why is it so important for you to be friends with him?"

"Well," Joan said leaning forward, "it's kinda hard to explain."

Jeb rubbed his upper lip with his finger. "Is that right? From where I sit, I see a man, and I'm using that term loosely, who put you through hell and—"

"I don't need you to tell me what he did to me." Joan slid back her chair and stood up. "I gotta jump."

Jeb put out a hand to prevent her from leaving, but stopped short of grabbing her. "Explain it to me, and I'll make things right."

She sat and looked steadily into Jeb's eyes. She drummed her fingers on the tabletop while she gathered her thoughts.

"Okay. In the beginning, in the Constitution Defense Legion, Kearney did everything to make me quit, and when I wouldn't quit, he tried to turn the leadership against me. He thought I wasn't right for Duncan. Said I was a screw up, even though I was good at my job. Then the you-know-what happened—"

"The torture. Call it what it is, Joan."

"*You* call it what it is, I'm telling you why I want to be his friend."

Jeb didn't reply.

"So we have all this bad history, then in Arizona he had some great epiphany or something and decided I was okay for Duncan. And his harassment eased up. Then everything went to shit during that sting and he was the only other member of the militia who wasn't dead or arrested. Pretty ironic, huh?"

"How so?"

"I couldn't save the man I love, but I somehow managed to save the one man I hated most in the world. What kind of screwed up shit is that?"

"If you ask me, your whole history with Kearney is FUBAR."

Fucked Up Beyond All Recognition—you got that right. "Yeah, tell me about it. Hey, come to think about it—" She waved her finger at him. "—you two should actually be best buds."

"Why would you say that?"

"You are always doing or saying some dumb shit to piss me off, then trying to make it up to me, and Kearney is being a royal pain in the ass trying to make up for everything he did to me over the last couple years." Joan nodded slowly and narrowed her eyes. "I have both of you by the short hairs."

"Power—that's your reason?"

Joan shrugged one shoulder. "So are you going to make it right with Kearney?"

Jeb rubbed his upper lip, as if considering the case she had just made.

CHAPTER 11

Jeb must have been watching for Joan because he opened the front door to his townhouse before she knocked.

"Come in and see where you could be living if you had taken me up on my offer a month ago."

Joan gave him a smirk that called him a smart ass. "Three and a half weeks."

"I stand corrected." He shut the door and the uneven slapping of his sandals led the way toward the back of the house.

The hallway skirted the stairs to the second floor. Joan slowed to look through wide doorways that revealed a living room and a dining room that had survived the renovations as two separate rooms rather than the open concept idolized by so many people.

"The kitchen is back here," he said.

Crown molding and built in cupboards nodded toward the original construction. Yet everything was crisp and fresh. The soft scent of lemon furniture polish tickled her nose.

"Did you refurbish this?"

"I'd love to say I did, but the previous owners put a lot of time and money into fixing it up. What do you think?"

"It's not what I expected." She pulled out a backless stool at the marble-topped island in the middle of the large kitchen.

The kitchen had been renovated and updated, but the choice of cabinetry reflected an early time.

"What did you expect?" he asked.

"I don't know. Glass and chrome and low-slung, white leather couches."

"I spent so much time overseas in hot, dusty, Godforsaken, insect-crawling, snake-infested countries, I wanted a couch I could sink into and a big kitchen to cook real food. You know what I mean?"

Joan took the bottle of beer he offered her. "I missed running water and flushing toilets the most."

"You'll love the upstairs bathroom. That was *my* part of the renovation. You want a glass?"

"Nah, this is good."

Jeb pulled several bags of vegetables out of the refrigerator and plopped them down in front of her. "You aren't a guest here. Your job is to make the salad. Can you do that?"

"I wasn't a fugitive all my life, you know."

"That didn't answer my question. Should I be worried?"

"Give me the damn vegetables." She got up to wash her hands at the porcelain farmhouse sink with faucets that sparkled in the sunlight.

Jeb laid a paring knife and a vegetable knife on the counter. "So how did your week with one-on-one training with the famous Frank La Costa go?"

Joan dried her hands and laid the towel across her shoulder. Frank La Costa owned a well-established bodyguard school. Because Joan did not have much time to train-up for the bodyguard job, and as a favor to Jeb, Frank himself had conducted the training.

"He didn't give you an update?" she asked, de-seeding and slicing a green pepper.

Jeb stopped at the sliding door to his deck, grilling tongs in one hand and a plate holding two New York Strip steaks in the other. His mischievous dimple winked at her. "Of course he did. I want to hear your side of the story."

"Put on the steaks and I'll tell you."

She had hesitated to accept Jeb's invitation to his home, but he had promised no talk of the past. She intended to hold him to that because the last thing she wanted was a repeat of the last time they had spent an evening together. He still had not set things straight with Kearney, but she was afraid if she snubbed Jeb, he would never do it. She harnessed her anger, stashed away her reservations about what she was doing, and put on a friendly face.

She slid the sliced pepper into the salad bowl and started tearing lettuce into bite-sized bits. "Okay, tell me what you think," Jeb said. "Was Frank too strict?"

She sliced several grape tomatoes before answering his question. "At first, I got the feeling he was being especially hard on me." She slid the tomatoes into the salad bowl and wiped her hands on the towel. "But by the time we got to the situations simulator, he lightened up a little."

Jeb checked his watch and headed to the deck. He said over his shoulder, "How did the mat work go?"

Joan followed him and stepped out onto the deck that was a nod to the twenty-first century. She soaked up the unseasonably warm mid-April day that hinted of the coming heat of summer. Automobile traffic noises filtered to the backyard. A plane flew over on its approach to Newark Airport. Laughter and squeals from children playing in the next yard made her smile. It was noisier than her place up-state, and the air had that city smell—a combination of car exhaust and garbage and, with the wind from the south, the noxious odor of the New Jersey chemical plants. Joan hugged herself and leaned on the railing.

After flipping one of the steaks, he turned to Joan and raised his eyebrows. "The mat work?"

"I've never been thrown to the mat so many times in ten minutes. And hard, too."

"You didn't take him down?"

"Let's just say I let Frank be the teacher."

Jeb turned back to the grill and shook his head.

"That's not to say I didn't learn anything," Joan said, sitting on a gliding chair with gold and red cushions. "I learned how to control people without killing them."

"I'm glad to hear that." He chuckled and sat in the chair next to her.

"I am still new at this," Joan said with a smile. Her smile faded. "Tomorrow I'm scheduled to go through all the training again with the mobile team, so they know my strengths and weaknesses."

"Why the rush?"

"The clients are going shopping Sunday afternoon…I don't get it."

"Don't get what?"

"She has a controversial talk show. Controversial enough to receive death threats, but she's going shopping. To a mall of all places." Joan shook her head and took a large swallow of beer. "And she's taking her kid. Why would someone do that?"

"First of all, she's been receiving death threats for a long time. The bodyguards are just a precaution, and maybe even a deterrent. She wants her kid to lead as normal a life as she can provide for her."

Joan shook her head. "Still don't get it."

"Why the rush to put you on the team?"

"Like you told me, The daughter is afraid of the big guys with guns. He thinks my unarmed, female presence will keep the kid calmer. Unarmed—that doesn't make me feel safe. But it's a job, right?"

"I'm impressed," Jeb said. "Frank doesn't put anybody on a team until he's sure they're ready."

"Well, tomorrow we'll know for sure."

They fell into a comfortable silence and let the warm spring air caress their bare arms. Joan's thoughts wandered to Jeb's invitation to stay at his home and wondered what it would have been like.

"You're going to be fine." Jeb patted her arm and pushed himself out of the chair. "Your abilities made a deep impression on Frank. He said you take instruction well, learn quickly, and have great instincts and reflexes." Jeb pointed the tongs at Joan. "He doesn't say that about everybody."

"'Take instruction well,' is that a euphemism for 'gets up each time she's slammed into the mat?'" Joan muttered.

"I'm surprised you know the word 'euphemism,'" Jeb said over his shoulder.

"Very funny, Jeb. I'll have you know, I was a nerd in high school."

A bird twittered in the tree a few feet from the deck. It hopped from branch to branch eyeing Joan and Jeb. Its feathers fluttered when it flew off across the backyards to the south. Joan mulled over going inside to get another beer. It would be a good excuse to check things out. Something might reveal Jeb's plan or motivations.

"I'm getting another beer. Want a fresh one?" she asked him, rising from her chair.

"Sure."

It took several seconds for her eyes to adjust to the darkness inside, but she found her way to the refrigerator and pulled out two cold bottles of beer and stilled at the immaculate interior. Not one little spill mark. No ring from the milk carton. It was marine clean.

She broke the trance and opened the bottles then, not wanting to upset Jeb's penchant for neatness, wondered where to put the caps. She set the bottles down on the counter, cringing at the sweat rings they would leave. The third cabinet she checked housed the trash can. She moved on to a drawer. Nothing unusual. The second drawer held unopened mail.

After a glance to see if Jeb was still busy with the steaks on the grill, she fingered through it. The usual marketing letters from insurance companies, a postcard announcing a sale at a local store. Nothing important or out of the ordinary. A wall calendar might have held clues, but he was fully invested in the electronic age. A shadow passed across the doorway to the deck. She quickly turned and pretended to admire the commercial grade range.

"Did you get lost?"

"Oh," she said, pretending to be mildly startled. "I'm admiring this stove. Five burners, a spigot to fill pots with water. Double oven. This is really nice."

"Yeah, it's a beauty. I can cook, but I don't think I do it justice." He picked up one of the beers, leaned on the counter next to the stove, and took a swig. "You'll have to show me how to use it right, Miss Rachel Ray."

"I can cook but..." The soft, lingering look in his eyes made her squirm inside. Backing up would make her look weak. He was blocking the way to the deck. The lack of options jacked up her discomfort.

"But what?" He put his bottle down.

"But I'm no Rachel Ray." She hoped her eyes didn't reveal her nervousness. If he came on to her, she wouldn't know what to do. Duncan had not been her first boyfriend, but he had been one of only a few. It had been so easy with him. Jeb was different.

And he was her boss. And her inheritance administrator. She couldn't lose sight of that.

He smiled and it seemed that his dimple brightened the room. "Let's go sit on the deck and enjoy the fresh air." He stepped aside to let her lead the way to the deck.

She returned to the same chair, looking out over the small, green backyard. *Jeb can be charming. And intimidating.*

"Would you rather drink something else?" Jeb tapped her shoulder with the bottle she had forgotten on the counter in her haste to get away from him.

"Beer is fine." She took the beer and smiled a thank you. She watched him turn up a corner of each steak. He was in good condition for a man whose workout must be compromised because of his hip. His polo shirt revealed muscular biceps and broad shoulders. His thighs looked thin compared to the bulkiness of his upper torso.

"What exactly was the injury to your hip?" she asked.

"Uh-uh," he said waving the tongs back and forth. "We

promised not to talk about the past." He sat in the chair next to hers.

"Okay. Let me rephrase that," she said. "How does your hip effect your workout?"

Jeb took a long sip of beer, watching her out of the corner of his eye. "Were you watching my ass?"

"No, because there's nothing to see," she said with a straight face, but she flirted with a tight smile.

Jeb pressed the beer bottle against his chest in mock injury. "You have cut me to the core."

Joan laughed out loud, which encouraged Jeb to laugh, too. When he laughed, he looked handsome. The pretentious camaraderie made him seem slick and disreputable, and she wished he would laugh more often. Pundits say laughter is good for the soul, and he seemed like a man whose soul needed some good.

They both sipped their beers and soaked up the sunshine. Their conversation gave way to the lilt of a songbird, children's playful squeals, the thump of a helicopter's rotor blades.

Finally, Jeb broke the silence. "You did a good job on the stalker case."

"How so?" The orange glow of sunlight through her eyelids soothed her mind and peacefulness swelled through her extremities.

"I assigned someone else to your shift. He said there was no sign of the stalker all week."

Thinking of that butt-bumping bastard would ruin her inner calm if she let it. "I think it has more to do with what Carmine and Claude did than me," she said, still not opening her eyes.

"Regardless, the client is happy." He leaned back in the chair and put his feet up on the railing. "And I'm happy with the way you handle things. You don't let adrenaline spiral a situation out of control."

Joan didn't know what to say to that. She opened one eye just enough to see Jeb.

He sank down farther in the chair, but he didn't look relaxed. "I've got something else for you."

The serene moment melted away. "Other than the bodyguard gig?" She took a swig of beer.

"There's an op Monday night. I'm short an operative."

"What kind of op?"

"There'll be a briefing. Show Time is twenty-two-hundred hours in the garages on Thirty-Fourth Street."

The paycheck would tell Joan the riskiness of the job. "For the usual amount?"

"Double." He looked at her. "Triple if there's hard contact."

Joan sipped her beer. Shadows were longer than when she had arrived. A breeze teased her arms into goose pimples. "I'll be there at twenty-two-hundred hours."

"Good." Jeb's triceps bulged when he pushed himself out of the chair. "Do you want to eat out here, or inside?"

"Inside. It's getting cooler now that the sun is going down."

"I'll meet you inside."

They settled at the dining room table with their steak and salad They ate their dinners without conversation.

"You want another beer?" Joan stood and picked up her plate.

"Sure." Jeb finished the last third of the bottle and handed it to her.

She reached for his plate.

"You don't have to clean up. I'll get it," he said.

"You said I wasn't a guest here. I'm doing my share." She felt his eyes on her while she stacked his plate on top of hers and balanced it with the empty beer bottle. She flashed a smile before heading to the kitchen.

She scraped the plates into the garbage can, set the plates in the sink, and turned to go back to the dining room. She stopped short to avoid bumping into Jeb. For a man with a bum hip he was quick and quiet.

"I would have thought you would have better situational awareness," Jeb said.

"I feel at ease here." For the second time that day, he blocked her escape.

They stood looking at each other until he glanced over his shoulder, took a couple steps back, and pulled a bottle out of the wine rack at the end of the counter. While he concentrated on the wine bottles, she walked around the opposite end of the work island and slid onto a stool.

"Would you like to switch to wine?" he asked, checking the labels on a couple bottles before settling on one of them. "This is a nice Pinot Noir."

Joan eyed the dozen bottles in the rack. "Hey, why did you bring the apology wine from the club, and not from your private stash?"

Jeb winked at her before skillfully de-corking the bottle. "Nothing gets past you." He opened a glass-front cabinet and took out two wine glasses with large, round bowls. After pouring a conservative four ounces in each, he slid one of the glasses across the island to Joan.

"To friendship," he said.

"To friendship," Joan repeated when they clicked glasses. She took a sip.

"What do you think?"

"I don't know much about wine, but it has a nice aftertaste. It's not quite as bold as the Cabernet Sauvignon."

Jeb smiled and turned his head slightly. "And you say you don't know anything about wine." He put his forearms on the counter and leaned halfway across the island. "You are such a liar, Joan Bowman."

A slight lilt in his voice made his statement playful, and instead of taking offense, she flowed with the mood he was trying to create. She flashed a flirtatious look over the top of the glass.

Jeb pushed off the counter and began putting the dirty dishes into the dishwasher. "So was Archer—hey, why do you call him Duncan?"

"It was his street name when we met, and that's all I've ever called him, except when—" Her thoughts went to Duncan's lovemaking. He had been a rough man, and his sexual appetite reflected that, but she had always felt safe with him. She watched Jeb fill the dishwasher and wondered exactly how safe she was with him.

"Except when?" he asked without looking up from his task.

Joan's face felt hot. She was a veteran, a battle-hardened freedom fighter, and a fugitive. She hoped she wasn't blushing from talking about sex.

Jeb leaned on the counter again. If she was blushing, he didn't point it out.

"I never called him Archer, and I only called him Dennis when we made love. He seemed to like that—" She could feel Duncan's weight on top of her. Hot, bare skin touching the length of their bodies, mixing their sweat. She swallowed the lump in her throat. "—a lot." She downed the wine in her glass. "I never called him by his given name in public."

Jeb wiped the counters with the hand towel. "When did you know you were in love with him? Was it at first sight?"

"I thought we weren't going to talk about the past."

"Indulge me."

Jeb refilled her glass. This time with a healthier pour.

"He always said he loved me at first sight, but he always told me I was a pain in the ass."

"I can't imagine why."

Joan threw a napkin at Jeb. He promptly put it in the trash can.

"You are a full-bore neatnik, Jeb Durham."

"Don't change the subject. You were talking about Duncan."

Jeb's use of Duncan's street name did not go unnoticed, but she decided against bringing it up.

They were getting into a flow, and she didn't want to get distracted. First, they would talk about her, then after the wine flowed and loosened him up, she would turn the conversation to him.

"Well, he professed his love for me when I was still cluelessly looking at him as a mentor and a friend. It took me a while to change gears."

"I can't imagine you clueless about anything."

Joan raised her eyebrows, nodded, and took a sip of wine.

"So I take it you didn't have a lot of boyfriends before Duncan."

"I hate wishy-washy men. I need a guy who'll stand up to me. And Duncan was the guy."

Jeb hitched around the island and sat on the stool next to Joan. "He really loved you. I knew him a long time. I never saw him so wrapped up with a woman as he was with you."

An emotional mudslide buried her words. Her eyes stung. "I have to—" She cleared her throat. "Where's your bathroom?"

"There's one under the stairs."

"I want to see the one you bragged about earlier this evening."

Jeb smiled with pride. "Top of the stairs, straight ahead."

The stairs creaked when she climbed them. When she turned on the bathroom light, all the pent up emotion about Duncan's love vanished in the luster of the glass and chrome she had expected downstairs. A hint of a rose scent softened the hard lines. Part of the adjoining bedroom had been commandeered for the walk-in shower surrounded entirely in glass—not a water spot anywhere. A sleek soaking tub sat in the alcove that must have been the original shower. Everything gleamed. The granite floor was so shiny, she hesitated to step on it, thinking it was wet.

⌒⌒⌒

Jeb pushed away the image of Joan and him in the shower, but not before he imagined the silkiness of soap lather on her wet skin and the pelting water from the three shower heads leaving water drops on her lashes. Her smiling up at him. It took all his willpower to remain in the kitchen.

Joan's phone caught his eye.

He picked it up, glanced at the stairs, and listened. He turned on her phone. He thumbed through her contacts. Checked messages. A slow smile curled the corners of his mouth—dozens of texts to Kearney remained unanswered. After another moment of listening for a hint of Joan's return, he opened the photo gallery, hoping for a picture that could reveal her partner in crime. The gallery held only five photos: four of her bike, and one picture of her sitting on her bike. She had leaned forward, resting her elbow on the gas tank, holding her head in her hand. A long earring dangled below spike hair. A coy smile graced her face. Her long, leather-covered leg stretched forward in front of the kick stand. He stared at it for several seconds before shutting off her phone and placing it on the counter.

The pose was one he would have never imagined from her, but now that he had seen it, he couldn't get it out of his mind. It revealed steamy, molten rock beneath her stony exterior. Who shot the picture? Who elicited that smile?

He rubbed his jaw before pulling another bottle of wine from the rack. *Brother, you better get your feelings in check or you are going to blow your plan.* He thought of the morning she had walked into his office strung out from wandering the city, her life in two bags. Braless.

Get your shit together, Bro—

The stairs creaked as Joan returned to the kitchen.

Stay objective. Don't blow this.

ͽৎ

Joan had checked the medicine cabinet over the sink to see if it would tell her anything about Jeb, but it held nondescript items that anyone would store there. The hardwood floors creaked too much for her to check out his bedroom or the spare room. Maybe some other time. She used the toilet and headed downstairs.

When she walked into the kitchen, Jeb was opening another bottle of wine.

"You need one more showerhead in that shower," she said dryly.

The wine bottle released the cork with a muffled pop. "What?" Jeb sounded distracted, as if his thoughts had been far away.

"You don't think three showerheads are a little overkill?"

"Don't knock it till you try it." Jeb smiled at her as he filled the glasses.

Joan picked up her glass. "Let's toast to long, hot showers."

The cork tumbled out of Jeb's hand and he caught it as it rolled across the counter. With cork in hand, he raised his glass with the other. "To long, hot showers." In one tip of his glass, he swallowed over half the wine. Then poured a hefty amount to replace what he had sucked down.

"What kind of women are you attracted to?" Joan asked as she sat on the same stool she had sat on before.

Jeb grabbed the bottle and walked clumsily around the island toward Joan. He sat on one of the stools and placed the bottle on the counter. The stool between them provided a safe zone.

"I liked girls who were the opposite of the rugged, coarse life I've known. I'd return home from some shit hole to a sweet, chatty fashionista absorbed with her nails and clothes and hair."

"You just spoke in the past tense."

"Did I?"

Joan nodded.

He set down the glass and looked at Joan. "I don't want you to get the wrong idea. I'm not saying anything other than what I'm saying." He swirled the dark red liquid. "I've always preferred girls—women—who would freak out when they saw a spider and who'd want me to kill it for them. That is, until I met you. I'm not saying I'm going to jump your bones. I'm just saying that getting to know you makes me wonder what it would be like to date a woman like you."

"Like me?"

"You know, a woman who kills her own spiders."

"I can see how that would make your life easier."

"You don't have a sister or cousin like you, do you?"

"So now I'm your matchmaker?" Joan said with a heavy, New Jersey accent. She took a breath before continuing. "Just remember, most tough women didn't start out that way. For us, life dished out one pile-driver after another. We have problems just like men who've seen war—you know what I'm talking about—and if you get involved with us, you're getting involved with those experiences. It's a complete package."

Jeb rubbed his upper lip with his finger. "I think that's been the downfall of my relationships. I get stressed out, and my girlfriends were naïve about the energy it took to get through each day."

"Copy that." It was Joan's turn to swirl the wine in her glass. "Sometimes people like us see things that aren't there. I don't mean hallucinations." Only her eyes moved when she looked at him. "I mean our perception of motivations or emotions is skewed."

Jeb's eyes flashed up to hers and she studied him. Her words had pushed a button. Possibly, somewhere inside he knew his thoughts were twisted, but consciously he couldn't, or wouldn't, try to get it right. Earlier, he had joked about lying, but jokes held a kernel of truth. And yet, he just offered her a job with greater responsibility.

But what lie would cause him to distrust me? What you see is what you get. "All the things Duncan told you about me, one of them must have been how honest I am."

"He also said you're good at bluffing."

Her eyebrows raised. At last, a nugget of insight. "And you think I'm covering up something."

"Are you?" Jeb took a long sip.

She was no good at talking around a point. Duncan had told her she needed to develop finesse. Well, her tool box still didn't include finesse. The only way to find out something was to ask.

"Jeb, what do you think I'm lying about?" So much for playing the game. Sometimes you just have to go for the Hail Mary.

He stood too quickly, winced, and rubbed his hip. "You have a busy day tomorrow and it'll take you at least an hour to get home."

"No."

He hitched to the end of the island and turned to look at her.

"I've had too much to drink to get on my bike right now," she said. "And, why won't you answer my question?"

Jeb thought for a moment. "It's nothing. Don't let it bother you. I'll make some coffee so you can get on the road and get to bed early tonight."

Joan watched Jeb make coffee. A veil of silence hung between them while each waited for the other to speak. He stood with his back to her, leaning on the counter, watching the coffee drip into the pot. Joan let him work through whatever was going on in his head.

After he placed a steaming cup of coffee in front of her, he said, "Look, Joan, when Archer died, I lost one of my best friends—"

"I'm sorry, Jeb. Sometimes I forget others are grieving, too. I'm so heartless at times."

Jeb ran his hand over his hair and cupped his neck. "That wasn't what I was getting at. I just want to know what happened to him."

"I told you."

Jeb shook his head at her.

"What's that head shake for?"

"I can't talk about this with you right now. I know enough to be dangerous. Like I said the other day, when Colavito and Darren return, we'll talk."

"Dangerous?" When Jeb didn't say anything she said, "Where did they go?"

Jeb pressed his lips together.

"When will they get back?"

"I am not going to talk about this now. With you." Jeb leaned against the cabinet on the other side of the island and sipped his coffee.

"You're acting like you know something I don't."

He sipped his coffee and watched her face.

"I was there. You weren't. And they sure as hell weren't."

"I know more than you think I do."

Jon narrowed her eyes. He was bluffing. But why? Absolutely nothing happened that she hadn't told him. "There is nothing else to know."

"The subject is closed."

"I don't know what you think happened, but what I told you is all there is."

"Talk about something else."

Dammit. I really need to develop some finesse.

CHAPTER 12

Joan scanned the crowd at the food court for anyone who looked like they were more than casually interested in the client. She glanced at Carl, her teammate about six feet to her right. He was built like a tank—imposing, broad and solid. His face was neutral. Good. He didn't see anything out of the ordinary either.

Melvin was a little farther away on her left. He was a short black man, more like a bowling ball than a tank, who stood placidly with his hands clasped in front of him. For the past twenty minutes only his eyes had moved. When she glanced at him he was watching two young men in their early twenties, who were excitedly talking on their phones and glancing over at the client. They could be fans, but if they weren't, things could slide out of control in a hurry.

While she scanned the swarming mass of people, her mind wandered to the training session the day before. It had gone well. Mel and Carl were highly-trained and capable, and she hoped they had faith in her. When they practiced threat control techniques, these men had been almost immovable. She had controlled them and taken them down a few times, but by the end of the day, the mat was shinier from the seat of her sweatpants than from theirs.

She looked up at the balcony that overlooked the food court and tried to remember the names of the bodyguards posted there, but their names evaded her. A man stood there, pointedly not looking below. He pulled out a phone and started talking. One of the bodyguards moved closer to the man before he turned and walked beyond the line of sight from the food court below. Joan wanted to sigh in relief, but trouble could pop up at anytime from anywhere. Her day wasn't done until the clients were returned to the safety of their home. She shifted the bulletproof vest, which was heavier than it looked, and frowned. Duncan would be alive if he had had one. And she wouldn't be standing there wishing her feet would stop hurting. *No time to think of that now. Stay alert.*

She had purchased the "uniform" of choice which was a black pantsuit, white shirt, black shoes. She shrugged her shoulders to rearrange the sleeves and back. It had been a long time since she had worn matching, dressy, girl clothes. A sleeveless tee shirt, cammo pants, and a holster strapped to her thigh would have been much more comfortable. But it wouldn't have been professional or appropriate.

A woman approached Carl and asked if she could get an autograph. The client heard and waved the woman over to the table. Joan tensed and moved within four feet of the client, but outwardly remained neutral. The client asked the fan a few questions, and after a pleasant exchange of words, the woman left.

The food court was noisy. Tables surrounded a cordoned-off a play area where children squealed while they slid on the plastic slide or rode the bouncy horses on springs. Kids at a table five feet to her right cried. A few feet away a couple argued quietly. Whoever had designed the wide open area had evidently not been concerned with acoustics—or security, for that matter—all the noises were magnified and echoed off the hard surfaces.

The client was trying to persuade her three year old daughter to finish her lunch. Joan watched the mother cajole and encourage her daughter to eat. The mother's patience seemed infinite. A thin smile edged onto Joan's face at the bittersweet vision of carrot-top children running around the house playing commando. In the few seconds she was distracted with the pleasant family scene, a man appeared next to the railing on the opposite side of the play area. When Joan looked at him, he turned around and leaned against the railing. Movement behind a fake plant next to him caught her eye, but when nothing else developed, she resumed scanning the people at the surrounding tables.

The two young men who had been excitedly chatting on their phones, started toward the clients with smirks on their faces. Melvin stepped into their path and put up a hand, signaling them to stop. "Whatever you're thinking of doing, it's not worth it."

They hesitated and noticed the two other bodyguards for the first time. They walked away.

Her earbud crackled. "Man on the opposite side of the play area. Time to exit."

Joan gave the client the Time To Leave Now signal. The client immediately stood and gathered the trash. People screamed and pushed away from the other side of the play area. Joan's eyes flashed to the disturbance. The man she noticed earlier now stood in a shooter's stance, pointing a handgun at them. Joan yanked the toddler into one arm and lunged toward the mother. She pulled the mother into her chest. Two gunshots echoed through the cavernous mall. Two hard strikes hit Joan between her shoulder blades, driving her forward. Her head whipped back. She fell to her knees. Her lungs seized. The room darkened. Screams in her ears. She shook her head to push back the darkness. She glanced back to reestablish the shooter's location. A man dove toward the shooter. A flash of copper. The shooter was gone, out of view behind the trash can.

Get up. Get UP! Ears ringing, thoughts hazy, surroundings drifting away, her survival instinct clicked on. The surrounding chaos seemed to go around them like water around rocks in a stream. A blur of people ran from the area in an uncoordinated mass of bodies and strollers. With her clients gathered in front of her, Joan headed for the ladies restroom—easy to defend, out of sight of the shooter. The little girl screamed in Joan's ear while she ran them to safety.

Carl grabbed her by the arm. "You okay?" He steered her in a different direction.

Joan nodded. She could hear him, but he was outside the deepening tunnel. She shook her head again, and the tunnel receded enough for her to navigate through the commotion.

"Hard contact," Carl said into his mic. "Possibly hot exfil. Primary exit." He pulled Joan toward the main concourse. "Go!" He followed close behind them, talking into his mic, the tone of his voice anchoring Joan in consciousness.

Joan held the little girl tight to her chest and guided the client through the mob running in different directions. They rushed down the side hallway to the north entrance. Over the bobbing heads around her, Joan saw the exit vehicle at the curb. Their driver leaned across the car roof supporting a semi-automatic rifle and scanning the roof above the panicking people. The crowd balked. Some splintered left and right. Others pushed back against the people rushing out of the mall. The confusion jammed Joan, Carl, and their clients in the area between the interior and exterior doors. Hysterical people screamed and shoved. Carl yanked and elbowed people out of his way, making a narrow path. Joan thrust the client ahead before squeezing through the small opening with the screaming three-year-old child in her arms.

They were outside. Police sirens grew louder.

Carl plowed a path through the chaos to the car and opened the back door. He pulled his sidearm and joined the driver in searching for a threat. The mother clambered into the backseat and took the child from Joan's arms. Joan followed right behind them, blocking any possible danger. The driver hurled himself behind the steering wheel. Carl jumped in seconds later, and car sped away from the curb.

Carl relayed their exit time to dispatch adding the ETA for the next checkpoint. He turned and looked at the clients. "Everyone okay?"

The mother held her crying daughter tight to her chest and nodded over the child's head.

Carl turned a little farther in the front seat to look at Joan. "Angel?"

Joan panted, trying to keep her lungs working and to control the nausea. The vest had stopped the bullets, but the pain was worse than the time Duncan had shot her in the leg. She leaned her head against the headrest to support her traumatized neck muscles. She grimaced and said between gasps, "I'm okay."

"You were shot," the mother said to Joan. "And you still got us out of there. I don't know how you did that. I—we're so grateful."

Joan raised a shaking hand and patted the mother's leg. "It's a team effort."

"I can't believe someone actually acted on a threat. Years. For years, I've received them." Her chin quivered and she pressed her daughter's head against her chest. "I never thought—I jeopardized my daughter's life."

"You couldn't have known," Joan said. "At least you hired protection and didn't disregard the threat completely."

The client looked out the window.

Joan looked to Carl for support, but he was reading traffic and talking to dispatch. Had she said something wrong? The silence was brutal.

"Where were you shot?" the driver asked, glancing in the rearview mirror.

"In my vest, in the back." She swallowed the saliva accumulating in her mouth. "I'm good." She rolled her head toward the mother, who was looking at Joan with thoughtful, glassy eyes.

"Is your daughter okay?" Joan asked. "I grabbed her pretty hard."

"She's shaken up, but she's okay." The woman swallowed hard. Joan could see her struggle with emotion. Finally, the woman said, "How did your parents have the foresight to name you Angel?"

Joan knitted her brows and sent a questioning look to Carl. He shrugged.

The mother must have seen the confusion on Joan's face. "You were our guardian angel back there."

A weak smile flickered on Joan's face before tightening with a grimace.

Carl called in the checkpoint time.

Good. That means less than five minutes to the house.

"How you doing, Angel?" Carl asked.

"Where's Mel?"

"He's right behind us." He gave her a long look. "Hang on. We're almost there."

She nodded and willed the pain to stop. After several minutes, the car slowed. She moved to sit forward but pain streaked across her shoulder blades. Stifling a groan, she craned her neck to see out the windshield. The gate guard detail had doubled. No doubt there were snipers in the tree line. She leaned back and relaxed.

The car pulled into the safety of the garage and Carl said to the clients, "The driver will escort you into the house. Angel, hold back."

The clients got out of the car, turning and thanking Joan again. She reminded them again it was a team effort. She opened the door. "I'm feeling better now."

"Stay put."

"Yes, sir." Actually, she was grateful for the extra time in the car. Her legs and arms trembled from the adrenaline draining from her veins. In the absence of the fight or flight response, nerve endings fired and misfired from the beating the two bullets gave her sympathetic nervous system. Her ragged breathing settled into rhythmic panting.

The door was pulled out of her hands. She looked up into Mel's worried eyes.

He checked her pupils. "Come with me to the guard house."

He helped her out of the car and locked his arm around hers. "Walking will help get your system back in order," he said, guiding her through a back door and into the pool area. The air had turned chilly and Joan shivered when a gust of wind blew across her neck. Mel picked up the pace as he maneuvered her around the emptied turquoise pool that yawned to their left. The surroundings blurred a little, giving the backyard a surreal quality. Then they were inside the pool house that doubled as guard central.

The brightly colored chairs and couches had been pushed back to line the room when it had been turned into a gathering area for the guards. Beachscapes still decorated the walls accompanied by a fake starfish and nautical wheel. Plopped into this beautiful oasis sat two utilitarian desks. One of them held an open first aid kit. Behind the desks stood two empty gun racks, security chains pooling around their bases. To the left stood Frank La Costa.

"Get that jacket off. Let's take a look at your back," Frank said.

"Wait. I'm going to puke."

Mel thrust a trash can at Joan. She bent over it, hands on knees, panting through the pain. Bile joined the extra saliva in the back of her throat. She swallowed it. Nothing came back up. When her stomach settled and she was sure it would retain its contents, she stood up and looked at Mel. "It passed."

"You're gonna be all right," Frank said. "It's a shock to your system, and right between the shoulder blades makes it worse. Just relax."

"You got here fast," she said, fumbling with the buttons on her jacket.

"I wasn't far away when I received the call. I hear you saved the clients."

"It was a team effort," she said. Her voice was weak. Her fingers shook and struggled to get the buttons through the holes. Thankfully, neither of the men offered to help her. That would have been uncomfortable and downright mortifying. She had been through many tough times, even stared death in the face. But if Frank or Mel had to help her unbutton her jacket, they would never believe that she was battle-tested. Of course, she had not been shot in the back before—lethal blows, if she had not worn the bulletproof vest. She took a deep breath and shook out her hands.

When the last button was undone, she pulled on the sleeves to shrug off the jacket, exposing the bulletproof vest. Frank separated the Velcro straps and pulled it over her head. She cringed, not from the pain, but at the thought of when Duncan got shot. Their small militia had not been able to afford vests, and he paid the ultimate price for that. At the time, she had not known how much Duncan was worth. With all the money he had—why hadn't he invested some of it in Kevlar vests?

She looked at the two holes in the back of the jacket. "I guess my karma can't stand new clothes."

Mel checked out the vest, leaving the bullets where they were for the police investigation. "Pull up the back of your shirt."

She did what she was told, bending away from him.

Carl entered the room, an assault rifle slung diagonally across his chest. "How's she doing?"

"No broken skin," Mel said. "But these babies are already black and blue. You're gonna be hurtin' for a while, Angel."

If there was a silver lining, the bruises were on her back, and she wouldn't have to explain the nasty scars on her chest and abdomen. It was a tiny blessing, but she lived in the Iron Angel Bad Karma whirlwind. She took what little pleasure life handed her, no matter how painful or obscure.

Mel rubbed a salve between his hands. "This is going to be a little cold."

When his hands touched her back, she jumped. "Geez, Mel, where'd you get that salve? The North Pole? What is it?"

"It has a topical analgesic in it. It'll ease the pain a little." After gently applying it to the two bruises, he pulled back her shirt collar and rubbed some onto her neck. The blow had caused a trauma just short of whiplash, and her neck was already tightening up.

Joan moaned. As Mel's skillful hands rubbed in the salve, the friction created soothing warmth, the kneading loosened her taut neck muscles. Her shoulders dropped, relinquishing control of her body to Mel's expertise. Her stomach stopped rolling.

"By the way," Joan said between moans. "Thank you, Mel for tackling that guy with the gun. Another second, and he might have gotten a bead on my head."

"I didn't tackle the guy."

Joan opened one eye and looked at Carl.

"Don't look at me with that one eye. I was right next to you. Remember?"

"Who else was there?"

"Just us three on the main floor," Mel said.

"Then who took out the shooter?"

The question hung in the air.

She had managed only a glimpse of the shooter before he was tackled. A vision of copper-colored hair flashed into her memory. It couldn't have been Duncan. He was dead. *Keep your shorts on, girl. Duncan wasn't the only red-haired man on the planet.*

The desk phone chirped, and Carl stretched across the desk to get it.

Mel patted her shoulders. "Massage is over. Put your jacket back on."

Carl hung up the phone. "The police were just waved through the front gate."

"Already?" Joan said, before she could filter her thoughts.

Carl and Mel exchanged looks.

Joan saw the look. "I don't like cops. They make me nervous."

"Is there something we should know?" Frank asked.

I'm a fugitive wanted in Ohio for assaulting two police officers. I'm wanted for sedition and possibly murder. "No.

I guess it's all that authority."

She reminded herself she was a witness. She saved the day. The police would photograph her back. She would act professional and cooperative. They'd ask their questions. She'd give her answers. And they'd all be on their way. *You're a player. Play the game.*

The tension returned to her shoulders.

Maybe not this time, but soon, one of them would recognize her. She recklessly flirted with her Iron Angel Bad Karma and snubbed her nose at her punitive destiny. She had beaten the odds far too long. It was only a matter of time.

CHAPTER 13

Against Jeb's better judgment—in light of taking two bullets in the back of her Kevlar vest the day before—Joan slouched in the front passenger seat of a cargo van and thought about the double paycheck for simply riding shotgun on what seemed to be a quiet operation. Jeb had assured her these ops almost always went like clockwork, and her presence was insurance. Almost always meant sometimes things turned into a bad time. Her Iron Angel Bad Karma meant almost always things went sideways.

Her back hurt like hell, and she shifted in the seat. Tension tightened her already traumatized neck muscles. She rolled her shoulders and changed position again.

She forced her body to relax in spite of the restrained nervousness that was always a part of waiting for the "go" command. Waiting was never one of her strong points and the act—or the lack of action—raised her anxiety level in and of itself. That was no comfort to Joan because she carried around the Iron Angel Bad Karma, almost ensuring an unhappy ending. She pulled her knife from its new sheath on her belt and thought, *Anyone who says they aren't nervous before an op is either dead inside or crazy—and I'm not either of those...yet.*

"I heard you're a hero. Saved the clients," Colavito said.

"How did you hear about that?" Joan asked. "I thought you just got back into town last night."

"I got in yesterday morning. Had drinks with Mel last night. He talked highly of you."

She toyed with a loose thread on her new cargo pants, cut it with her knife, and searched for another. She watched Colavito out of the corner of her eye.

"Got shot in the back," he continued. "But you stayed alert, didn't pass out from the shock."

"It was a team effort."

He sat in the driver's seat radiating a cool diffidence, which added to her nervousness. His posture communicated a controlled tension. Something must have happened on his trip to Phoenix. Whatever it was, he was jumping over fire trying to talk around it. Opening the conversation with praise didn't fool Joan. Jeb had tipped her off about Colavito and Darren, where they went, what they found, or rather what they thought they found.

Colavito turned in the seat, draped one arm over the steering wheel, and put the other over the back of his seat. He must have come to a decision. "What was Archer's condition when you last saw him?"

Joan stilled. No one had ever asked her that question. "Where did this come from after all these months?"

"I'm curious. Was he dead when you left him behind?"

Joan sat up straight. "I didn't leave him behind," she said through clenched teeth. "I couldn't get back to him. I tried, but I was—I just couldn't."

"But you claimed to Jeb that he died. Why would you feel compelled to get back to him, if he was dead? It wasn't a war on foreign soil."

Joan looked out the window of the van. Explaining how things went down in Phoenix was difficult. No one seemed to understand the desperation she had felt, fighting her way through the building, fighting more than one group, trying to get back to Her Life.

"Angel, I'm not trying to start something here," Colavito said. "I'm just trying to understand. What was his condition when you last saw him?"

She looked out the window several seconds, and answered without looking at Colavito. "He was shot through the chest. I bandaged the entry and exit wounds. Right before I left him, he passed out."

"He was alive when you left him?"

"Yes. Barely."

"I have to ask you something, and don't get upset. I'm not trying to upset you." He hesitated before continuing. "Why did you show up here to collect his estate if you didn't know for sure he was dead?"

"There were gunshots—" Joan wondered how anyone would understand who wasn't there. The leadership got dropped into her lap when Duncan was fatally wounded. The militia was fighting three groups—bikers, *La Espada*, and the feds. Opposing forces popped out of everywhere. She finally looked at Colavito. "There were people there to—"

"*La Espada.*"

"Yes, somehow *La Espada* got wind of the gun deal and they showed up. Members of the Demon Brotherhood Motorcycle Club were there to avenge what I did to their president. And of course, the ATF was on site because it would have been too easy without them." She swallowed her sarcasm. Colavito seemed sincere. "There were lots of people who wanted to bring down the militia. What better way than to take out the leader?"

"And you assumed those gunshots finished off Archer."

Joan nodded. Her eyes stung, but no tears formed. "And just for the record. I didn't show up here to claim his estate. I didn't even know there was any money. I thought Duncan sent me here for assistance in going into hiding or getting out of the country."

"But you took the money."

"I took what Jeb gave me—enough to get started—to pay rent and the security deposit, clothing, kitchen items. You know, to finance things like that. I didn't take any money after that."

"Why not?"

"Spending it was like giving pieces of Duncan away. If the money was there intact, he was there, too." She looked out the window again. "It's hard to explain."

"So you didn't get the whole estate all at once?"

"No. I said that. Jeb advanced me start-up money."

"And nothing after that?"

"No. Well, he kept giving me a monthly 'allowance.'" She curled her fingers in air quotes on the last word. "But I never spent any of it. I have my own money. The money Jeb gave me is in a cache until I can get him to take it back."

"Archer told me he set it up for you to get the money so you could buy a new identity and disappear. You'd have to have all of it to do that." He tapped the steering wheel. "You don't think it's odd, getting the estate in…installments?"

"It doesn't matter. I don't want the money anyway," Joan said. "All I want is what I'll never have again."

"If you have your own money, why don't you take off? Why are you doing this?"

She had asked herself that same question several times. It all came back to the connection she had to the area. "I have a connection to the area."

"When the feds find it, they'll find you, you know that, right?"

She rubbed forehead. "I circle the New York Tri-State Area like a duck over a pond, knowing it's not safe to land, knowing there are hunters in a blind waiting to open fire."

Colavito nodded in understanding.

"And Kearney's still here," she continued. "He's like a bad habit. Not good for me. A pain in the ass. But I still can't walk away."

"What about Kearney? Didn't he get part of the estate?"

"Yeah, he takes and spends his allowance. He doesn't seem to have any problem with that."

Colavito thought for a while.

She misunderstood the silence and added, "I'm not judging Kearney. I'm okay with whatever he does about the money. I just can't bring myself to spend any of it."

"Did Kearney say he saw Archer's body?"

"He never saw Duncan that day. Why do you ask?"

"No reason. Forget I asked."

"You can't just start an idea and drop it."

Colavito didn't answer her.

Joan went back to her own thoughts about the mission. She was calm on the outside, but inside her nerves were thrumming like guitar strings. They were the exfiltration team, and she hoped this extract would go better than the one in Phoenix. Colavito had backed the panel truck into a dead end alley. The wait was taking longer than they'd been told in the briefing, and Colavito's conversation filled her with dread. His tone was soft, but his questions made her talk about things she didn't want to think about.

She didn't have to look up to know he was staring at her. She slid the knife into the sheath on her belt—turning in her boots every time she used it was inconvenient, to say the least—and looked out the grimy side window. She forced her thoughts away from Colavito and onto the team carrying out the mission. They were executing a vigilante mission for people who were unable to exact justice on their own. They were middle class, normal, everyday people whose daughter had been strangled, dismembered, and thrown away like trash. The justice system didn't come through for the family. Sure, the courts prosecuted the man who had killed the girl, but the prosecutor's office refused to go after the group who used and abused misguided young girls—then discarded them when they were used up. It was rumored at the time that the reason no further charges were sought was that someone with political clout was involved with the group. It was uncorroborated, but there was enough evidence for Jeb to take the case. Justice was being served while she and Colavito waited in the dark alley three blocks away.

"I'm just making conversation." Colavtio leaned forward trying to make eye contact. "What would you do if Archer turned the corner up there and walked toward the truck?"

She glanced at Colavito. His eyes had hardened since he came back from his last assignment. Actually, she could trace it back to that awkward moment in Jeb's outer office. Her leg started jiggling. "Where are those guys? Shouldn't they have radioed by now?"

"When they need us, they'll call." He stretched his arm across the opening to the back of the truck and placed his hand on the back of her seat. "Duncan. Walking toward us. What would you do?"

She clenched her teeth. "Stop. It." She could feel his hand even though he wasn't touching her, just like she could feel his eyes on her. "You're playing with fire."

"What are you going to do? You swore off killing, so I know you won't kill me." He turned to face front, draped both arms over the steering wheel and snorted. "Big bad-ass Iron Angel."

"There are things worse than death, you know." She looked at him, but he was looking out the windshield. "I could make you wish you were dead," she said in warning. "There's no telling what could happen. It might be like a dam breaking." It was time to put an end to this…whatever it was.

"Oooh, I'm a-scared. The boogey angel will come after me," he said shaking his hands and looking at her out of the corner of his eye.

Joan fought laughter at his silly words. She could appreciate his attempt to break the tension with humor. She turned her head to look out the window, and lost the battle. "You are one stupid bastard," she said, rolling down the window. It was an older truck, and the cranking motion helped hide her laughter. She inhaled a lungful of night air. And coughed. The alley was rank, and the exhaust building up in the tight space only made it worse.

He laughed but stopped abruptly. "We're up." He

pressed the ear bud to his ear. "Roger that." He tugged on the gear shift lever, pulled out onto the street, and made a sharp left that threw Joan against the door. She would have bet against the tires squealing on the bucket of bolts they were riding in, but they were at top speed in seconds. He wove around slower cars.

"Better grab that rifle on the floor." His glance directed her toward the canvass-covered lump on the floor between the front seats.

She picked up the canvass to reveal an M-16. "Why? What happened?"

"They had hard contact." He swerved around a car making a slow left turn. "This is going to be a hot ex-fil."

"Shit." She released the magazine, checked it, and reinserted it. The action and familiar metallic sounds filled her with a sense of purpose. Her training kicked in.

She reached down for the other three thirty-round magazines. "Any injuries?" She shoved the magazines into the pockets of her cargo pants.

She stopped and looked up at him. The lack of an answer was answer enough.

"Coming up on the street in ten," he said into the micro-transmitter plugged into his ear.

She slid between the front seats and headed for the cargo area of the truck. The lurching truck threw her two steps left. She used the roof to brace herself and fought to get in sync with the rocking motion. "Which side?"

"Your side."

She slid the side door until it latched open.

"Coming in hot. In three," he said as much to her as the team on the other end of the radio.

She knelt on one knee and braced her back against the side of the doorway with the toe of her boot tight against the other side of the opening. She raised the rifle to her shoulder. The force from taking the corner almost threw her out of the truck. She steadied herself, and when the truck straightened in the street, she sent cover fire against the building. The truck slid to a halt. Return fire ripped through the side of the truck, making dull, metallic clunks. She fired back. Spent casings tinged inside the truck.

"Taking fire," she yelled over her shoulder.

Men appeared in the doorway. They waited while she changed magazines. She slapped in another, nodded to the men, and sprayed bullets over their heads.

Three men smelling like blood and fear dove and tumbled past her. She grabbed the pant leg of the last man and pulled his leg inside. "Go, go, go," she yelled over her shoulder.

The truck squealed down the one-way street.

Joan stumbled over someone's leg and staggered toward the back of the truck. She grabbed the handle on the side door to stop her momentum. She flung it closed and looked down at the moaning men. The only one she had met before this op was Darren, who was already assessing the conditions of the other two.

Before she could offer assistance, popping sounds from behind them and three quick clunks above her head got her attention.

"Hang on. They're following us," Colavito yelled.

Several more rounds hit the roof the van. Followed by breaking glass and the sound of bullets whizzing past her head. The barrage ended with several thunks into the dash.

"Holy shit," Joan said plastering herself to the side of the truck. "Everybody okay? Stay—"

The truck lurched, bounced off a parked car, and kept going.

"Colavito!" She grabbed the backs of the front seats to brace herself. "You okay?"

He gave her a wobbly thumbs up. The truck came to a stop against a parked car. Darren pushed her into the front compartment of the truck, slamming her against the dashboard.

"Help me pull 'Vito out of the driver's seat," he said.

She knelt on the passenger seat and pulled Colavito's

legs free from the driver's area. "Can you push?" she asked him.

He nodded and gave a weak push. It was enough to enable Darren to manhandle him out of the seat. Joan supported his legs until he was past the front seats. More bullets sprayed the inside of the truck. Colavito's body jerked with each round that hit him.

Joan's blood turned to ice. Battle spiders crawled up her neck and across her scalp.

"You're shotgun. Shoot 'em for Chrissake!" Darren yelled. He jumped into the driver's seat and yanked the truck into reverse. It slammed into the vehicle behind them.

The first motion caught Joan by surprise and threw her against the dash. The sudden stop threw her to the floor. She scrambled to get her legs under her. She dropped the empty mag from the rifle and slapped in a full one. Her heartbeat pounded in her head. Icy fingers of fear sliced across her shoulders. Her body prickled. She braced the butt of the rifle against her shoulder, leaned out the window. And all sensation stopped. Sounds were muffled. The inside of the truck took on a surreal quality. She seemed to watch herself in slow motion, leaning out the window, firing. The rifle recoiled with each shot. Hot, spent casings flew against the side of the truck, and bounced into her face and neck. She was barely aware of their sting.

Her bullets went wide.

More rounds thwunked through the van, one of them cracking the windshield.

Darren was saying something. She turned to look at him and real time returned. Her ears rang. Acrid burnt gunpowder stung her nose.

"Are you shooting at them or playing patty cake?" Darren yelled. He ran a red light and the truck went up then down over the crest of the intersection. "Girl, you better get a shitload of lead down range in a hurry."

She patted the pocket in her cargo pants. One mag left. *Better make every round count or this is going to end very badly*. She put her left leg out the window and straddled the door, gripping it between her thighs. She brought the M-16 up to her shoulder, aimed at the grill of the car directly behind them. Fired. The chase car didn't slow down. With both vehicles bouncing on city streets, aiming was impaired, if not impossible. She leveled the barrel to the area just above the dashboard of the car behind them. She sent five rounds across the vehicle. The passenger slumped.

Joan ducked her head into the cab of the truck. "Shift left so I can get a bead on the driver."

When Darren pulled the truck to the left, the driver in the car behind them pulled to his right, directly into view. She fired three rounds, hoping for the best. His head blew back, then slumped forward. The car hit a parked car and stopped.

A second chase vehicle crunched the fender of the disabled car, forcing its way past the disabled vehicle. It gave Darren enough time to lengthen his lead.

He swerved to the right then back to the left so sharply, Joan had to grab the HSH—Holy Shit Handle—just inside and above the door. Darren slid the truck to a stop.

"Why are you stopping?" She ducked her head to lean inside the truck. "What's—" She was talking to an empty cab. Darren had already jumped out.

Loud automatic gunfire filled the street. She slid out the window. Her foot caught on the lock button. She quickly righted herself and ran in a low crouch toward the rear of the truck, rifle braced against her shoulder. Her ears rang from the gunshots, but she recognized larger caliber rounds being fired. She peeked around the rear fender.

An older car, something out of an old gangster movie, faced their pursuers. Using the large fenders for cover, Claude and Carmine fired fifty-cal handguns at the occupants of the second chase car. Large holes opened up in the grill. A side door opened. The large rounds tore fist-sized holes through it. Blood spattered. Bodies fell. The gunfire stopped.

Sirens sounded in the distance.

"Time to go," Claude yelled. "Darren, you okay to drive?"

Darren nodded and motioned for Joan to get in the truck. Speeding toward the safety of the Durham Security garages, she looked through the shot-out back window. Carmine had told her that Claude owned a '39 Merc, and the gangster car behind them looked the part. Claude drove in reverse, staying on the truck's bumper. At the first intersection, Claude did a power turn, tires squealed, and he was right on the truck's bumper.

Minutes later Darren pulled into the Durham Security garage, Claude and Carmine right behind them. Before Joan could move out of the seat, the back doors swung open.

"This looks like the bad end of a good idea," Carmine said before climbing into the truck.

Darren slid between the seats to help Carmine assess the casualties. Joan jumped out of the truck and slid open the side door. She climbed in next to Darren to check the men.

He gave her a grave look that sent chills down her spine. "We got this. Give a sit-rep to Jeb. You know, a situation report." He said the last two words like she was a six-year-old child.

She backed out of the truck, stung by his dismissal. In her confusion, she barely flinched when a Durham Security employee bumped her shoulder and rushed by her. Claude eased past her and leaned into the truck.

Darren looked over his shoulder at her. "You still here?"

Joan froze. Duncan had said those words to her a long time ago. But his words had lacked the animosity of Darren's.

He shook his head. "We don't need your help." And returned to continue helping the wounded men.

"Lay off her," Claude said.

She snapped out of it. "Hey, Darren, I just saved your asses, and I—" She jumped when a heavy hand landed on her shoulder. She looked up into Jeb's eyes. Instead of feeling relieved, she flinched at the same hard stare Darren and

Colavito had given her. "Um…it was a hot ex-fil. Everyone except me and Darren have been hit. And except—"

"Carmine already gave me the sit-rep."

"When? We just—"

"On the way in." He watched two men being carried past him. He turned his hard eyes onto her. "Get cleaned up and go home."

"Is there a problem?"

He turned to walk away. "Get cleaned up before the guys get up there."

"Jeb," she called after him.

He kept on walking.

She fell in beside him and grabbed his arm to get his attention. "Jeb, if I did something wrong, I need to know what it is. What the hell did I do?"

He stopped and turned his head slightly, but didn't look at her. "Like I told you before, don't internalize—until it's necessary." He walked away.

She followed after him. "Jeb, Talk to me."

He stopped, and she almost bumped into him. "You did good today. You handle every situation well. Think straight in the middle of chaos. At times…" He looked past her, as if lost in thought, and shook his head, "…you perform at the point of perfection. Other times…" He looked into her eyes. "I don't know you."

Joan took a step back at the bite of his words. She did well during the operation, but he and Darren were acting like she was lower than fly spit. Colavito had been acting strangely in the truck before everything went to hell. And what did "I don't know you" mean? He spent months trying to convince her to be on one of his teams, weeks trying to be her friend. He already knew everything he had to know.

He looked at her impassively. "Get dressed. Get out of here. I'll see you in my office tomorrow."

"When?"

"I'll let you know. Now get moving." He disappeared around a twenty-foot delivery truck.

Jeb's words sounded more like a warning than a suggestion and she headed for the stairwell at a trot. She took the stairs two at a time. Why had these guys, who had always been friendly, turned on her? The last time everyone turned on her in the Constitution Defense Legion…She blocked the memories of how she had barely survived that ordeal. Jeb's last words echoed back to her, bringing her out of her stupor. *Get dressed. Get the hell out of here.* He hadn't said the word "hell," but it was in his tone.

CHAPTER 14

Joan's hands shook from the adrenaline dump, which made changing clothes an effort. She fumbled with the button on the pants, dropped the tee shirt twice before putting it on—inside out. She righted the shirt and finally stashed her operation clothes in the plastic bag. She headed out of the makeshift locker room, but didn't get far before her legs gave in to the weight of the events of less than an hour before. No more adrenaline to keep her going, she slumped onto the end of the crude bench, rested her elbows on her knees, and covered her face with her hands. The sudden let down left her confused.

Colavito had died in front of her. She couldn't shake the feeling of his body jerking from the impacts of each hit. Or the dead weight when he went limp. The hollow space in her core radiated heaviness into her extremities. Did he leave any family behind? The realization that she hadn't taken the time to get to learn about his personal life slashed her like a knife.

And, worse than that, she had broken her vow of no more killing. She was only supposed to keep him company, be an extra set of eyes, ride shotgun. *Damn Iron Angel Bad Karma*. Now there were more deaths. The slide back into a dark lifestyle that threatened her freedom and her sanity drove the heaviness into her bones. The specter of more phantoms added to those already clamoring for attention in her dreams made her want to give up on life. She looked at

Colavito's M-16 leaning against the bench next to her. It had a shortened barrel—it would be so easy. A line of poetry filled her head *...From this world, I struggled downward, of coming death, his purpose told me...*

She shook her head to clear it. She couldn't think of her mother or her poetry right now. Those lines were suppressed a long time ago. She steeled herself, determined to prevent her demons from ruling what was left of her life.

The outer door banged open. The weight of the evening's events prevented her from pulling her knife or grabbing the M-16. She was too drained for a response to the plodding male footsteps in the briefing room, and resigned herself to the harsh words that would surely come.

"He—e—ey, Annie Oakley." Carmine mimed riding a horse—one hand in front of him holding invisible reins, the other over his head swinging a make-believe lasso. He came into the locker room and passed behind her in hitching hops. "Yeee-ha-a-a. Ride 'em, cowgirl."

Apparently oblivious to her mental state, he pointed a beefy finger at her. "You shoulda seen yourself. We was zoomin' to the spot where the...whaddaya-call-it?...GPS told us you were. We almost blew past you guys, but Claude whipped a sharp turn and we headed down the street to where you guys were making tracks. And whadda we see? You straddling that door like one o' them fuckin' broncos, shootin' at the guys behind you." He held a plastic water bottle like it were a rifle. "Pop, pop, pop, pop, pop."

Joan looked up at him, barely raising her head from her hands. Jeb, Darren, and Colavito had been cold and, at times, harsh with her. But Carmine was acting buddy-buddy. That meant Carmine wasn't in on whatever was turning Jeb and Darren against her. Claude's defense of her in the garage indicated he wasn't on the uplink either. Why were some of the guys but not others mad at something that involved her? And Darren was an outsider. What the hell could be his problem?

"Yeah, well, if I didn't do something," she said, "we

would have been dead before you guys got there."

Carmine took long, glugging swallows from the water bottle, then pulled his polo short over his head. "Yeah, you guys were on the south side of Shit City, that's for sure. But, hey, you did your job. We did our job. We're here talking about it." He reached into his locker. Thick black fuzz covered his muscular back, except where substantial scars lay bare and menacing. They looked like the result of torture. She should have felt something—empathy, affinity, even curiosity—but the emptiness in her bones only produced numbness.

"Coulda been worse," he said, looking around inside his locker.

We're here talking about it. "How can you be so light hearted? Colavito died." She wanted to leave but couldn't make her legs move. She crossed her forearms across her knees and rested her head on them. "He died in my hands."

"Don't let my joking around fool you. I loved Colavito like a brother. Humor is just a defense mechanism. The reality of what happened will kick in later, after a couple o' shots at Notches." He glanced over at her and stopped rummaging around inside his locker. "Hey, Colavito knew the risks."

Struggling with a surge of emotion, and not wanting to break down in front of a man she didn't know very well, she returned her face to the comfort of her hands. Carmine was another man she didn't know anything about. Another man flirting with death. *Flirting. Was that all I knew about Colavito?* She wiped the emotion from her face and looked over at Carmine.

A religious medallion hung around his neck on a silver chain. He straddled the bench, plopped down onto it, and watched her with his dark brown, sleepy eyes. His hairy chest and bulked-up arms were covered with tattoos—a pin-up girl tat on his side had been slashed by a wide, ugly scar and never touched up. Several smaller scars peeked between the chest hair that started as a broad band across his muscled pecs then narrowed into a line that dropped across his round belly and disappeared at the waistband of his camouflage pants.

"We all know the risks," he said. "And you do, too. You're no dummy. This isn't your first road show."

"Yeah, I guess."

"You stepped up. Saved lives today. Remember, Iron Angel, in self-defense and the defense of others, the only sin is cowardice."

"But I put myself in that position—to possibly have to take lethal action. It's like I'm on a treadmill and keep going, when all I have to do is step off. But I can't make myself do it."

"Stop beating yourself up. You need to decide if what you do for the people who have been screwed by the system is worth the risks we take for 'em."

"Is it? Is it worth the risks?"

Carmine stood up, stepped one leg over the bench, and wiped the sweat from his chest and armpits with his shirt. "Only you can decide that."

"And taking justice into our own hands…what is right about that?"

"Some people can't seek justice for themselves. They don't know how to shoot and fight these guys. We do."

"But we have a justice system in America. It's not perfect, but it's one of the best in the world."

"And sometimes it's too convoluted, corrupt, or just plain inept to deal out justice. The ones who are able to seek their own justice—and are brave enough to do it—get that satisfaction only justice can provide. Those who don't have fighting capabilities hire us."

Joan shook her head. "So it falls into our hands to meet it out?"

He started unbuttoning his fly. "Justice is justice, no matter whose hands it's in."

She grabbed the rifle and willed her legs to leave.

Claude barreled into the room. "Well, if it isn't Iron Angel—the Angel of Death, eh?"

She walked past him.

He followed her, reciting a parody of a Lord Byron poem, sweeping his arms as if spreading wings, turning for
dramatic effect, and widening his eyes.

"'The Angel of Death spread her wings on the blast,
And breathed in the face of the foes as she passed;
The eyes of the jerk-offs waxed deadly and chill,
Their guns fired but once and forever were still!'"

Joan shook her head and walked across the briefing
room to the hallway. Seeing the big man with a shaved head
and mutton hands reciting Lord Byron would have been
funny under different circumstances, but the events of the
afternoon sucked the humor out of it. And the thought of
crossing paths with Darren or Jeb added a sense of urgency
to her steps.

"What? You don't like culture?" Claude said with a
mock Brooklyn accent.

She turned and saw him standing in the briefing room,
hands out, palms up, in a questioning pose. Taking a couple
backward steps, she said, "I never took you for a poetry reciting kinda guy. And Lord Byron of all people."

"I'm from Canada. We learn this stuff in school, eh. See
you downstairs for a couple."

"Not tonight. I have to get home."

"Notches is there for you to unwind. Use it."

"Thanks, Claude. Maybe some other time."

While Jell-O legs carried her down the stairs and into the
alley behind the Durham Security garages, thoughts of the
change in her position with the company filled her head.
Everything was going okay until Darren showed up. Jeb
said he was from the Chicago group. What was he doing in
Yonkers? If he had some special skill that would have
helped Colavito—in whatever his mission had been—it

would be understandable to pull him in. But why was he on the operation this afternoon? Why didn't he hightail it back to Chicago where he belonged?

And the Phoenix mission changed Jeb and Darren—and Colavito to a lesser degree. They couldn't possibly have found out anything she didn't already know. Jeb had warned her against internalizing events. Tonight he had changed his position to, "until it's necessary." Did that mean she should internalize now? In view of the corkscrew feeling in her gut, the answer to that question was most likely a "yes."

The cool night air brushed her cheeks and she realized she still had Colavito's M-16 in her hands. The thought of going back up those upstairs and the possibility of crossing paths with Darren was not appealing. She silently thanked Kearney for loaning his car to her, and she put the rifle under a blanket on the floor. Before she climbed into the front seat of the Jeep, something told her to look up. When she did, she saw Jeb watching her from an upstairs window. She waved.

He turned and walked out of sight.

∾⌾∾

Kearney lay in bed, propped up by pillows, hands behind his head. Elaine slid out of bed to go to the bathroom, and he savored the candied scent of her perfume until it wafted away from him. He watched her pick up his white dress shirt from the floor where it had dropped in a rush of passion. Before she wrapped it around herself, he caught glimpses of curves and hollows he had explored for the past hour. The door closed behind her, leaving him alone with the memory of her silky skin over Pilates-toned muscles. His smile broadened. She was a mature, successful woman, but her body and playfulness were youthful. Not even a year ago, he would have used her for one night's satisfaction, but something had changed in him. He wanted more of her—and only her.

She was an ambitious real estate broker, which left odd pockets of free time. He liked the thrill of rushing to im- promptu trysts. This evening had been a rare exception. They had enjoyed a long, luxurious dinner at an expensive restaurant then retired to his room for a night of making love. He smiled. The ruggedness of the bungalow added to his bad boy persona.

He rubbed his eyes. Unfortunately, he and Joan couldn't stay in the area much longer. Remaining in one place too long was a surefire way to get snagged by the feds. They would have to move on soon. But whispered words, soft hands caressing his skin, a naked body rubbing against his—benefits of a settled love life—were calling him away from caution. Conversation with a mature woman that didn't involve bawdy sex talk or paramilitary tactics tugged at something inside him that had lain dormant for decades. Too bad he couldn't stay. Staying was a death knell to his and Joan's liberty. A little more time, that was all he asked. This passion would run its course, like it always did, and he'd move on when it was time.

The pale light from the lamp on the bedside table created a soft glow that muted details. But when Elaine slipped back into the room her facial expression was one of unmis- takable worry and fear. She closed the door behind her, the shirt held at her chest in a death grip.

Kearney sprang out of bed and grabbed his semi- automatic handgun from the night stand in one fluid motion. "What's wrong?" he asked, rushing across the room. He leaned in close to her, looking into unblinking eyes. She was shaking.

He understood things that were commonplace to him could scare her, and he was trying to guide her through the maze of his rough lifestyle without jading her outlook on life, give her just enough to keep her interested. A little thrill at a time. Not too much. Not too illegal. He liked her and the last thing he wanted was to scare her, for her to run away, or worse, go to the police.

But things may have just gotten slippery. Could something from his past popped up? Someone he interrogated who lived, and was now seeking revenge? Or was it one of the rowdy punks living in the next bungalow? A burglar? It could be anybody.

He put a hand on the side of her face to calm her. "What did you see?"

"There's someone sitting on the couch."

Calmly sitting on his couch—sounded like a professional. Precious time was being wasted. "What's he doing?"

"It's a woman. She's slouched on the couch with a rifle of some kind in one hand and a bottle of alcohol in the other." She clutched Kearney's arm with her free hand. "She's just staring at the television with the volume turned way down."

"Does she have short brown hair?"

Elaine nodded.

"Shit. What the hell's she doing here?" He walked around the bed, searching for his pants. "It's my sister, Angel. I told you about her." Elaine didn't relax at that revelation—maybe he had told her too much about Joan too soon. He zipped his fly on his way back across the room to Elaine. "Watching Animal Planet relaxes her so she can fall asleep." *Or she's gone off the deep end.*

"Liquor and firearms are never a good combination. That's what you told me at the firing range, right?" Elaine's voice quivered slightly.

He put a hand on the side of her face. "You're right. It'll be okay," he said in hopes of comforting her, but his mind was on Joan, wondering what could have triggered a downhill slide. He gave Elaine a peck on the forehead.

She looked down at the semi-automatic in his hand.

"Don't worry. This is…I don't know…habit." He slowly opened the bedroom door and peeked into the living room. "I'll take care of it. Stay here."

The plaid couch faced the television on the wall between the two bedrooms. The flickering light from the television revealed Joan with hair matted on one side and spiked on the other, chin to chest, blank eyes staring straight ahead. One hand held the muzzle of an M-16, with the butt against the floor like the image of a despondent queen with her scepter. A square bottle of Avion tequila was in her other hand, resting on her thigh, tipping precariously away from her.

Kearney remembered Elaine had been heading to the bathroom when she was stopped by the scary sight of Joan. Over his shoulder he whispered, "Go ahead to the bathroom." He waved her behind him. "There's nothing for you to worry about."

There was an ottoman directly in front of Joan, but she had chosen to leave her feet on the floor. He knelt next to the ottoman to be eye level with her.

༄༅༄

Somewhere in the murky edges of her consciousness Joan was aware of Kearney's presence. Her mind was filled with spattered blood, the recoils of the rifle, the tings of ejected casings, the loud reports of the rifle. Men diving past her into the van. The smell of fear. The weight of Colavito's limp body. The jerks when bullets hit him, killing him. But the worst was the horrid feeling deep in her gut, a gnawing alloy of pain and pleasure—pain at another loss of life and the morbid pleasure that what fails to kill you makes you feel alive.

She sensed more than saw Kearney reach past her to turn on the floor lamp. Low light instantly formed a small circle that encompassed them. The visions faded in the light, but vestiges of the emotions clung to her, releasing its hold only at the sound of Kearney's voice.

"Want to tell me what happened?" he asked, holding the

nine-millimeter semi-automatic beside his thigh, the barrel resting on the area rug beside his knee.

On the television, a gazelle raced away from a cheetah that followed every dodge, every attempt at escape. She eyed the gun in his hand then took a long pull of tequila. "Colavito was killed." The clear liquid sloshed around the inside of the bottle when she plopped it back onto her thigh.

"You can't save everyone, Joan." The corners of Kearney's eyes hardened. There was a brief silence. "Want to talk about it?"

A toilet flushed. Joan's blank eyes moved toward the sound and saw Elaine standing just outside the bathroom door in a man's shirt.

"I'll make some coffee," Elaine said, and soon familiar sounds of running water and clinking silverware emanated from the kitchen.

With two fingers, Kearney lightly pulled on the muzzle of the rifle. "Want to let me have this?"

Joan refused to let go. "It's…" She swallowed twice. "Colavito's."

"It won't be far from you." Another little tug on the rifle barrel. "It would honor him if it was cleaned and oiled."

"Afraid I'll go on a shooting binge?"

"Nah. If you were going to do that, you would have done it already."

She nodded and relinquished the rifle to Kearney. He leaned it against the end table out of her reach and placed his handgun on the floor next to it. He slid onto the otto-man, partially blocking her view of the scene of zebras hesi-tantly approaching a waterhole full of crocodiles. He leaned his forearms on his thighs. Her eyes were still focused past him, on the zebras.

Picking up the remote and turning up the volume to muf-fle their conversation, he said, "Talk to me."

Her eyes shot to his. *Talk to me* was how Duncan always answered the phone. *Talk to me*…The words echoed in her head. She pressed her lips together as if they would hold back the flood of emotion building up inside her. Her gaze slid back to the television. Another team member shot in front of her. Another man she couldn't save. Her eyes were awash with tears, blurring her vision. When she blinked, they overflowed her eyelids and streamed down her cheeks. She wiped them away with the back of her hand.

"Take your time," Kearney said softly.

She sniffed and rubbed her nose. "I don't have the energy for your head games, K."

"No head games. Just a friend listening to a friend."

"Friend." The word was flat, but spoke a volume of emotion. Her eyes moved from the television to Kearney. "When were you ever my friend?"

"Longer than you think." He leaned forward. "I'm here for you now. That's all that's important."

Elaine's gestures caught his attention. She had a coffee cup in one hand and mimed pouring milk into it.

Joan saw her, too. "Milk with one sugar and one packet of sugar substitute."

Elaine gave her a thumbs up and returned to the kitchen.

"Where'd you get the tequila?" Kearney asked, trying to get Joan to start talking.

"At the liquor store just up from the five-corners in Vails Gate. You know the one owned by that nice gay couple? Leonard asked about you." A slow smile tugged at the corner of Joan's mouth. "You two have something going on?"

Kearney frowned and shook his head. "Don't they close at eleven?"

"I bought this before the op, and I drank in your car for a while."

"It looks like you drank quite a bit. Want to give me the bottle?"

She held up the bottle to see what was left in it. "I didn't drink *all* of this. The cork stopper was hard to get out and…Well, your car might not smell so good in the morning."

Kearney's frown deepened. "That's okay. That's what detailers are for."

When Elaine appeared with three mugs, Joan leaned forward, took one. "I'm Angel, Kearney's sister."

"I'm Elaine," she said. "It's nice to finally meet you. Kearney has told me a lot about you."

"Yeah, I bet." Joan eyed Elaine's hand on Kearney's shoulder and his hand covering hers. Joan had never seen Kearney with a woman before, but it was obvious Elaine was special to him. "I interrupted your evening. I'm sorry. Spend time with your girlfriend, K. We can talk tomorrow."

"Actually, I thought I'd head home," Elaine said. "I'll leave you two to talk in private."

Kearney stood and pulled her into his arms. "Are you sure? You could wait in the bedroom."

She kissed him lightly on the mouth, freed herself from his embrace, and went into his bedroom to get dressed.

"I'll be right back," Kearney said before following her.

"I'm not going anywhere," Joan muttered, returning her attention to the television where the zebras had left the waterhole, but now a lioness was in the tall grass watching the herd, looking for the weakest one.

Elaine re-emerged wearing a red, strapless dress that ended mid-thigh.

Through bleary eyes, Joan stared at the dress, lamenting the life that had scarred her so extensively that she'd never wear a sexy dress like Elaine's. "Nice dress."

Her gaze slid to Kearney. They locked eyes. The mutual stare said it all: her scars, both mental and physical, were his handiwork.

"Humor him," Elaine said, breaking the uncomfortable silence.

Joan looked up at her with a tilt of her head and raised eyebrows.

"I have two older brothers," Elaine continued. "They just want to protect their sisters. Talk to your brother." Before Joan could protest, Elaine gave Kearney a quick peck on his lips, then disappeared into the kitchen to go to her BMW parked in the back of the bungalow.

Kearney walked Elaine to her car and returned few minutes later. "Nice parking job. Were you blazing a new trail up the mountain?"

"Yeah, but a tree stopped me." After a brief silence, during which the documentary narrator talked about the lioness getting ready to attack, she added, "She knows we don't get along, right?"

Their life together was like a carnival fun house—floor underfoot all atilt, mirrors reflecting disturbing images, dark shadows. Expectations of something popping out of the darkness without warning.

He sat on the ottoman. "She chalks it up to normal sibling contention."

After a couple gulps of coffee, Joan said, "She's nice. What does she see in you?" She had her own nice person nudging into her life. "A nice guy asked me to a poetry reading," she added. *Where were all these respectable people before I got caught up in this ugly subculture?*

"A date? Well, that's something new for you. Do you think you're ready?"

She shrugged. "I keep telling myself it's not a date—just a poetry reading, but…I don't know."

"When are you getting together with this nice guy?"

"Tomorrow night. But poetry is…I don't know…depressing, and with Colavito's death…" Her voice trailed off. "What would we talk about?"

"Same things you talk about with other guys. But I wouldn't recommend describing your extensive knife collection. It might scare him off."

She snorted and poured tequila into her coffee. She reached to set the bottle on the end table, sunk back into the couch, and took a deep breath.

"Well, you have a day to think it over," Kearney said. "If it doesn't feel right, you can call it off."

Joan nodded her head. After a few seconds of silence she

said, "Did Jeb ever talk to you about that night at the house?"

"No. As a matter of fact I haven't had any contact with him since then. Why?"

"He was supposed to make things right with you." Joan thoughtfully stirred the tequila-coffee with her finger. "I never told Jeb you killed Duncan."

"I figured as much. He's up to something."

"Why didn't you answer my texts?"

"Just in case he got a hold of your phone and checked it. I knew you would eventually show up at my door."

Joan nodded. "I'm playing him, and I think he believes you and me had something to do with Duncan's death."

"Maybe he wants to keep all the money for himself."

"Maybe." She studied Kearney while taking several sips of coffee.

"I've forgiven you for what you did to me, but I can't forget it," she said. "Consciously, I know I can't change the past. I know I have to let it go. But I can't." She hiccupped. "I'm sorry, K. I know you're trying to make things right. And I know it doesn't seem like it at times, but I am trying. I have to because…" Her chin quivered with pent up emotion released by the alcohol. She pressed the back of her hand against it and gulped down a sob. When she spoke her voice was thick with alcohol and emotion. "This distance between us over the past couple weeks made me realize that you're the only person left alive who understands me. You're all I have…almost family."

"Wow. Those words must have burned your mouth on the way out." He gave her a gentle backhand to her calf. "But you aren't going to change the subject that easily. That's a conversation for another day." He leaned forward. "Let's discuss what put you off your stride tonight. Sorting through it will put things into perspective. Just set the scene for me, and we'll go from there."

"Fucking psychiatrist."

"Psy—cho—lo—gist," Kearney corrected, emphasizing

each syllable. He smoothly moved to the couch beside her and put arm around her shoulders.

She nestled her head onto his shoulder and hiccupped.

"Talk to me, Joan."

∽∾∽

"Yeah, I'm leaving now," Elaine said through the Bluetooth in her car.

A voice came through her speakers. "How'd it go?"

"We had a great evening until—"

"Until what?

"His sister showed up tonight."

"I thought she moved out."

"She did." There was a silence while she pulled up to a traffic light. "She showed up with an assault rifle, bummed out about something."

"Did you hear what happened?"

"They were talking low. I didn't want to arouse any suspicions, so I left to give them time together."

"Well, you're the one who was there. I'll trust your judgment."

"She's messed up enough that she isn't going to give us a problem," Elaine said.

"It would have been nice to know what she was bummed out about. That information might come in handy."

"Kearney'll tell me tomorrow."

"You sure?"

"Trust me. He'll tell me."

CHAPTER 15

Joan inhaled deeply, stretched, and fingered the plaid wool blanket, wondering where it her came from. "What time is it?"

"Time to get up, sleepy head." Kearney squatted beside the couch with a mug of coffee in his hand. "It's eleven-thirty."

Sometime during the night she had fallen asleep on the couch and Kearney must have covered her. It was thoughtful and kind. Before she could thank him, memories of the previous night made her groan. She sat up, rubbing the kink out of her neck.

She took the offered coffee. "I scared your girlfriend away, didn't I?"

"You weren't that scary: loaded M-16, drunk, hair matted down on one side, spiked on the other. Nah. Nothing scary there."

She took a sip of coffee. "Was I that bad?"

Her phone vibrated in her jacket pocket.

"Oh, yeah, someone's been blowing up your phone." He reached into her jacket pocket and pulled out her phone.

"Man, I feel like shit," she said, tapping the icon to bring up the messages. They were from Jeb.

The first was time-stamped eleven-eighteen: *I need you to come to my office*.

Five minutes later: *Did you get the last message*?

Three minutes later: Come to my office now.

After a two minute break: *Text back, dammit.*

This last one was: *Text me and come now.*

She texted back: *Kearney, too?*

She went to the bathroom while she waited for his reply. After relieving her bladder, she looked in the mirror. A pale, drawn face with black circles under her eyes looked back at her. *What the hell are you doing to yourself? Better yet, why? Get your shit together, girl.*

Kearney hadn't lied. Her hair was a weird combination of plastered down and wild abandon.

Her phone vibrated: *No. Be here in an hour.*

She pulled out her shirt and sniffed. She wrinkled her nose and texted: I'm at K's. I have to go home first to change clothes, then drive down.

He texted back: *you now have fifty-eight minutes.*

"Shit. Something's climbed up Jeb's ass. He wants me there in an hour."

"How are you going to do that?"

"Hell if I know. But I can't go smelling like a bottle of tequila."

"Elaine left some clothes here when she changed to go out to dinner last night. Maybe they'll fit you."

"I hate wearing someone else's clothes."

Kearney turned her around to face the bathroom door. "Take a quick shower and I'll put Elaine's clothes on the bed in your old bedroom. If you're a few minutes late, screw Jeb and his inflated sense of importance."

An hour and ten minutes later, wearing Elaine's denim skirt and one of Kearney's tee shirts knotted at the waist, Joan heeled down the kickstand on her Honda in the parking lot behind the Durham Security building. She checked her appearance in the mirror. The circles under her eyes defied the makeup she had swiped over them in the rush out of Kearney's house. She fingered her helmet-hair into some semblance of a hairdo, and headed inside to find out what was so damned important.

The back parking lot had several cars. The bullet holes in

Claude's '39 Merc had been repaired and primed. *Already*? Jeb's SUV was in its usual place. Carmine's Cadillac was parked crooked, taking up two spaces. There was a sleek, black GTO with Illinois plates—probably Darren's. A white Harley Davidson Sportster slowed her pace—special lighting package, extra chrome…nice. She looked up at Jeb's office window. Someone closed the blinds.

She took the stairs two at a time to the second floor. When she walked into the reception area, a man stood in the center of the small room, arms crossed. Black tee shirt, desert scarf, muscled chest and arms—the foul-mouthed operative from the night she got Jacked. The pizza delivery guy. His cocky smirk made the sour alcohol in her stomach roll. She tightened her mouth and looked at him.

"A woman in a skirt, riding a bike." He looked down at her skirt and boots, then back up her body to her eyes. "That is fucking hot."

"You're a pig. I don't have the energy or patience for you."

Unruffled, his smirk widened into a grin. "You're late."

"Screw you. I'm here to see Jeb." She headed toward Jeb's office.

Foul Mouth stepped to block her way. "Leave all your weapons with me."

"No." The request didn't set off any alarm bells, but it should have. She moved again to get past him.

"Jeb's orders."

Dread prickled down her spine. She reached under her motorcycle jacket, pulled the knife from its sheath, and handed it to him. "Take good care of this. It's a Fairbairn-Sykes—"

"World War Two Commando knife," he finished her sentence. "I know. I've seen them before." He inspected the knife and nodded. "Don't worry, I'll keep it safe."

He put out his hand. "The helmet." He put the knife in her helmet. "Any more weapons?"

"No. And you're not going to frisk me to find out."

"No gun?"

"Jeb hasn't gotten me a concealed carry permit yet. So, no."

He rested his hand on the doorknob to Jeb's office. "You might want to check your shitty attitude. You're already on thin-fucking-ice."

"You know what they say: if you're already on thin ice, you might as well do a triple axel."

"Your funeral." He turned the knob and opened the door.

After taking a deep breath to control the adrenaline pumping into her arteries, and straightening her shoulders, she walked into the office with a slow, self-assured stride. The room was gloomy, the closed blinds filtering the bright afternoon sun. A dog barked somewhere outside. Several different scents of aftershave—and the wretched patchouli—assailed her nose. She rubbed her nose and studied each of the men.

Jeb was behind his desk, leaning back in his chair. Darren sat in the chair to the left of the desk, elbow on the armrest, chin in hand. He took a double take when he saw her in a skirt. Claude sat back on the window sill on right side of Jeb's desk—he must have been the man she saw when she looked up from the parking lot. Carmine leaned against the wall below the empty spot where Duncan's photo had hung. Foul Mouth was behind her.

Four operatives, two of them from out of town. This must be a big deal. Foul Mouth's words about being on thin ice pumped up the adrenaline, and her mind raced to find some action or word that was sufficiently out of line to warrant this reception. Nothing stood out, but this had something to do with her. And it was so big it compressed the air in the room, making it hard to breathe.

Her mouth was dry. Jeb didn't offer her anything, so she walked to the small refrigerator and helped herself to a bottle of water. She looked at Carmine while she took a long pull of the cold water. His words came back to her: *If we were going to strong arm you, we would have multiple op-*

eratives and we'd catch you by surprise. Her anxiety level ratcheted up several notches, but she calmly screwed the cap onto the bottle. The two bruises on her back throbbed.

Darren watched her cross the office. Her racing blood heated up—he was sitting in her chair. When she walked toward him, only his eyes moved. She stopped next to him in front of the desk. She positioned herself so none of the men were behind her and kicked the side of Darren's boot. "Get up. That's my seat."

Darren continued to look up at her, his chin still resting in his hand.

"Sit in the other chair," Jeb said.

"What's going on here?" she asked, making no move toward the other chair.

"I told you the landscape was changing and I sent Colavito to check things out."

"Yeah. You said it didn't have anything to do with me." She kicked Darren's boot again. "Get up," she growled.

"My exact advice was for you to not internalize."

She planted her gaze on Jeb and kicked Darren's boot. "Yeah. And I didn't." Adrenaline was giving her a false sense of courage. The strong-silent-men act was grating on her nerves. The lost opportunity to catch up on her sleep and mourn Colavito was pissing her off. "What's with all the muscle?"

"I'm asking the questions here."

Joan leaned both hands on the desk. "Really? I haven't heard any." She turned to Darren. "Get the fuck up."

Jeb leaned forward. "Dammit, Angel, if you must sit down, sit in the other chair."

"No. That is my chair."

"This is my office. Technically, that makes it my chair."

She pointed a thumb over her shoulder. "Why did I have to give my knife to Bozo back there?" She fought the anger and fear that was pushing her toward an edge she did not want to approach. "You know, Jeb, the knife is just a tool. I'm the weapon."

"Is that a threat?"

They glared at each other. A faint rustle of clothing hinted that Darren had shifted in the chair.

Jeb's words told her he felt threatened by her. She respected him and had no reason to attack him. That meant she was called in for something that might set her off. What could he say that would make her go ballistic? She broke away from Jeb's stare and scrutinized the other men in the room. Four operatives, two of them Titans. If she went off the deep end, she wouldn't have a chance in hell—at least Jeb still respected her abilities.

She settled her tired eyes on Jeb. "I'm running low on patience. Just tell me what's going on." She toed the side of Darren's boot in a last, half-hearted attempt to get him out of her chair.

"Remember I told you we are part of an umbrella company called Stillwater?"

Joan nodded.

"There are five teams. New York, Chicago, Dallas, Denver and L.A. In order to keep electronic communications private and untraceable, Stillwater launched its own satellite two years ago. We've never been hacked until…well, until maybe now."

"You guys can afford your own satellite?"

"It's a lucrative business."

"I guess so. But I'm not an electronics expert." She swept the room again. "Why am I here?"

"I'm getting to that." Jeb leaned on his desk and pushed himself to his feet. "I have a communication that was sent to you."

"To me?" She did not see that coming. The shock deflated her bravado. "Who would send something to me through your private satellite?"

"That's what we want to know." Jeb motioned for her to come around the desk.

Carmine locked eyes with her and refused to move in a show of dominance, making her squeeze past him. Jeb's chair squeaked when he swiveled it, and indicated for her to sit down. She hesitated. Sweat broke out over her whole body at the flashback of ligatures binding her to a chair in a dark motel room. If she sat down, it could happen again, and she would be helpless to stop it.

"Take a seat," Jeb said.

He had a gun holstered on his hip. On the way into the room, she noted the other four men had guns under their jackets. Most operatives carried two weapons, usually more. Outnumbered and outgunned. Joan's control of her adrenaline slipped.

"Sit down," Jeb said.

She scanned the impassive faces and the lack of support they conveyed. She never missed Duncan's strength more than she did at that moment. He would have intimidated them. He would have had her back.

She wiped the sweat from her upper lip and noticed her fingers shaking. She put her hands on her hips to steady them.

Jeb must have noticed the shaking, too, because he stepped to the side of the chair and put a gentle hand on her shoulder. "I just want you to look at an email. Verify its authenticity, if you can."

Then why the show of power? Her nerves strummed in waves down her legs, up her neck, across her scalp. The bullet impact bruises bored into her, making her stomach roll. She clamped her eyes shut and blew the air out of her lungs. She had foolishly allowed herself to be maneuvered to a position farthest from the door. Unarmed. Trapped behind a desk, within feet of very large, very trained men, she was helpless. Resisting fate was useless. She opened her eyes and sat down.

Jeb leaned over his laptop and typed what she assumed were a USERID and password. After a short wait, he turned the laptop to face her and stepped back.

Joan looked at the screen. The room darkened. The testosterone-infuse room disappeared. The hardened eyes, somber faces, bad attitudes—gone. The words burned into her eyes:

Nena,

You aren't going anywhere without me. We're a team.

Duncan

PS. I'm coming for you.

She checked the timestamp: three-oh-eight a.m. Less than twelve hours ago.

Duncan's alive?

She stared at the message. "You aren't going anywhere without me." Joan tried to swallow the emotion scrambling up her throat. Blood rushed to her head, flooding it with memories. *We're a team.* Each breath came shorter and faster. She grabbed the armrest on the chair. *You aren't going anywhere without me.* She heard the deep timber of a man's voice.

"Does this mean anything to you? Who's nena?"

We're a team. The room was slipping away. *You aren't going...*

"Does this mean anything to you?"

Everything was getting darker. *I'm coming for you.*

Duncan is alive.

A heavy hand on her shoulder made her jump.

"Angel, are you all right?"

She leaned forward to put her head on her knees and willed herself to remain conscious. Blacking out would leave her at the complete mercy of these thugs. *Stay alert. Breathe.*

"Does this mean anything to you?" Jeb asked.

She nodded.

"Who's *Nena*?"

"It was Duncan's pet name for me."

"Who else knew of it?"

Joan slowly sat up and wiped her face, smearing the make-up with which she had tried to cover the dark circles under her eyes. "A few people, I guess."

"We have to determine if this is real or fake." Jeb

snapped his fingers for someone to get a tissue. Everyone jumped to find some, but being a man's world, there weren't any. Foul Mouth slipped out to the reception area. Darren leaned across the desk and placed her bottle of water closer to her.

She took a couple sips. The act of swallowing the cool liquid brought back some of her strength. "It's real." She pulled her phone out of the back pocket of her skirt. "I have to tell Kearney."

Jeb slapped the phone out of her hand. "Why do you have to tell Kearny? Tell him the con is up?"

"Kearney deserves to know." *We're a team.*

Jeb spun the chair around.

You aren't going anywhere without me.

He leaned on the arms of the chair.

We're a team...you and Kearney...I'm coming for you.

Jeb shook the chair. "Is that it?"

Nena...I'm coming for—

She shook her head to clear it. "Is...what?" Her mind was on overload. She heard Jeb's words, but couldn't focus on him. "It's real," she said, misunderstanding his question. And why wouldn't Duncan just walk up to her instead of sending an email? That meant he wanted Jeb to know, and maybe even wanted this confrontation. Why would—

Jeb leaned in to get her attention. "Is this a con perpetrated by you and Kearney?"

"Con?" She shook her head slowly. "I thought you—" She took the offered tissue and wiped at her eyes. "I thought you wanted me to authenticate the email to verify that Duncan is alive. What con?"

"We already know Archer is alive. And you just verified this email's authenticity."

"Where is he? Why did you..." Her voice trailed off at Jeb's clenched jaw and piercing glare.

"Colavito and Darren snooped around in Phoenix. No death certificate anywhere."

"That's a strong indication that he's alive," Darren said.

Jeb straightened, ran his fingers over his hair, and cupped his neck with his hand. "I'm not sure if you're dazed because you just found out Archer is alive or because you've been caught red-handed. But, okay, one thing at a time. How do you know the email is from Archer?"

"It's the message. He said those words, 'You aren't going anywhere without me. We're a team,' to me during the last battle in Phoenix."

"But who else heard those words? Could they—"

"Everyone else who heard those words is dead."

"Are you sure?"

Tears blurred the room at the grievous loss of life. "Everyone on our team died that day except me." And here she was again, in the middle of another violent subculture. *Never again.*

"And Archer," he pointed out.

She blotted her lower lids with the tissue.

"Why did you have to call Kearney so suddenly? To warn him the con was exposed?"

"No. To tell him about—" Her eyes darted from man to man. She narrowed her eyes. "What con?"

Jeb leaned on the chair again, pinning her with his stare. "Did you know Archer was alive?"

She looked at the tissue in her hand. "No. I thought I saw him a couple times, but no. I thought he was—"

"Look at me."

She looked into his eyes.

"Did you and Kearney claim his estate, knowing he was alive?"

"No." The idea of stealing from Duncan was ludicrous. "Why aren't you asking Kearney these questions?"

"Don't worry, a couple of my guys are taking care of that at this moment. I'm searching for answers from you." He leaned closer, scanning her eyes. "Have you two been conning me?"

She shook her head. "We thought he was—"

"Dead, yeah you told me." Jeb pushed off the chair. He

studied Joan while he clenched and unclenched his jaw deep in thought. "You can go."

She didn't move. She knew from experience if someone said you can go, when you weren't previously free to leave, there was more to it than that.

"I want you to call in to Carmine four, five, six times a day. I want to know where you are every minute. I want access to you within minutes, at a moment's notice."

She bent over to pick up her phone. "For how long?"

"Until I make a final decision about what to do with you."

She wanted to throw his words "Is that a threat?" back at him, but opted for something less antagonistic. "Which is…when?"

He took a step toward her. "Get out of here before I change my mind."

She hesitated at the thought of squeezing past Carmine again.

"And the rest of the estate is frozen until I sort this out," Jeb added. "No more money."

Joan smirked. "Does this mean we're not friends anymore?"

Jeb's glare got her feet in motion.

Once she had settled in, she hadn't used any more of her allotments. But that wouldn't convince Jeb there was no con. Being slow and unassuming was how cons were successful—lead the victim on, reassure them, keep them calm and distracted. Even Duncan showing up would not clear her name. Jeb would still think she was part of a con, and that Duncan was unaware of it. There had to be another way. She had to get out of that room and find a place to think.

When she slithered between the desk and Carmine, he whispered, "Every hour, lady. Every hour or else."

She didn't acknowledge his warning or ask what "or else" meant. She had a good idea what that would entail. Besides, the micro-second she cleared her name, she was out of there. Not one look back. She had a secret cache with some cash. Maybe she'd go to the middle of nowhere. Buy some land. She would play along until then.

She put her hand out to Foul Mouth. "My helmet and knife."

He shoved them into her midsection. "I still think you're hot."

She looked at each person in the room, "I know you don't know me that well yet. But I've been nothing but loyal to you. Don't push me to the point where I don't give a damn." She turned on her heel and walked out of Jeb's office.

❧❧❧

"Darren, you're Colavito's replacement," Jeb said. "Stay on her."

"I'm in no hurry." Darren got up and stretched his legs. "She's tired and hungover. She'll go home."

Jeb glared at him. "If she eats a bologna sandwich, I want to know. You and Carmine stay in close contact." While Carmine and Darren punched their numbers into each other's phones, Jeb asked the group, "Do we cut her loose?"

"Keep your friends close, your enemies closer," Foul Mouth said, quoting Sun-Tzu.

Claude turned from the window, where he had been watching Joan get onto her bike. "Did you see the look in her eyes when you told her to sit in the chair? She has some serious issues, but she toughed it out, eh? I've seen operators like her before—resolute, resilient, fearless—

"Fearless? Something about sitting in that chair scared the shit out of her," Darren said.

"Something triggered a flashback, eh? But she stepped-up and sat in the chair—outnumbered and outgunned." Claude pointed toward the door through which Joan had left. "That, my friends, is fearlessness in action."

"What do you suggest?" Jeb asked.

Claude leaned against the window sill and crossed his arms. "She's an alpha female. I say keep her in tight for as long as she tolerates it. If you throw her to the wolves now, she'll just lead the pack back to us, eh?"

CHAPTER 16

Joan jumped off Route 9W. A more circuitous route home would give her more time to think. She soared past the north gate of the West Point Military Academy, leaning hard through the wide curve that narrowed into the winding two-lane road that hugged the mountain above the Hudson River. Shifting her weight through curves between a rocky mountainside and a three hundred foot drop to the river was cathartic. The Honda purred between her thighs, surrendering its power to her. She downshifted and skidded to a stop in a scenic pull-off. Energized and feeling more in control than she had in a long time, she texted Kearney.

While she waited for him, she thought through what could be going on with Duncan. Sending the email to Jeb was an odd thing to do. It could only mean he wanted Jeb to know before her. There could have been more emails that he only wanted Jeb to see. She and Duncan had always shared everything—well, not exactly. Their honesty pact didn't require them to tell each other everything, just that whatever they told each other had to be the truth. But they always shared enough to have each other's backs. She knitted her brow—he didn't trust her to have his back anymore. And Jeb had developed trust issues with her. She frowned. Turning state's witness when she was in the Legion had branded her a security risk. Her loyalty and actions in Phoenix should have made up for that.

She shook her head and sat on the broad stone wall. The beauty of the Hudson River Valley distracted her. The mountains on the other side of the river had the pink haze of tree buds that were about to break open and unfurl their tender new leaves in the warm spring sunlight—unlike this side where the mountain blocked the sun. The breeze was cool. It fluttered through her hair and sent a chill across her shoulders.

Fifteen minutes after she had called him, Kearney pulled his Jeep Wrangler into the turn-off and parked next to her bike. He stretched when he got out and sauntered to the front of the vehicle. "Nice view," he said.

Joan closed her eyes and smiled into the breeze. "Yes. I like it here."

"Too bad we can't stay much longer."

"Why not?" Her eyelids begged to stay closed. When was the last time she had a good night's sleep? It seemed like eons. She forced them apart at the sound of Kearney's voice.

"We're fugitives. We can't live like other people. We've already overstayed a prudent length of time. And last night you had a severe episode. Do you really want to continue this work?"

"We have aliases. Nobody knows we're here." The wind picked up and fluttered her skirt. "I have some money secreted away."

Kearney didn't respond.

"You haven't talked much about your relationship with Elaine," Joan said. "But I get the feeling you don't want to leave her any time soon."

"It isn't whether I *want* to leave or stay." He put a foot on the wall and leaned on his knee. He watched a train snake its way south along the base of the mountain on the opposite side of the river. When it disappeared from view he added, "Life for people like us is incompatible with getting attached to someone or putting down roots."

"In time, they'll give up the hunt for us."

"Do you really think Woyzeck is going to give up looking for you?"

"If he doesn't get any leads…" Her voice trailed off.

Who was she kidding? She was kidnapped out of his car while he escorted her to prison, then she managed to elude him in Phoenix. And then there was that phone call at five in the morning. That could have been Woyzeck on his way to arrest her. With any luck she'll never know. That was two, maybe three, times she got away from him. Something told her there would not be another. He was a man on a mission, and he'd find that one bit of information that connected her to this area. Then it would be just a matter of time before he tracked her down.

"Agent Woyzeck is a bulldog," Kearney said. "He won't retire until he puts you in jail."

She stood and brushed off the back of her skirt. "Maybe I should just turn myself in. Save him the trouble."

"We have to be watchful, that's all. Now, why did you lure me out here? Something tells me it wasn't to share the view—as beautiful as it is."

"I found out what crawled up Jeb's ass."

"Did it have anything to do with those two guys who paid me a visit? The timing of your call to Yonkers and them appearing at my door is too coincidental."

"That depends. What did they want with you?"

"They accused me of running a con with you to get Duncan's money. Can you believe that?" He watched a hawk circle overhead before continuing. "I admit, I'm not a saint, but I wouldn't steal from Duncan—even after death. I saved his life twice. Why would I do that just to steal from him in the end?"

"Duncan's alive, K."

"That's what they told me. They seemed absolutely sure."

"So is Jeb. And I am, too. He showed me an email that was sent via their private satellite. Did you know he has his own satellite?"

"His own satellite? That takes mega bucks—three, five million. I know this business is lucrative, but—"

"There's a consortium or something. Did you ever hear of Stillwater?"

Kearney whistled. "Durham Security is part of Stillwater? That explains the money for the satellite. They did a lot of private security work in the gulf before the Arabs got their hands in the till."

"Anyway, the wording in the email was something Duncan said to me during that last battle in Phoenix."

"Anyone could have heard it and used it to pretend they're Duncan."

She frowned. "Everyone who heard him say those words is dead except me and him."

"Are you sure?"

Joan blinked in disbelief. "Dumbass, *everyone* is dead except for you and me and Duncan. And you were in the other building." *This is going nowhere.* Fatigue flooded her bones, making her limbs heavy. Her joints ached. "I'm so tired I have to make a concentrated effort to stay awake. I only got a few hours of sleep in the last thirty-six hours. I'm going home before I'm too tired to make it." She grabbed her helmet and plopped down onto the bike seat.

"You okay to drive? Wanna stay at the bungalow? It's closer."

"I'm okay. The wind in my face will be enough to keep me awake for a while." She pushed the ignition button to let the engine warm up. "Think about it. Duncan is alive and around, but not making contact. He could have sent that secure email at any time. Hell, why didn't he just walk up to me on the street? He's up to something."

"If he sent the email, by now he knows you know. He won't take long to come to you."

She heeled up the kickstand. "That's what I'm afraid of."

"What do you mean?"

"The last line of the email read: 'I'm coming for you.'"

CRCR

Joan downshifted and leaned into the driveway to home sweet home. With fresh air no longer blowing into her face, the fatigue returned, dragging down her arms and legs. When she puttered down the lane, the grazing horses looked up, munching on grass. The white board fencing funneled her toward her new home.

Although she was dead tired, it would take a while to unwind. A long, hot shower and donning her sweats sounded relaxing. She would fall asleep eventually, but it wouldn't be a deep, refreshing sleep.

I'm coming for you. She couldn't get those words out of her head. Six months ago she had promised the wounded Duncan she would come back for him, but circumstances in Phoenix had overwhelmed her and she hadn't been able to retrace her steps. During the past seven months all she had wanted was to be held his strong arms. But now he was alive and coming for her.

As she parked her bike near the entrance to her apartment, she shook her shoulders to throw off the dread enfolding itself around her. She had been on the white-hot side of Duncan's wrath once before, and she wasn't looking forward to facing it again—once was one too many times. His anger made him seem massive and dangerous. He didn't hurt her the last time, but this time she wasn't so sure. The number one rule for soldiers is to never leave anyone behind. And if Duncan was anything, he was a soldier.

Her helmet felt like it weighed fifty pounds when she pulled it off. Her boots were lead weights around her ankles. Too tired to notice the door was already unlocked when she turned the key, she dragged herself into her apartment. She hung the keys on the rack by the door and toed-off her boots. A mental "Ah" flowed the length her body.

A wide, saliva-ejecting yawn obscured her view of the

room. When her mouth closed, she stood still, eyeing a rosewood box on the coffee table. She rubbed her eyes to clear them, but the box was still there. It was the hand-carved box Master Yu had presented to her as a reward for her diligent training. Her eyes watched it as if it were a crouching tiger ready to leap at her. *How in hell did this get here? When Kearney and I escaped from Phoenix, we left everything behind.*

Focused on the box, oblivious to her surroundings, she took a step toward it. Another step. Her fingers shook when she released the clasp and lifted the lid. A sob escaped from her throat—all her precious throwing knives were cradled in their respective, velvet-lined indentations.

Arms encircled her waist. Out of reflex she spun and hit the attacker's jaw with a back elbow, and recoiled immediately with a back elbow on the other side. She spun around, grabbed the attacker, pulled him in to her, and kneed him— missing the groin and instead hitting the thigh.

The attacker stumbled backward. "Geez, Joan. It's me." He shook his head to clear it.

"Duncan? Oh, my God." She put a hand on each side of his face and looked into his eyes. They were a bit unfocused. "Jeez, I am so sorry." Her hands traced his shoulders, his arms, his chest. He was there, for real, right in front of her.

He shook his head again. "Over the past several months, I imagined this moment a dozen different ways. This was not one of them."

"Why didn't you say something?"

"I wanted to surprise you." He rubbed his jaw. "I've never been on the business end of your skills. Damn, Joan, you are deadly."

Joan's face dropped.

He must have seen the effect of his words, because he pulled her against him. "I'm sorry. I didn't mean to say anything to upset you."

"No. I'm sorry," Joan said, her words muffled against his chest.

"You have nothing to be sorry for."

"Yes, I do. I left you behind. I couldn't get back to you because of my lack of leadership skills and you—you—"

"You saved my life. You bandaged the wound."

"No, that wasn't enough. I—"

"If you had returned and dragged me through the buildings out of there, I would have bled out before I got medical attention. By leaving me, the feds rushed me to the hospital. I was stabilized and filled with antibiotics. You saved my life, Joan." He gently rocked her. "You were right," he said into her hair. He swallowed hard and whispered, "You were always right."

"About what?" She tried to pull away to look into his eyes, but he held her tighter.

"About everything. That last fight in Phoenix was a sting. I never should have authorized the deal." He turned his head to peck a kiss on the side of her head. "You were right to not come back for me."

You were always right. Duncan was alive because of her. She relaxed in his arms and groaned. The weight of the past seven months escaped in sobs that left peace of mind in their wake. She let go of the weight she had been carrying and cried for the burden she no longer carried, for the clearing of her conscience, for finally feeling his strong arms around her. And most of all for the forgiveness she had withheld from herself for far too long.

"Was that you at the food court?" she asked, pulling away far enough to look into his eyes.

"I couldn't let that guy shoot you. But I was too late. Thank God you had a vest on."

"But you ran away."

"You were in good hands, and seeing me while you were physically traumatized wouldn't have been a good idea."

Joan thought about that for a few seconds before asking, "How long have you been in town?"

"About a week."

"A week?" She hit him with a percussive push, knocking him back a couple steps. "Why didn't you contact me sooner? Why did you use the secure server and make me go to Jeb's office? Why didn't you just walk up to me?"

"I had things to take care of, and I didn't want to take the chance of exposing you or Jeb's company, but as it turned out—"

"What things?"

"I'll tell you in time."

"No, Duncan. Tell me now."

"Right now I just want to make love to you."

"Not until you tell me what's going on."

Duncan pressed his lips together and searched Joan's eyes as if mulling over something. "I love you and will do anything to keep you out of jail."

"What things, Duncan?"

"I—a day after I arrived, I crossed paths with Agent Woyzeck."

"What? Where? How are you still free?"

"I was watching the Durham Security Building, knowing that would be the easiest way to find you. And I caught him watching the building, too."

"What did you do?"

"He was alone. No backup. So I walked right up to him."

Joan knitted her brow. "He didn't arrest you?"

"He's smart enough to know he couldn't take me down without help." A slow frown worked its way across Duncan's face. "We had a long talk."

"About what?"

"You. He wants you. Not me. I mean, he'll arrest me if he gets a chance, but for some reason I couldn't get out of him, he really wants you."

"Probably because on the way to prison I was abducted out of his car by the Legion."

"Maybe, but I think it's more than that."

"Like what?"

"I don't know. Whatever the reason, it's important enough to keep secret, even under threats of violence."

"You didn't threaten a federal agent, did you?"

Duncan shrugged. "I like to think of it as an intense interchange of ideas."

"But wait. How does he know about Durham Security?"

"He didn't say it in so many words, but I think Durham Security is under investigation, and somehow through that, he learned about your involvement with them. You don't go there often, do you?"

"No. I have no need to be there or to socialize with the other operators. You still haven't explained why didn't you come to me right away."

"I wanted to make sure he didn't put a tail on me. The last thing I want is to lead him right back to you."

Joan cocked her head. "But why a week?"

A sheepish look came over his face. "I'll admit that after being separated from you for so long, I savored the sight of you being so strong and self-reliant. And beautiful," he said, tracing the line of her jaw. "But it was just that one time in the food court."

Joan traced the indentation between his pec muscles. "You didn't want to savor me?"

"That's why I'm here." He kissed her softly. When he broke off the kiss, he frowned and stepped back. "There's something else I need to tell you."

"Like what?"

"When I was in Arkansas I made a—"

Joan smiled up at him, her anger at him not coming to her sooner drifted away on the tide of her joy at having him back again. To say nothing about what that loving kiss did to her libido.

"I made a—" He hesitated at her smile. "I made a vow to put you first from now on."

She pulled away just enough to see his face. "Let me look at you."

His eyes were the same harsh, piercing blue that bored

into her heart. The pale, red beard was full, untrimmed. It was scruffy, but it softened his battle-hardened features. His cheeks above the beard were wet. When she reached up to dry them, his lips found hers. His passion mashed the inside of her lips against her teeth. Her fingers grasped his curls at the back of his head. His hands were everywhere, searching, sensing, stroking.

She pulled back from the kiss. "What's with the flannel shirt? It's so...Appalachian." Flannel was light years from the black tee shirts he had always worn under denim or leather jackets.

"It's part of my disguise," he said between kisses that trailed down her neck. "It goes well with the beard. Do you like it?"

"I don't know." She moaned at the hot trail his lips blazed toward her throat. "I could get used to hillbilly love."

"Oh, you want hillbilly love? I'll show you hillbilly love." He picked her up and threw her onto the couch. He kicked the coffee table out of the way and strode toward her.

Joan's eyes widened is surprise, then softened into passion. She leaned forward and grasped the front of his shirt and pulled his lips onto hers. He pushed her shoulders against the back of the couch. She fumbled with the buttons. Desperate to feel his skin, she yanked the shirt open, popping buttons across the room.

"Let's go into the bedroom," she said into his mouth.

Duncan pulled her to her feet and in one smooth movement slung her over one shoulder like a sack of grain. "Come on, hillbilly momma." On the way down the hallway to the bedroom he said, "There's something in here I want to ask you about."

He eased her onto her back on the bed and stood over her. He pointed at the nightstand. "Want to explain this to me?"

Joan pushed herself up and leaned on one elbow. The makeshift altar to Duncan had seemed like an honorable thing, but now explaining it to a living Duncan, it seemed foolish. "I toasted to your memory every night before going to sleep." She looked up to see his reaction.

"And the second shot glass?"

She fingered the waistband of his jeans. "That was your shot. It was never emptied."

He picked up the full shot glass. Downed it. Smiled. And reached for her.

The warmth of his hands on her thighs pulsed heat waves through dormant neural pathways. When he kissed her, she savored the smoky-sweet taste of whiskey.

He lowered his body on top of her, shielding her from his weight.

CHAPTER 17

The violent swaying of the van woke Joan with a start. The pops of automatic gunfire echoed away with it. The nightmare faded with each wild beat of her heart. Reality seeped into her mind. She wiped the sweat from her forehead and reached for Duncan.

He turned toward her and wrapped her in his arms. "Bad dream again?" he asked sleepily.

Joan snuggled her head against his arm and nodded.

"I'm here." He kissed her forehead. "Go back to sleep, *nena.*"

Joan emptied her mind and concentrated on her breathing. A fog encircled the vestiges of the dream, obscuring them until nothing remained. Her heart rate and breathing slowed. Contentment flowed through her body. *I'm here.* She wasn't alone anymore.

She awoke a few hours later, stretched, and looked over at Duncan. Panic seized her breath. Had Duncan been a dream, too? She wildly eyed the room and spotted his black duffel bag. Her breathing slowed, and she slipped out of bed to find him. She padded past the bathroom. Empty. Kitchen. Empty except for a pot of coffee cooling on the burner that had shut off automatically. When she grabbed a mug out of the cabinet she spotted Duncan's note telling her he went to the stable to check out the horses. She smiled at his thoughtfulness.

She jogged through a cold drizzle, dodging puddles in the muddy driveway, and stopped inside the stable door to shake the rain out of her hair like a wet dog.

She stomped the mud off her sneakers and squinted in the darkness. In front of the fifth stall down the wide, cement aisle, Duncan stood scratching a horse's chin. The horse's ears turned toward Joan and a deep-throated whinny signaled her presence.

"There you are, sleeping beauty." Duncan smiled at her. "Come over here and say hello to your counterpart in the animal kingdom."

Joan crept down the dim center of the stable, expecting the strong odors of manure and wet livestock. But the stable had been scrupulously cleaned, and the sweet scent of hay pulled her along. The aisle had been swept and hosed down. The varnished stall doors glistened in the filtered light. Only the faint rustle of hooves in bedding indicated horses were there.

She had never seen a horse up close—it was bigger than she had imagined. Its power was both ethereal and real. The horse smelled her then snorted. She jumped back.

Duncan laughed and scratched the blaze on the horse's forehead. "There's nothing to be afraid of. She won't bite."

"Horses don't bite?"

"Well, some horses bite, and when they do, it's bad. But biters are only reacting to ill treatment by mean humans. Horses aren't mean by nature." He brushed the horse's forelock to the side. "This pretty girl is a sweetie."

"How do they like to be petted?"

"Just scratch right here, under the chin."

Joan scratched the mare's chin and caressed the muzzle with her other hand. "It's so soft."

Duncan watched her with soft eyes. "You haven't been around horses much, have you?"

"I've never been this close to one before. You seem to be comfortable with them."

"I grew up around them. My parents loved their horses.

Someday we'll have horses of our own and I'll teach you to ride."

"You seem positive that we have a normal life ahead of us."

"I am."

Joan turned from the horse to Duncan. "Then I am, too."

He placed his hands on the sides of her face and kissed her gently on the lips then pecked a trail across her jaw to her throat. "I can't wait to see you ride a horse. Two powerful animals flowing as one across the landscape with grace and beauty. Damn, that's sexy."

She moaned. Last night's sexual reunion hadn't been nearly long enough. After the second round of lovemaking, she fell asleep in his arms. He had let her sleep. But she was rested now.

He slipped his hands under her tee shirt. "Have you ever made love in the hay?"

"We can't do it here. Someone might come."

"No one will come," he said between kisses.

"Are you sure?" She wanted to give in. Love him hard. Make it fast and hot. She remembered her housesitting duties. "I can't do it here. It'd be like screwing at work."

"C'mon, *nena*. The possibility of someone coming...that's what makes it exciting. Then we'll go inside and make long, slow love on that brass bed."

"No." She pulled away and turned to scratch the horse's jaw. After a thoughtful silence, she changed the subject. "You never talked about your life growing up. You haven't told me much of anything."

"During my long recovery, I spent endless hours thinking about how I had taken you for granted, and how I had put other matters before you. I was alone, struggling desperately to get better." He frowned and seemed lost in thought for several seconds. "Things are going to be different. I'm going to make it up to you—for all of it." He gently pressed on her shoulder until she faced him. "I was a fool to keep anything from you. I'll tell you whatever you want to know. Ask me anything."

Joan thought for a moment. There were so many questions. "What kind of jobs did you do for Jeb?"

Duncan turned back to the horse. "My specialty is silent assassination."

"Kearney told me you were an assassin, but I didn't believe him."

Duncan's hands stilled. He looked out of the corner of his eye, but didn't face her. "When did he tell you that?"

"A couple years ago, in Youngstown, when he was recovering from that gunshot."

"Is it going to be a problem?" he asked, still not looking at her.

She tugged on his arm until he looked at her. "Who am I to talk shit about killing people? I have my own phantoms who haunt my dreams at night."

He put his arm around her shoulders. "How often do you have those bad dreams?"

"Almost every night. This morning I woke up reliving that operation where Colavito got killed." She hesitated. "It was easier to deal with knowing you were there."

Duncan didn't say anything. He just rocked her in his arms.

Joan broke the silence. "So the man who loves me is an assassin. That is pretty darn cool." She fingered his coppery-brown curls. "What's your ethnic history? Irish?"

"I don't know. Maybe on my mother's side."

"You don't know?"

"I was adopted."

"Oh." Joan couldn't imagine not knowing where she came from. She thought of her parents and how happy they had been at one time, and how important family had been to her father. "Did you ever try to find your biological parents?"

"Yes. I asked Kearney to look into it. With his connections...I felt it was the safest way." He sat on a bench and indicated for her to join him. "My mother died a month before he identified her."

"And your father. Did you find him?"

"Yes. I met him."

"You did? What did he think of his handsome, world-saving son? Did he tell you why he put you up for adoption?"

"No." Duncan placed his forearms on his thighs. He looked at the floor in front of him. "I met him, but he didn't know who I was—that I was his son."

"You didn't tell him? You didn't give him a chance to explain?"

"It seemed pointless. The people who raised me gave me everything. The best education. Opportunities. When I joined the Army, they were disappointed, but they supported my decision. They were my parents."

He hesitated as if trying to find the right words. "And my biological father, what would he say? That he did it to give me a better life?" He rubbed his mouth with the back of his hand and shook his head. Moisture teetered at the corner of his eye. "Only to discover his son is a fugitive wanted for treason, murder, terrorism and dozens of other charges? He—all his life he pictured me a success."

Joan threw her arm around Duncan's shoulders. She grabbed a handful of beard and pulled his face toward her. "Baby, you are a success. Fuck the government and their opinion of what you do." She gave his shoulders a squeeze. "He would understand if you told him why you fight—that you do the ugly things so nice people can sleep safely at night."

"You say that like you know who he is."

Champ's mischievous, coy smile and stocky, boxer build filled her vision. She pressed her thumb and forefinger on her eyes, but she could not erase his catlike agility when he walked. She should have known. In a way, a part of her always knew. It explained why Jeb and the other operatives tried to keep her and Champ apart. They weren't keeping her from him. They were protecting her, afraid he would seek revenge. But Champ had been the better man. He had as much as told her he would wait for the facts to reveal the truth—just like Duncan would have done.

When she looked into Duncan's eyes. "Champ," she said softly.

He nodded.

She threw her leg over his legs and hoisted herself up to straddle him and pulled him into her.

He buried his head in her shoulder. "I love you, *nena*. I trust you with everything: my fortune, my heart, my life. My future."

"And I trust you."

He pulled back to look into her eyes. "You sure?"

"Of course. Always have. Always will."

He squeezed her tight. "Promise to trust me. No matter what happens."

Okay. That's weird. "No matter what, baby."

He looked at her and flashed a coy smile. "Good. How about that roll in the hay?"

"No."

"What if a SWAT team shows up now? You'll regret not getting in that last bump."

"No SWAT team is coming."

"Are you sure?"

A car door slammed in the driveway. They both froze.

"Expecting someone?" he asked.

"No. You?"

"Nope." He pressed on her hips, but she had already stood up. "Better go see who it is," he said.

She started for the doorway with Duncan on her heels. She stopped short and turned around. Her shoulders slumped. She dropped her head onto his chest in mock resignation. "Shit. I was supposed to go to a poetry reading with a guy named Rob."

"A poetry reading?"

"He was in the meditation class—you know the one with

the stalker I told you about and… well he felt sorry for me, said I looked sad, and asked me to go to a poetry reading with him. He's just being a friend and—"

Duncan shook his head. "I thought I was the poetic part of this duo. I can't picture you at a poetry reading."

Joan shook her head and smiled. Some things about Duncan didn't change. Not a shred of jealousy. "I better go tell him I can't go."

"You can go. I'll just stay here all alone with—" He traced the neckline of her tee shirt with his fingertip. "—nothing to do."

"Stop it. You know I'm not going anywhere without you—unless you want to go to a poetry reading?"

He gave her shoulders a gentle push. "Go. Get rid of him."

She stepped into the doorway. The rain fell straight down, obscuring the distance between the barn and the house in a murky gloom. "Hey, Rob, over here."

He jogged down the porch steps and across the muddy driveway. He stepped into the shelter of the stable, rain dripping off his nose. "Hi, are you ready?" He wiped his wire-rimmed glasses on his shirttail.

"I'm sorry. My cousin came into town last night, and I haven't seen him for a while and I thought I'd spend the day with him."

Duncan appeared behind her. He offered his hand, leaning around her, brushing her shoulder with his chest. "I'm Vic."

"This is Rob Reddington," Joan said weakly. The thought of Duncan's muscular, naked torso under the flannel shirt sent a tingle down her back. She wished she had taken him up on that roll in the hay.

As the men shook hands, whole conversations passed wordlessly in a silence. Duncan's strong posture and hardened jaw spoke of ownership and his higher position in the pecking order. An intensity flickered in Rob's eyes before sliding his gaze to Joan. The glare disappeared and the boyishness returned. Joan squinted at Rob, wondering what just happened. Rob's reaction flashed by quickly, too quickly to read correctly. Events over the last couple days had her on edge, possibly leading her to see things that weren't there.

"So…Bob—" Duncan said.

Rob pushed up his glasses. "It's Rob."

Joan elbowed Duncan to tell him to stop toying with Rob.

"Yes, of course, Rob." Duncan fought the corners of his mouth. "I'm concerned about my cousin's welfare. The world can be a dangerous place. Would you be able to defend her if something were to happen?"

Joan elbowed him again. He dodged it without taking his eyes off Rob.

Rob looked back and forth between her and Duncan. "I have a purple belt in Tae Kwon Do, if that's what you mean." His gaze settled on the edge of Duncan's shirt. The lack of buttons. The scarred skin peaking from beneath the shirt. His gaze worked its way past the beard to Duncan's face.

But Duncan was smiling at Joan. "A martial artist. Good." He said to Rob, "I wouldn't want anything happening to my angel."

"Oh, no, she'd definitely be safe with me. You don't have anything to worry about."

Duncan scratched his beard. "I'm going inside for some coffee. Can I get a cup for you, Bob."

"Uh…it's Rob…no thanks."

Duncan slipped between Rob and Joan. He raised his eyebrows and mouthed to her, "A purple belt." He pulled up his collar and jogged across the driveway, dodging puddles.

She glared at his back. When he disappeared into the house, she looked at Rob. "Family. Can't live with them, can't eat their livers."

"So what does he do for a living?"

"He's a private investigator."

"Oh. Is he licensed here, in New York?"

"No. The last I knew he had a license in…you know, I'm not sure."

Rob shrugged. "Huh. Like out west somewhere?"

Joan narrowed her eyes. "I saw that look you guys exchanged. What was that about?"

"What look?"

"I don't know. Like some male *non*-bonding thing."

Rob shrugged. "Don't know what you're talking about."

She shook her head to clear it. "Don't mind me. His showing up out of the blue has put me out of sorts."

"No problem." Rob flashed a honeyed smile. "Family first. Hey, I have to run if I'm going to get to Poughkeepsie and find the location of the reading."

"I'm so sorry I made you drive all the way out here to find out I couldn't go. I should have called, but with Vic showing up, I—"

"Don't worry about it. Family is important. You seem really close." He waved and rushed back to his car.

She waved back and leaned on the stable door. He hadn't made any reference to calling her in the future. She shrugged it off and watched Rob until he disappeared at the end of the fencing, then jogged to the house.

When she got back to the apartment, Duncan was leaning against the kitchen counter, legs crossed at the ankles. He looked up when she passed the kitchen on her way to the bathroom.

When she reappeared, drying her hair with a towel, the microwave beeped. She walked around him to get the warmed up coffee.

He put both hands on the counter, pinning her from behind. His breath warmed her ear when he spoke. "All the time I was recovering from the gunshot wound, I pictured you hooking up with one Jeb's battle-hardened operators. And here you are bumping some wimpy guy."

She turned around to face him and had to bend backward because he crowded her. "Jealous?"

He smirked. "No, I'm not jealous. I just thought if I had

to win back your love, it'd be a worthy opponent. Not Bobby Bookworm."

"Well, I'm not 'bumping' him. We're just friends. Well, not even that…acquaintances, really." She did not fear Duncan, but something about his questioning made her hesitate. His too casual stance had turned into too-intense intimidation.

"I sensed something, Joan. Something more than friendship. If you're having sex with him, it's okay to tell me because I'm here now. He won't be coming back." He began pulling up the edge of her tee shirt. One corner of his mouth curled up. "This tee shirt's wet. You should take it off."

She slapped his hands away. "You felt something odd? Me, too."

His hands rested on her hips. "What do you mean?"

His eyes searched hers as if trying to detect insincerity, which he had never done before. He wasn't acting jealous per se, but the inference of having a boyfriend made her uneasy. The close call with death could have weakened his self-confidence, and the ensuing separation may have intensified that inclination.

Joan overlooked his odd behavior. "I thought there was…I don't know…an intensity I had never seen from Rob before. It didn't last long, then it disappeared, or—"

"He suppressed it."

They exchanged a long look before she opened the refrigerator and grabbed a carton of milk. She thoughtfully stirred the milk into the coffee. "Do you think we imagined it?"

"Maybe if only one of us noticed it, but not both of us. No. How much do you know about him?"

"Champ vetted him and—"

Duncan lowered his brows. "Why did he vet him?"

"I asked him to. Well, actually I asked Jeb to have Colavito…" She waved her hand to dismiss the digression. "Anyway, I thought maybe he was the stalker or the stalker's accomplice."

"What stalker?"

"Remember, last night, I told you about the stalker and Nirmala?"

Duncan nodded. "Go on."

"Well, one night he followed me part way to Nirmala's house then turned down a street. It made me goosey so I asked Jeb to vet him."

"And?"

"And he came back clean." She took a sip and grimaced. She put the cup down and opened a cabinet door to look for sugar.

"Could his route home be partially the same as the route to Nirmala's?"

The searching stopped. She slammed the cabinet door. "Dammit. Dammit." She gripped the counter and leaned into it. "God dammit. I didn't make the connection before. Jeb said Rob lives in Putnam. Nirmala lives in Scarsdale. He should go due north up the east side of the Hudson River. Nirmala lives northeast. "

"Maybe he's interested in you and wanted to find out where you live, or see if you're seeing someone else. Are you?"

She released her grip on the counter and grabbed Duncan's arm.

He winced at her fingers sinking into his bicep.

"He seemed to know I lived north—farther than the suburbs. How would he know that?"

Duncan peeled her fingers off his arm. "It could have been a lucky guess. Let's not get wrapped around the axle." He pulled her against his chest. "That boy looked like a lovesick puppy."

"Except for whatever we saw in his eyes."

"Yeah, except for that." He released her and swatted her butt. "Go shower and change. I'll call Kearney. See if he wants to meet us for dinner. Help sort this out."

She stopped before disappearing into the hallway. "You don't want to get in a...bump? You know, just in case a

SWAT team shows up in the next thirty minutes?"

His eyes tracked a line from her lips to her crotch. He flicked the towel at her. "I didn't say that."

She dodged the towel and said from the hallway, "I can't believe I'm bumping an assassin who can't say the word, 'fuck.'"

❧❧❧

By the time Joan climbed out of the shower, Duncan had filled the sink with hair trimmed from his beard. He had been in the middle of edging it when she dragged him into the bedroom. An hour and a second shower later, they were dressed and ready to go. They weren't meeting Kearney for dinner until six o'clock. They had plenty of time.

Duncan looked like his old self wearing his usual arboreal camouflage pants. The traditional black tee shirt had been replaced with a black compression shirt, the short sleeves stretched to their limit across his biceps. He had lost weight during his recovery, and his thick waist had given way to a narrower version. Joan felt underdressed in her yellow I ♥ New York tee shirt, beige, wrinkled cargo pants, and scuffed up boots.

"Maybe I should change."

Duncan shook his head. "Come here. I have something to ask you."

❧❧❧

Jeb cursed the traffic as he raced up Rte. 17. He thought accusing Joan of running a con before he had any evidence would intimidate her. So determined to prove his suspicions, he had failed to get to know her—really know her. His harshness, telling his other operatives and having them present—it had all been over the top. Any other woman would have been reduced to a quivering pile of goo. He had misjudged Joan, and he wasn't used to making mistakes in judgment.

She had not called in to Carmine since she stormed out of his office the day before. His intimidation tactics had not worked. And why would they have? Her past experiences overshadowed anything he could do or say to get her to admit to wrongdoing.

Darren was keeping an eye on her, and his report convinced him there was a con, and that someone else was with her. She was being manipulated by someone. But after yesterday, she was going to skip town and disappear. He could feel it like he could feel the leather seat beneath him. Before she took off, he had to talk to her. Get her to calm down. Rework the connection he had spun between them.

A call came in from Claudia. He disconnected it without talking to her. It was the third call from her during the trip upstate, and he probably should have taken them, but he would not be deterred from his task. He missed doing field work, and being out of the office with a stated goal revived something inside that had withered for many years. The freedom of the road, the exhilaration of having a purpose. Whatever was going on at the office could wait.

He looked at the bottle of wine on the seat beside him. It was from a wine store, not part of the inventory at Notches. Joan had her standards, and he was willing to comply with them. He leaned his arm against the door and rubbed his lip with his forefinger.

How far would he go to keep her around? She was a promising new operative, and his other operators were showing signs that the lifestyle was grinding them down. She had heavy baggage, but comparatively speaking she was fresh, eager, and diligent.

And if she skipped, he would miss her company.

He activated his car's Bluetooth.

Darren answered on the first ring. "Yeah, boss."

"Anything new?"

"Her bike is still here, and so is the black sedan. No

signs of movement inside, but that doesn't mean they're not in there."

"Other than the two visitors yesterday, no other people in or out?"

"No, sir. The red-bearded hillbilly is still there. The Harry Potter wannabe has not returned."

"Copy that." Jeb's stomach clenched and he looked over at the bottle of wine. He had hoped to talk to Joan alone. But this could be where he learned the truth. "I'm turning onto the property now."

"I see you. Take care. Hillbilly looks like he's paid his dues at the gym."

"Roger that." Jeb disconnected the call as he turned between the white plank fencing.

He parked out of sight of the door to Joan's apartment, and closed the driver's door with a soft click. He repositioned the holster at the small of his back and walked quietly toward the door. He peeked around the corner and froze.

Joan had her legs wrapped around the hillbilly's waist.

ᏇᏇᏇ

Joan traced the edge of Duncan's beard. "Ask me anything."

"Will you marry me?"

"You already asked me that, remember?" Her eyes tracked from his beard to his mouth.

"I mean, let's get the marriage license and get married before anything else comes between us."

"Don't you think it's tricky getting the marriage license? I mean, we have to use our real names and identification."

"They won't run a background check. Besides, if we're going to get caught, I want it to be while we're doing something we have wanted to do for a long time. What do you think?"

"Yes, yes, yes." She jumped up, wrapped her legs around his waist and kissed him.

He took a step back to keep from falling over, and squeezed her hard.

She broke the kiss. "We have a lot to do. I don't want a cold, impersonal—oh my God. Duncan there's someone sneaking at the door."

He dropped her, spun around, and grabbed his pistol off the breakfast bar. The man was gone. Duncan cautiously opened the door. He stepped through, gun raised.

Jeb backed away, hands held out waist high, the wine bottle forgotten in his hand.

Duncan kept Jeb in his sights. "What are you doing sneaking around here?"

"I was checking on Joan. She hadn't called in today."

Duncan glanced at the wine bottle. "And she won't be. What's your fucking problem?"

"I was concerned." Jeb cautiously lowered his hands. "We have to talk." He looked past Duncan at Joan. "Alone."

"Whatever you have to say, you can say in front of Joan."

"Can I come inside?"

Duncan looked around for other threats. "Call off your surveillance." He nodded toward Darren's position in the tree line. He lowered his gun, but did not move to make way for Jeb.

Jeb gave the signal to Darren to button up and head off.

Jeb looked at Duncan. "You're lucky he didn't shoot you."

"No." He nodded toward Joan. "*You're* lucky he didn't shoot me."

Jeb offered his hand. "It's good to see you, Archer."

Duncan shook Jeb's hand. "It's nice to be back. Let's go inside."

Jeb pulled Duncan into a shoulder bump and whispered, "We really should talk privately."

"Not happening, buddy."

They went inside and closed the door. "What's so damn

important that you tried to put Joan on a short leash?" Duncan asked.

"Now that you're back, we need to get the money back into your hands."

"I'm okay with that," Joan said.

Duncan turned and put out a hand to silence her. He pinned Jeb with a look and said, "The money is right where it belongs."

"We need to talk first."

"You put Joan's safety at risk," Duncan said, taking a step toward Jeb. "Making her stick around by giving it to her like an allowance. Whose bright idea was that?"

"If I had given it all to her, she would have disappeared." A weak smile worked its way across Jeb's mouth. "You wouldn't have found her. I did you a favor."

"Colavito was right? I was supposed to get it all at once?" Joan closed in on Jeb. "You've been suckering me all this time, being buddy-buddy, pretending to be my friend?"

Duncan put an arm around her shoulder and pulled her back.

"And you weren't very good at it," she said as a parting shot.

"Sit down, Jeb." Duncan stepped back, pulling Joan with him, making a path between Jeb and the couch. "And start talking."

CHAPTER 18

Her wedding day had arrived, and the whole thing seemed surreal. It made her more nervous than she had been during her torture, any gun battle, or any high speed chase. The past two weeks had been filled with frenetic activity pulling together a wedding that wasn't a cold and unceremonious act in a city hall or magistrate's office. Everyone they knew had pulled together. Carmine called a guy who knew a guy to line up a caterer. Nirmala charmed the florist. Elaine opened her beautiful home for the wedding and reception. Jeb had overcome his negative suspicions of Joan and organized a guard detail—Joan joked it was to prevent Duncan from disappearing again.

Claudia had taken Joan to her salon where the hairstylist trimmed and highlighted Joan's hair—a minimal trim. Joan was letting it grow out. The manicurist tipped and polished Joan's nails. With the pampering complete, the only thing that remained to be done was the Big Deed.

She took a deep breath and stole a look into the living room. Her future husband sat on the sofa, chin tucked, thumbing his phone, legs relaxed—a man waiting for his date. Her breath caught in her throat. He was beyond handsome with his trimmed and edged red beard. His rowdy, curly hair had been clipped short to keep them under control. He looked as at ease in the black three-thousand-dollar suit, as his usual black tee shirt and cammo pants—a man comfortable wherever he found himself.

But was she doing the right thing? This new Duncan differed from the Duncan she had always wanted to marry. Without leadership responsibilities he acted relaxed and constantly doted on her. He seemed to savor every minute with her, indulging her, loving her. Joan bit her lip and silently chastised herself. Other women would give anything for that kind of attention. Cold feet. That's all it was.

She bit her lip at the memory the shopping trip for her wedding clothes...

෴

Nirmala had seemed pleased to be invited to help Joan pick out a dress. The usually soft-spoken Indian woman had been talkative and animated on the way to the mall. Her inner peace kept Joan calm while they went store to store trying on dresses, and kept her nerves at bay in the mall with its surveillance cameras and crowds. The security nightmare distracted Joan, but Nirmala kept Joan focused on the shopping. No dress seemed to be right, but Nirmala good-naturedly steered Joan on to the next rack of clothes in the next store until they hit pay dirt.

After two hours of trying on clothes, one dress stood out and Joan asked Nirmala to bring a different size. When Nirmala returned, she slipped into the changing booth with Joan. Without a second thought Joan pulled off the too large, two-piece dress and took the smaller sized one from Nirmala. The sound of Nirmala's sucked in breath seemed to echo through the whole changing area. Someone would surely open the door to find out what dire thing had happened. Joan stilled and watched Nirmala's eyes.

"How did you get those scars?" Nirmala asked.

Joan gave her standard response. "I had tattoos removed."

Nirmala shook her head and touched the scar on Joan's upper chest with her fingertips. "No. This is not a tattoo removal." She seemed to think twice about her query and gracefully added, "You don't have to tell me what this is from, of course."

Nirmala didn't know that the scar she touched was actually from the removal of a tattoo, but not in the way to which Joan had so offhandedly alluded. It had not been removed with laser precision by a trained technician, but had been peeled off her body with an unsanitary knife, a symbol of her betrayal of the Constitution Defense Legion.

"I have never seen scars like these on your belly and your thighs." Nirmala looked deeply into Joan's eyes. "Whatever happened must have been terrible."

Joan quickly slid the top of the outfit over her head and bent to pull up the skirt to cover her thighs. She zipped the skirt and said, "I'll tell you, but not here. We'll go someplace for coffee, where we can talk."

Joan paid for the dress and she and Nirmala went to a quiet café a mile from the mall. Joan chose a corner table separated from the rest of the café by a plastic plant and a large garbage can.

She told Nirmala how the Legion had their resident expert interrogate her. She didn't want Nirmala to become fearful of Kearney, or be so incensed by his actions that she would go to the police. A name-free, detail-free account of what happened was far better for their future security. Nirmala had wondered what Joan could have done that elicited such harsh treatment. Joan explained that she had been the Operations & Security Chief in the Constitution Defense Legion and knew enough to put a lot of members away for a long time, and that she was, in fact, in the process of giving State's Evidence when she had been kidnapped and interrogated.

She wanted to tell Nirmala that it had been Kearney—an attempt at catharsis, but she would never be able explain how she could still be friends with him after what he had done to her. That he had been Duncan's life saver, and if not for Kearney's actions, Duncan would not have been alive—or mentally stable enough—for Joan to have fallen in love with him. She tolerated Kearney in deference to Duncan, and her love for him. How could she explain how over the past several months, when she and Kearney were the only people who truly understood each other, they had formed a bond? They would never be bosom buddies, but they could express themselves without spelling out everything. And without fearing reprisal or being turned in to the police. Words could not explain the effort Kearney made to make amends for what he did to her. The remaining soft side of Joan, small as it was, had to acknowledge his efforts. She had wanted to give Nirmala Kearney's name, but had not been able to bring herself to do so…

ৼৣৼ

Duncan's voice pulled her out of her reverie.

"Kearney will be here in a few minutes." Duncan's voice indicated that he thought she was still in the bedroom. He glanced up and saw her standing barely in sight. "What are you doing?" His eyes smiled. "Watching me?"

"Oh, I—" Joan smoothed the skirt over her thighs. "I think the skirt might be too tight across the hips."

"Let me see."

Joan stood in front of him in a sapphire, two piece dress covered in beads of the same color. When she moved the beads glittered a swirl pattern from her hips down the front of the ankle-length skirt. A slit in the skirt showed a little leg but still covered the scars on her thighs. The asymmetrical top draped over one shoulder to cover the scar on her chest and bared the other shoulder. It fell so that one side fell a few inches below the waist. On the other side it fell a few inches above her waist, revealing a slender, fit waistline.

"Turn around," Duncan said moving his fingers in a circular motion.

Joan turned and looked over her shoulder at him. He covered his mouth with his hand in a thoughtful pose. She turned to face him. "It's too tight, isn't it?"

He shook his head. "It's those shoes. How high are those heels?"

"Three inches, why?"

"You can't run very fast in them."

Joan looked down at her feet. "Run in them?" She looked up at him. "Do you think I'm going to have to run?"

"If you knew what I was thinking, you'd already be running." He smiled and motioned for her to come to him and sit on his lap.

Joan shook her head and motioned with her fingers for him to come to her. She pointed at the spot right in front of her. They locked eyes. Duncan stood and walked toward her. His slow approach radiated masculinity and power. When he stood inches away, his intensity compelled her to step back.

He rested his hands on her shoulders. "Stand your ground, *nena*. It's unbecoming of a warrior." He traced the slanted edge of the top. "It's unbecoming of you."

Heat raced through her. She swallowed and said, "I'm never be afraid of you. It's just that you were so intense." One corner of her mouth curled upward. "What if I had run?"

Duncan chuckled. "We'd be in the bedroom by now."

Joan cupped his face with her hands, smelled his musky cologne, and smiled into his eyes. "Is this really going to happen?"

He wrapped his arm around her. "Nothing is going to stop us from getting married. You will be wife in less than an hour."

"And you will be my husband." She looked up at him and they kissed gently.

His hand traced a path down the side of her neck to her throat. "Where's your jewelry?"

220 Janet McClintock

Joan reflexively put her hand to her throat. "I forgot to buy jewelry when I was out with Nirmala."

"I didn't forget." Duncan pulled a black box from his inside pocket. "This is my wedding present to you."

Joan opened the box and gasped. A pair of diamond pendant earrings sparkled against the black velvet. The teardrop diamonds had to be at least two carats each. A matching necklace with a larger, solitary diamond on a chain completed the set. Tears blurred Joan's vision. All she had gone through: the firefights, getting trapped in a fire, so much burnt gun powder it choked her, the fear of death, the grief of losing Duncan, the overwhelming emotion of having him back. The torture. What had been a lead blanket for years came out all at once in cathartic, throat-constricting sobs.

Duncan held her and let her burn out all the emotion.

Kearney opened the door and stuck his head in the living room. "Now what?"

"I just gave her the wedding gift and she burst out crying."

"I told him you'd prefer a gun," Kearney said.

Laughter pushed its way through the sobs. "It's just after all we've been through this is so beautiful and..." She fingered the jewelry, "sophisticated."

Duncan put the necklace on Joan and she put on the earrings.

He put his hands on each side of her face. "This jewelry pales in beauty compared to you."

Kearney looked at his watch. "We have to leave."

"Okay. In a minute," Duncan said without taking his eyes off Joan.

"Jeb is being so hard on the armed guards, well...a mutiny would not be surprising. Nirmala's fussing with decorations and driving the guys crazy. Elaine's arguing with the caterer," Kearney said. "We have to get going before pandemonium sets in."

Duncan nodded to his friend. "Give us a minute."

Kearney headed toward the car, leaving the bride and groom a few more seconds alone.

"We are going to be together for the rest of our lives," Duncan said with confidence, as if saying it would make it true.

"How can you be so sure? The feds always get their man."

"Believe in me, Joan, and we will spend the rest of our lives together." He pulled her into his arms again. "Do you believe in me?"

She pulled back to look into his eyes. "I do."

"Then let's make this happen."

CHAPTER 19

Elaine pulled into the parking lot behind the federal building, wondering if she should have called ahead. She sipped her coffee and wondered what the hell she was doing. She loved Kearney. No man had ever made her feel so important and beautiful. He was worldly, articulate, well-mannered, and passionate. He made her feel protected.

His friends made her feel like she needed protecting. Angel was haunted by some past trauma. Duncan intimidated Rob without saying or doing anything. The rest of Kearney's friends were armed thugs. What she was about to do would either allay her fears or get those people out of Kearney's life. If they went down, would he go down with them? How would she feel about that? She was in over her head. Her gut told her to take action before something happened where she would have to clear her name.

She pulled down the visor, reapplied lipstick, and got out of the car. She pulled up the collar of her jacket. The May afternoon was cool, but the breeze smelled like spring, promising warmer days ahead. A third of the way across the parking lot she hesitated as a car pulled into a parking spot to her left. She looked back at her BMW. If she was doing the right thing, her stomach did not get the message. It jumped around inside its cavity. Her hands shook.

A well-dressed man got out of the car. "Can I help you with anything?"

"I made a mistake. I'm not sure I'm doing the right thing."

"Maybe I can help."

"Do you work here?" She looked at his suit and noticed the bulge on his right hip. "Of course you do. What am I thinking?"

"Did you have an appointment?"

"No. Maybe I should go." She headed toward her car.

The man turned and headed into the building.

Elaine stopped, turned. "Excuse me, sir. Can you show me where to go?"

૭૦૯૦

Agent Lyndon offered a seat to Elaine. "Can I get you anything?"

Elaine shook her head and slid onto the chair. Agent Lyndon looked young compared to the stereotypical image Elaine held. The agent had a girl-next-door face, hair pulled back into a ponytail, her eyes were friendly.

"Okay, let's get started. The agent downstairs said you had information on a couple fugitives."

Elaine nodded and looked over her shoulder at the door through which she had just entered. The FBI headquarters was not anything like she had imagined. Agents sat at desks in cubicles quietly talking on the phone or going over paperwork on their desks. Phones chirped, a copy machine whined, the water cooler behind her glugged. Many cubicles were empty.

"Okay, let's get started. What's your name?"

"Why do you need my name?"

"It's just for our records. It's strictly confidential. Do you have a fear of reprisals?"

Elaine shook her head.

Agent Lyndon smiled. "Okay, let's start with your full name."

"Elaine. Elaine Reddington." After prompts from Agent Lyndon, Elaine gave all her contact information and related how she met and knew Kearney, but stopped short of the plan to con Kearney out of his money.

"And you don't know any other name for him."

"I'm here about his friends, not him."

"And why have you decided to come forward at this time with this information?"

"I—his friends scare me. I think they're fugitives." Elaine flinched when a man strode past Agent Lyndon's desk.

"Okay. What are their names?"

"There's a woman he calls his sister, but I don't think she is—"

"Is he cheating on you with her?" the agent asked.

"No. I'm sure of it. But they're very close."

"Her name?"

"She goes by Angel, but her name is Joan Bowman...well, Archer now. She just got married. I think she has a lot of issues."

"Why do you say that?"

"Kearney is very protective of her and she drinks a lot."

The agent nodded and typed Joan's name into the computer. When the information came up, her eyes darted to Elaine. Her face remained calm. She hit a button Elaine assumed was the print button.

"What makes you think she changed her name?"

"She got married to a man named Dennis Maurice Archer at my house about two weeks ago."

"Is he the other fugitive you talked about earlier?"

"She calls him Duncan, but—" Two agents on the other side of the room laughed at some inside joke. Elaine looked over her shoulder and slowed her speech. "His real name is Dennis Archer."

Agent Lyndon typed Duncan's name into her computer. The agent's outward appearance remained the same, but she watched Elaine with interest. That made Elaine more jumpy. She had trouble making eye contact and focusing on follow up questions.

Agent Lyndon excused herself and headed to the printer. After talking to one of the other agents, she returned to the desk with the printouts. She showed photos to Elaine.

"That's them. Angel and Duncan."

"Ms. Reddington," the agent stood, "if you would come with me."

Elaine stood. "Why? Am I in trouble?" she asked, following the agent down a short aisle between cubicles.

The agent opened a door to a glass-enclosed briefing room. "We have to ask you for some more information, and we thought you would be more comfortable in here."

A steely-faced agent joined them and they sat across the table from Elaine. Elaine repeated the information she had previously told Agent Lyndon.

When Elaine completed her re-iteration, another agent motioned to Agent Lyndon and shook his head. He whispered into Agent Lyndon's ear. She nodded and returned to her seat across from Elaine.

"Is something wrong?" Elaine fidgeted and looked from the steely-faced agent to Agent Lyndon.

"Your background check came back clean."

Elaine did not say anything.

Agent Lyndon smiled. "That corroborates your story that you don't have anything to do with Archer and Bowman and anything they're up to. Do you have any idea who they are?"

"No." Elaine shook her head. "I just know there's something going on with them. Did you find anything?"

"And you don't know anything about Kearney's past?"

"Just what he told me. What I told you."

"Ms. Reddington, you seem like a nice person, so I'm going to be up front with you." Agent Lyndon paused for effect. "You are nervous about something. Are you in any danger?"

"I suppose if they found out about my trip here, they

would be upset, but I don't think Kearney would let them do anything to me."

"Is there anything you want to tell us? Something you want to get off your chest?"

"Oh…coming here…I'm not sure I'm doing the right thing," Elaine said.

"Let me assure you, Ms. Reddington, you did the right thing by coming here. These people are armed and danger-ous—"

"I knew it. I knew there was something about them."

"I'm afraid Kearney is one of them, and you were right to think he is not Joan Bowman's brother. She is an only child," the steely-faced agent said. "I must warn you to stay away from them until we get them into custody.

"Kearney, too?"

"All of them."

"If I stop seeing him, won't he think it's odd. Maybe suspect something."

"Use your best judgment," Agent Lyndon said. "But keep in mind you are not safe with them. At any time."

"Okay," Elaine said. How was she going to handle this without tipping off anyone of what she had done. And what exactly had she done? The realization that Kearney would be arrested hit home. Elaine put her head in her hands. The reality of Kearney being taken away in handcuffs spotlight-ed her love for him. She hadn't thought of Kearney that way until his absence was imminent.

Agent Lyndon softened her eyes, but stopped short of a smile. "You are not in any trouble. You have done the right thing by coming to us. For now, we need you to tell us eve-rything you know about them." She pulled out a notebook. "All their friends, where they live, what they drive, what they do to unwind. Everything you can recall."

CHAPTER 20

Joan watched the wiper on her side of the windshield push the rain to the driver's side, then the driver's side wiper swiped the windshield clean. The repetitive movement mesmerized her into quiet reflection on the wedding and the honeymoon.

Elaine had opened her lovely home to Duncan and Joan. Kearney and Nirmala had been the witnesses. The ceremony took place in front of the fireplace in Elaine's formal living room. Nirmala had gone above and beyond Joan's expectations for the decorations. There were giant vases of fresh flowers in every room, and the mantle dripped with a thick, green garland laden with lilies and daisies. After a brief edginess at the sight of stern armed guards, the ceremony had gone off without "outside interference," as Jeb called it. Joan cried, Nirmala cried, Elaine cried. Even Carmine palmed something from his eyes. With cheers and toasts ringing in their ears, the newlyweds had left for their honeymoon.

They had spent two wonderful weeks at a hunting cabin in the Adirondacks. The time spent with nature and each other had been relaxing—more than Joan had expected considering the outhouse and the hand pump for water. They both loved being in the woods, and they had spent many hours hand-in-hand absorbing the beauty and pungent aromas of the primitive forest. Long hikes drained the tension out of them.

The fresh air made them content and sleepy. It had been easy to unwind with the freedom from surveillance cameras and prying eyes, possible tails and federal agents. Having Duncan's undivided attention for two weeks reinforced the bond they had formed years before. They had never had time for undivided attention unencumbered by responsibilities of, at first, the Legion and after that the militia.

Upon arrival at the hunting cabin, they had made a pact to talk only about their relationship and their future. No past. No rationalizations. No regrets. Even Joan's phantoms had disappeared in the power of Duncan's presence. At first, Joan feared they wouldn't have anything in common outside of the military arena, but she needn't have worried. Their days were filled with the simple pleasures they both enjoyed, the outdoors, pleasant conversation, and passionate love making. Plans for a rosy future.

But reality demanded its due, and they were headed home at the end of their two-week respite in the mountains.

"Why don't we take another week?" Joan asked dreamily.

"Where would you like to go?" Duncan asked.

"Hmmm…maybe the Gulf Coast. Sand and sunshine sound good."

"I know it's corny, but there's always Niagara Falls."

"Too many cameras."

"Yeah, and people," he added.

She looked over at Duncan in time to see him rub his chin with the back of his hand. "Are you okay?" she asked. "Want me to drive for a while?"

He smiled at her—mountain quiet and seclusion had softened the hard lines around his eyes—then returned his gaze to the road. "I'm fine. Relax, Mrs. Archer."

Mrs. Archer. Joan leaned her head back on the headrest and watched the windshield wipers. She smiled. "Do you think I should officially notify Agent Woyzeck of my name change?"

"Somehow I get the feeling he knows." He squeezed her hand. "Like a ripple in the force."

"Yeah," she snorted, then muttered, "fucking bastard."

"He's only doing his job, babe." He hesitated before adding, "Like you do yours."

"So you're okay with me continuing to work for Jeb?" She put her stocking feet on the dashboard and frowned. She loved the adrenaline from the type of missions she did for Jeb, but she chanced something going horribly wrong. Fatally wrong. Mountain climbing or whitewater rafting would give her the adrenaline rush without bullets whizzing past her head. They had enough money to spend the rest of their lives doing those things. The decision to keep working remained cloudy in Joan's mind. She had decided to keep working, yet all the negatives kept crawling around her insides.

"You don't have a problem with my decision?" she asked again, hoping Duncan would nix the idea.

"We've already talked about this, and I'm still okay with it."

Joan remained quiet and watched the wipers working together to clear the glass. She knitted her brow and recalled the conversation about her future with Durham Security. Duncan had not been gung ho about the idea, but he had listened to her and in the end agreed with her reasoning.

"You get edgy and off your stride if you aren't doing something challenging or constructive," he said, as if reading her thoughts. "I understand that. I've had my time in the field. This last gunshot pulled me up short and made me realize I've had my fun. It's time for me to relax and—" He took his eyes off the road and squeezed her hand again, "take care of you."

"You got shot, Duncan. You aren't worried the same thing could happen to me?"

"That was different. I didn't listen to you. If I had…" He looked over at her. "Of course, I'm worried. But you are good at what you do. I have faith in you and your abilities.

Promise me you will listen to your instincts and act accordingly."

Joan pointed through the windshield to indicate for him to keep his eyes on the road. *Trust my instincts and act accordingly. That's what I'm trying to do.* She glanced at him and smiled.

"I just want what's best for you," he said, returning his eyes to the road ahead.

"You're a good husband."

He checked his mirrors before changing lanes. "I'm not a *great* husband?"

She reached over and rubbed his thigh. "You have your moments."

⌘⌘⌘

Claude lounged on the couch in Jeb's office with his feet on the coffee table. "Anybody hear from Angel?" He looked like he didn't have a trouble in the world.

"Duncan texted from the road this morning," Jeb said. He took a sip of coffee. "They're on their way back. Champ got them tickets to the Ottmar Liebert concert tonight."

"Who the hell is Ottmar Liebert?"

Jeb scratched his fledgling beard and exhaled loudly. "He plays nouveau flamenco or some shit. I guess they like Latino music."

"Where's it at?"

"Poughkeepsie somewhere." Jeb stopped rubbing his jaw and looked at Claude. The lines on his face appeared deeper, and dark rings had formed under his eyes. "You're extraordinarily inquisitive this morning."

"I don't know, boss." Claude thumbed the rim of his mug. He glanced at Jeb. "There's something about her I don't trust, eh."

"I've come to believe she is who and what she says she is. I don't get any deception from her."

"She's good at bluffing. That's what Archer always said."

Jeb leaned back and rubbed his new moustache. After a moment of thought he added, "I have something to tell you in confidence. Don't go sliding sideways on me."

Claude shrugged as if to say, "What is it?"

"I heard through the grapevine that the feds have their eyes on Durham Security."

"What's that mean?"

"I think maybe there's somebody inside."

"Any idea who?" Claude said before taking a sip of coffee.

"No. If I did, they'd be gone."

"Gone? As in…gone?" Claude's fingers made a slicing motion across his throat.

Jeb nodded.

Claude put his feet on the floor and slid to the edge of the couch. "It's her."

"Don't go jumping to conclusions. We have to keep level heads and stay alert."

"Why can't you see it? What does she have on you?"

"That's enough, Claude. No more talk like that." Jeb leaned his elbows on his desk. "She doesn't have anything on me. I just don't sense deception from her."

"Aw, come on, Jeb. Everything ran smooth. Then she showed up and we think there's a con—"

"We straightened that out."

"Maybe, eh." Claude used his fingers to emphasize each point. "She comes here claiming Duncan is dead, then he shows up alive and well. Colavito got killed in that messed up op. The shooter at the mall—"

"She saved people both times."

"We never had an incident at any of our guarding jobs. She shows up and—"

"Let's not concentrate on one person." Jeb stood to get a refill. "And that messed up op wasn't on her. She saved those guys' asses—" He gave Claude a hard stare. "You were there. You know that." He raised the pot to offer coffee to Claude.

Claude waved off the refill.

"What about Kearney's girlfriend, Elaine?" Jeb asked. "She opened her home to complete strangers to hold a wedding for people she barely knew. It could have been a set up."

"Nothing happened."

"Maybe nothing was supposed to happen. It would have tipped us off." Jeb took a sip of coffee. A car alarm went off, and he fingered open the blinds to check the Durham Security parking lot. "It coulda been an intelligence gathering op."

"That's a stretch."

"I think I'll have Joan get close to Elaine. Get her to talk."

"Yeah, that's good—have one suspicious broad check out another one. Good luck with that."

"We have to keep our eyes on everybody."

"Yeah? You do that." Claude crossed his arms. "I'll keep my eyes on Joan."

Jeb narrowed his eyes. "I could say the same about you. All this shit happened when you returned from jail."

Claude's face reddened and his body stiffened. "What are you saying? You think I'm the mole?"

"I'm saying it could be anybody."

⋘⋙

Joan followed Duncan as they sidestepped to their seats, excusing themselves and avoiding people's toes, until they reached the middle of the row. Champ had given them tickets to the Ottmar Liebert concert for a wedding gift, and the seats were perfect—orchestra level, five rows back, center stage.

When they were settled in their seats, Duncan searched

for Joan's hand. He kissed her on the cheek and fingered her wedding band. Her stomach fluttered. After all they'd been through over the past few years, his touch still sent her blood soaring and her head reeling. She nuzzled him back.

As the low, mumbled din of conversations in the concert hall further relaxed Joan, she thought back over the past two weeks. It had been the longest stretch of one-on-one interaction with Duncan without interruption—no tactics, responsibilities, and problems vying for attention. It could be that way all the time if she quit working for Jeb. They had the money for new identities. They could afford to live anywhere in the world. The quiet life with Duncan was within her grasp, but she had decided to wait a little longer. Her gut again reminded her to rethink the decision. Duncan's support of her staying with Durham Security was heartwarming and encouraging.

She looked at Duncan, but he had turned away from her to talk to the woman on his other side. Could his support of her staying at Durham Security have something to do with his unusual conversation with Agent Woyzeck? What was the connection? He must have felt her eyes on him, because he turned to look at her. She smiled. She trusted him. He had asked her to believe in him, and she did.

He squeezed her hand.

The lights slowly dimmed and the curtain opened revealing a stage full of conga drums, a small brass section and a couple violinists. A stool sat to the right of center in a pool of light. The emcee offered a few housekeeping announcements then launched into the introduction of Ottmar Liebert. The audience applauded and hooted his entrance.

An hour and a half into the concert Joan looked at Duncan head-dancing to the music. She looked past him to soak in the beauty of the hall. The detailed, gilded scrolling on the balcony was beautiful art that modern halls lacked. Her gaze followed the scrolling to the side exit. Her blood turned to ice. A uniformed policeman stood in the alcove, scanning the crowd. She nudged Duncan and looked over her shoulder. Another policeman stood in the exit alcove on the other side.

"Good music, right?" Duncan said.

"Look over my shoulder. There's a cop under the exit sign."

"It's just security," he said. "The promoters want to do everything they can to keep us safe."

Joan couldn't shake the deadly stillness that filled her insides. "Hold me, Duncan."

He put his arm around her shoulders and whispered, "Relax. We're fine."

She kept shooting glances over her shoulder and past Duncan.

Ottmar Liebert announced his final selection, and after a brief introduction to the piece, the band played "Passing Storm."

Duncan must have felt her tension. "The concert is almost over. I'll take you for some dessert and coffee on the way home."

Joan forced a smile and nodded. She looked toward the back of the hall and saw a man wearing a different, olive-colored uniform that, even in the dim light, showed a bulletproof vest.

With heart racing and her mouth drying, Joan put her lips next to Duncan's ear and said one word, "SWAT."

Duncan looked over his shoulder, then locked eyes with Joan. "They won't take us down in here. Too many people. They'll wait until we're outside."

"How can we get away?"

"Give me a minute." After another glance over his shoulder, Duncan watched the musicians on the stage, but he did not hear the music—the head-dancing stopped.

Joan watched his profile. When the piece ended and the audience jumped to their feet in a standing ovation, he muttered, "Fucking bastards."

Joan stared at him. This could be the last time she would see him, and she wanted to remember this moment forever.

When he turned to look at her, his sad eyes said it all.

"Hold me, Duncan. Don't let me go. Make them tear us apart."

After several bows, the band left the stage. While the audience chanted, "Encore," Duncan and Joan remained locked in a forever kiss.

When the people around them realized there would not be an encore, they stood and slowly inched their way to the aisles.

"Let's go," Duncan said. "Maybe we can get lost in the crowd."

"This is it. Isn't it?"

He clenched his jaw muscles so hard they swelled through his beard. "Afraid so, *nena*."

Joan shuffled along with the other concert goers, shoulders hunched, chin on chest, Duncan directly behind her. His hands on her shoulders blazed heat through her body. She had to will her lungs to breath and her heart to beat.

When the opportunity arose, he moved from behind her and slipped an arm around her shoulder. He lifted her chin with the knuckle of his forefinger. "Chin up. Shoulders back. They may take our freedom, but don't let them take our dignity."

Joan gave him a weak smile and straightened her shoulders. She looked back to see how many people were behind them. The woman behind her smiled and commented on the music. Joan smiled and nodded before turning back to look at Duncan.

He squeezed her shoulders, but didn't look at her—his eyes scanned the area in front of them. "How many at our rear?"

Joan locked her gaze on the back of the head of the woman in front of her. "Twenty-five, thirty."

People toward the back of the hall shuffled into the aisle, making forward movement a lazy, sluggish pace. The urge to push people out of the way and make a break for it roiled Joan's insides. Though calm on her exterior, she valiantly fought the urge shove the crowd. She stared at the woman in front of her.

A man somewhere at the front of the throng raised his voice. "We ask that you move along. Do not linger in the lobby. Please exit the building in a calm and orderly fashion. There is no emergency. Keep moving through the lobby."

Two-thirds of the way up the aisle, Duncan dropped his arm from Joan's shoulder and entwined his fingers in hers. "Ready?"

"No." His palm was moist. Duncan, who had always been her rock, was nervous.

He leaned in. "Scared?"

She nodded. His breath on her ear made her long for another year with him. Another month. Or day. Fear blanketed every sense. She floated in a blurred Monet painting of a crowd of people. The low din of people talking reminded her of the movie *Jaws* where a horrific event was preceded by the haunting music.

"Me, too." He squeezed her hand. All confidence in a life together forever dissipated.

The man raised his voice again, repeating the directions to keep moving. Although his voice seemed louder, he seemed farther away. Terror singed with panic warped her sense of time and space. Every step they took toward the back caused the rear wall to recede. Joan could see the brighter light of the lobby through the doorway. She looked toward the man giving directions out of the corner of her eye.

Duncan looked straight ahead. The man looked directly at Joan then at Duncan. The man's eyes slid past them. He repeated the instructions in a jarring voice.

And they were in the lobby.

Uniformed police were herding the people through the lobby. Although a few voices demanded an explanation, the bulk of the people went where the police pointed. There were several individuals who were hyper-alert, watching the faces in the crowd—plainclothes officers. When the nearest one looked at Duncan, Joan tucked her chin.

They were twenty feet from the door to the street where they would be ordered to the ground. The swish of street traffic carried the toxic odor of car exhaust through the open doors. A rush of air brushed her face. Her heart pounded and sweat broke out over her whole body. Duncan squeezed her hand so hard she should have cringed, but she barely felt it.

Eighteen feet.

"Freeze! Let me see your hands."

She felt his hand pull from hers. They raised their hands.

The officer repeated the words several times. The few concert goers left in the lobby milled around, not sure how to stay out of the way. A SWAT officer approached Joan and Duncan.

She blinked. The officer approaching them held his finger outside the trigger guard, the barrel pointing toward the floor. He motioned for her and Duncan to come toward him. They obeyed. He pulled them alongside him. Then past him. Another SWAT officer on the street side of the doorway waved them toward him.

As they walked toward the officer, the SWAT team rushed toward them, guns drawn, yelling to get on the ground. They washed past Joan and Duncan, taking down a man behind them.

They were in the street. Joan stared at Duncan's face, mouth open, incredulous at what just happened. She tried to speak, but words escaped her.

He looked past her then over his shoulder. "No one's looking at us. Let's get the hell out of here."

They hurried to their parked car. Exhaust laden air never felt so wholesome and fitting. Their pace put distance between them and the police, but not so fast it drew attention.

In the relative safety and anonymity of the car, Duncan sat back, hands gripping the steering wheel. With eyes straight ahead he asked, "What the hell just happened?"

Sharp inhales cut off Joan's nervous laughter. She sat stiff in her seat, leg jiggling from the adrenaline coursing through her body. She wiped her forehead with the back of her shaking hand.

He leaned across the front seat and put his arm around her shoulder. "I thought they—I thought it was over for us." He kissed her then rested his forehead against hers.

"I was so not ready to be separated from you," she said.

"I can't believe they rushed right past us."

"Drive, Duncan."

"Yes, ma'am."

CHAPTER 21

Joan woke with a start to a dream of lying on her stomach, hands cuffed behind her back and looking over at the backlit profile of Duncan mouthing, "Fucking bastards." The more she tried to remember the dream, the more it melted into the mist between dreamland and reality. She rubbed her wrists and looked over her shoulder to Duncan's side of the bed. He had gotten out of bed early, leaving behind the indentation in his pillow and cold sheets.

She got out of bed and pulled on a tee shirt and shorts. The deep murmur of Duncan's voice floated from somewhere else in the apartment. She padded barefoot toward the sound.

He stood in the living room, back to her, looking out the door. Unaware of her presence, he continued to talk on his cell phone. He ran his hand over his curly hair. "I'm married now. I'm not doing this." He must have sensed her presence because he half-turned to look at her and said to the caller, "I gotta go."

"Who were you talking to?" Joan asked when he hung up.

He walked across the room and put his arms around her. "Jeb."

"What can't you do?"

"He has a job for me, but the last job had bad intel, and I won't do it unless the surveillance is done right this time."

He pulled her tightly against his chest. "How did you sleep last night?"

"Like a baby—once the adrenaline wore off." She pushed away from him and leaned back to make eye contact. "What kind of job does Jeb have for you?"

He slid his hands under her shirt and stroked her back. "Mmm, let's go back to bed, Mrs. Archer."

"If you take this job, can I go with you?"

"No." He nuzzled her ear. "But I know something else you can do with me."

His romantic mood sent flames licking down her spine, and she knew she shouldn't ask a sticky question now, but she had to know. "Remember on the way home from the honeymoon, you said to not be mad at the feds because they were just doing their jobs?"

"Mmhmm," he answered while he trailed kisses down her neck.

"Then why did you say 'fucking bastards' last night when the police were in the theater?"

"Did I?" Duncan murmured between planting kisses across her sternum and down between her breasts. "I don't remember that. I was a little stressed out, if you recall. Now stop the straight talk and sweet talk me."

"Or," she said, pulling his head up near hers, "let's stop talking altogether."

He smiled. "Now you're talking." He covered her mouth with his.

လာလာ

After they made love, Duncan left with Kearney to go to Yonkers for a lunch meeting with Jeb. Joan did her first two-hour workout in a long time. The tightened muscles, heightened speed, and fluid agility created the All Is Right With The World feeling, which relaxed her. After a quick snack to replenish her carbs she took a long shower.

While she let the cool water rinse the soap from her body, she thought about Duncan and his lovemaking. Strong. Commanding. And sexier than ever. He had promised to meet her at Durham Security at six o'clock before going out to dinner.

While she dressed, the job that afternoon took greater importance. Jeb had told Joan to talk to Elaine, get insight into her life, plans, and motivations. Build rapport. Elaine had agreed to show a few houses for Duncan and Joan to rent. It would be a busy afternoon, but there was plenty of time to build a rapport with Elaine. What better way than to let Elaine do what she was comfortable doing—showing houses. With her relaxed and distracted, it would be a great opportunity to connect with her and get her to give up some information.

She turned her attention back to her life. Everything appeared to be going well, but she couldn't shake the heavy, black spot at the base of her spine. Duncan was attentive. Kearney was his usual annoying self. She felt healthy and fit. Her life was on an even keel for the first time in months. But her instincts were setting her nerve endings on fire. Sliding the sheath onto her belt, she decided to stop picking apart her circumstances. If her life went the way it usually did, the good times would end soon enough. She would enjoy them while they lasted. She grabbed the keys and headed to Duncan's car.

Duncan had ridden to the city with Kearney, which left his car for her use. Leaning back in the driver's seat, she drove to Elaine's office. The soothing ride on rural roads turned out to be the perfect time to sift through all the conversations, facial expressions, and body language of everyone over the past few days. Nothing stuck out. Duncan had been a loving groom on the honeymoon. Several times she had caught him looking at her with an expression somewhere between love and sorrow. When she had asked him about it, he changed the subject or teased her into bed—just like he did this morning.

She chalked up his unusual behavior to the mysterious job Jeb had for him. She shook her head. He didn't know about the job before this morning. She shrugged off her thoughts and pulled into the gravel-covered parking area outside Elaine's office. It could simply be jangled nerves from the close call at the Ottmar Liebert concert. She stowed her misgivings and applied herself to the job at hand.

On the way to the first house, Elaine filled the silence with real estate babble. She pulled into the driveway and repeated the specs for what seemed like the tenth time. Before she slid out of the driver's seat, Joan gently caught her arm.

"How are you doing?" Joan asked.

"Fine." Elaine squinted. "What do you mean?"

"You seem nervous."

"I do?"

Joan nodded. "I've never heard you say so much in a short length of time."

"Oh." Elaine reached for the folder with the description of the house. "I'm just excited for you and Duncan getting your first house together."

"We're not buying—"

"Oh, I know, but it's still exciting. Aren't you excited?"

"Sure." *I should be, I guess.* "Let's go inside and take a look." Maybe once Elaine started her sales spiel, she would relax.

The whole time they wended their way through the house, Elaine chatted up the house's good points and pointed out repairs that would have to be made before moving in. Her words and phrases hit the mark, but her dialogue seemed stilted, as if she was afraid of saying the wrong thing. Joan put her hand on her forehead and squeezed her temples, struggling between her instincts, which had never been wrong before, and not wanting to think negative thoughts about Kearney's girlfriend. *I'm getting soft, if that's even possible at this point in my life.*

"Are you okay?" Elaine asked. "We can look at the other two houses another day."

"No, no. I want to get this done today so I can drop it in Duncan's lap to make the decision. It's just a mild headache."

Elaine returned the door key to the lockbox. "I have some aspirin in the car."

❧❧❧

After two more houses and a long ride to Yonkers, Joan parked in the Durham Security back parking lot and cut through Notches. Duncan and Kearney were not in the bar. She had arrived early and did not really expect Duncan there yet, so she headed to Jeb's office. She found it deserted and stood in the center of the quiet, empty room. Honking horns from the street below filtered into the office lit only by the desk lamp. She looked around trying to figure out what unsettled her. Elaine's odd behavior that afternoon, Jeb and Kearney's absence in Notches, Duncan's cut-short phone conversation that morning all brought a chill to her spine. Consciously tempering her growing sense of dread with a caution to maintain focus, she slid into her chair. She texted Duncan pictures of the three houses with a short comment on each, then waited alone with her churning thoughts...

❧❧❧

Sometime during the showing of the third house, Elaine had relaxed. Words rolled off her tongue easily, making cracks about the outdated counters in the kitchen and the weird closet under the stairs. Her body language changed from tense to fluid and confident, and she made more frequent eye contact.

Joan had taken the plunge and asked Elaine to have a

late lunch. Jeb had ordered her to get tight with Elaine, and what better way than over food.

During lunch, the two women shared Kearney stories. The ones Elaine told were probably true. Joan's stories were lies. There wasn't anything about Kearney she felt comfortable revealing, especially to a woman who had weaseled into Kearney's life at a time when he was vulnerable. The purpose of this lunch date was meant to form a bond and get Elaine to trust Joan and open up to her, not the other way around. When the lunch wound down, Joan could not shake the feeling Elaine withheld important facts.

When Elaine pulled into the real estate office parking lot, Joan jumped headfirst into the gist of the problem. Wishing she had taken the time to learn finesse, she said, "Jeb says someone ratted to the feds about his company. He thinks it's you."

Truthfully, Jeb had no idea who it was, but his suspicions were enough for Joan to take a leap and accuse Elaine of it.

Elaine gripped the steering wheel until her knuckles were white. She stared straight ahead at a budding azalea bush. "I—" She licked her lips and glanced in Joan's direction without making eye contact. "I don't know what you mean. I wouldn't even know where to start to do something like that."

Joan didn't respond. A heavy silence could be more effective at getting people to talk than anything she could say or do.

"And if I did that, and I'm not saying I did, that would bring down Kearney, too. Wouldn't it?"

Again Joan didn't respond. Elaine was doing fine without any outside help.

Elaine finally made eye contact. "I don't know what you want me to say." Her voice shook.

"Let's go inside and talk," Joan said.

Joan checked the empty parking lot and the surrounding area. The real estate office stood alone, set back from a quiet road that had some traffic, but not a lot. And the sound of cars whizzing by masked any sound, the speed precluded seeing anything to report.

She followed Elaine into the small building and quietly locked the door behind them. They walked into a messy office with file folders stacked on the credenza behind the desk, leaving the center of the desk clear for doing paperwork. A flat screen monitor and keyboard took up one corner of the desk, several framed photos lined the front edge of the desk. Joan picked up one—a family vacation photo.

She replaced the picture and tried another tack. "What's the story with you and Kearney?"

"At first it was different, but after a while I really became—" She shrugged. "—fond of him."

"Yeah, I bet."

Elaine perched on the edge of the desk and looked at Joan. "You have to believe that before I tell you."

"Tell me what?" Joan kept her face neutral, but her mind buzzed at Elaine's possible revelation.

"You have to tell me you believe that I really care for your brother."

Joan looked out the window. The whole brother-sister scenario lost its charm months ago. "Just tell me what you did."

Elaine shook her head. "Say you believe me."

This high school, locker room banter exasperated Joan. She grabbed Elaine's arm and squeezed. The pussy footing around had just kicked its last life. "I don't know what Kearney told you about me," Joan said with a clenched jaw. "But believe me, he sugar-coated it. If you aren't afraid of what I can do to you, you should be. Now, why are you with Kearney?"

"Ow! You're hurting me."

"If you think this hurts, you have no idea where this is going if you don't tell me what I want to know." So much for building rapport.

She hoped Elaine would give up something. The last

thing she wanted was to become a person like Kearney—
like Kearney used to be.

"Okay, okay. Lighten up."

Joan loosened her grip, but didn't let go. "What is going
on and who did you talk to?"

"My friend met Kearney when he was drunk and—"

Joan tightened her grip. "Get to the point, Elaine."

She cringed from the pressure. "I'm getting to it.
Kearney bragged about inheriting a lot of money. My friend
called me with a plan to con him out of his money." She
looked at Joan with wide eyes. "But I really fell for him."

"But not enough to call off the con."

"I was going to call it off but…" She clamped her eyelids shut and a tear trickled down her cheek. "Then all those
scary men with automatic weapons at my house at your
wedding…I got scared." She flinched. "I panicked. Okay?"

Of course, the most beautiful day in Joan's life brought
about this ugly unraveling. Joan's breathing became short
and rapid. Her neck prickled.

"What is your friend's name?" When Elaine didn't answer, Joan shook Elaine's arm. "His name, Elaine."

"I won't tell you his name."

"Oh, you will. How quickly will depend on how much
pain you can stand." Joan didn't want to hurt Elaine any
further than squeezing her arm. Inflicting mental pain could
be more damaging than physically hurting someone.

"You wouldn't." Elaine wiped her nose with her free
hand. Something in Joan's face must have convinced her
otherwise because she said, "Rob."

Joan stopped breathing. "Rob who?"

"Reddington. Rob Reddington. There I told you."

Friend, my ass. "What relation is he to you?"

Elaine cowered away from Joan. "He's my brother."

Joan shoved Elaine's arm before letting go. "So you
guys were going to con me, too?"

"Until Duncan showed up." Elaine rubbed her arm. "Rob
backed out then. Something about Duncan scared him."

Joan's instincts had been right on target about Rob. She rubbed her forehead, stared at Elaine and ran her fingers through her hair.

"Are we done?" Elaine asked.

"Hell no. We still have to talk about you being a snitch."

Elaine started backing away.

Just like a guilty person would do. Joan snatched Elaine's wrist, put her in a hammerlock, and smashed her face into the bookcase. "What did you tell the feds?"

"Ow, ow, ow, you're hurting me."

"Believe me, this is nothing compared to what Kearney will do to you." Joan pressed her weight against Elaine's back, wrenching her arm, adding strain to Elaine's shoulder. Joan spoke into Elaine's ear. "If you talk to me now, you won't have to endure his grisly interrogation techniques. He was a CIA interrogator. Did he tell you that?"

Elaine nodded.

"Did he tell you that when the CIA had someone they couldn't break, they called him in? Most people he interrogated didn't survive. I don't hold out much hope for you."

"Let me go. Please."

"Did he tell you that he interrogated me?"

Elaine shook her head. A tear dragged mascara down her cheek.

"I survived. That should tell you how strong I am. How determined." Joan clenched her jaw and said through her teeth, "How resilient."

She hated hurting someone unable to fight back. If Elaine did in fact go to the feds, she could hurt everyone Joan knew much more than Joan could ever hurt her. Duncan had just come back into her life. She was not about to lose him again because of some woman's fear. Elaine had not fought back physically, but in the only way she knew. Joan clenched her jaw harder, resisting the urge to dislocate Elaine's shoulder.

"You're a survivor," Elaine said.

"That I am. And I hope you are, too." Joan eased the

hammerlock. "Because if you are, you'll tell me who you talked to, and what you told them."

"I didn't talk to anybody." Tears rained from Elaine's eyes. She spoke through sobs. "Let me go."

Elaine was not going to talk. Not now. *Not to me*. She let go of Elaine's wrist.

Elaine rubbed her shoulder. "When I tell Kearney what you did to me, he'll be pissed."

"Really?"

Joan's face must have hardened, because Elaine took a step back.

Joan stayed in Elaine's face. "Go ahead. Tell Kearney. Remember that interrogation incident? He had to have two goons sucker punch me and tie me up to do anything to me. He doesn't scare me, but he should scare you." She poked Elaine's sternum in time to the last two words.

"Are we done here?" Elaine asked in too-late defiance.

"Just one thing," Joan said, still in Elaine's space.

She flinched.

"Knowing what you were going to do—or what you may have done, for all I know—why are you helping us find a new place to live?"

"I want to try to make amends for what I was going to do. The con." Elaine inched around the desk out of Joan's reach. "And I really do care for Kearney."

Joan had studied Elaine's body language, her furtive looks around the office, her lack of eye contact at times. "Okay, but since we're being honest here, Kearney is not my brother. We're longtime friends."

"I know." Elaine winced and bit her lower lip.

She had slipped. Honesty, finally, but she had revealed something she should not have known...

ନ୍ଦ୍ରନ୍ଦ

The office lights came on and Jeb strode into his office.

"Joan. What are you doing here?" he asked. "Did we have an appointment I forgot about?"

Joan put the Elaine puzzle away. She looked from Jeb to the open door.

CHAPTER 22

"Where's Duncan?" Joan asked.

"Want a drink?" Jeb said over his shoulder. Ice cubes clattered into a glass.

"No thanks."

"Jeb." Joan stood and took a step toward him. "I thought he had a meeting with you."

Jeb turned with a glass in his hand. "I haven't seen him since lunch."

"You didn't have a meeting with him about a job?"

"Duncan, Kearney, and I got together for lunch. We talked about old times, that's it. Why? What's up?"

"Where'd he spend the last couple hours?"

"I don't know. He didn't elaborate beyond saying he said he had something to take care of."

"What?"

Jeb smiled and hitched around his desk. "Relax. There's nowhere in the world he'd rather be than with you. He'll be here." He sat down.

Joan plopped into her chair. "Yeah, maybe he's with Kearney." She rubbed her head and wished she had taken the offer of a drink.

Jeb did not agree with her, which suggested he knew Kearney's whereabouts, and it did not include Duncan. Or maybe her mind was too muddled with the Elaine bullshit to understand his silence.

"Do you know if he's with Kearney?" Joan asked.

Jeb picked up the desk phone handset and punched keys. "Yeah, Tony. Duncan and Kearney, if they show up, tell them to come up to my office...thanks. Feel better?" he asked Joan.

"Thanks." She stood. "I think I'll take you up on that offer of a drink. Do you mind if I help myself?"

Jeb gestured for her to go ahead.

She put some ice in a glass and leaned on the liquor cabinet, rolling the cold, sweating glass across her forehead. When Kearney strode into the room, she expectantly looked past him.

He looked over his shoulder then back at Joan. "What's up? Tony said to come up here."

"Do you know where Duncan is?" Joan asked.

Kearney stopped midway across the office. "No. He wasn't with me."

"Want a JD and coke?" Joan asked. She started fixing it before he answered.

"I get the feeling I'm going to need it."

When she had finished making the drink, she looked at Jeb. "You said he had something to take care of." She handed Kearney his drink. "Do you know what it was?"

"He didn't go into details," Kearney said, taking the glass from her. "He looked upset. I thought it had something to do with you."

Jeb looked at Kearney then at Joan. "What's going on here?"

"I only know what he told me." Kearney took a sip. "He said he had to meet with someone. It sounded important." He motioned toward Jeb with his glass. "If it didn't have anything to do with Joan, was it for you?"

Joan put her glass on the tray that held several bottles of liquor. "I'm going to go find him." She headed toward the door.

"Joan. Stop," Jeb said. "What are you going to do? Knock on all one million doors in the surrounding area? Sit. You don't know where he is, but he knows where you are.

He'll show when he's done with whatever he's doing."

She grabbed her drink, spilling a little on the carpet. "You're right." She sat in her chair with a sigh. "I just hate being separated from him, not knowing where he is, or if he needs me." She took a long sip from her glass.

"I'm sure he didn't mean to worry you." Kearney patted her shoulder then sat in the chair next to her. "You're a little early. He probably thought he'd be back before you got here."

That still doesn't tell me where he is or if he might need me. Joan took in a long breath and let it out slowly. The room fell quiet while she thought through the situation. "He's been acting odd lately. Something's going on with him." She wanted to use Jeb as a sounding board about Duncan's contact with Agent Woyzeck, but Duncan had sworn her to secrecy.

He did not want anyone other than the two of them knowing about that conversation. He had said others would not understand and get stressed over a harmless chat.

"What did he say when you asked him about it?" Jeb asked.

"The first time I asked, he gave a vague answer. When I asked again later on he changed the subject, so I just let it go."

She rubbed her eyes.

"A brush with death can change a guy," Jeb said.

"I know, and I try to take that into consideration." She took a sip while searching for the right words. "Why won't he let me in?"

Jeb shook his head. "That's something you'll have to ask him yourself."

"Don't worry," Kearney said. "I'm sure whatever this is about, he will tell you when the time is right. Do you want us to see if we can get him to talk to one of us?"

"No, you're right. He'll tell me when I need to know." She crunched on an ice cube. "But if he says something to either of you, you'll tell me, right?"

"Sure. If you're distracted by something, you aren't focused, and you're no good to me." Jeb must have realized how harsh that sounded because he added, "I mean no good as part of a team on a job. You are important to me as a person. You know that, right?"

Joan walked to the bar to refill her glass. She held up the bottle of Jack Daniels. "Anyone else?"

Jeb waved her over. "Bring the bottle."

Without looking up from refilling the glasses, Joan said, "I don't suppose you talked to him on the phone this morning?" She looked up at Jeb.

"Me? No. Did he say that?"

Joan flopped into her chair and rubbed the sweating glass on her thigh, wiping the condensation onto her jeans.

"I can have someone do a check. Get a list of his calls," Jeb said. "Do you want me to do that?"

Joan shook her head. She didn't want the subject of this conversation to go beyond this room. "I—he'll—" She shrugged and swirled the whiskey in the glass. City sounds of horns and a faraway siren filled the room. Duncan's words came back to her. '*If you believe in me, we will spend the rest of our lives together.*' If his actions were strange because of that promise, she had a choice. She could hound it out of him, or she could wait out his timetable, let him work through it, and tell her at his discretion.

"Why did he marry me?" she mused aloud.

"What?" Jeb and Kearney said in unison.

"Why now?"

"He said he had missed out on all that time with you, he didn't want to wait—" Kearney started to say.

"Yeah, yeah, yeah. Got that." She sat straight in her chair and looked directly at Kearney. "Why now? Why not last year? Why not next year?" She raised her brows. "Why *now*?"

"The time was right?" Kearney said hesitantly.

"Right." Joan looked at Jeb. "The time was right. Right for what? Do you know and you aren't telling me?"

"Joan," Jeb said softly. "If I knew, I'd tell you. I don't like secrets any more than you do. It's bad for business."

"Why don't you text him? Find out where he is and when he'll get here," Kearney suggested. "I'm sure it will clear up everything."

"I texted him the rental information about five minutes before you guys came in. He hasn't answered that, yet."

A look passed between Jeb and Kearney. The eye contact and length of contact suggested they were worried.

Joan straightened in her chair and leaned on the desk. "What? What don't I know?" She looked back and forth between the two men. "You know something, don't you?"

"No, Joan, we don't, but it's becoming more evident there might be a need for concern," Kearney said. He leaned toward her. "Don't worry. Whatever it is, we'll take care of it."

"We aren't going to know anything until Duncan shows up or contacts you. When he does, we'll get to the bottom of it. Until then, let's talk about something else like how your afternoon with Elaine went."

Joan's eyes darted to Kearney. She took a breath and switched gears. "Well…" She leaned both forearms on Jeb's desk. "The whole 'build rapport' thing might be out the window."

Kearney shifted in his seat.

Jeb leaned forward. "Tell me she's not dead."

Joan grinned. "You talk like I'm a cold-blooded killer."

"Well…" Jeb made a motion with his hands like fanning cards on a table, indicating her reputation spoke for itself.

"Just for the record, I only killed bad guys—and only after they made the first move. So that said, she's still alive." Joan looked at Kearney. "She might boo-hoo to you about a bruised wrist, but other than that, she's not only alive, but well." Joan grimaced. "Her shoulder might be a little—"

"Dislocated?" Kearney offered.

"Strained. I shoved her arm into a hammerlock a little too aggressively. In my defense, I thought she was in better physical condition—but I did it for her own good."

"I gotta hear this," Jeb said.

"If you had been there," Joan said to Kearney, "you would have done worse. The way I see it, she got off light."

"Aren't you the benevolent one?" Jeb said.

"Were we right about the con?" Kearney asked.

"You were right, but that's not all. Rob—" Joan looked at Jeb. "You remember Rob Reddington?"

Jeb nodded.

"They planned for him to con me out of the rest of Duncan's estate." Joan snorted. "Yeah, like that would happen. I didn't have access to the estate until—" She looked at Jeb and decided to move on. "Anyway, Rob called off his part of the deal when he met Duncan." Joan's breath shallowed. She looked from Jeb to Kearney and back to Jeb. "You don't think Duncan went after Rob."

"Nah, he would have told me if he planned to do that," Kearney said. "He'd know I'd want to be part of it."

"Did Duncan know about Rob's part in all this?" Jeb asked.

"Not exactly," Joan said. She thought about the conversation in the kitchen after Duncan had met Rob. "But he voiced a feeling that something wasn't on the up-and-up with Rob."

Joan chewed her bottom lip, not wanting to think of the other possibility. She looked at the two men who were the closest thing to friends she had. "Unless…"

"Unless, what?" Jeb asked.

Joan shook her head. "Nothing. I'm thinking crazy."

"Go ahead, try us," Kearney said.

"You don't think—" It was too ridiculous to verbalize. She said it anyway. "You think there's another woman?"

"No, for God sakes, Joan," Jeb said.

"There's never been any other woman than you," Kearney said. "Why would he marry you, if there was another woman?"

"I'm trying to think outside the box."

"That's way outside the box," Jeb said.

Kearney placed a hand on her arm. "There is no one but you for him, Joan. And if he's nothing else, he's loyal."

She looked at Jeb who nodded in affirmation.

❧❦❧

Duncan looked over his shoulder at the other patrons in the café. They were absorbed in their own conversations. It didn't look right, a forty-six year old man sitting with a twenty-two year old girl...woman, holding hands. His skin stung where it touched Lucinda-Mae's hand. He finally married the woman he loved more than life itself. This country girl could ruin not only his marriage, but his ticket out of this life. She had to go home.

When Lucinda-Mae gawked at a man in a multi-colored Mohawk, Duncan snuck a peek at his watch and winced—five-thirty—not enough time. He had less than a half hour to button this up, and put an end to this mistake that had followed him from the Ozark Mountains to Yonkers, NY.

He knew she wasn't pregnant. He had used protection. A baby would have caused devastating ripples in his relationship with Joan, but he could have worked it out. Given time, Joan would have honed in on the fact that an innocent life carried a part of him. Pregnancy would have been difficult to work through, but do-able.

This was worse. Lucinda-Mae was acting like she was in love.

She turned her blue eyes back to Duncan and he felt...nothing. He couldn't even muster hatred. She represented nothing more than a problem to be solved.

She had to go.

He thought back to the first time he had seen Lucinda-Mae. He had stopped at the ma-and-pa combination general store, bait shop, and gas station at the intersection of roads that went to Nowhere and Some Unknown Place. She stood with her back to him, pumping gas into a beat up, red pickup truck. She looked over her shoulder at him and a breeze that smelled of rain blew a strand of straw-colored hair across her face. Denim cut-offs revealed athletic legs— long and firm. After a long recovery that had been touch and go at times, he finally felt healthy and strong. He had been alone for a long time. She had locked eyes with him and he had walked over to her. Even then, he had felt something wasn't quite right. Off-center enough to feel it, but not enough to bring it into focus. He should have listened to his gut.

What had he been thinking?

"What are you thinking, honey?" Lucinda-Mae's mild Southern accent brought him out of his reverie. It had been enticing at one time.

"You have to go home, Luci." Maybe blunt words would sink in. Twenty minutes of talking nice had gotten him nowhere.

"I know you don't mean that. You said you were leavin' only because you had to take care of some business." She squeezed his hand. "When you didn't come back, I came lookin' for you. That must show you how much I love you."

This back country girl navigated her way across country and through a large, international airport. Her eyes, once soft and alluring, now looked more like they were hiding something. Again, too vague to pinpoint. "Look, I told you I'm not a nice guy. You shouldn't get attached to me." He gave her a hard look. "I never told you I loved you."

"Oh, honey, I know you didn't actually say it, but you were so loving and attentive. Your actions spoke louder than any ol' words."

"I'm married. I'm happily married. There's no place for you in my life."

"You told me you weren't married. Or I wouldn't never have—"

"I wasn't married at the time, but I am now."

She looked at his cell phone. "Is that who that text was from? Your wife?"

"Yes, and I have to get back before she gets suspicious."

"I don't believe for a second that you're married. Honey, it's easy to buy a ring and put it on." She reached out to touch his cheek. "You're just afraid of a little commitment."

He grabbed Lucinda-Mae's hand before it reached his face. "I am committed. To my wife." He squeezed her hand. "Very committed."

"Ow." Lucinda-Mae shook out her hand. "Maybe I should tell your wife about me."

"That, Luci, would be a very bad idea."

"She'll leave you?" A spark of interest glittered in her eyes. "You'll be in big trouble?"

"No. *You'll* be in big trouble. You won't fare well against her."

"I'm tougher than I look. I grew up on a farm with two brothers."

"It won't be enough." Duncan leaned back and raised his hands as if to say 'look at me.' "I'm no slouch, and I'd have a hard time dealing with her. You have no idea, Luci. None. Let it go. Go home."

"That's what I'll do. I'll call her." Lucinda-Mae grabbed for Duncan's phone, but he got it first.

"Don't even think about it," he said, emphasizing each word. He slid the phone into his pocket. "Then there's the age difference."

Lucinda-Mae's eyes tracked from his pocket to his eyes. "You kept up with me just fine."

"It was only a few times. And we can't stay in bed twenty-four hours a day."

"We could have a great life together. We have so much in common."

"No, we don't. You don't know anything about me." This nice talk grated on his nerves. He clamped his eyes shut and longed for a to-the-point conversation with Joan. "I'm not a nice guy, Luci-Mae."

"I don't believe that. You were nothing but nice with me."

Duncan leaned across the table. "I acted nice because I wanted something from you." His voice got low and menacing. "And I wanted you to keep giving it to me." He cringed inwardly at saying mean things to this girl who had so willingly given it all to him. She didn't deserve the bad side of him, the side he had so diligently hidden from her. He mentally kicked himself in the ass for pretending to be an honorable person, for denying her the opportunity to make the decision to be with a crude, violent man or walk away. It would have made things easier now. Or possibly this whole conversation would have never come to pass.

Lucinda-Mae's eyes got glassy. She sniffled and reached into her bag.

Oh, no. After tears comes revenge. I have to fix this fast. "Don't cry. I didn't mean what I said just now. When I met you I wanted you to feel comfortable and safe in my presence."

She blew her nose. "But you're a different man now."

Why hadn't he thought of this good-man-bad-man track earlier? "Yes, I'm a different man now. In the city I am the man I've become."

"So come back to Arkansas with me." The corners of her mouth turned up into a coy smile. "Be the sweet, sexy man you were when you were there."

His gut told him something was not right. It was a million-to-one shot that she could have followed and located him in New York City. Her voice was fake. Coyness—phony. This whole scenario—bogus. But fake or not, he had to deal with it and put an end to this slip-up.

"I'm a city man, Luci." He held both her hands, and recognized the mistake right away. A look of hope came into her eyes. He plowed forward. "Let me buy a plane ticket for you so you can go home."

She yanked her hands out of his and stood up. She poured into her words every ounce of southern cachet she could muster. "Buy me a plane ticket home? Honey, you can't just use me then send me away. I am not a call girl. I'm not going anywhere."

Everyone in the café turned their attention to them now. Lucinda-Mae had just made their personal business the world's business. He didn't need the world in his business. It had far greater consequences than a jilted woman telling his wife he had cheated on her. That would be bad enough, but if he didn't pull this off, Joan would go to jail, and he needed her trust and love to keep that from happening.

He stood and guided Lucinda-Mae out of the café. She pulled her arm away from him, but went along anyway. He would continue this conversation in the cab—on the way to her hotel to pick up her things then to the airport. Acting like a groveling, sweet man not only depleted what little manners he had, it was degrading and distasteful. Everything about Lucinda-Mae aggravated him.

He would have to text Joan and tell her…what? He got caught in traffic taking the "other woman" to the airport? No. She couldn't find out about Lucinda-Mae and the horrid mistake he had made.

Lucinda-Mae would get on that plane.

෴

"Hey, Woyzeck, I got a hit. Archer used his cell," Agent Liz Merrill said into her phone.

"And?" Special Agent Woyzeck said. A hint of urgency tinged Liz's voice.

"He just bought a one-way ticket to Little Rock."

"What?" He could not have heard her correctly. Joan was here. Duncan wouldn't run off and leave her. A one-way ticket. Could he be sending her away? "Do you know his location?"

"The Holiday Inn downtown."

"What's he doing in a hotel in Manhattan?" Agent

Woyzeck shoved his feet into his shoes and grabbed his sport coat. "Meet me there."

"They aren't there anymore. Wait where you are," Agent Merrill said. "I'll pick you up. We'll travel faster in a car with flashing lights and a siren."

"I'll be out front waiting." Agent Woyzeck ran his fingers over his hair. "Do you think Danielson could send a couple agents over to the hotel to check that out?"

"You know I can't do that. If he finds out I'm helping you with this investigation against his express orders, I'll lose my job. And so will you."

"Okay, I guess I owe you some thanks for all your help."

"You bet you do. I'll be there in five."

When they reached the departures drop-off area Agent Merrill showed her ID to the security while Agent Woyzeck ran in to the ticket counter to see if Duncan had already checked in.

On his way back to the drop off area, Agent Woyzeck shook his head, indicating Duncan had not checked in yet. The two agents parted, found an inconspicuous spot, and waited. Agent Woyzeck hoped for an uneventful takedown, but past experience did not give him a lot of hope.

Special Agent Woyzeck settled on the terminal side of the exterior glass wall. If Archer spotted him, he would be tipped off. He wanted Archer, but wanted the takedown to be uneventful and safe. Without Archer, there would be no Joan Bowman.

∽∾∽

Duncan sat in the back of the cab, thumbing through Joan's email, and looking out the corner of his eye at a much quieter Lucinda-Mae. She had vehemently refused to pack her bags, and stood with arms crossed yelling threats while he had jammed her clothes into her suitcase. When he swept her personal hygiene clutter into her carry-on with a

sweep of his arm across the bathroom counter, the name
calling started. They had left the room with his hand tightly
on her elbow. She yanked it out of his grasp in the elevator
and pouted the whole ride down to the lobby. At least she
had had the presence of mind to refrain from making a scene while he had checked her out of the hotel. The act of getting into the cab and heading for the airport must have
brought a sense of reality, because she sat quietly on the
other side of the cab, watching the city sights slide past.

He reached out and held her hand, not because he felt
anything toward her, because he didn't want her jumping
out of the cab before they got to the airport. This calm un-
nerved him.

He concentrated on his phone and sent a text to Joan: All
three houses look good. I especially like the split level.

He looked up at Lucinda-Mae smiling at him. His shoulder muscles prickled, and his neck muscles tightened. She
could have come to grips with going back to Arkansas, but
the sweet smile didn't fit in with her behavior in the room.
He couldn't get her out of his life fast enough.

He leaned forward and spoke to the driver. "How much
longer until we get to the airport?"

"We are almost there." The driver spoke with an Arabic
accent and his words were barely intelligible. He spoke over
his shoulder. "Fifteen minutes. Maybe thirty with this traffic."

Dammit. Thirty minutes too many. "Thank you," Duncan
said and leaned back. When he did, Lucinda-Mae slid
across the seat and leaned her head against his shoulder.
She put her free hand across his waist and sighed. He covered her hand with his just to make sure it did not wander
anywhere else. If this position kept her calm and quiet, he
would endure the thirty minutes.

The traffic slowed to a stop, and he looked out the window. He thought of the meeting with her two brothers when
they had found out about him and their sister. They were
big boys, one older and one younger than Lucinda-Mae,

who were living proof of how farm work can chisel a man's body. Living in synergy with nature gave them a clearheaded perception of the situation. They knew the deal. His relationship with Luci-Mae was physical, nothing more—and they didn't like it. Not that they had not done the same thing at one time or another, but Duncan perpetrated it on their sister.

It had been two weeks into the relationship when they warned him off. He had had his release. He should have taken the opportunity to take his leave and ended it then. He should have come to Joan, but his pride wouldn't let him be chased off by a couple farm boys. He shook his head and looked down at Lucinda-Mae leaning on his chest. If he had been well enough for sex, he had been well enough to travel. If only he had swallowed his pride and listened to her brothers. He would have left them feeling like they had done their duty protecting their sister from a dog like him. So what if she would have thought less of him for running from her brothers? He would have never seen her again. Now, in this taxicab, in this worrisome jam, that sounded like a great idea. A sudden urge to be with Joan made him want to get out and jog to the terminal, Lucinda-Mae and her purple luggage bouncing behind him.

His muscles must have responded to his desire to get out of the car because Lucinda-Mae looked up at him. "Is everything all right, honey?" She tried to move her hand, but he held it tight against his waist. "Are you thinking about your wife and how mad she'll be?"

Duncan's lips tightened. *Fucking bitch.* The impulse to slap her and shake the meanness out of her surged through him. "No." She had no clue how easy it would be for him to find a corner of the terminal out of the range of the cameras and snap her neck. But it was her lucky day—in the glow of Joan's love, that man no longer existed. He looked out the window and added, "I can't wait to get you on that plane."

His cell beeped that he had a text. He released her hand on his waist and pulled his phone out of his pocket. He read it and texted back: *Stuck in traffic. I can't explain now. Soon.*

Lucinda-Mae watched him thumb out the answer to the text, and her eyes followed the phone all the way to his chest pocket. Then up to his hard, blue eyes.

ↄ∕ↄↄↄ

Joan set her phone on Jeb's desk. "He says he can't explain now, but says he'll be here soon."

"May I?" Jeb asked, pointing to the phone.

Joan waved her hand in permission. She watched him read through the texts.

"Do you have codes for trouble or duress?" Jeb asked.

"Yes. And he hasn't used them."

Jeb frowned. "You said he was distracted, like he was working through something."

"Yes, why?"

"I don't know." Jeb looked at Kearney. "You know him better than me." He motioned with the phone toward Kearney. "Do you mind?"

"No. Go ahead," Joan said to Kearney.

He reached for the phone.

"Maybe you can read something into those texts." She looked at Jeb. "Why did you ask me about him being distracted?"

Jeb rotated a silver pen end over end between his fingers, his eyes focused on the middle of his desk.

"I don't read anything other than what the words say," Kearney said, looking up and seeing Jeb's thoughtfulness.

"If you have an idea, share it, Jeb," Joan said.

"This is going to sound ridiculous." He shook his head and looked up at Joan. "But I received a tip that Durham Security is under investigation. There might be someone on the inside."

"And you think it's Duncan? That's the most outlandish—"

"I said it was ridiculous. But I have to look at everybody. And that includes Duncan. And you two."

Silence fell between them.

"Look," Jeb finally said, "to be perfectly honest, I don't think it's Duncan, but the safety of my other employees depends on me ferreting out this rat." He exhaled loudly and had an "I'm sorry" look in his eyes. "Until I can exclude someone for certain, I can't allow myself to play favorites."

"But surely—" Joan looked to Kearney for back up. "Duncan is the most loyal person I know. And he would never turn on you...on any of us."

"Have you excluded anyone?" Kearney asked.

"Champ. He has been here from the beginning. It has to be someone who is relatively new."

"Then that excludes Duncan," Joan said.

"I would tend to agree. He has been a part of Durham Security for a long time, but he was away over the past few years fighting other battles, as you well know."

"Claude fits then, too," Kearney said. "He was in jail for a while. And you have to admit he got out on a real sweet, good conduct deal."

Jeb nodded. "And you two are the newest additions."

"What about Darren?" Joan asked. "He came after me."

"He worked for the Chicago group before moving here, but you're right. And he's on the short list." Jeb poured another drink and refilled the other glasses. "Don't say anything to anyone. I'm keeping this close to the vest."

"Who else knows?" Kearney asked.

"Just Champ and Claude." Jeb's brow wrinkled and his eyes flashed up to Joan. "For the record, Claude thinks it's you."

Joan leaned back in her chair, ignoring the refilled glass. "Well, I can see why I'd be suspect. There's my history of being a state's witness during my time in the Legion, and I've been acting a little squirrely lately." She rubbed her forehead. "But I know it's not me." She looked up at Jeb. "You know that, right?"

Jeb leaned forward and said, "For what it's worth, I don't really think it's either of you two. Or else I wouldn't have told you." He pointed two fingers at his eyes, then swiveled his wrist so they were pointing at Joan and Kearney. "But I have my eyes on you."

Joan relaxed and fought a smile at Jeb's lame joke.

❧❧❧

When the taxi slowed and pulled up to the curb in front of the Southwest departures terminal, the hair on the back of Duncan's neck stood up. He tried to shake the feeling, but it only got worse.

"Wait here," he said to Lucinda-Mae.

"You were in such a hurry to get me here, now you don't want me to get out?" She slid across the seat, but the door closed on her.

Duncan nodded to the driver who had popped the trunk to get the luggage. While he placed it on the curb, Duncan scanned the long expanse between the terminals trying to pinpoint anything out of place. Spiders crawled across his shoulders. There were too many cars at the curb, too many people lacking a sense of urgency. They passed a car on their way in, and it was still parked in the same spot. He studied people getting out of cars behind them and the car that just pulled up in front of them. But there was nothing he couldn't explain away. They were people simply going about their business

He paid the driver then opened the door and pulled Lucinda-Mae's arm. "Let's go."

Lucinda-Mae threw her arms around him. Her words were muffled against his chest. "Don't make me go. I won't tell your wife. Just let me stay."

He pushed her shoulders until he could look her in the eyes. "This is the best thing for you. You don't have any idea what you're getting into."

Lucinda-Mae hung her head, sniffled, and slid something into her pocket. She wiped her nose with a tissue and turned toward the terminal.

They took two steps and Agents Woyzeck and Merrill descended on them, shouting to show their hands and get on the ground.

Duncan eyed the taxi that had just pulled in a few feet from him. The driver got out of the car, opened the trunk, and started offloading the luggage. Duncan made a break for the driver's door of the cab, climbed in, and took off away from the terminal. In the rearview mirror he saw Lucinda-Mae facing the federal agents and handing them something.

CHAPTER 23

When Duncan finally walked into Jeb's office, Joan, Kearney, and Jeb stood and faced him.

He strode up to Joan, threw his arms around her, and squeezed her. "I love you, baby. More than you'll ever know."

She pushed away from him. "I think you owe me an explanation." She gave his shoulder a friendly shove. "I was worried about you."

Duncan looked at Kearney and Jeb. "Can I speak with Joan alone?"

"Under other circumstances I would let you two be alone," Jeb said. "But you have misled all of us, involving all of us in some hazy scheme. I guess you thought we wouldn't talk to each other."

"I intended to be back on time, but I got caught in traffic."

"So much traffic that you are two hours late? No, Duncan, you owe all of us an explanation."

"I really need to speak to you alone." He looked at Joan for so long, she shifted under his gaze. He pulled her into his arms and said over her shoulder, "Let me talk to my wife, then I will explain to the rest of you why I was so late."

Jeb's phone rang. He listened for a few seconds before looking up at Kearney, then Duncan. "I'm needed downstairs. We have a situation. Kearney come with me. Duncan, I guess you got your chance to talk to Joan."

Duncan spotted the bottle of Jack Daniels on the desk. He grabbed Joan's glass and downed the amber liquid. "Man, I needed that." He filled the glass and motioned for Joan to sit on the couch. He sat down beside her.

She shook her head when he gestured with the glass to offer her some. He took a couple sips and set the glass on the coffee table. He gripped both her hands and looked into her eyes.

She stiffened. *Oh, God, please don't let it be another woman.*

"Joan, I love you more than I've ever loved any other woman. And I know you love me the same."

"I hear a 'but' coming," Joan said.

"No 'buts.' I have something to tell you. I tried to tell you the day I came back but couldn't. Something has happened, and I have to tell you before—"

Kearney slammed through the door, out of breath from running up the stairs. "Duncan do you know where your phone is?"

Duncan patted his shirt pocket. His hand stopped at the spot where the phone should have been. A sweat broke out all over his body. He looked at Joan. "I must have lost it somewhere."

"We know where it is." Kearney glared at Duncan. "You need to come downstairs. Now." He jerked his eyes to Joan. "Joan, you need to stay here."

She stood when Duncan stood. "Why? What's wrong?"

"Stay here, Joan, please," Duncan said. He pulled her into his arms. "Promise me you'll stay here until I can talk to you."

"I will not stay here. Since when do you *not* want me by your side?"

She brushed past him. Kearney blocked the doorway. "Let me past."

"Joan." The severity of Duncan's tone made her flinch. She didn't turn to face him when he said, "Stay here. I wouldn't make you stay out of this if it wasn't important."

She looked at Kearney.

"Joan, it would be better for everyone if you stayed here," he said in a controlled voice. "We'll call you when it's clear."

"Okay," Joan said. "But if you don't call me in five minutes, I'm coming down."

Duncan hugged her and kissed her on the lips. "Fair enough. I'm sorry about this."

He disappeared with Kearney.

☙❧☙

Joan waited ten seconds, then followed them. These men weren't going to tell her what to do. They lumbered down the stairs in front of her, unaware of her quiet descent behind them. By the time she reached the kitchen, they had already disappeared through the other door into Notches.

She slipped into Notches, took one look around, and the world stopped turning.

A skinny blonde girl stood in the middle of Notches looking around at the tense, scary men. These men could handle anything, but looked unsure how to handle this situation.

"But, Dennis, I love you," she whimpered.

"I told you," Duncan said. "You have to go back to Arkansas. There is no place for you in my life here."

"In your life…here?" Joan asked, standing just inside the bar. "Like this woman would have a place in your life somewhere else?" She took several steps forward. "And she calls you by your given name in public? I don't even call you 'Dennis' in public."

Every eye in the room turned to Joan. She strode across the creaking floor. Darren tried to stop her, but she blocked his arm and planted a palm heel into his ribs. He cringed, held his side, and let her pass. Kearney grabbed her arm and she knocked him on his ass with a palm heel uppercut. She continued her march toward the woman, who took a couple steps back, seeing Joan layout two men with hardly a break in stride.

Carmine stepped between Joan and the woman. "We have this under control. Take it easy before someone else gets hurt."

"Get out of my way."

"Step back," Carmine said, one hand on the butt of his gun, the other in front of him, palm forward. "There's more going on here than you and Duncan and this chippy."

"Like what? This is damn important to me."

Carmine crossed his arms and rested them on his belly. "I am the Sergeant-at-Arms, and I can use whatever force necessary to maintain order."

"A title isn't going to protect you."

"You may take me out, maybe not," he said, nodding past her right shoulder. "But you can't take both of us."

Joan turned her head just enough to glance over her shoulder and see Claude standing right behind her.

Duncan grabbed Joan's arm to turn her toward him. "I wanted to tell you before—"

"Before I came face to face with your other woman? Another woman, Duncan?" She stepped into his space and poked a finger at his chest. "I thought you were different. I believed you when you said you would never want anyone else." Tears blurred the room. She pushed her way past the men to the relative safety of the kitchen.

She felt Duncan behind her and wanted to be anywhere, except in his presence. But she stopped to steady herself on the stainless steel prep table. Life drained out of her. Questions spilled out of her emptiness. "Why? When? How long?" She took a breath. "How old is she?"

Duncan encircled her with his arms. She elbowed him to get him to back off.

He ran his hand over his hair and shook his head. "She is—"

"Undamaged?" Joan blurted out. Her shoulders slumped. "I bet she isn't covered in scars and doesn't have the ghosts of dead people keeping her awake at night." Tears over-flowed her lids and rolled down her cheeks.

"I was going to say 'nothing.' She is nothing to me."

"Yeah? Well, she must have been *something* to come all the way from Arkansas to get back into your life."

"It was a mistake."

Joan turned and glared at Duncan. "No fucking shit."

He reached for her but hesitated. "It was nothing but a tragic mistake."

"And how old is she? Twenty? You had to pick someone who checked all the boxes I don't?" Joan used her fingers to count off the differences. "Innocent, perfect body, young?"

"Don't, Joan. Don't do this to yourself."

"Myself? I did this to myself?" She shook her head and turned her back on him. Her eyes were awash with tears that had not yet flowed. Her nose stung. She pressed on it with the back of her hand.

"I mean don't put yourself down. You are way better than her in so many ways." He took a tentative step toward her. "You are beautiful. Your scars don't bother me. To me they're signs of your strength and fortitude. You don't play games. Dealing with Lucinda-Mae's youth and manipula-tions is draining."

"Oh, poor baby." Joan wiped her cheeks with the shoul-der of her tee shirt. Then turned to face him. "I'll bet all that sex with a twenty year old was so exhausting."

"She's twenty-two and—"

Joan squared off and took a step toward him. Duncan took a step backward.

He put his hands up palms out. "I'm not saying this right. I should have come straight here when I felt healthy. After many weeks alone in a hunting cabin in the moun-tains, I was lonely. I should have—"

"Thought farther than the tip of your dick?" Joan fin-ished for him. She pointed toward Notches. "So this is why you were in New York so long before coming to me."

The words must have stung because he rubbed his eyes with his thumb and forefinger. "No. What I told you about that was the truth. I'm sorry. If I could go back in time and undo this I would. I never meant to hurt you."

"Why did you do it?"

"I struggled to get well. There were infections, then the physical recovery. I was finally healthy—"

"Healthy enough for sex but not healthy enough to travel?"

"I should have come straight to you when I was healthy. I know that now." He reached out and caressed her arm. "It didn't mean anything. It was only a couple times, and it was purely physical. It—I know this doesn't excuse what I've done, but after being on the brink of death for so any weeks, it made me feel alive for the first time in months."

"Sure, now that you've had your fun, you're ready to settle down with the older, used up woman scarred from having your back. I don't want pity love, Duncan."

"It's not pity love. You are the greatest woman in the world, and I'm lucky you chose to marry me. I owe you for everything that I am. Tell me you'll work through this with me."

She didn't respond right away. "Why did you marry me?" she asked in a soft, barely audible voice.

"What did you say?" He took a step closer.

"Why did you marry me?" Joan waved her hand toward Notches. "You obviously still want to be with other women. Was it guilt?"

"I married you because I love you. And only you."

"Oh, that's just so sweet," Joan hissed at him. She wished the tears would stop. She didn't want to be weak in front of Duncan. Not now.

"I married you because I want the world to know that you are the woman I want to wake up next to every morning for the rest of my life."

"The rest of your life could be staring you in the face, right here, right now."

"Please, Joan, don't be like this. We can work this out. I'll do anything to make this up to you. I can't stand seeing you in so much pain because of my stupid mistake. I am so sorry."

She saw the hurt in his eyes. She had never seen him in pain. He was probably telling the truth, but it was too late for that. He should have thought about the consequences before he gave in to temptation.

"I'm sorry, too, Duncan. But we've been through too much. I'm tired. I'm spent." She brushed past him. He tried to stop her, but she blocked his arm and kept going. "We're spent."

He followed her. "Joan, don't go. We vowed to be together for better or for worse. It won't get any worse than this. When we get past this, it'll be clear sailing. I'll make it up to you for the rest of your life."

She spun around. "So that's why you married me."

He stayed silent, looking unsure where she was going with that statement.

"You know how I am with oaths. I see it now. Get me to vow to be with you forever." She waved her arm in a large circle, a gesture to take in the world. "And you can go about your merry way fucking any woman who will open her legs for you."

"It's not like that. If you'll just let me explain how it happened—"

"Do not say: 'It was an accident. Or I swear, I'll drop you where you stand.'"

"I...she—" The look of discovery on Joan's face stopped him in his tracks.

"Jeb said there was someone on the inside working the feds' investigation. I bet you're the inside guy," she said. "Yeah. You don't have an ounce of loyalty. It would be easy for you to give up your friends."

"Jeb knows?" Duncan let go of Joan and paced to the far

end of the prep table. "Jesus Christ. I wanted to take care of it before he found out." He shook his head and rubbed his beard with the back of his hand. "Dammit. I'd hoped for more time." He turned and studied her face before continuing. "Joan, you gotta trust me. I know it's going to be really hard now, especially—" His glassy eyes looked past her at the door to Notches. "But I promise you won't go to jail."

Joan studied his demeanor. *What the hell? This has rocked his world more than Lucinda-Mae's appearance.* The urge to comfort him surged through her body. This was something more than an ill-considered roll in the hay. She crossed her arms. *I don't give a shit if his world is falling apart. I don't care about him or his problems anymore. He's on his own.*

She put up her hand in dismissal. "You know, Dennis—if I may call you that. I don't know and I don't care what's going on in your head. I am done. Done with this life and done with you."

She flung open the door and strode into Notches. She heard Duncan rushing behind her to stop her, but kept going.

She walked across the floor without looking at the operatives who stood in place watching her pass. When she stood face to face with Carmine, she shrugged off her leather jacket, dropped it to the floor, and pulled off her tee shirt.

Carmine put out his arm to stop her. "Joan, you're out of control—" he started to say, but something about Joan exposing herself—and the nastiness of the scars—in a roomful of men made him hesitate.

"Lucinda-Mae, see these." Joan stepped around Carmine and pointed to her chest and stomach.

Lucinda-Mae gasped. Her eyes darted from the knife in the sheath on Joan's belt and back to the scars, unsure of which to concentrate on.

Joan hesitated. There was a maturity to Lucinda-Mae's eyes. A hardness. A lack of fear. Quiet restraint, but no fear. Joan had just pulled off her tee shirt, exposing gruesome scars. Horror, or at least shock, would have been more fitting.

"There are more I can't show you," Joan said, barreling on. "And many more you can't see because they're up here." She pointed to her head. "But this is your future if you stay with Dennis. Go. Go now. Go fast."

"Joan, stop," Duncan said. "You've gone too far."

"Oh, really?" Joan put her tee shirt back on and turned to face Duncan. Her face felt hard, wet, and lined with heartache. "I suppose I went too far the day I led that assault to save your worthless, cheating ass when *La Espada* kidnapped you. Do you know how many men I killed to get to you?" She leaned toward him, stopping inches from his face. "You probably don't even care." She pointed a finger at him. "I rue the day I saved you from *La Espada*. They were going to beat you to death. I should have let them."

She turned on her heel and walked out the door.

When she got into Duncan's car, she broke down and cried long, loud sobs. She had to get out the emotion before driving on the city streets, but it seemed like the sobbing would never end. Her mother's poem flashed into her mind: *And broken now upon the ground, Within his sick embrace—*

A commotion outside Notches made her look over her shoulder.

Jeb pushed Duncan backward. "You messed up the best thing that ever happened to you."

"I should have known you'd move in on my woman." Duncan squared off with Jeb. "It's not like it's the first time."

"This is different." Jeb stood face to face with Duncan. "Get in there and clean up the mess you made," Jeb growled. "I'll take care of Joan."

Kearney appeared and said something Joan couldn't make out.

She opened the car door to get out to break up the argument before it got physical, but a rap on the passenger window made her stop and turn around. She expected to see Duncan, but instead Jeb stood there holding up her jacket.

"Where are you going?" he asked through the closed window.

"Why would you care? Go be the wingman for your friend. He's free to womanize openly."

"You're my friend, too, and I'm concerned about you." He pointed at the door lock. "Let me in. I'm not going to try to talk you into going back inside. I just want to sit with you for a while."

Joan unlocked the door, and when Jeb slid into the passenger seat, she said, "So now we're friends again?"

"'Together again, my tears have stopped falling,'" he said, mocking the Buck Owens Country Western song.

His comic response cooled the heat of her anger.

He opened the glovebox and rummaged around before pulling out several crumpled up napkins. "Here. You have snot under your nose."

She eyed the wad of napkins.

"They're clean, I think." He picked up her hand and placed them in her palm. "Even if they were used, they're better than that crap on your face."

"Aren't you the sweet talker?" she said before blowing her nose. She rested her forehead on the steering wheel. "I thought he was different. You knew, didn't you?"

"No. No, Joan, I didn't. If I had, I would have made him own up to it. If it makes you feel any better, I don't think this…whatever it was…happened here. I get the sense it all went down in Arkansas, and he left it behind. But the mistake followed him."

Sobs gave way to sniffling.

A raindrop plopped onto the windshield. A second or two later, another hit. They watched the rain pick up its rhythm until it blurred the alley around them.

"He loves you," Jeb said.

"Yeah," Joan snorted. "He has a funny way of showing it." She took a long inhale and let it out. "I'm going to move on from this. I'm going to move to the middle of nowhere. Maybe set up a meditation ashram. Make trails for walking meditation. Become one with nature."

"Trouble will find you. You know that, right?"

"So now you're an Iron Angel Bad Karma believer?"

Jeb ticked the list on his fingers. "I lose an operator in a routine mission. Kearney attracts a con. *You* attract a con. After ten years of clear sailing, my company is under investigation—maybe with the help of an insider. Lucinda-Mae shows up. You and Duncan are at odds." He turned so he sat in the corner of the seat and the door. "Yeah. I guess you could say I'm a card-carrying member of the Iron Angel Bad Karma cult."

"Things will be different. It'll be a different me. I'll create a bubble of peace around me that the Iron Angel Bad Karma won't dare to invade."

"Good luck with that. Let me know how it turns out for you."

The renewed sense of purpose didn't fill her gut-wrenching emptiness or ease the pain of betrayal, but it cleared her head and gave her mental momentum. She tossed the keys to Jeb. "You drive."

After they had switched seats, he asked, "Where are we going?"

"New Jersey."

eɔɐɔ

"We've circled these same eight blocks twice," Jeb said, forty-five minutes later. "Do you even know where we're going?"

"I know where we're going," Joan said. "I'm making sure federal agents aren't sitting on the house yet."

"What house?"

"Park there." Joan pointed to a dark spot where the road was shaded from the street lights by an ancient chestnut tree. She unclipped her seatbelt and proceeded to unbuckle her belt.

Jeb turned in the seat and tensed. "What are you doing?"

"I thought since Duncan cheated on me, I'd fuck one of his best friends." She motioned to the backseat with her eyes.

"I appreciate the proposition, and I must confess to fantasies of taking you for a test drive. But I'm uncomfortable with this."

"I was kidding."

"I have a confession to make," Jeb said.

Joan hesitated, her hand on her belt buckle.

"I was playing you. In the beginning. I thought you were complicit in Duncan's death somehow. Or at the very least, you were trying to con me to get his money. I guess it was just my way of mourning the loss of a longtime friend."

Silence filled the car.

Her stomach felt like barbed wire cinched around it. "You still think that?"

Jeb pulled the keys from the ignition and dropped his hands into his lap. "Dammit. I shouldn't have said anything. The short answer: No. I think you are who you say you are."

"Back in the alley behind Notches, when Duncan accused you of making a play for me, were you?"

"No. Yes. Shit." Jeb rubbed his jaw where a five o'clock shadow blurred the edges of his fledgling beard. "Since I've already stepped into the honesty arena, let me say I was playing you, until I began to see what Duncan had seen in you. Then I started to…have feelings for you."

Joan remained silent.

"When Duncan arrived on the scene I saw how much you loved each other."

Joan snorted and looked out the side window.

"Regardless of what he may have done in Arkansas, he loves you. It's painfully obvious, and I can't interfere with that."

After a brief, harsh silence, Joan said, "In the spirit of being honest, I thought you were playing me. So I was…in the beginning, I playing you. To find out what your game was. Now I know."

"Joan, if there's ever anything you need—money, fake ID, anything—promise me you'll come to me and let me make this up to you."

Both tired domestic soldiers gazed out the windshield. They sat alone with their own thoughts, Jeb's offer floating between them.

Jeb broke the silence. "What are we doing here?"

"Right now, I'm taking off my knife." Joan pulled the belt out of the loops and tossed it with the sheath into the back seat. "I don't need it anymore and it'll scare Auntie Gertie."

"Who's Auntie Gertie?"

Joan opened the car door. "You'll see."

On the way out of the car, Jeb muttered, "I can't wait."

They walked along the damp sidewalk. Joan stopped and listened. The siren of a police car got louder. She watched the blue lights blink through the intersection behind them as it raced past. Joan continued her walk as if the sirens never sliced the night. She greeted a man standing at a bus stop. He nodded and turned to look up the street for the arrival of his bus.

Jeb swiped the back of his neck. The rain had stopped, but the leaves still dropped their wet payload when it became too heavy. "How much farther?" he asked.

Joan took in large gulps of air—New Jersey air, but it brought back a sense of comfort and familiarity. She felt Jeb's eyes on her.

"What?" she asked him.

"You're different here."

"How so?"

"You're calmer. Almost light hearted."

"Yes." She tugged his sleeve and stopped walking. "Yes, I am."

They stood, hands in pockets, looking across a tree-lined, street at a brick, suburban house in the middle of a block that looked like any other block. A glassed-in porch spanned the front of the house. Similar houses flanked it. A handcrafted, cloth patchwork wreath hung on the front door. In the front window one candle glowed, presumably one of those electric ones with a light sensor so it would come on at dusk. A yellow outside light on the side of the house lit the driveway that disappeared into a detached garage in the back.

"What are we looking at?" Jeb asked.

Joan linked her arm in his and smiled up at him. "Home."

"Funny. I never would have pegged you for a Jersey girl."

"Come on. Let's go see Auntie Gertie." They crossed the street. When Jeb headed for the front walk, Joan jerked him toward the drive, almost pulling him off his feet.

"We aren't going to the front door?" he asked.

"That's for company." She banged on the side door. "I'm family."

"Why did you bang so—"

"'Test drive' me?" She banged again, harder this time. "What the hell is that supposed to mean?"

"You know, kick your tires, see how you handled the curves." He smiled a crooked smile. "See how you hugged the road at high speed."

"Funny. I never would have pegged you as a pig."

He shrugged. "I'm not a pig, but I am a man."

Joan shot him a glance before pounding harder on the door.

"Why are you banging so hard?" he asked emphasizing each word.

The metal clicking of deadbolts pierced the night air. The door opened to reveal an elderly woman with a cane and a cast on one leg. "Whatta you want?" The old woman's voice cracked with age.

"It's me, Auntie Gertie. Joan." Joan yelled so loudly, Jeb looked around to see if lights came on at the neighbors' houses.

Recognition sparked in the woman's eyes. She opened the door, admitted her two guests, and checked to see if any of the neighbors saw anything before closing the door and flipping three deadbolts. She hugged Joan for a long time before letting go.

"I knew if I kept that candle in the window long enough, you'd find your way home."

Joan started to cry again in the elderly woman's arms. "He broke my heart."

"Who? This man?" Auntie Gertie smacked Jeb with the cane, hitting his shoulder and the top of his head.

He backed up until he bumped into the door and rubbed his shoulder.

"No. Duncan broke my heart. This is Jeb," Joan bawled into Auntie Gertie's ear.

"It's going to be all right, Joanie. You're home now." Auntie Gertie patted Joan's back then stepped backward. "Come in. Come in," she said in a loud, grating voice. She led them through a kitchen where frilly café curtains with red cherries covered the windows and a red clock shaped like a teapot hung on the wall over the sink. The followed her through a dining room where a white, lace tablecloth glowed in the darkness. "And who is this man?"

"This is Jeb."

Auntie Gertie cupped her ear. "Who?"

"She's a little hard of hearing," Joan said to Jeb.

"A little?" he said with raised eyebrows.

"This is Jeb," Joan said louder and closer to Auntie Gertie's ear. "My friend."

"He looks like a good catch," Auntie Gertie said behind her hand, as if sharing a confidence, but her voice could easily carry to the neighbors' through the closed windows. She led the way into the living room, tottering on one good leg and one bad one, the cane thumping every other step.

The backs and arms of the dark green couch were covered with antimacassars. More doilies were tucked under lamps and knickknacks on the tables. She turned off the blaring television, filling the room with a blessed silence interrupted only by the ticking of a cuckoo clock over the maple stereo cabinet.

"I feel like I'm in an antique shop," Jeb said under his breath. He studied a wall of photos. "Is this you?" he asked pointing to a young girl with big hair in a karate uniform.

"Yes. My dad was a martial arts instructor. Had his own dojo."

"And this is you in hunting gear? Ever shoot a buck?"

Joan shook her head. "I had the chance a couple times, but I just couldn't pull the trigger. I'd get all shaky. I can skin a deer faster than any man, though."

"So that's what you and Kearney have in common," Jeb said. He stepped back and looked at Joan. "I'm sorry. I didn't mean anything by that."

"Someone's being overly sensitive," Joan said, hiding a smile.

"You *are* different here." He glanced over Joan's shoulder at the old lady and said, "Just don't sic Auntie Gertie on me."

"You have to speak up, young man," Auntie Gertie graveled to him from her rocking chair.

"You have a very nice house," he said to her.

She nodded in deaf understanding.

"I'll fix some tea." Joan pointed to the sofa. "You stay here. Keep Auntie Gertie company."

"Don't leave me alone with her," he said, touching the bump on his head and checking his fingers, as if expecting blood.

"You've been a mercenary in hot spots all over the world, for crying out loud."

Jeb eyed the elderly woman rocking in her chair. "I may have met my match."

"Suck it up." Joan pushed him onto the couch and headed for the kitchen.

After what seemed like forever, Joan returned to the living room with a tray holding a rose-patterned tea service, two matching cups and one mismatched one, and a plate of ginger snaps. Joan prepared Auntie Gertie's tea with a cookie on the saucer before preparing her own tea.

Auntie Gertie slurped her tea. "Armed men in suits came to the door looking for you." She winked. "They thought I didn't see the bulge under their jackets." She snorted. "Can't fool a Jersey girl, right, Joanie?"

Jeb coughed up tea that got stuck in his throat.

Joan elbowed him and said to Auntie Gertie, "When did they come?"

"What?" Auntie Gertie asked.

"When?" Joan said louder.

Auntie Gertie waved her hand. "Oh, a little over a year ago. Then again last week or maybe it was a couple days ago. I made 'em show me some goddamn ID. Said they were from the FBI."

"What did you tell them?"

"I told 'em you had a tough life and they should give you a goddamn break." She nodded with a flat smile on her face. "I told them FBI guys a thing or two."

Jeb wiped his mouth with a napkin and talked behind it. "Way to go, Auntie Gertie."

"They left a card. I got it here somewhere. Told me to call them if you showed up."

"Are you going to call them?" Joan asked.

"Hell, no." She looked indignant at even being asked that question. "You're family. Family don't snitch on family."

"Remember the money I left with you?" Joan asked.

"Saw your picture in the paper a while ago. They were looking for you. Never got it straight what they wanted you for. Uncle Job explained it before he died—he died a while ago, you know—but I didn't believe any of it. You were the do-gooder in the family—took after your mother, rest her soul."

Joan raised her voice. "Remember the money I left with you?"

"Money? What money?"

"Uh-oh," Joan said under her breath. "I hope she isn't senile."

Auntie Gertie laughed and shook her head. "Don't mind me. That's what I practiced saying if those goddamn G-men ever came back and asked about it. Do you want it?"

"Yes, if it's not too much trouble."

"I'll be glad to get it out of my house. That much cash makes me nervous." Auntie Gertie struggled to her feet. Joan jumped up to help her, but Gertie waved her off. "I can get around my own damn self."

Auntie Gertie took a framed oil painting off the wall to expose a safe. She dialed in the combination. "Here's a third of it. Don't worry I didn't spend any of it, even though you said I could use whatever I needed. I have plenty of money of my own thanks to your Uncle Job. He invested in IBM and something called broadband. You wait here. I'll get the rest."

"Where is it?"

"I had three safes installed in case I got robbed. So the thieves wouldn't get it all, you know? Who would think there's more than one safe?" Auntie Gertie raised her eyebrows. "Used three different installation companies, too, in case a robbery was an inside job. Can't be too careful these days. Those drug-using thugs are everywhere. Before they showed up, you were safe walking down your own goddamn street." She hobbled into another room her voice trailing off, railing about drugs and the danger they posed.

"What's the story?" Jeb asked. "She looks too old to be an aunt to you."

"When my mother was killed, my dad and I moved in with Auntie Gertie and Uncle Job. She's my great-aunt— my dad's aunt. Then when—"

"Wait." Jeb put a hand on Joan's arm. "Your mother was killed? How?"

"It doesn't matter." Joan's face fell at the thought of her mom. "My mother was a pacifist. A gentle person who wouldn't even kill a mosquito. Dying violently went against everything she stood for."

"It does matter, Joan. I want to hear the story, but we can talk about it later. Go on."

"Right before she died, she wrote a poem that foretold her death." Joan's eyes focused on the space between her and Jeb.

> "'I saw a flashing light of darkness,
> As hands, unloving, grabbed and stole me,
> From this world I struggled downward,
> Of coming death, his purpose told me.
> And broken now upon the ground,
> Within his sick embrace,
> I yearned for shining glimpses of my life,
> But only saw his face.'"

"Joan."

"I yearned for shining glimpses of my life, but only saw his face," Joan whispered, thinking of Duncan's hurt expression at Notches.

"Joan, stop." Jeb grabbed both her arms until she looked up at him. "We'll talk through this later."

She focused on him and continued her narrative. "When my dad went...away...my Auntie Gertie and Uncle Job got custody of me and raised me until I joined the army."

"Where did your father go?"

"Here's some more," Auntie Gertie said, putting three bundles of fifty-dollar bills in Joan's hands. "I'll get the rest." She started a slow ascent up the stairs. "There are bags in the pantry. Might want to get one."

Joan dumped the bundles of cash in Jeb's arms and headed for the kitchen.

"Where did your father go?" he asked following behind her.

Joan ignored him and rummaged through the pantry. She found a reusable, cloth grocery bag with the name of a local store on the side. She grabbed several bundles of cash from his hands and put it in the bag. When she reached for the last bundle, he held it tight.

"Where did your father go?"

Jeb blocked the pantry door, trapping her inside. Other than beating up the only friend she had left, she would have to face her past where she stood.

"My father went to prison."

"How long was he there?"

"He died after two years. Gran mal seizure—they called it. If you ask me, he died of a broken heart."

"What was he in prison for?"

"Later, Jeb. I don't need this now. I'm too emotional already—"

"It's okay to tell me. Give me the short version."

She rubbed her forehead.

He opened the bag and dropped in the last bundle.

"When I was almost seventeen I started dating a guy I thought was the love of my life. He was older than me—twenty-one. My mom took an instant dislike to him, but my dad knew I could take care of myself, so he let me date the guy with strict boundaries. Anyway, after less than a year of dating, he—" Joan's eyes stung. Tears filled her eyes, but didn't flow. She licked her lips before continuing. "—after a year of dating, he raped and killed my mother. My dad was never the same after that. He worshiped my mom."

"Like Duncan worships you," Jeb mused.

Joan's jaw muscles tightened. "Don't even compare that piece of shit to my father."

"Did the police catch the guy?"

Joan shook her head. "Not enough evidence, they said—it was before DNA testing. Finally, something snapped in my dad and he hunted down that bastard and killed him—

beat him to death with his hands." Joan fought the tears. "I miss them so much."

Emotion muffled a sob, mucus trapping it in her throat.

Jeb pulled her into his arms. "So you lost both parents."

Joan nodded against his chest. "My mom died because I made a stupid decision. And my dad died like a caged animal because of me."

"It wasn't because of you. He was in jail because of a decision he made. *He* chose to hunt the bastard down who dishonored your mom. In my book, that makes him an honorable man who sought justice for your mom."

"How do you know he was honorable?"

"He raised you, didn't he?"

Joan sniffled against Jeb's chest.

"Does Duncan know any of this?" Jeb asked.

"I assume so. He said he vetted me more than anyone else when I joined the Constitution Defense Legion." Joan stepped back and wiped her eyes with her palms. "As if he ever cared."

"Did you two ever talk about it?"

Joan shook her head and a couple errant tears trickled down her cheeks.

"Jesus, Joan." Jeb thumbed away her tears. "I'm sorry this happened to you."

"Here's the last of your money," Auntie Gertie said behind them.

"Thanks, Auntie Gertie," Joan hugged her aunt. "We have to go. I'll stay in touch. I promise."

Jeb gave the old woman a hug and yelled into her ear, "You did a good job raising Joan."

Joan pulled his arm and they left by way of the side door to the driveway. The deadbolt clicked behind them.

"Where to now?" Jeb asked.

"To my caches."

"Caches? You have more than one?"

"Yeah, just in case the feds find one of them."

Jeb exhaled through his teeth and shook his head. "The nut doesn't fall far from the tree."

CHAPTER 24

The door to the storage unit clattered up, revealing an almost empty area. In the center of the swept, cement floor sat the rosewood box with her throwing knives. Next to the beautifully carved box sat an olive green, metal ammunition box. In the back of the small unit a ten speed bike leaned against the wall surrounded by biking gear and a backpack.

"This is it?" Jeb asked. "This is your cache?"

"Like I told you, I have two in case the feds locate one," Joan said, removing half the cash from the bag.

Jeb flipped the latch on the ammo box and fingered through the contents of the box. "There's only one fake ID here. You'll need more if you ever have to disappear."

"The other cache?" She put her hands on her hips and looked down at him. "You remember me saying I had two caches, right?" She handed him the cash bundles.

"How could I forget?" He put the documents back into the box, tucked in the new cash, and stood. "I know a guy who will make you a couple more fake IDs in case you can only get to one cache. You'll need at least two to disappear completely, if it ever comes to that."

"You're like the pain in the ass big brother I never had," Joan said while locking the storage unit.

After they pulled out onto Route 80-E, Jeb broke the silence. "Any thoughts where you're going to stay tonight?"

"We could always go back to Auntie Gertie's. She sure took a shine to you."

"Does she always assault people she likes?" He drove for several seconds before adding, "The offer to stay at my place still stands."

Joan looked out the window at the familiar landscape sliding past. "Do you think Duncan will stay at Durham Security or go back to the apartment upstate?"

"Oh, he'll be at the apartment to talk to you. He's probably there right now, pacing through the house." Jeb glanced at Joan then focused on the road before speaking again. "You should give him a chance to explain."

"I don't want to talk about him."

"Give him a chance, Joan. You two belong together."

"I thought you said you weren't going to try to talk me into going back to Duncan."

Jeb's smile seemed to glow in the dark. "I said I wasn't going to talk you into going back inside Notches."

"Let's go to your place."

"Are you sure you don't want to go home?"

Joan looked out the window.

"How much cash do you have?" he finally asked.

"Aren't you full of questions tonight?" Joan muttered.

"It will take a lot of cash to buy land with a house on it to make your ashram."

"I have the money Duncan left me when he made me think he was dead." After a pause, she added, "And he's dead to me now."

"You aren't going to take all his money and run, are you?"

Joan thought for a moment. "No. I can't take all his money and leave him broke. I can't do that, not even after what he did. I'll just take what I've been given so far, and leave the rest of it for him—it's his money."

"I would be disappointed if you became a money grubber." Jeb looked at Joan and smiled. "You are your parents' child."

"Why do you say that?" Joan pointed straight ahead. "Eyes on the road."

"You said your mother was peace loving and gentle. And so are you."

Joan snorted. "Yeah, right. I'm so peaceful, I'm a fugitive from justice. The feds consider me armed and dangerous—that's how much of a shrinking violet I am. When they take me down, it won't be a day on the playground."

"You don't go looking for trouble. And from what I've heard, you avoided trouble until you could no longer avoid it. You wanted a quiet, peaceful life with Duncan. That was all you asked out of life."

Joan shrugged.

"Your father was a highly trained martial artist who lived a quiet life with his beloved wife and daughter. He gave you advice, shared his skills with you, and believed in you when you insisted on a relationship against his better judgment. Sound familiar?"

"No." It did sound familiar. It was a carbon copy of her relationship with Duncan—but he wasn't going to get away with betraying her. She wouldn't let that happen. She would not swallow her pride on this issue.

"When life dealt him an injustice," Kearney continued, "your father flew at it like an eagle to prey—a justice seeker. Like someone else I know." He looked across the dark car at Joan.

"What my dad did differs in a big way from what I've done."

"Only in scope. The passion is the same."

Joan didn't respond.

"You're going to give Duncan another chance. I'd bet my boots on it."

Joan reflexively looked down at Jeb's mud-flecked loafers. "Why do you say that?"

"Say there's this guy, and he calls a girl to try to get her to break up with her boyfriend. If she stays on the line, he knows there's a chance. She's interested. If she hangs up on him, he knows he is shit out of luck. You, my friend, are still on the phone."

"No. You are still on the phone. I've not only hung up, I've ripped it off the wall. Speaking of phone, someone is blowing up my phone—probably Duncan trying to sweet talk me into coming back to him."

"Yeah, mine, too. What I'm saying," Jeb babbled on, "is you didn't grab money and get out of Dodge. You are still lurking around the area."

Silence fell between them.

Joan pulled out her phone. There were three voice mails, but she didn't pull them up. She thumbed through the messages. Her heart started beating fast. He mouth went dry.

"That's why I think you're going to give Duncan another chance."

Joan grunted, but didn't say anything.

"You have to work through this, or that cozy, little ashram you want—"

Joan threw her phone out the window.

"What the hell'd you do that for?" Jeb asked.

"Lucinda-Mae found Duncan by the GPS tracker on my phone."

Jeb snorted. "She didn't look smart enough to know how to turn on the phone."

"Yeah, but the feds are smart enough."

"What about the feds?"

"Duncan left Lucinda-Mae on the sidewalk in front of the departures terminal in the hands of federal agents. They could have been tracking me all night."

Jeb quickly thumbed through her texts. "Carmine has ordered everyone to the safe house." He looked at Joan. "Evidently Lucinda-Mae isn't exactly who she says she is."

"What do you mean?"

"Carmine isn't sure, but he thinks she may be working with the feds."

"What?" Joan bit her lip while she thought back to the lack of fear in Lucinda-Mae's eyes at the sight of Joan's scars and her over the top behavior. "I knew there was something about her. Do you think she's an undercover agent?"

"It's possible."

"The feds wouldn't send a civilian into a dangerous situation."

"Unless they didn't know the danger potential."

"Your company is under investigation," Joan said. "They knew." She chewed the inside of her cheek, sorting out what few details she knew. "But how did they target Duncan? He was in hiding."

Jeb stepped on the gas.

"Where're we going?"

"Carmine is opening the safe house."

"You think this is that dangerous?"

Jeb glanced over at her. "Carmine seems to think so. We'll go and check it out. See what's going on."

Joan gripped the arm rest to steady herself. Her mind brought up instances in the past few weeks that were suspect. The vision of Duncan's profile in the theater when he said, "Fucking bastards" came into her head. Jeb's speeding around slower cars faded to the background. Duncan's lips were moving, but now she couldn't make out the words. Law enforcement had been doing their jobs, like he said to her on the ride home from their honeymoon in the Adirondack Mountains. But something had been different with the appearance of the cops in the theater. She zeroed in on his lips. Those lips that had been so loving. She frowned, those lips had touched Lucinda-Mae.

"Watch, Jeb," Joan said stomping on the non-existent brake pedal on her side of the car.

"Got it." He whipped around a Honda Civic entering the highway at a snail's pace.

Joan relaxed and thought of Duncan's lips. His lips were mouthing "lying bastards," not "fucking bastards." *Lying* bastards? If the cops were the lying bastards, and Duncan thought they were after her and him, and he had thought they had lied to him, he must have made some kind of deal? But what? And why didn't he tell her?

"Duncan is up to something," Joan said.

"Just because he made an error in judgment and cheated on you doesn't mean he would betray his brothers in arms."

"It doesn't have anything to do with that. In a fit of temper I accused him of being the mole. He didn't ask, 'What mole?' Instead, it bothered him that I knew about the mole, and he seemed even more upset that you knew about it."

"When?"

"In the kitchen at Notches, right before I came out and exposed myself to everybody." Joan cringed. In her whirlwind of emotions, she hadn't thought about that action in quite that way. *Man, I gotta pull my shit together.*

"How did he know about the mole?" Kearney asked.

"Exactly. How did he know about the mole?" She smacked her palm against her forehead. "God, I'm such a jerk. Duncan's betrayal blinded me to the real problem. Carmine tried to warn me that there was more going on than Lucinda-Mae. Why didn't I listen?"

"You were betrayed by the man you love. That is more than enough to distract anyone."

"You're right," Joan said, thinking through what had happened over the past few hours. If Lucinda-Mae was an undercover agent, and things didn't quite go as planned at Notches, the feds could make a move.

"Carmine might be onto something," Joan said. "The feds might think their investigation is going to pieces. They might jump early."

⸙⸙⸙

Duncan rang the doorbell a second time before a man in a gray sweater came to the door. He had reading glasses perched on the end of his generous nose. He folded a newspaper and tucked it under his arm before opening the front door.

"Mr. Chesterton?" Duncan asked, knowing full well the answer to his question. He was impressed the Director of the New York/New Jersey Office of Homeland Security answered the door himself.

"Yes. I'm Randolph Chesterton."

"You don't know me, but you owe me a big favor."

"I don't owe anyone a favor. Good night." The door started to close.

Duncan had already jimmied open the storm door and he quickly pulled it open and pushed on the interior door. The older man did not have a chance against Duncan's speed and strength.

"I'm going to call the police."

"Sir, you can do that after I speak with you, but you will give me a few moments of your time." Duncan pulled a small revolver from his jacket pocket and backed the man from the door. "Now, where can we talk privately?"

A middle-aged woman with short, gray-streaked hair and a round midsection appeared at the end of the hall. "Who is it, dear?"

Duncan pulled his gun out of sight.

Mr. Chesterton turned to his wife. "It's just someone from the office. I have to clear up a few details. I won't be long."

"Okay, dear." The woman disappeared.

"Follow me," Mr. Chesterton said. "We can use my study off the living room." He led the way into a small study. When he turned on the desk lamp, it illuminated a pile of papers on the corner of the desk that looked like it would spill onto the floor with the slightest movement. He moved to sit in his office chair.

"Keep your hands on the desk where I can see them," Duncan said, sliding into the chair opposite Mr. Chesterton.

"I won't give you any trouble. You can put the gun away," Mr. Chesterton said.

Duncan placed the gun on the edge of the desk where he could reach it if he needed it.

"You said I owed you a favor, but I don't know you. Who are you and what is this about?"

"Sir, you had a son who was abused and murdered."

"That's public record, I don't see—"

"The abuser got off on a technicality. The DA failed to provide full disclosure of facts in the case, isn't that right?"

"Again, that's public record."

"There is something not in the public record," Duncan said. "You sought justice outside the court system."

"I did nothing of the kind. I'm a law-abiding man."

"I'm sure you are, but this involved your son. And it was a most grievous tragedy." Duncan leaned forward. "You hired a vigilante to meet out justice."

"I...I never..." Mr. Chesterton was at a loss for words. "What would make you think such a thing?"

"I know because I was the assassin who got justice for your only son."

"I'm not admitting to any of this, but let's just assume I did this thing—for the sake of playing along. How can I be sure what you are saying is the truth?"

Duncan reached into his pocket and pulled out a green matchbox toy truck and set it on the desk. "When I fulfilled my contract, I found this in the abuser's apartment."

Mr. Chesterton could not pry his eyes from the tiny tow truck with a BP sticker on the hood. It had been his son's favorite toy, and it had gone missing at the same time his son disappeared. "Anyone can buy one of those and place it on my desk."

"If that anyone knew your son's favorite toy," Duncan said. "And if that someone could find this particular match-box toy. You see, this particular truck is rare. Very rare."

"I'm going to call the police."

"You do that, Mr. Chesterton, because I'll be glad to tell them who hired me to take care of this for you."

"It'll be a thug's word against the word of a Regional Director of Homeland Security. Who do you think they'll believe?"

"I'm not just any assassin. I leave particular details with each job that only I know. And I am meticulous with details. The police won't doubt my story." Duncan pressed his lips together and shook his head in a show of confidence. "You might want to consider how this will affect your career path."

Mr. Chesterton reached for his son's toy. "If this is about blackmailing me, I won't pay you a cent.

Duncan covered the green toy truck with his hand. "This isn't about money, sir. But there is something within your power that you can do for me."

CHAPTER 25

Forty-five minutes later, Jeb slowed, looking for the driveway to the safe house. The lane ran beside a closed gas station, and he missed it the first time they passed by the station, which affirmed its inconspicuous appearance. At the end of the overgrown, tire-track lane stood a large nineteenth-century, two-story, stone house. Weeds had grown to a height of five feet in what must have once been flowerbeds along the front of the house. Golden light flickered through a crack at the edge of a window covering to the right of the front door. A half dozen cars, a couple vans, and several motorcycles filled the front yard. The foul-mouthed operative must have pulled valet duty, because he waved Jeb forward and showed him where to park.

Jeb and Joan went up the two stone steps and went inside. The front door opened into a dark foyer with worn, wooden stairs straight ahead. Footsteps and voices came from the rooms beyond the top of the stairs. In a stark, sparsely furnished dining room on the left, several men sat around cleaning weapons to the light of a Coleman lantern. They talked in low undertones until someone looked up and saw Joan. Jeb guided her into the living room on the right. Men sprawled on a beat up couch facing a fire blazing in the fieldstone fireplace. Others leaned on the mantle. The first ones to see Joan tapped the others and nodded toward her. Conversations stopped. They all stared at her.

Carmine broke away from the group standing around the

hearth and approached Joan. "That was quite a display at Notches."

"I should have listened to you. I had my head screwed on backward."

"You had a lot on your mind. There's coffee in the kitchen and there might be some cold cuts left for sandwiches."

"I took the last of it," a Hispanic-looking operative said with a mouthful of sandwich.

Joan had seen him before, but his name escaped her. "Is Kearney here?"

"No. He went—" Carmine looked at Jeb. "He went to a meeting to get some inside information. We're holed up here until he returns with some intel. Make yourselves at home."

Joan left Jeb to talk to the men. She walked across the creaky floor to the kitchen, feeling the burning heat of the attention of the men in the room. When she reached the sanctity of the kitchen, a petite brunette turned from a take-out box of coffee.

"You finally made it," she said. "We never met. I'm Zelda, Carmine's wife."

"Did you hear about what happened at Notches?"

Zelda chuckled. "I heard you gave quite a show."

Joan winced.

Zelda looked up from pouring coffee from the spout on the front of the coffee-filled takeout box. "The guys didn't know about the scars." She leaned toward Joan. "And they're a little upset that you implied they would do that to that other women. They aren't like Kearney."

"I know. I was just trying to scare her off. Where is she, by the way?"

"She's still at Notches. Carmine figured it was only a matter of time before the feds raided the place. They'll find her when they do." Zelda's put her arms out to Joan. "I am so sorry. Where the hell was your husband's head at?"

Joan had to bend a little to receive the hug, but it felt

good to commiserate with a woman. Her life had been so full of men the past two or three years, she had forgotten how comforting a female friend could be. The softness and gentleness, without being prissy, was a breath of fresh air. She would have women-only days at her ashram.

Champ stuck his head in the kitchen. "Kearney just pulled up. Thought you'd like to know."

"Okay. Thanks," Joan said.

"How can you be nice to Kearney after what he did to you?" Zelda whispered, nodding toward the front room.

Joan picked at the parsley garnish on the empty cold cuts tray. "If he hadn't been with me these past several months, I don't know what I would have done. I gotta go. I have to talk to him."

Joan walked into the living room where the men were standing in a group. They saw her and parted to reveal who they had been talking to. Duncan gazed at her. He looked haggard with tired eyes above dark circles, ragged stubble, and wrinkled clothes. She wanted to hold him and comfort him. Tell him everything was going to be okay.

Instead she looked at Kearney, who stood next to Duncan. "What's he doing here?"

Duncan's shoulders dropped. He wiped his mouth with the back of his hand. He drew in a deep breath. "I have to tell you something." His voice rasped with emotion.

"There isn't anything else for you to say to me." Joan turned on her heel and headed for the back door.

The sweet aromas of spring greeted her. She wanted to breathe it in and enjoy the woodsy freshness, but her respirations were short and labored. She paced the length of the back terrace, hands supporting the small of her back. Where had her plans gone wrong? Duncan was supposed to be by her side, sharing her life. Together. Even if they stayed in the counterculture of revolutionaries or mercenaries, they would each be there to have each other's back. Instead, she was alone, on her own—again. The screen door squealed behind her.

"Please let me explain," Duncan said.

Joan spun around at the sound of his voice. "If you say 'we can work through this' one more time, I swear I'll kill you."

"You have too much pride to forgive me and take me back. That train has left the station, and I'll just have to accept it." He stepped toward her. "I have something else to say to you."

Joan's heart ripped in two at Duncan's acceptance that she would not take him back. She wanted him more in that second than she ever had in all their time together. She wanted to reach for him, but couldn't will her arms to move. She felt weak, as if watching someone else's body, unable to make it do her bidding.

Again she couldn't say the right words. "Say what you have to say and go away."

"What I did was a bigger mistake than even you can imagine—"

She snorted and turned away from him.

"I need your love and support to…"

She turned to face him when he stopped to search for words. She crossed her arms.

"Damn, I've made a mess of things. Without you, I can't see straight." He wiped his mouth with his hand and scratched his beard. "I know things got…chaotic, but there is a plan."

She threw up her hands. "A plan? A plan to screw with my head even more? A plan to drive me away from you?"

"Without you, I'm nothing but a screw up."

"Yeah, and when you're with me, you don't listen to my advice."

"That'll never happen again. From now on—"

"Is there anything else you want to say to make me more miserable?"

"No, but I do have one more thing. I got the investigation into Durham Security squashed."

"Really? *You* got it squashed?"

"It was always supposed to be that way—an integral part of my plan, but I didn't want to pull the trigger on it just yet. When Jeb found out, I had to move up the timetable."

"Pull the trigger?"

"Metaphorically speaking, of course."

"And just how did you get the investigations stopped?"

"The Regional Director of Homeland Security owed me a favor."

Words formed but would not leave her mouth. She realized she knew little about the man she married. The Regional Director of Homeland Security owed him a favor. When and where did that happen? She wanted to know the details, but it had to wait. She rubbed her eyes in a futile effort to rub away the vision of Lucinda Mae and Duncan panting, naked next to each other after a rowdy round of sex.

Words finally formed, but anger changed them before they were spoken. "Anything else?"

"No. That's it." Duncan turned to go.

Say something, damn it. "Duncan?"

"Yes?"

Joan swallowed and loosened her jaw to soften her words. "I never really thought you were the inside guy in the investigation."

Duncan nodded. Before going back inside, he stood under the pale outdoor light and said, "I will always love you."

Joan wanted to say something more to him, but he was gone. The words probably would not have come out right anyway. *Besides, what would I have said? I'm sorry for making you miserable because you made me miserable? I'm sorry I can't forgive you for betraying me?*

She gave him the finger, although he wasn't there to see it. She walked the length of the terrace, around the house, and down the dirt drive. Her footsteps were muffled in the soft dirt. She edged around a GTO parked at the end of the driveway. It had Illinois plates.

That's an odd place to park. I think that's Darren's car.
She had to clear her head.

About fifty yards down the road past the closed gas station, the bright lights of a Seven-Eleven beckoned her. She felt around the pockets of her jacket and found a rolled up a five-dollar bill. The idea of eating a candy bar appealed to her, and she couldn't resist. She cruised the candy aisle, taking in the variety, the deep aroma of chocolate oozing through the colorful wrappers. There were so many different brands—some with caramel, some with peanuts, some with both—and she hadn't bought a candy bar in years.

Two cars pulled in while she munched on the first of two candy bars—she couldn't make up her mind, so she bought both. A van pulled in and the driver got out and talked to the driver of one of the other cars. All the passengers in the two cars and four more men from the van got out. She couldn't see what the men at the rear of the van were doing, but the men in the cars had the trunks open and they were gearing up. Strapping handguns to their thighs. Putting something over their heads. She had seen that before. Even in the dark she recognized body armor. One of the men turned and *US Marshall* reflected in the pale light. *Someone's getting arrested tonight.*

Joan took a casual bite of her candy bar. It felt weird to be this close to men who would arrest her in an instant if they knew who she was. It was exhilarating and heart-stopping at the same time. There but for the grace of—the men got into the van and took off in the direction of the dirt drive toward the safe house. *Oh, shit. They're going to get Durham Security.*

Joan pulled out a burner phone she had taken out of the cache, dialed Kearney's number and started jogging toward Darren's car. "Pick up, pick up, pick up," she begged out loud, hoping he would answer a call from a number he didn't recognize.

She nearly choked on a small chunk of candy bar when she heard him answer.

"Yeah."

She dropped the remainder of the candy bar. "Feds are heading toward the house. Get out. Go out the back. They're—"

"Whoa. Slow down. What's this again?"

"You have no time. *No* time." She picked up her pace, and her words breathed out between her panting. "I'll get Darren's car. Go out the back. Go now."

Yelled warnings, scuffling, a door slammed, then the phone went dead. Joan broke into a run. Darren's car came into sight. She slowed for a quick scan. The feds had overlooked putting a guard on the car.

But the doors were locked. *Shit, shit, shit.* She spied a rock in the pale light from the street lamp. She chucked it at the rear driver side window. It bounced off, just missing her foot. She grabbed it and whaled it against the window, this time putting her body weight behind it. The window smashed. She unlocked the driver's door.

She pressed the horn in three short bursts—the international sign of distress—several times. All the while looking for keys.

Keys, keys. Joan looked behind the visor and in the console. The glovebox was jammed with papers and junk. And a screwdriver. She grabbed it, jammed it into the ignition, and pounded the end with her palm. She shook out her hand and started the engine with the other. The engine rumbled to life. She pressed on the horn three more times, put the car in reverse, and stomped on the gas.

෴

They heard three more short blasts of a horn.

After grabbing Darren and pushing him into Duncan, Kearney led the way out of the house and across the back patio. Men grabbed weapons and rushed out the door behind them. They slipped into the mottled shadows of the overgrown bushes that lined the once-upon-a-time yard. Instead of crashing headlong through the underbrush, they slowed their pace and moved slowly picking the placement of their feet with attention and care. Sometimes slow is fast.

"My car's at the end of the drive," Darren whispered, when they were a good thirty yards from the house. He gestured and led the way to the left. "Arc this way."

"Joan has it," Kearney whispered.

Darren stopped and turned to look at Kearney.

"She told me when she called to warn us," he said. "We should head for the road."

Without comment, Darren adjusted his path to head for the road, head on a swivel. After only a few steps he knelt and put up a fist, indicating for the other two men to stop. Men's voices, low and firm, drifted toward them. Law enforcement. The officers fanned out just past the spot where Darren, Kearney, and Duncan knelt in the tall weeds.

When they were out of earshot, Darren motioned Duncan and Kearney forward. They squatted in the underbrush along the shoulder of the road. The shadows covered them.

"Did she say where to meet her?" Darren asked.

"The call was too short. But if I know her—"

Darren put up a hand. "I hear it." He stood and looked in the direction of the sound. "I'd know that engine anywhere." He stepped toward the road.

Duncan grabbed Darren's arm. "Are you sure?"

Darren boldly stepped into the open and waved down the car.

❧❧❧

Okay. If they manage to get away, where would they go and where would they come out on the street? She drove a hundred yards up the street. Then circled back. On the second round she saw a man step out and wave his arms back and forth over his head. Darren.

She blew past him, unable to stop in time. She executed a perfect power turn, sped toward the men, and slammed on the brakes, screeching to a halt. Three men jumped into the car—Darren in the front passenger seat, Duncan and Kearney in the back. She stomped on the gas. Tires squealed, caught, and took off down the road.

"First you crack a rib, then you break the window of my car." Darren spied the screwdriver. "And the ignition switch," he said, holding his side with one hand and bracing himself against the dash with the other. "You are one destructive woman."

"Welcome to my world," Duncan said.

Joan glanced in the rearview mirror. Duncan and she locked eyes briefly. Eyes back on the road ahead, Joan resolved to worry about her future when they were safely tucked away somewhere.

Kearney twisted to look behind him. "We have company."

"Getting away without a high speed chase would have been too easy," Joan groused. The lights were getting bigger in the rearview mirror. She powered through the gentle curve. She flew through the five corners in Vail's Gate. Cars slid. Horns blew. She checked her mirrors again.

The cop car behind them slowed and worked its way through the cars that blocked the intersection. It pulled away from the congestion, but Joan had gained valuable ground. Route 32 was relatively straight, and she powered through the curves, increasing the distance between the GTO and the police cruiser. A car pulled out of a side street. She swerved. The powerful GTO spun out. She over corrected, but skillfully centered the wheels on the road and hurtled away. Telephone poles whizzed by in blurs, corners came up fast.

Joan glanced around the car. All three of the passengers were holding onto the car for dear life. "It should get smoother. We're almost to Route 17."

"I don't know about you guys, but I'm fastening my seat belt." Kearney said.

Two clicks came from the back seat.

"You aren't going to click yours?" Joan asked Darren.

He smiled through the pain in his ribs and shook his head. "I like living on the edge."

"It's your safety." Joan whipped around a slow moving car and jerked back into the lane to avoid a head on collision with a delivery truck. The truck's blaring horn faded into the sound of air rushing past the car. Joan passed yet another car. The oncoming car drove off the road to avoid the imminent collision.

A barrage of traffic lights at the entrances to a shopping center loomed ahead. They turned red. The car in front of Joan stopped at the light. She leaned on the horn, pulled into the oncoming lane, and raced past the cars. Oncoming traffic swerved to avoid a collision. Horns blared behind them. She pulled back into the right lane, but a car pulled off the Route 17 ramp directly in front of her. She turned the wheel, skidded left, over corrected, and slid sideways up the embankment.

She gunned the engine. Tires spun. Caught traction. She fishtailed back onto the road.

Darren fastened his seatbelt. "You're gonna kill us. I'll be safer with the damn police."

"If there's anything I can do, it's drive," she said.

"You could've fooled me," Darren said looking over his shoulder to see if Kearney and Duncan agreed with him.

"Just get us out of here," Duncan said.

"You're doing fine," Kearney said.

Duncan narrowed his eyes and looked at Kearney.

Kearney put out his hand palm up. "What? We're still alive, aren't we?"

Joan blew through the intersection and raced south down Route 17. The road became a smooth four-lane. The curves were long and smooth. She picked up speed.

Darren braced himself with one arm on the dashboard

and pointed left, past Joan. "There. Go into the park."

"Where?"

"There. There. There." Darren said pointing across the front seat of the car. "The brown sign. Turn there."

Joan braked. Turned the steering wheel hard. The power in the rear tires drifted the car into a slide. She straightened the wheels and gunned the engine. Turned into the park. The car fishtailed into the park entrance.

"Turn off the lights," Kearney said.

"Where's the switch?"

Darren pointed it out. Joan flipped the switch and slowed to see the road in the dark.

"They won't find us in here," Darren said. "They'll race on down Route 17."

Duncan turned to look out the rear window. "There they go."

Joan turned the headlights back on and stepped on the gas. "This place is freaky in the dark."

"You don't have to go so fast. Slow down," Darren said.

"I just want to get out of here."

"Look out!" Darren warned.

Joan slowed to make a sharp left turn. The road evened out into a long, slow curve. She sped up. "Holy shit." She turned into a sharp right turn.

The car drifted into the other lane. The corner sharpened into a hairpin turn. The car drifted farther. The door panels wailed in misery as they scraped along a boulder blocking the car from flying off the road into the woods.

Darren winced.

"You're gonna kill us," Kearney said.

"I got it. I got it." Joan pulled the car back into the right lane. The road straightened out. She stomped on the gas. Zero-gravity flipped their stomachs when they flew over a bump in the road. The rear bumper scraped.

"My car," Darren moaned.

Joan checked her rearview mirror—no tail. She kept the needle hovering at sixty miles per hour, a dangerous speed for the winding, bumpy road. Fast enough to make time, but not so fast that they would fly off the road at a sharp turn. She downshifted going into the corners. Gassed the engine coming out of them. The narrow two-lane road wound around outcroppings of bare rock and between tranquil, dark lakes. The trees had just begun to unfurl their new leaves, but the foliage was still not thick enough to obscure her vision.

"This is a pretty park. Nice old growth foliage—yow!" She skidded around a turn that was sharper than it looked and sloped the wrong way. She downshifted. The car bounced off another boulder. "I'd love to come back and spend some time here when I'm not in a hurry."

"Yeah," Duncan said, looking out the back window. "Cops have a way of sucking the joy out of nature." He gripped the armrest. "Watch it!"

"I don't know how you can tell in the dark," Darren said.

She slowed just enough to stay on the road.

Darren looked behind them. "Can we slow down now? Nobody is behind us."

"Not yet," Joan said. "I want to get to the other side of the park and in the midst of other cars before a helicopter is called in to tail us."

A traffic circle loomed out of the darkness.

"Which road do I take?" Joan asked, downshifting to follow the road around the circle.

"Second road to go straight."

"No. This first one," Duncan said. "It goes south."

"Straight across," Darren said again.

Joan drove around the circle and, on the second pass, took Duncan's suggestion. "Look a beach. I bet that's nice in the summer."

"Yeah, we'll have to come back and check it out," Kearney said with a heavy hint of sarcasm.

They passed a sign that said the dark, calm lake was Lake Tiorati. The road straightened, and Joan picked up speed. Even at sixty-five miles per hour in the unlit, dark passage through the park, the untouched, natural landscape was breathtaking.

Kearney stuck his head out the window and looked up. "I think it might be time for a change in plans. I think I hear a chopper overhead."

Joan looked upward out the side window and stepped on the gas. The car rammed everyone against the back of the seats.

"Slow down," Darren said. "You can't outrun a chopper."

"I can try." She looked for the chopper through the side window before returned her eyes on the road ahead. "Oh, *shit*."

CHAPTER 26

Another circle. Too late. Without thinking, Joan stomped on the brakes and the powerful engine combined with momentum threw the car into a slide. It drifted sideways through the soft dirt in the center of the circle. The car slammed into a tree. The side windows shattered. A chink in the windshield crackled across the glass in spurts.

Joan shook the glass shards out of her hair. She gently pressed the gas pedal, but the sodden ground sucked the car down. The tires spun, digging in deeper.

"Not so much gas," Duncan said.

"I'm not giving it too much gas. The ground is too muddy." After a couple more tries she stopped and flopped back on the seat.

"Everybody out," Duncan said. "We all go in different directions. Meet up in Suffern by the War monument. Noon tomorrow."

Everyone bailed out of the car, but stopped when Darren said, "I'll go slow. Let the police catch me. I can slow them down and give them misinformation."

"No, Darren," Joan said running around the car. "You have to get away."

He shook his head. "I can't with this rib. I can barely breathe when I'm sitting still."

"Oh, God, Darren, I'm sorry," Joan said grabbing his arm.

"Don't be sorry, be gone." He looked around. "That goes for all of you."

Duncan hesitated. Joan locked eyes with him. He wrapped his arms around her. "Make it out of the woods and get to safety. That's what this whole thing has been about—your freedom." He gave her a hard peck on the lips and disappeared into the woods heading south. After good-bye pats on Darren's back, Joan took off east. Kearney headed north.

꿍꿍

The helicopter pilot headed northwest from Clarkstown, scanning the dark park below with his thermal imaging camera. The occasional hits turned out to be nocturnal animals prowling through the woods, probably hunting for dinner. The glowing image outlined animals, but did not reveal which animals they were. They did not have the movement characteristics or general outline of a human. Human arms and legs would show up on the image. He kept searching.

On the verge of changing direction, the pilot saw the image of a human.

After giving his call sign he said, "I have a person walking south just east of Seven Lakes Parkway."

"One person heading south. Copy. Any sign of any others?"

"No. Do you want me to make a circuit and look for others, or follow this one?"

"Give me your coordinates and make a circuit for others."

The pilot gave his GPS coordinates. "How many am I looking for?"

"Three."

"Three Tangos. Copy that." The pilot turned westward to begin a search grid.

❦❧❦

The eastern skies showed signs of morning light, but the woods were still dark making navigating the obstacles tricky. Joan guessed it was close to four-thirty in the morning. She picked up speed. She had to get out of the woods to find out what Duncan meant by this whole thing being about her freedom. It could have been just a teaser to get her to meet up with him, but he was not by nature a manipulator. It meant something, and she had to make it out of the woods to find out. She looked around. Nothing but untouched forest everywhere she looked. Underbrush, fallen logs, granite boulders jutting out of the piles of dried leaves. Injuries waiting to happen.

Without a compass she couldn't even be sure she still headed east. The trees and rocky slopes made seeing the skyline challenging. She came out on a granite outcropping and stopped to get her bearings. The view was breathtaking. Who knew New York had such a beautiful panorama of old growth forest? She adjusted her course and picked up speed through the thick underbrush and over the rocky terrain. She was sliding down an embankment watching her footing to make sure she didn't catch a rock and sprain her ankle when pain filled her head with a dull thunk. Her feet flew out from under her, and she landed flat on her back with a breath stealing *oomph*.

❦❧❦

Kearney grumbled and griped his way in the dark, batting away the thick underbrush. If he were fighting an enemy, this would be great terrain, but it made trying to escape a pain in the ass. He climbed up a crevice between two boulders. When he got to the top, he looked around and found nothing to give him hope that there was civilization nearby.

Hints of light brightened the sky to the east, so he adjusted his course to try to intersect Joan. He didn't like being in the woods alone, and he didn't like the idea of her being alone in the woods either. She could take care of herself, and she was much more at home in the woods than he was, but he had to find her. The gentleman in him demanded it.

Gentleman in me? Where the hell did that come from? It has to be Joan's influence. She has a way of making a man a better man. She doesn't do it on purpose. And probably if she tried to do it, it wouldn't happen. Just by being competent and expecting everyone around her to be at the same level, it raised the bar. She was tough, sensible, and straightforward. It made a man want to be more of a man than she was.

But she is human, he reminded himself. She had her moments when emotion could cloud her decision-making process. It was for those moments that men wanted to be there. To give back for all that she had unintentionally given them.

Dammit! A branch swacked him in the face and when he cleared his vision, he stood on the edge of a marsh. An army of cattails stood in his path. *Damn it to hell and back.* He looked at his loafers, said farewell to them, and hopped onto the nearest mound of earth.

៚៚៚

What kind of husband am I? My wife was in my arms and I let her go. I don't believe her when she says we're through. She let me hold her, didn't she? That has to count for something. I'm not going to give up on our marriage. And I don't think she has, regardless of what she says.

Duncan walked into a spider web and made a path through it with his hands. While he followed a game trail he pulled remnants of the web from his stubble and hair.

It comforted him to know Joan headed off east, which was the shortest way out of the park. He stopped and looked toward the east. He wanted to cut a diagonal and try to catch up to her. It would be almost impossible to find her in this primitive forest. The undergrowth had never been cut back. From what he could see there hadn't been a fire to thin out the trees. And the rock outcroppings—this region was littered with boulders and rocks that jutted out of the ground—made navigation difficult at best. *It's hard to tell how fast she's traveling, or if she is even traveling in a straight line. I'll catch up to her in Suffern.*

He smiled and shook his head at the memory of the meeting at The Woods, the training area for the Constitutional Defense Legion. She had outshone every other rookie and the leadership bumped her up to an operative the first day with the Legion. She had said she did dead reckoning through the woods at a run. A woman who could do that with confidence was the kind of woman he wanted in his life.

And he got her. Then through his own stupidity, he lost her. A few days with Lucinda-Mae had made him feel whole and masculine. He had kept a twenty-two year old satisfied, letting him know he still had it, but at what cost. Keeping Joan happy and content was much more satisfying. *Damn Lucinda-Mae. Why did she have to follow him to New York City? Joan would have never found out about it, and it would have been his cross to bear. And his cross alone.*

Now it was Joan's cross, too.

He never wanted that—never wanted it to add to Joan's problems. If he could get her to come back to him, he would gladly make it up to her for the rest of his life.

He used trees to break his slide down a long, jagged slope until he hooked an arm around a birch tree. He should go back and catch up to Joan. He didn't care if she never said a word to him again. He would remain by her side and bear her silence, forever if he had to.

He debated changing course, but continued south. He had to get to Suffern.

౿ఎఴఎ

The New York State Troopers set up a tactical operation post at the Visitor's Center at Lake Kanawauke, less than a half mile from where they had found the abandoned car and had recovered one of the targets.

Darren Callahan had been transported to the nearest hospital, and it would be a while before they would get any information from him. Special Agent Woyzeck did not expect him to be forthcoming with information on finding Joan, Duncan, and Kearney. Darren had refused to talk to them while waiting for medical transport, and getting him to give up any information in a timely manner would be futile. His file indicated he had been a mercenary in several hotspots around the globe, with most likely a lot of training in resisting interrogation.

K-9 teams were en route. Agent Woyzeck had pushed for them to go after Duncan, but they had overruled him. Until local federal authorities were on site, they would conduct the manhunt their way. They cited the "if you find the woman, you find the man" tactic. But Woyzeck knew the dynamics of this group was backward from other people. If they got Duncan, and, if any chance of rescuing him presented itself, Joan would come for him. They could set up an ambush and get her. Kearney was former CIA. If they didn't get him right away, he would be gone, never to be seen again. It made no sense to waste resources on him.

Agent Woyzeck had just arrived on site when the chopper pilot had reported three individuals making their ways in three separate directions. That confirmed the investigators on the ground who had traced three separate paths—the smallest footprints headed east. That's the direction they would send the dog. Woyzeck rubbed the back of his neck.

Something did not fit the profile. Duncan had taken off, leaving Joan to make her way through the woods on her own. Even Kearney went his own way.

"Hey, Danielson," Woyzeck called to the Special Supervisory Agent in Charge.

Danielson looked up from the map he had been studying. "What's up? Do you have something?"

"What do you make of this? Duncan heads off in his own direction, leaving his bride to make her own way. What man does that?"

"Didn't you say she was tough and woods savvy?"

"Yeah, but still…" Agent Woyzeck rubbed his chin. "I can understand Kearney taking off and leaving her. She and he have a bad history. But Duncan was a forty-six-year-old bachelor who loved her enough to put a ring on her finger. And he runs off and leaves her?"

"Maybe there's trouble on the home front," Danielson offered. "I'm sure Joan didn't take too well to the other woman showing up. We might be able to use it to our advantage."

The wind picked up and gusted across Lake Kanawauke. The roof of the visitor center creaked in protest.

"Yeah, you're probably right," Agent Woyzeck said. "But damn, it would have been easier to get them if they were together."

⌘

Joan moaned and shook her head. She propped herself up on her elbows. Something warm dripped into her eyes. She gingerly touched her forehead. The lump throbbed and stung at her touch. When she pulled her fingers away, they were covered in blood. She wobbled to her feet and hit the back of her head on a tree branch. *Dammit. I must have been clotheslined by a damn tree.* Mother Nature could be just plain mean at times.

A gust of wind sucked the air out of her throat. She ducked under the branch and took a few steps away to avoid hitting it again. She brushed off the leaf debris and continued her march east. She didn't know how long she had lain on the ground, and time was of the essence. She picked up her pace again, but after a few steps her head began pounding and she slowed to a walk. The ground sloped upward. She climbed over rocks and deadfall. When the slope steepened, she used saplings to keep from sliding back down. The ridgeline loomed less than twenty feet ahead and the desire to get to it drove her forward. Her thigh muscles burned from the effort and by the time she reached the ridge, her breathing was fast and gaspy.

She put her hands on her knees until she regained her breath. Voices filtered through the undergrowth. Her breathing stilled. Her first inclination was that the feds had caught up to her, but a softer voice said something about breakfast. Hikers would have a map and water. And car keys. She thought about her knife in the backseat of Duncan's car. Without a weapon, she would have to fight for the keys. She listened to determine direction.

The voices were to her left and she could now smell the smoke from an early morning campfire. She scrambled over the rocks and fallen trees. The campsite was only sixty feet from her and the campers were chatting and not paying particular attention to their surroundings. They looked like they were in their fifties. Maybe they wouldn't be inclined to put up too much of a fight.

Joan stepped into the clearing. When they saw a bloody woman in the path, they rushed to her. They gave her water and dampened a tissue to wipe the blood from her face and to put pressure on the wound on the lump on her forehead.

"You have been very nice to me," Joan said. "So I hate doing this, but I need your binoculars, your water, and your car keys. And your map, if you have one."

"What do you mean?" the woman asked.

"We're not giving you our car keys," the man said.

"Please just give them to me. I don't want to hurt you."

"No. You aren't—"

Joan grabbed the woman and applied a rear naked choke. She locked it in, but didn't arch her back to apply more pressure. Doing this to this kind lady turned her stomach. The last thing she wanted to do was put the woman into unconsciousness, but desperation required desperate measures. The woman grabbed Joan's arm and gasped for air. She struggled, but not enough to break the hold.

The man picked up a big stick. He approached Joan in an arc.

"Please, I don't want to hurt you." Joan turned to keep the man's wife between them. "Put the stick down. Just give me the car keys before your wife dies."

"She's still breathing, so I know she's still alive."

Great. A know it all. "If you know that, then you know I can change that in less than nine seconds."

He continued to circle Joan.

Joan continued to turn with him. "Please just give me what I need. I really don't like doing this."

"Hey, what's going on here?" Kearney said from behind Joan. "Do you need any help?" he asked the man.

"This woman is trying to rob us."

"Oh, really, then it's a good thing I came along." He walked up to the group. "Let the woman go, Joan."

The man looked dumbfounded. He didn't even reach for his wife when Joan let go of her and she ran to her husband's side.

During this action, Kearney reached to the small of his back and pulled his gun. "Give my friend what she wants."

The man froze, hands in the air, typical of someone who had never had a gun pointed at them before. The woman gasped and grabbed her husband.

"Give me your car keys, water, and binoculars," Joan said. "And your map."

The man gave her the canteen and the map. The woman handed over her the binoculars.

Joan flicked her fingers at the couple. "The keys."

The man reached into his pocket and gave Joan the keys.

"Sit." Kearney indicated with the barrel of the gun. "You are going to stay here for five minutes before leaving."

The couple sat with their arms around each other and nodded.

Joan and Kearney turned and headed toward the trail.

"What happened to your head?" Kearney asked.

"I got clotheslined by a tree. What are you doing here?"

"I had to cross a fucking swamp, and decided I don't like being in the woods alone. I know you are quite the woodsman. I felt I would be safer with you."

"Let's see if we can find Duncan in this miserable forest."

Kearney stopped. "Are you sure?"

Joan opened the map.

They found a trail that headed in a general southward direction. According to the map, it crossed a stream, then turned eastward. They would have to leave it then to continue their southward movement.

The well-maintained trail made walking easier. Occasionally a fallen tree blocked the path, the rain had left muddy patches and ruts from rain run-off, but it was clearly marked and they made good time. They were actually surprised when they heard the rushing water before they saw it.

Joan didn't like the sound of the rushing water, and she voiced her concern about crossing it.

"Let's cross that bridge when we get to it," Kearney said, not aware at the time of how portentous those words would turn out to be.

They followed the trail along the stream for a while. Joan eyed the fast-moving water, knowing the rocks beneath the surface would be slippery. The map indicated the trail crossed the stream about thirty yards ahead. Maybe the stream was shallower there. They walked around a curve and the crossing came into view.

A hanging rope bridge with four-inch wide planks for

the deck spanned the creek. Thick ropes spanned the stream, and other ropes connected the deck to the top ropes. On each bank, the deck was secured by thick ropes tied to metal rings. It looked well-maintained and sturdy enough.

Kearney went across first without any trouble. He turned when he got to the other side and said, "Piece of cake. Just keeps your eyes on me. Whatever you do, don't look down."

Joan started across keeping her eyes on Kearney. Half-way across, the breeze that had been refreshing the past half hour picked up into a gust. Joan grabbed the vertical rope support to steady herself. And looked down. The deck moved upstream. Joan hugged the supporting ropes for dear life. The deck had not actually moved, but the rushing water beneath it created an optical illusion that convinced her mind the bridge was moving.

"Joan," Kearney yelled over the water and the wind. "Look at me." He stepped onto the edge of the bridge. "Look at me."

She looked up at him, but hugged the ropes harder. "I can't move. I'm going to fall in."

"You won't fall in. Just keep your eyes on me."

Joan looked at him. Eyed his outstretched arm. She eased her grip on the ropes. He took one step toward her and nodded encouragement.

"That's it. Eyes on me," he said.

Joan locked eyes with him. Reached her arm out. Side-stepped a couple steps, reaching with her fingertips for the next vertical rope.

He took another step toward her. "Come to me. Do it now."

Joan let go and dashed across the bridge. Kearney grabbed her arm and pulled her onto land.

"Holy shit," Joan said staring at the bridge. "I guess when people say don't look down, they mean Don't Look Down."

"Let's keep moving," Kearney said.

The wind picked up and pushed the front of their clothes flat against their bodies. They had to lean into the wind to make forward progress. Then, in the flick of a second, it would stop and they would stumble a step or two before getting their feet under them.

"This has ceased to be fun," she said.

"Was it ever fun?"

They found the place where they had to leave the trail. They didn't have to bushwhack too long before finding a game trail. Walking became a little easier and they picked up their pace. About twenty minutes along the trail, Joan stopped and put up her fist, signaling to stop and be quiet.

She turned her back to the wind. "I hear a car engine."

"We can commandeer it and get the hell out of this limb-smacking, spider infested place."

"It could be law enforcement. We've been in here for a couple hours, maybe more. They have to have boots on the ground by now."

They walked more carefully through the brush, avoiding sticks and using hand signals. The foliage wasn't very thick yet, so they stopped just short of the ridge of a small hill. Joan checked the map.

She nudged Kearney and pointed at the map. "We're making horrible time," she whispered. "We've only gone about four miles from the traffic circle. All the doubling back and screwing around on that damn bridge has put us behind the curve."

"There are men along the road." He pointed to their left. He looked through the binoculars, taking time to adjust them. "They're police, but they don't seem to be doing a search."

"What the hell are they doing?" Joan asked.

Kearney put his finger across his lips to indicate no talking. He waited for the next gust of wind. "They have a parabolic receiver. Talk only when the wind gusts." He stopped when the wind died down and continued when it gusted again. "They're mostly facing away from us to our

left. Where do you think Duncan is? Should we keep looking for him or get the hell outta Dodge?"

"I want to find him, but we're moving so slowly it's
hopeless," Joan said. The wind quieted and she took the
time to look at the map, hoping something would jump out
at her. She spoke when the wind returned. "We'll never find
him in these woods. He probably took off like a rocket. He
could be anywhere."

"Or right there," Kearney said, handing the binoculars to
Joan and pointing at the intersection below.

ഏൟ

"The pilot can't fly in this wind," Agent Danielson reported.

Agent Woyzeck frowned and looked out over Lake Kanawauke. No chopper. The dogs hadn't arrived yet. Joan
would get away again. They had a plan to lure her out of the
woods, but he was sure it would not work. He scanned the
woods. She could be anywhere.

"We're going ahead as planned. Archer is in plain sight.
Snipers are in place."

"It isn't going to be enough to catch her."

"We have handheld thermal imagers and a parabolic an-
tenna. A mouse can't fart without us seeing and hearing
him. Don't worry. If they're anywhere nearby, we'll get
them."

"Yeah, I've heard that before," Agent Woyzeck said. He
saw ripples in the lake and wondered how the turtles survived in such cold water. He turned away from the window
and crossed the room to get another cup of coffee.

ഏൟ

"Where?" Joan grabbed the binos from Kearney and
looked where he pointed. She stopped scanning. "What the
hell are they doing?"

At the bottom of the slope, a grassy area divided the north and southbound lanes of Seven Lakes Parkway. Police cruisers blocked off the parkway where it divided and again where it rejoined. A road intersected the division. Cruisers with flashing lights partially blocked that road. In the center of all the commotion, in the headlights of one of the cruisers, stood Duncan with his hands cuffed behind him.

"I'd say they're setting up an ambush," Kearney said, taking the binoculars back from Joan. He searched the rock outcropping on each side of the road. He frowned. "There are snipers on the cliffs to the east and west of the road that heads south from where they have Duncan," he said with the wind in his face. "Take a look."

She took the binoculars and checked out the two ridges, and, like Kearney said, there was a two-man team just back from the edges.

"Do you see what else I saw?" Kearney whispered in Joan's ear.

She scanned down to the intersection in time to see a blonde, female officer release one of the cuffs on Duncan's wrists. A badge glittered on her belt. The officer said something and Duncan clasped his hands behind his head. The officer snapped the open cuff back on the wrist, then motioned for him to kneel.

"Those fucking bastards. That's cruel to make him kneel like that on the pavement."

While she watched from the ridge, the female officer shielded her eyes and scanned the woods around her. When she looked directly at the ridge where Kearney and Joan were hiding, Joan sucked in her breath.

"Lucinda-fucking-Mae." In the length of time it took to say those words, Joan redirected her anger from Duncan to federal agents in general, and Lucinda-Mae—or whatever her real name was—in particular.

In that flash of insight Joan realized the FBI had purposely seduced Duncan and ruined her happy marriage, short as it was. On purpose. They set about destroying the one thing that meant everything to her. Joan looked at Kearney and put her hand out. "Give me your gun. I'm going down there and make that bitch pay."

"That's just what they want you to do." He poked his finger on her arm. "They want you. And they want you to come to them."

"That's exactly what I'm going to do."

"I thought you walked out on him."

Joan frowned. "I don't hate him. If I hated him, it wouldn't matter to me what those bastards did to him." She looked through the binoculars again. "She seduced him. *They* are at fault." Not that Duncan didn't have a small part in the destruction of their relationship. She put binoculars down and waited for the next wind gust. "What's the plan?"

"There is no plan, Joan. It's over."

"No. It can't be. There has to be something we can do."

They sat with their backs against the slope. Joan tried to formulate a plan, but they were adrift in the woods. Two people. One gun. No water. The sound of car doors and raised voices came from below.

She looked over the hilltop. "What are they doing now?"

"It looks like they're packing up and leaving," he said.

After the roads were clear, she said, "Let's go."

Kearney pulled her down and laid his finger across his lips. "What? They're gone."

He shook his head. "They made too much of a show of it," he said when the wind gusted. "You can bet there are some agents in the woods, waiting to see if we think the coast is clear and make a move."

The next gust, she whispered, "What do you think happened to Jeb and Carmine and the others?"

"We may never know unless we see a newspaper or something."

"I had a sweet deal here, but my Iron Angel Bad Karma struck again."

"Maybe you should get a rabbit's foot or burn some sage or something."

Joan snorted quietly and they sat in silence.

"Did you know Duncan knew the Regional Director of Homeland Security?" she asked.

"He knew the Regional Directory of Homeland Security?"

"That's what he said. Said the director owed him a favor."

"News to me," Kearney said. "It must have something to do with his jobs for Jeb. He never talked about that."

"Who do you think was the mole?" she asked after several minutes.

He shrugged. "I'd put my money on Claude. Something about him—"

A car engine idled below them. They ventured a peek over the hilltop. Three men, one of them fifty yards below them, jogged to the car and got in. The car took off.

"How did you know they would do that?" Joan asked.

Kearney stood and brushed himself off. "It's what I would have done."

"What are we going to do now?" she stood and did the same.

"I'll tell you what I'm going to do."

"What's that?" she asked.

"Disappear."

"Oh, no. I—can't leave—I—" She looked at the empty road where Duncan had knelt.

Kearney put his hands on Joan's shoulders. "You can. And you will. We have to move before they get dogs in these woods." He took the map from her hands. After looking at it for a while he said, "We're going to cross this road, here." He pointed at the map. "We'll go behind this outcropping, and circle Lake Kanawauke which is just beyond those trees. If we can scoot around their flank before they get the dogs out here, the woods behind them will be the last place they'll search for us."

"I don't think it's going to work. It's too tricky."

"Yeah, well, staying right where they think we are isn't going to work either."

"Okay," she said, eyeing the road below. "I'd rather get taken down doing something than sitting here talking about it." She looked at the sky. "Besides, it's getting lighter as we speak."

"That's my girl."

They stumbled down the slope to the edge of the tree line along the road. Not hearing any sounds of approaching cars from either direction, they ran full bore across the road in a westerly direction. They slid under the brush on side of the road and stopped to catch their breath. When their breathing evened out, they bushwhacked their way toward civilization.

"Kearney, wait," Joan whispered. "I think I hear something."

They dropped to a squat to listen.

CHAPTER 27

They topped a rise and laid out before them a ribbon of highway wound its way to the left and right. The occasional car or eighteen-wheeler whizzed past. Civilization, warmth, and food would be nearby. Before those things could materialize, they had to find a way across the four-lane divided highway closed in by a chain link fence on both sides. Nothing was ever easy.

Kearney took out his phone and checked the bars. He smiled. "Who do we call?"

"Who can we trust?" Joan asked, plopping onto a cold stone to rest her legs.

"Everyone in Durham Security is using burner phones. We don't know all those new numbers. And we don't know who got away and who didn't. That leaves someone outside our circle of friends."

"How about Nirmala?" Joan asked, pulling out the candy bar she hadn't had a chance to eat before all hell broke loose. She tore it apart and gave half to Kearney.

He traded the phone for the meager sustenance. "It's worth a try."

She took the phone and scanned left then right. "How do we tell her where to pick us up? This section of the Thruway doesn't have any distinguishable features."

"If she agrees to help us, tell her to start heading this way. When we hole up somewhere, we'll call her again."

She punched Nirmala's number into the phone. Joan

frowned and shook her head when the fourth electronic ring burred in her ear. When Nirmala's voice came on the line, Joan jumped in surprise.

"Nirmala? It's me, Joan."

Silence.

"You know, I used to call myself Angel?"

"Oh, yes, I did not make the connection right away. How are you doing?"

"Well, I'm kind of in a jam. I was wondering if you could come and pick me up." She winced, expecting a turn-down.

"I am free for several hours this morning. Where are you?"

Joan turned her back to the win an gave a thumbs up to Kearney. "I'm in between places right now, but if you head west and pick up Route 17 and head north, when I get to a place that's easy to find, I'll call you back."

"This sounds very cloak and dagger."

She couldn't tell through Nirmala's accent if she was joking or balking. "No, nothing like that. I'll explain when you get here. So will you come?"

"I will come. My curiosity is piqued."

"Thanks, Nirmala. I'll call you as soon as I'm some-where easy to find."

"Okay. Bye."

"Bye."

Joan rubbed her hands together. "Let's find a way across this highway."

After following the chain link fence about a half mile it crossed a narrow, two-lane road.

"That isn't..." She didn't want to believe it was what she thought it was.

"I think so," Kearney said. "I think that's the road we drove in on."

"How the hell—" She looked over her shoulder than back, trying to get her bearings. "We must have been traveling a little north through those woods back there. You know, before we called Nirmala."

He grunted an answer while he checked the lay of the roads. They ducked when two cars rushed by.

"This could be our way across the Thruway." He pointed to the overpass below them. "If we can make it down there, go under the overpass, and to the other side of the road, we'll have it made."

"Is that all? Just go out in the open for, say, sixty to ninety seconds, then back into the woods? That's it?"

"Cowards never start…" He raised both eyebrows in a covert dare.

She stood and prepared to slide down the embankment. "Yeah, and the weak die along the way." She started down the bank.

He followed close on her heels. "Good thing you're not weak."

She ran in an off-kilter gait the last dozens steps, controlled her speed, and leaned herself against the round, cement support post for the overpass. Kearney ran past her to the next post. They listened.

The faint sound of an approaching car turned them to stone.

"Which way?" Joan asked.

Kearney pointed toward the left, toward the direction they wanted to go.

Was there time to make it? They'd be running toward the oncoming car.

Joan opened her hands in a silent question.

Kearney motioned to stay where they were. He moved to the east side of the post and flattened himself against it.

Joan nodded and moved to the east side of her post.

The car got closer.

Her mouth dried.

Headlights illuminated the highway.

Her breath caught in her throat.

The headlights lit up the area beneath the overpass.

She slid to the right to stay on the opposite side of the post from the car as it passed.

The area around them returned into darkness. She peeked at the retreating car, its dashboard lights glowing inside the car. When it was gone, she looked over at Kearney.

"Whooo," he said with an arm pump. "Take that, hotshot federal agents."

"You are one screwed up dude," Joan said. "Let's get out of here."

They listened for another car before jogging across the road to the other side of the overpass.

Kearney vaulted the guardrail without looking. "Oh, *shi—i—t*!" Rolling gravel and stones ended in a splash.

Joan stopped at the guardrail and looked at a ten foot drop-off. "You okay?"

"Yeah, but watch out for that first step."

She went to the end of the steel rail and walked around the edge of it. It wasn't as steep at this point and she carefully stepped onto the slope. Her boots slipped out from under her, and she did a three-point slide down the steep embankment. Gravel and stones followed behind her and when she stopped, they rolled on by, plinking into a creek at the bottom.

Kearney helped her up. "Let's follow this stream. I think that deserted, rundown rest stop is just north of here somewhere."

"Yeah, I think I remember seeing that." Joan wiped the mud off the seat of her pants. "The Red Apple something-or-other."

"We'll follow this upstream until we find a way across."

"Roger that," she said, dropping in behind him.

After stumbling over stones and getting slapped in the face by tree branches, they came to a place in the stream where stones provided a way across the fast-moving stream. Kearney balanced himself as he stepped from stone to stone. His foot slipped on the last stone, and he got wet up to his knee. The other leg remained dry. "Be careful. Those stones are slippery," he warned. He stood on the bank, hand out as an offer of assistance to help Joan on the last step across. She only had to make it that far on her own.

She hesitated. The memory of losing her balance on the rope bridge sent flutters through her stomach and up her spine. She stepped on the first rock. Good. Second rock. Good. The third stone was more slippery than she planned for and she fell toward the creek. She caught herself and soaked only one leg. She climbed back onto the rock, slipped again, and fell full force into the icy, fast-moving water.

He stepped into the stream. She grasped his hand, and with his assistance pulled herself out of the freezing water. Shivers started in her shoulders and radiated throughout her body, following the neural pathways. Her teeth chattered. Her wet leather jacket weighed a ton, and the cold wind syphoned off any body heat she still had.

He grabbed her hand. "Let's get to the Red Apple Rest and out of the cold air." He pulled her, shaking and chattering, the final thousand feet.

When they saw the decrepit building, Joan called Nirmala, and told her where they would be and how to signal for them to come out. She lay in the tall grass on the bank beyond the Red Apple Rest's weed-lined parking lot while Kearney looked for a way into the building. In the wind, The shivering got worse. The shaking was uncontrollable. She was sure her teeth would crack from the chattering. Finally, she saw Kearney, crouched low, motioning for her to go to him.

He led her to the window where he had kicked in a plywood barrier. He slid through first then helped her down to the dust-covered basement. He returned the plywood to the opening, blocking out the pale morning light, and leaving them in darkness. Joan slid to the floor. She willed her body to stop shaking, but it shook even harder than before.

"I can't stop shaking, K."

"Take off your jacket." He slid off his jacket. "Here put this on." He laid her jacket to the side and helped her put on his. He sat down and put his arm around her to share his body heat.

"All that I've been through," Joan said, looking over at Kearney, "and I'm going to die from hypothermia in the basement of a deserted restaurant."

"Nirmala will be here soon. Just hang on."

"What if she doesn't come? What if she sends the police?"

"Well, we made it this far. No one can take that away from us."

"Copy that," Joan said between her chattering teeth.

CHAPTER 28

Joan slumped at a computer in a library in Clarksburg, West Virginia. The exhaustion from staying on the move sapped her energy. A new town every day, not knowing anyone, the sight of a police cruiser sent shivers down her spine. She had handled this well in the past, but not this time. Hope for a normal life withered with every mile she put behind her.

She thought back to the last time she saw Kearney. They stood in front of her second cache, loading the last of her meager stash into a trailer made specifically to be pulled by a ten speed touring bike. They had already been to his cache, which held enormous treasures—an arsenal of weapons and corresponding ammo. He had offered her a beautiful Ruger, but she had declined. No more weapons. Maybe a peaceful demeanor would beget a peaceful life.

Kearney had asked if she was going to be okay. What could she say to that? If she had said, "no," he would have changed his plans and stayed until she could handle being on the run. But that would have put them both in danger. The authorities were looking for a man and a woman. A man alone, or a woman alone, wouldn't be as obvious. It was better this way.

He had given her a disguise kit and showed her how to apply the fake scar and change the tint of her skin. There were contacts to change the color of her eyes, gooey stuff to change the shape of her nose, and a couple wigs. She tried something different each day for a couple weeks, but gave up because no one seemed particularly interested in a forlorn woman pedaling a bike alone on back roads.

Kearney had gone over the steps to take to remain undetected: don't stay in the same town for more than twenty-four hours, save the third fake ID for an emergency, and never contact anyone that she knew prior to going on the run. Even the most trusted people would give in to the lure of a reward.

Before she had climbed onto her bicycle, he had given her an email address—the only exception to the no-contact rule. They could leave messages for each other in the Drafts folder. He would check it every week to ten days to see if she needed anything. She memorized the email address and the password then pedaled to the end of the drive out of the storage facility. He had pulled up next to her, nodded farewell, and turned left in his Mustang convertible. She pumped the pedals to get her bike and trailer moving, and didn't look back.

After a month of traveling the highways alone, she had to contact someone she knew. She had input the email address and the password. And hesitated. *Just hit Enter.* She bit the inside of her cheek.

She tapped the button, then looked over her shoulder to see if federal agents were ready to swoop in and take her away in handcuffs. She silently chastised herself. Even if it could be traced, it would take a while to pinpoint a location and get there.

There were two messages in the Drafts Folder. One from Kearney, and another marked *IMPORTANT!* She opened the one from Kearney first. It turned out to be exactly what she had expected. He had checked three times and hadn't heard from her. He pleaded for her to simply write a few words so he knew she was all right. She thought about the rain-soaked, suburban streets outside the library and typed: *I am fine. Today I'm enjoying the beach. Tomorrow it will be some points of historical interest. Your concern means a lot to me. ~ J.* She saved it to the Drafts Folder, and opened the second, more recent email.

Joan pushed the chair back from the computer terminal and caught her breath. The monitor blurred from tears not willing to fall over the edge of her eyelids. She blinked to clear her eyes. It was a long email from Duncan. But that was impossible. She looked around the library. No one seemed the least bit interested in her. She wiped the tears off her cheeks, rolled the chair back up to the computer desk, and read the email...

My dear, dear Joan,

If you are reading this, then Kearney shared with you the email we have used for a long time to stay in touch when far apart. (And Kearney: if you did not give Joan this email address please find her and give her this message.)

Remember on the day we got married when I told you if you believed in me, we would spend the rest of our lives together? You said that you did believe in me. I hope that you meant it and that you still feel that way...

She wiped her cheeks again. If only she could take back her mean words and hold him again. She crossed her arms and leaned them on her thighs before reading on...

The FBI wants to make a deal. They want to make it with you, but it could benefit both of us. I don't know any details about the deal, you have to discuss it with them, and you have to do it face to face. That means you have go to the nearest lawyer and turn yourself in. Have the lawyer contact Special Agent Woyzeck in the Pittsburgh Office. He will go to wherever you are and arrest you personally. He assured me you will be safe and treated with dignity. I know this sounds frightening and goes against every ounce of will in your body, but trust me when I tell you that this is the only way.

Make the best deal you can for yourself, and if you can

Janet McClintock

find it in your heart, please remember me. My promise to
you to be together for the rest of our lives hinges on what
you do during the deal-making process.
I know you will do the right thing.
Your most humble and loving husband,
Dennis

Joan wiped her cheeks and looked around the library again. If anyone noticed the woman crying in front of the computer, they weren't letting on. She read the email again, then closed out of the email provider, deleted the browsing history, and returned to her motel room.

When she cycled toward the blinking vacancy sign of her roadside motel, she thought about her options. She could continue on the move for another five months or so, staying under the radar. And eventually find a safe haven to settle down with her third and final fake identification, with the hope that no one recognized her and turned her in.

Or she could trust the man who betrayed her. For all she knew, the deal did not exist, and Duncan simply wanted her to be incarcerated like he was. But his parting words in Harriman State Park had been that his every act had been calculated to make sure she stayed free. Well, she was free. If she turned herself in, she would be in jail for a long time. Somewhere in that progression of facts lurked a logic that at this time only Duncan saw or understood.

She shook off the rain and wearily unlocked the door to only the fourth motel room she had rented in a long string of campsites. Many days pedaling endless stretches of unfamiliar roads gave her a sense of freedom, but that freedom teetered on whether an alert sheriff or trooper recognized her. The better campsites had showers, a few had rental cottages, none had television. The urge for a hot shower, a solid roof and four walls, and a television had been too great to resist. She could get those comforts in jail, but there would be no freedom.

She flopped onto the bed.

She had been in the underworld so long that every way out looked like the road to hell. There would be no fairytale ending. Not for her.

She groaned when she realized she hadn't answered Duncan's email. Her body refused to move at the thought of going back to the library. She turned on the television and convinced herself the night would give her an opportunity to think through her answer to Duncan.

The next day she answered his email…

My dearest Dennis,

I have been meditating every day. I no longer listen to my mind because it is concerned with logic and morality and, at times, deception. It remembers the horrible things I have done for which I am very sorry. It embraces the demons that torment me. It leads me to do things that are the opposite of what my heart wants.

Meditation has taught me to listen to my heart because it will never mislead me. The demons have no power there, because my heart does not remember the past things I have done, but leads me to a better life. It will lead me to redemption—only redemption wipes the slate clean.

As for your request, I will do the right thing.

Your humbled and loving wife,

Joan

Two days later, Joan sat, arms resting on the armrests, participating in small talk with Ira Levine. After writing the email to Duncan, she had packed everything she could into her backpack and jumped on a bus, leaving everything else behind. If she had turned herself in while in Clarksburg, she would have sat in a county jail cell waiting for Agent Woyzeck to come and claim her. If she showed up in Pittsburgh, she could turn herself in—again—to Ira Levine, whom she had hired when she had been a member of the Constitution Defense Legion. She knew Ira and she knew Agent Woyzeck. After four long weeks alone, she had to talk to someone she knew, even if they were the means to her incarceration.

The secretary rang Ira, and his eyes flashed up to Joan.

Her stomach fluttered. Ira didn't have to tell her the caller's name. By the half of the conversation she could hear, she knew this was it. This was the end of her life from hell. The end of her freedom—freedom that was merely an illusion. The bars were there, she just couldn't see them closing in around her. The gatekeepers were there, they only had to focus on her to lock the gate behind her, blocking her escape. The bars and gatekeepers were there, the only thing missing was freedom. Real freedom.

"That was Special Agent Woyzeck," Ira said when he hung up the phone. "He is on his way over here to take you into custody himself. It's very irregular, but he says he has a vested interest in you."

Relief flooded Joan. Her nose stung. "Thank you, Mr. Levine." Any more words and she would break down. Her tears would wash away the dignity Duncan had told her to maintain during the close call at the Ottmar Liebert Concert.

"I'll ride to the police station with you," Ira continued. "They'll get you into the system, and when you're arraigned I'll be there with you. He says you'll be released into my custody."

"What does that mean?"

"It could mean there's a deal in the offing. Do you know anything about a deal?"

"No." She didn't know how to explain the email from Duncan without giving away too much information.

"Don't talk to them unless I'm there. If they offer a deal, make sure I see it before you sign or agree to anything."

She didn't respond.

"Hear me?"

"Yes. I'll have you there during questioning."

"Good."

The wait seemed endless. Ira took a couple calls while they waited, and Joan sipped the coffee his secretary had offered her. She thought about Duncan and how little time she had spent with him. And now, they would never be together again. With a plea deal, she might get out in a reasonable length of time, but what about him? He'd be a very old man when he got out, if he ever got out of jail.

The phone rang.

Ira picked up the receiver. He looked at Joan. "Are you ready?"

She nodded.

"Send him in," he said.

A strange sense of calm draped around Joan, enfolding her and supporting her. The thought of using jail time to rediscover her true self, offered comfort and hope. The long, tumultuous, violent trip was over. No matter what happened from this point on, it had to be better than looking over her shoulder, pretending to be someone else, and enduring the draining loneliness.

The door opened.

Joan turned in her chair.

Special Agent Woyzeck walked in with two uniformed police officers and a woman in civilian clothes. "Please stand up, Mrs. Archer," he said.

Mrs. Archer. Whatever the future held in store, she was still married to Duncan. Joan stood, chin up, shoulders back.

"Joan Bowman Archer, you are under arrest for sedition, terroristic activities, and felony escape." The handcuffs clicked into place. "This officer will read you your rights."

While the uniformed officer read her rights to her, Ira Levine gathered his briefcase and walked around his desk.

"Do you understand your rights?" the officer asked.

Joan looked at Ira then at Agent Woyzeck. "Yes."

Special Agent Woyzeck grasped Joan's arm and walked her out of Ira Levine's law office.

On the way down the stairs, Joan said to Special Agent Woyzeck, "You can say it."

"What's that?"

"Gotcha."

Special Agent Woyzeck smiled at Joan as he opened the door to the street.

ഗൈഗ

Three weeks later…

Joan absorbed every sound along the way. The buzzer to unlock the door, the heavy, solid sound of the barrier sliding away. Her heels clacking on the shiny, tile floor. The click of a latch when her escort opened a door into a visitation room.

She hesitated. She would face Duncan for the first time since she signed her deal with the federal District Attorney. She had insisted that no one tell Duncan the details of her deal. It was important to her to face him when he heard what she had agreed to.

She took a deep breath and walked into the room.

Duncan was sitting back against the edge of a table. He looked like he had lost weight over the past seven weeks, but he still looked handsome and sexy, even in an orange jumpsuit. He watched her with what appeared to be hope. She doubted if he would look at her the same way at the end of their conversation. The door clicked shut behind her.

"They say we can touch during this visitation," he said. "May I—"

She threw herself into his arms and kissed him hard and long.

He held her tightly searing into his memory the way her breasts felt against his chest. The scent of her shampoo. Her slender waist under his hands. This would be the last embrace for a long time, maybe forever depending on what she said here today.

When they came up for air he said, "I guess that's a yes."

She nodded. "I planned out everything I wanted to say to you, but I can't think of one thing right now...except I love you."

"I love you, too, *nena*." They kissed again.

"Are they listening in?" she asked, looking around for cameras.

"This is where lawyers meet their clients, but you never know."

"So this was you plan all along?" she asked. "For you to take all the charges, then have me make a deal to get our sentences commuted?"

He nodded. "After that meeting with Woyzeck, I saw the possibilities. Man, I thought that investigation in Durham Security would crack a cog in the whole delicate plan."

"How so?"

"Timing was everything. When I heard about the investigation, I was afraid they'd pull a sweep and arrest everyone—you along with them—and all my planning would have been for nothing. Good thing I had that ace in the hole to get the investigation quashed."

"And Lucinda Mae? How did she fit in?"

"I really thought that was the end of the whole thing. The whole plan hinged on you coming through for the both of us."

"Did you know she was an undercover federal agent?"

"Not until she showed up in New York and I saw her hand something to the feds when I escaped them. But something wasn't quite right from the beginning. It was just too odd after only a few days together."

Joan chewed the inside of her cheek. She didn't want to ask, but had to. "And you married me so I couldn't be forced to testify against you?"

"I always wanted to marry you." He pulled her into his arms. "Be you anchor and your protector. To love you and wake up next to you every single day." He touched her cheek. "Be your strength. I figured if you couldn't be forced to testify against me…it was the only way I could be your strength from in here."

A silence fell between them.

"I have to tell you something that may not make you happy," she said. "But I thought it offered the best future for us."

"I have a feeling I need to be sitting for this," he said.

They took seats facing each other, and Joan held both his hands. "I want to say first of all that I no longer harbor bad feelings about what happened in Arkansas. That's history, and has nothing to do with my decision. People make mistakes."

A sweat broke out on his face and sadness filled his eyes. "What am I going to be unhappy about? Just tell me straight out."

"Let me tell you what you are going to be happy about first. You will be transferred to a medium security prison. And we will be granted one conjugal visitation over the next one to one and a half years."

"And after that?"

"I'm getting to that. At the end of eighteen months, or sooner if things go well, our sentences will be commuted. And the FBI will—"

Duncan took his hands from Joan's and rubbed his eyes with his palms. His shoulders shook.

Oh, my God! "I hope those are tears of joy," she said.

He nodded and, when he looked at her, his eyes were red and glassy. He stood and pulled her into his arms, squeezing her. She thought he'd never let her go.

Get this over with before you break down. "Do you want to hear the rest of it?"

"Yeah, sure." He released her and sat down in his chair again, pressing on the inside corners of his eyes

"When it's over, the FBI will put us in the witness protection program." She waited until this sank in.

He blinked. "Why are we—you did say us, right?"

She nodded.

"Why are we going to need witness protection?"

She bit her lip. This part had the potential for setting him off. "I have to go undercover in the Demon Brotherhood Motorcycle Club."

He leaned back in his chair, avoiding her eyes. "What exactly do you have to do?"

"I have to cozy up to Bill Torrence."

His eyes flashed up to hers. "The President of the Brotherhood. And just how cozy do you have to get?"

She tensed. "As cozy as it takes."

He pushed back his chair and stood. "Why did you agree to this? To get back at me for what I did in Arkansas?"

She looked up at him. "I told you this doesn't have anything to do with that. Did you even bother to ask the feds why they wanted me?"

"Of course I did. Those bastards lied to me. I see it now." His face flushed from anger. His posture was tense and aggressive. "They sent an agent to put a wedge between us so you'd be broken and hurt and do anything to get even."

"That's not why I'm—"

"I believe you when you say that's not why you did this is, but that was their plan. When that didn't pan out, they worked me to get to you. I was used, Joan." He shook his head. "Oh, they were good. I didn't even see it coming. If I had known their plan to put you in danger, I would never have told you to turn yourself in. You know that, right?"

"Well, this is what they wanted."

"It's too dangerous, Joan. You left their president unconscious in the middle of a highway for Christ's sake. They'll be out for blood."

"I did undercover work for the Legion. I can do this."

"Nothing like this. You'll never be safe. And I won't be there to protect you."

"You taught me how to survive."

"This is a deathtrap. Cancel the deal. Say you won't do it."

"I can't do that, and you know it. You had a plan for our future. This is what it morphed into. So now it's my plan for us to be together. Together in separate prisons isn't my idea of together."

Duncan rubbed the back of his neck and paced the room. His jaw muscles clenched and released. She let him work through his thoughts.

"I never did a job without knowing how I'd get away afterward." He turned to face her. "You have to have an exit plan."

"I'll contact Kearney if I get in over my head."

"No. You need a safe house. A team. Support."

"My handler will make sure I'm okay. They said he'd call in back up if I need it and get me out if my life's in danger."

"This whole thing puts your life in danger." He snorted. "You really trust the feds after what they've done? No, you need your own back up."

"This isn't a military operation."

"Maybe not, but treat it like one. Have an endgame. Plan for it. Work toward it."

She looked around the room for any surveillance. None was evident, but she still got close to Duncan and whispered, "What do you suggest?"

"Contact Jeb as soon as you get out of here. Today. Set up signals. Tell him you need codes, logistics, communication lines. He'll know what to do."

"Won't the bikers get suspicious with all that going on?"

"They won't have a clue. Hell, you probably won't even see them, and you'll be looking."

"I don't know. It seems like a lot of commotion for something I probably won't need."

"Today, Joan. Contact Jeb today. If you don't feel comfortable talking to him, promise me you'll at least call Champ."

The look in his eyes was a combination of concern and determination. She knew he was doing what he could from the helpless position he found himself in. Listening to his advice wouldn't hurt and could only help. *It's better to have an umbrella before it rains.*

"Okay. I'll contact Jeb, but I don't see the urgency. There are at least two months before the operation steps off."

"Promise me you'll do it today."

She hesitated, still debating the necessity of mobilizing resources, or whatever Jeb would do. Duncan's eye contact didn't waver.

"Today. I promise," she finally said.

"You know how?"

She nodded. There was an outside chance they were being recorded, and she didn't want to jeopardize Jeb or the ability to contact him. She pulled Duncan toward her and they held each other, transferring strength between them one last time, until they were together again.

"How am I supposed to live in this shit hole while you are out there with…I can't even say it."

"I've done some horrible things over the past few years, and I'm sure you've done worse for longer. We have to fix this. We have to be redeemed."

"Redeemed. That's a cute little word. Did you learn it in one of your meditation books?"

"Redemption is a big-ass word. I signed away my soul, and now I have to dance with the devil to make things right for both of us."

"You don't have to do this, *nena*. You won't get as much time as me. If you were in jail someplace, at least I'd know you were safe."

"You think I want to do this? I am scared every second of every day, but since that first night together all I ever wanted was to have a quiet life with you. I'm in a position to make that happen. And I'm going to grit my teeth and claw my way through the muck each and every day until I can hold you in my arms, in our own home, planning our future together."

"I don't want to lose you."

"That won't happen." She stepped back so she could see his face. "Remember that time we thought we were going to be arrested? At the Ottmar Liebart concert? In those few excruciating minutes, I knew I could not bear living without you in my life. That I would do anything to make that happen. Anything, Duncan."

"You'll be dirty, contaminated."

She squared her shoulders. "My street name is Iron Angel, but I'm not made of iron. I'm stainless steel. When the filth is washed away, I'll be untouched, like uncontaminated spring water. As clean as—"

"I get it." He pulled her back into his arms. "You'll be redeemed."

A rap at the door deadened a part of Joan's heart. Her escort stuck his head in. "It's time to wrap this up. You have one minute."

"Okay." When the door closed, she continued. "I'm going to make this right—all of it." She held her husband's face in her hands and committed it to memory. "Do you believe in me?" she finally asked.

He looked at her. "I do."

About the Author

After twenty-two years in the Army, Janet McClintock exhaled and settled down in Pittsburgh with her aging Pit Bull. She has completed three novels of her four-part Iron Angel action series. She is also trying her hand at a paranormal novel before returning to her passion—action.

Action comes easy to McClintock. Over the years, she has owned motorcycles and horses and driven a tractor trailer across the country. She has trained in various martial arts over the past 38 years and is currently training in Kali and Jeet Kune Do. She is also a certified Edged Weapons Combatives Instructor.